"*DANTES' INFERNO* has everything readers crave: a full-throttle plot, top-notch psychological suspense, and—as always with author Lovett— gorgeous prose. And to top it off, the book features one of my all-time favorite characters, Dr. Sylvia Strange. Welcome back, Doctor. Good to see you again."
—Jeffery Deaver, author of *The Stone Monkey* and *Speaking in Tongues*

PRAISE FOR SARAH LOVETT AND DANTES' INFERNO

"Lovett creates some of the most mesmerizing serial killers since Hannibal Lecter."
—*Library Journal*

"[A] wild saga . . . [Lovett's] forte has always been a darkly fertile imagination untrammeled by the focus or discipline that could harness it."
—*Kirkus Reviews*

"An exhilarating read."
—*Midwest Book Review*

"A scorching tale."
—*Booklist*

ALSO BY SARAH LOVETT

A DESPERATE SILENCE
ACQUIRED MOTIVES
DANGEROUS ATTACHMENTS

SARAH LOVETT

DANTES' INFERNO

A DR. SYLVIA STRANGE NOVEL

POCKET BOOKS
New York London Toronto Sydney Singapore

This book is a work of fiction. Names, characters, places and incidents are products of the author's imagination or are used fictitiously. Any resemblance to actual events or locales or persons, living or dead, is entirely coincidental.

POCKET BOOKS, a division of Simon & Schuster, Inc.
1230 Avenue of the Americas, New York, NY 10020

Copyright © 2001 by Sarah Lovett

Originally published in hardcover in 2001 by Simon & Schuster, Inc.

ISBN: 0-671-02646-1

First Pocket Books printing October 2002

10 9 8 7 6 5 4 3 2 1

POCKET and colophon are registered trademarks of Simon & Schuster, Inc.

For information regarding special discounts for bulk purchases, please contact Simon & Schuster Special Sales at 1-800-456-6798 or business@simonandschuster.com

Cover design by Tony Greco

Printed in the U.S.A.

ACKNOWLEDGMENTS

Special thanks to

David Rosenthal and Marysue Rucci • Theresa Park,
Julie Barer, and Peter McGuigan • Miriam Sagan
Julia Goldberg • Sharon Neiderman • Carolyn Guilliland
Michael Mariano • Maggie Griffin • Brian Wiprud
Charles Knief • Bruce Mann, M.D.
Reid Meloy, Ph.D., A.B.P.P.
James Eisenberg, Ph.D., A.B.P.P. • Russ "Dynamite" Deal
S.A. John Hoos, FBI • LA County Flood Control
Paul Cooper • Jad Davis • Peter Miller Alan Zelicoff
March Kessler • Don Opper • Tom Johnson
Dorothy Bracey • Phil Schnyder and "AskSam"
Peter Schoenburg, Esq. • Alice Sealey • Reilly Johnson
Jill Ryan • Anne Pederson • Mark Donatelli, Esq.
Sandy MacGregor • Marilyn Abraham
Jim, Katie, Stephanie, and Jim Jr. Gallegos
Pat Berssenbrugge • Michael Gelles • Larry Renner
Jacqueline West • Peter Miller • Ron Schultz
Hope Atterbury • Tuko Fujisaki • Ana Matiella
Stephanie Marston • Rod Barker
Donald Fineberg, M.D. • Rich Feldman • Loretta Denner
Lew Thompson and, of course, Tim Thompson

For Lew, Miriam & Michael

1st Circle . . .

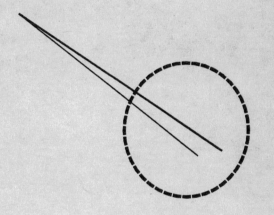

with a newfound enthusiasm, the animated painter expertly gripped the T-shirt of ten-year-old Jason Redding

CHAPTER ONE

INFERNAL MACHINES—Contrivances made to resemble ordinary harmless objects, but charged with some dangerous explosive. An innocent looking box or similar receptacle is partly filled with dynamite or other explosive, the rest of the space being occupied by some mechanical arrangement, mostly clockwork, which moves inaudibly, and is generally contrived that, when it has run down at the end of a predetermined number of hours or days, it shall cause the explosive substance to explode.

Dick's Encyclopedia, 1891

Another gunpowder plot. A gift of Greek fire for ancient Babylon of the New World. Know each of these missives as infernal machines.

Anonymous letter to the *Los Angeles Times*, March 2001

April 23, 2000—11:14 A.M. Los Angeles was wearing her April best: cerulean sky, whipping cream clouds, rain-washed air that whispered promises of orange blossoms and money. An LA day of sweet nothings.

Wanda Davenport, schoolteacher and amateur painter, expertly gripped the T-shirt of ten-year-old Jason Redding just as he was about to poke a grimy finger between the sculptured buttocks of a 2,500-year-old *Icarus*. Antiquities were the thing at the Getty Center. And so were toilets. The *lack* of toilets. Four of her fifth-graders needed to pee, and her assistant was nowhere in sight.

"Line up, guys," Wanda barked with practiced authority. "Jason, you get to hold my hand."

The boy moaned and rolled his eyes, but his face was glowing with excitement. Her class had been planning this trip for six months. Given a choice between Universal Studios and the Getty, they'd gone with art. Fifth-graders! Who woulda thunk?

But then again, Wanda Davenport wasn't your everyday teacher. She was so passionate about Art a wee bit of her passion rubbed off on just about anyone who spent a few weeks under her tutelage. She loved the realists, the impressionists, the dadaists—from the classical artists to the graffiti artists, she was a devoted fan.

She smiled to herself as she gave the command to march. Jason caused her a lot of grief, but secretly he was one of her favorites. He was smart, hyper, and creative. One of these days he could be a famous artist, architect, inventor, physicist, whatever.

"Turn right!" Wanda should've had a night job as a drill sergeant.

Jason nearly tripped over his own two feet, which were audaciously encased in neon green athletic sneakers, one size too big. Wanda knew that his mother, Molly Redding, was a recovering substance abuser; she was also a single mom supporting her only child by waiting tables. These were rough times in the Redding household, but there was love and hope, and Jason was a terrific kid.

"Turn left!" Wanda ordered her students, watching as Maria Hernandez accepted a fireball from Suzie Brown;

the bright pink candy disappeared between white teeth.

Twenty minutes earlier, Wanda had herded her troop of ten- and eleven-year-olds onto the white tram car for transport to the hilltop. The 1.4-mile drive had provided a startling view of Los Angeles and the Pacific Ocean. The moneyed view. The new J. Paul Getty Center was situated in Brentwood, nuzzled by Santa Monica, nosed in by mountains.

From the tram and the marble terrace fronting the museum at the hilltop, Wanda had called out city names for her children: Ocean Park, Venice, LA proper (the downtown heart of the metropolitan monster, with its constant halo of smog), San Pedro's south-end industrial shipyards, a tail in the distance . . . then back to Santa Monica and the ocean pier extending like a neon leg into blue waters . . . and last but not least, up the coast to movie-star Malibu, which had incorporated just as mud slides devoured great bites of earth and forest fires grazed the landscape down to bare, charred skin.

With that lesson in geographic and economic boundaries, the kids had marched into the reception building; Wanda barely had time to glance at the program provided for the tour; her students demanded 110 percent of her energy. No matter—she knew this place by heart. In her mind the architectural design was Greek temple married to art deco ocean liner. She'd wandered Robert Irwin's chameleon gardens for hours; each season offered new colors, new scents, new shapes and shades. Santa Monica's Big Blue Bus ran straight to the grounds. She'd lost count of her visits. Nobody had believed Culture could draw a crowd in LA. Well, just look at her kids!

With one expert swipe, Wanda removed a wad of gum from behind the ear of one of her oldest charges while simultaneously comforting the youngest, who was complaining of a stomachache. She couldn't wait to get them into the garden, her very favorite part of the facility. They began the trek across the first exterior courtyard. Water ran like glass between slabs of marble. The children shuffled and slid their shoes across the smooth stones.

"Hey, guys, remember the name of the architect? We covered this in class."

She barely caught Jason's mumbled response: "Meier."

"Richard Meier. That's correct, Mr. Redding."

They were almost to the stairway leading to the museum café and the outdoor dining deck. Within seconds, the central garden would rush into view. Lush with primary color and geometric form (chaos and pattern all at once), it overflowed the space between the multilevel museum and the institutes.

Wanda felt a tug at her sleeve and turned in surprise, looking down at the agitated face of another of her kids.

"Please, Miss Davenport, I have to *go*," a small voice announced.

"Break time, guys," Wanda called out cheerfully. "When we reach the bottom of these stairs, we'll use the rest rooms and regroup for the garden. Carla, hands to yourself. Thank you. No *running*, Hector."

They turned the corner, only to be welcomed by the sight of bougainvillea, jacaranda, orchid, daisy, iris, wild grasses, each as lovely and as ephemeral as a butterfly.

Wanda Davenport's last view in life consisted of the gardens she loved so much.

Jason Redding discovered the treasure chest beneath the stairwell. He opened it curiously, saw an intricate, whimsical, handmade collage—an infernal machine constructed of polished wood, ivory, colored wire, and spiked metal pipe filled with black powder.

The puzzled child heard a hissing sound, saw smoke and

soft petals, twisting and turning, floating upward: *initiation*.

One neon green sneaker survived unscathed.

1:03 P.M. Edmond Sweetheart didn't look at the bodies. He had nothing to offer the dead except his ability to focus—on the living, on an unknown bomber or bombers, on the wreckage that awaited him a hundred yards uphill. If he lost his center at this particular moment in time, his world would shatter.

Swift and surefooted, he moved through the garden on muscles that were taut and flexible, with arms held close, spine erect, with steps measured instinctively. His senses were painfully alert, ears filled with the implacable cry of sirens, dark eyes wide to the brightness reflected from the cloud-covered sky.

Los Angeles has a taste; here at the Getty, between the Santa Monica Mountains and the Pacific Ocean, Sweetheart registered an alkaline palate tinged heavily with carbons. There was comfort in the order of chemical compounds; he took no such comfort in the chaos of human motivation, action, reaction. The destructive evidence—now just a stone's throw away—was all too visible.

Out of choice, he rarely attended active crime scenes. Instead, his life was spent poring over printouts, comparing and contrasting data sets—a day's currency to linguistic morphology, four days to chemical compounds, an entire week to geographic spatial patterns. A dry exchange that made your eyes go red, your vision myopic. Unless it happened to represent both your passion and your sanity.

Sweetheart had spent more than a decade tracking terrorists and consulting with various federal and international agencies—he maintained research privileges at UCLA; he had an office at Rand Corporation—but because he was both practical and paranoid, his most delicate jobs were undertaken from his own home in the Hollywood Hills, where he could control the flow of information.

The results of forensic analysis of physical evidence (extortion notes, digitized threat calls, re-creations of bombs and incendiary devices, blood spatter patterns—a criminal's work product) were far removed from the location of the destructive action.

But this midday in April, Sweetheart was present at a crime scene for personal reasons—however mentally contained, however psychically encased those reasons might be—and it was vital that he keep his emotional, if not physical, distance.

He'd left his car parked at the end of the fire road alongside various emergency response vehicles. The half-mile jog hadn't begun to test his lungs. As he navigated the last fifty yards to the scene of the bombing, a familiar-looking man in an FBI jacket passed by, moving swiftly down the path toward a mobile forensic van. The agent glanced with wary suspicion at Sweetheart, who kept his focus on a living, breathing target at the base of the damaged stairwell ahead: a red-haired man named Church, who was wearing an LAPD vest and a fierce expression.

Barely two hours ago, a child and his teacher had died when a pipe bomb exploded. No one had claimed responsibility. No clues to the identity of the terrorist or terrorists. Not yet. Sweetheart knew that much from a telephone message.

Now his heartbeat fluttered dangerously as containment threatened to fail. His pace slowed; he almost faltered. A child had died . . .

Cleanse the mind of all emotional distractions.

He picked up speed again, shallow breath quickening, inhaling through his nose, exhaling through his mouth, the athlete's nonverbal mantra. When he was ten yards from the stairwell, he willed law enforcement to make eye contact.

LAPD's Detective Frederick "Red" Church gazed intently back at Sweetheart. The detective was one of a cluster of investigators that included FBI and ATF cowboys; they had gathered at the base of the damaged stairwell and were engaged in the early stages of crime scene analysis, a laborious process that included the documentation and collection of forensic evidence. Breaking from the group and cutting quickly downhill over carefully shaped earth, the LAPD detective couldn't mask his discomfiture—shock, even—at the sight of Sweetheart.

When he was within tackling range, Church whispered harshly, "You shouldn't be—" But he didn't finish the sentence, breaking off as he sensed the wild emotions trapped in the other man's eyes.

"My niece called," Sweetheart said distinctly. "I drove straight from LAX."

Twelve hours on Nigeria Airways, most of that time spent on the ground in hundred-degree heat, 90 percent humidity; twenty hours on Japan Airlines, much of that spent in transit, first class, oh-so-fully insulated from the famine, disease, poverty that plagued the rest of the world. Then the emergency phone call as they were circling LA's international airport.

"I need access *now*. Before all these bastards trample the scene. It's already turning into a circus." Sweetheart's voice was ominously controlled; no expression showed through the mask of his handsome face.

"I heard you were in Africa," Church said, ignoring the declaration, using his body like a closed door. He kept a wary distance from the larger man; there was no way he could head off 280 pounds of solid muscle mass.

"Nigeria was pathetic." Sweetheart was eyeing the scene possessively, as if it were his own private treasure. "Another embassy bombing." Taking one step toward Church, he finished in a quiet voice. "Seventy dead, twice that injured. Nothing but rubble and bodies."

"Bin Laden?" the detective asked, not budging. He was curious. He was adrenalized. He was also stalling. He didn't have the time or the strength for a confrontation—not with Edmond Sweetheart.

"We should send him a gift—a couple of Tomahawks." Sweetheart waved one hand abruptly, perhaps deflecting the emotional impact of tragedy past and present—almost making the detective jump. He was too damn calm, too controlled as he gazed straight at Church. "We should do what we did in Afghanistan six months ago—turn the rebel camp to dust."

He didn't have to add that the Afghanistan attack—which, in addition to wiping out a terrorist training camp, had also caused the death of an international fugitive—had been based on his intelligence. Antiterrorist circles were small and incestuous; players knew one another's business. Just like today, present circumstances, news would be circulating swiftly, Sweetheart thought, anger rising like a tide inside his chest.

Sensing movement, the detective stepped forward just as Sweetheart contracted his muscles. Church said quickly, "You aren't authorized to be here, Professor."

Sweetheart's black-brown eyes glittered with a sheen not unlike compressed metal. His mouth was a flat line against smooth, naturally bronzed skin.

"I'm asking you to leave," Church insisted in a low voice.

"No." Sweetheart might have been a tree or a structural column, so rooted, so *embedded* was his energy. For all his mass, he was powerfully agile, dauntingly strong, a formidable and athletic opponent. He said, "I'm not going anywhere, *Red*."

Church heard his nickname used as a warning—he also heard the hard note that communicated Sweetheart's frightening level of self-control. The detective's blue eyes reflected tiny images of the surrounding world, including this man he knew as a hotshot data junkie, a free agent sought after by federal and international agencies. For the dozen times their paths had crossed, Edmond Holomalia Sweetheart remained a total fucking enigma.

If he—Red Church—had been in the other man's shoes . . .

In slow-blink motion Church's eyelids dropped like a curtain, then lifted again. His words, a reluctant gift of information, were expelled with a sighing sound. "We've got the end cap from the pipe—blew off in most of one piece."

"Show me."

Church turned heel, resigned, his uneasiness channeled into manic movement as he led the other man up the short incline to the damaged stairway, past emergency personnel, past the investigative team. He came to a standstill. Sweetheart stopped a half step behind.

Balanced below the edge of the terrace where the wall had been peppered by shrapnel, both men now stood at the inner perimeter of the scene. Behind them gardens filled the shallow canyon. Sweetheart registered the view, abstractly appreciating its formal symmetry, but his attention was on the twisted cap of metal twelve inches from his shoes. Amid chunks of wood, contorted steel, and other explosive debris, a small orange evidence marker with the numeral 1 had already been placed next to the cap. Sweetheart squatted, his thighs spreading until the linen fabric of his slacks pulled taut over highly developed quadriceps. His fingers contracted, exposing the tension in his body.

The eight-inch-diameter, half-inch-thick metal cap was blackened, the lip stretched back in places as if it were a lid chewed off a can. The force of the blast had left pits and scratches in the surface. Balancing on the balls of his feet, Sweetheart eased closer, eyes intent and straining, mind blocking distractions. His breathing softened; he seemed almost asleep.

Detective Church remained standing, shifting nervously on the balls of his feet. He murmured, "It's scratched to all hell—but maybe something's there." His watchful stare landed on two ATF agents examining numbered evidence ten feet away. Would Sweetheart's attendance be challenged? Fortunately, the professor's presence was a badge of sorts.

Church squatted down beside the bigger man and said, "The bomb came in a pretty package, but our perp—or perps—packed the casing with nails, scraps, made sure there was plenty of effective shrapnel, enough to rip the head off—"

With horror, Church registered his own words, but he glanced swiftly at Sweetheart and saw no reaction. That blank face was worse than any display of rage, the detective thought, swallowing hard.

After a moment, Church continued: "Until we reconstruct the device, this could be the work of a hundred different scumbags. The closest witnesses were kids—they're totally freaked out. No usable descriptions, but the Bureau's psychologist is going to keep working with them."

Sweetheart knew Church was talking; he paid scant attention. Instead he studied the rough lines on the cap, fairly certain now that they predated the explosion. He allowed their arrangement to guide his thoughts, noting the associations triggered by familiar configurations that dissolved immediately into *un*familiarity; it was like gazing at the clouds overhead as they created form and identity, then evanesced, all in a matter of seconds. The complexity of communication was on his mind; almost daily he studied symbols as arranged to build language—from morphology to lexicon to syntax, the process of word formation, meaning, and structure in a larger context.

Deftly, Sweetheart pulled a pencil and a small pad of paper from his jacket pocket. With his large body still perfectly balanced on the soles of his feet, he executed lines very slowly on the page. He reminded Church of a man playing a solitary game of hangman. Marks appeared in a pattern that seemed simultaneously random and ordered.

Why the hell couldn't he *get* it? Church wondered, looking closely at the end cap, studying the scratches until they did coalesce into a rough language, albeit one he didn't comprehend.

"C—a—n—t—o—l—l," Sweetheart said deliberately.

"Who the hell is Cantoll?"

"Try *what*."

"I'll bite." Church nodded restlessly. "*What* the hell is Cantoll?"

"A letter, or a numeral, is missing, here at the end—where the metal was particularly twisted," Sweetheart said, closing his eyes. "If we take *canto*, then we . . ." He ran his index finger through air, marking three strikes.

Church shook his head, expelling frustration with a harsh whisper. "You lost me."

"It's famous poetry, Detective. The third canto," Sweetheart said deliberately, as if speaking to a thick-skulled schoolboy. "'Through me you enter into the woeful city, through me the way into eternal pain . . . ' A work originally composed in fourteenth-century Italian, and posthumously retitled the *Divine Comedy*. In *Commedia*, the inscription over the gates to hell."

Sweetheart's jet black hair was pulled back from his face; he fingered the knot with unadorned hands. As he waited, impatient for the obvious connection to be made, he turned to canvass the architecture of the building, in particular the graceful arched gate fronting the damaged terrace. His gaze moved with the linear curves, and the final line of the stanza returned to memory.

"Through me the way to the population of loss."

His mind—always running, mining data, sorting—made connections: a pipe bomb as antipersonnel signature device; a pattern of secondary antiproperty explosives capable of massive structural damage; a linguistic clue that would implicate a bomber.

Sweetheart's body stiffened. "The gates of hell," he whispered harshly. He lifted his eyes to the massive columns marking the entrance to the public courtyard. *A synthesis of pipe bomb and a more powerful antiproperty device . . .*

He pivoted to face Church. "Have you checked for additional devices?"

"We're still searching the grounds—"

"The columns? Those *pillars*," Sweetheart interjected. "Did you check the internal structure for bombs? It's been two hours since the explosion. If there's a second device targeting response personnel—" Sweetheart broke off, barking out a command: "Move everybody away from the scene. *Now.*"

Church hesitated only an instant, then the decision to act telegraphed across his face, and he wheeled around to head off an ATF agent. The alarm went up. The evacuation of investigative and emergency personnel took less than four minutes.

Sweetheart and the others were five hundred yards away—at the bottom of the hill—when detonation occurred. The explosion was deep and sharp, and it shot tons of concrete, rock, steel—the flesh and bone of the structure—in a quarter-mile trajectory. Immediately, a cloud of dust debris swirled up, almost as if it were deliberately covering such obscene devastation. The whole thing seemed to occur in an instant, while everyone dropped for cover.

Everyone except Edmond Sweetheart, who stood immovable, staring into the eye of the beast. He didn't even flinch when a ten-pound marble missile missed his left ear by inches.

Instead he recognized the quickening, the potent cocktail of adrenaline and dread; he'd come to identify it as a chemical threshold, a gateway to the altered state of terror. It was as pungent as the chemicals that make a bomb. It happened on the inside. Outside, all around him, the signs of disaster were familiar: panic on the faces and in the eyes, a heightened surreal atmosphere of smoke, gas, and fumes.

The reverberation of the blast faded as emergency crews and investigators went into high gear for the second time in two hours. The worst of the damage had knocked out three pillars, but the building face was intact. Through the smoke, the cries, the chaos, Sweetheart remembered other words of the great poet.

"Perched above the gates I saw more than a thousand of those whom heaven had cast out like rain, raging: 'Who is this approaching? Who, without death, dares enter the kingdom of the dead?'"

He felt, rather than saw, Detective Church at his side. When he turned to stare at the man, his eyes were dull, unnerving. He spoke in a lifeless monotone. "Six centuries ago, Dante Alighieri wrote the *Inferno*, the most famous book of the three-part *Commedia*."

Confusion showed on Church's sunburnt, freckled face. "Are we talking about *Dantes' Inferno?*" he asked, taking a logical mental leap to the four-hundred-page manifesto written in the 1990s, published in 1999. He was referring to its author, John Dantes, a twenty-first-century fugitive bomber who had claimed responsibility for a dozen crimes spanning more than a decade, causing immense property damage and, most important, taking lives.

Forget long-dead Italian poets, however famous; unless you believe in ghosts, they don't set bombs.

"Yes," Sweetheart said grimly. "We're talking about John Freeman Dantes."

"Maybe." Church looked skeptical. "Dantes has been known to leave a secondary device—"

"He's killed before."

"It's not his style to target schoolkids—he hasn't been tied to a bombing for three, almost four years."

"He went underground," Sweetheart said sharply. "Now he's resurfacing." Nodding toward the scene of the destruction, he reached down to scoop up a handful of sandy soil. "He wants everyone to know it."

He gazed past Detective Church to see a young woman staring back at him. She wore a stricken expression, and she looked frail as a crushed honeysuckle blossom. His belly hollowed. His breath disappeared, his mind went blank as slate. It took him several seconds to put a name to her face. Molly Redding. His own niece. She was holding a child's tennis shoe, clutching it against her breasts, swaying on her feet. A thin, keening wail escaped her lips.

A child and his teacher had died in the first blast . . .

The air stopped. Nothing entered Sweetheart's lungs, and nothing left. For however many seconds in time the tragedy registered, Sweetheart stopped breathing, poised between life and death.

Hakkeyoi—he commanded himself—*move!*—*get going!*

The dam holding back his emotions broke suddenly, and all his rage and pain washed through the canyons of his complex psyche. As denial gave way, information flooded the synapses of his brain: the dead child was Jason Redding, his own grandnephew. Molly Redding was Jason's mother.

Sweetheart's honeyed skin blanched white. The dirt in his hand ran through his fingers until only dust remained.

Jikan desu. Time is up.

His burning gaze settled on the detective's face. He said, "Let's bring in John Dantes, or I swear I'll track him down and kill him myself."

2nd Circle . . .

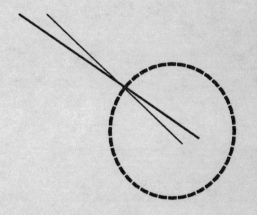

CHAPTER TWO

Utopia in the classic sense defies humanness in its necessary and constant striving for homeostasis. City, the built environment, with all its flaws, its dust and grime, its chaos of lies and secrets, must stand in for any dream of perfection. I'm a grown man crazy in love with LA and all her beauty, all her faults.

John Dantes, *Dantes' Inferno* (Athena Press, 1999),
excerpt published in the *LA Times*, November 7, 2001

April 16, 2001—Monday—7:59 A.M. One Year Later   A ziggurat rose above the shimmering sands of downtown Los Angeles.

Sylvia Strange slid ebony-framed sunglasses over her pronounced cheekbones and brown eyes. Seen through Polaroid glass, the morning glare of rush hour traffic retreated, the desert sands coalesced into a mishmash of urban high-rises fading from a half century's wear and tear; nomadic caravans were transformed into commuter lanes on the Harbor northbound; the ziggurat redefined itself as the terraced pyramidal tower atop City Hall.

The twenty-eight-story structure was just a stone's throw from her destination: Metropolitan Detention Center—aka MDC—home of the mad and the bad.

So much for visions of the Holy Land.

Still, it was hot enough to be the Negev desert. Even with air-conditioning, sweat dampened Sylvia's neck and trickled between her breasts. She punched up climate control settings and aimed arctic air at her throat. Almost instantly her skin raised goose bumps. No such thing as a happy medium this Monday morning.

Nudging unruly shoulder-length auburn strands away from her face, she took a deep breath, checking her reflection in the mirror. Olive skin a little wan, lips chapped and bare of lipstick, pupils dilated behind dark glasses. She knew she needed more than blush, eyeliner, and a jolt of chutzpah to pass for a member of the psychological-profiling elite.

Welcome to the majors, Strange. You hit the big league, the chance to contribute to the biggest forensic profiling study of bombers—ever. The chance to tag along while the FBI and ATF, LAPD and UCLA—all under the elitist and watchful eye of Rand Corporation—take an up-close-and-personal look at members of the Notorious Bombers' Club: McVeigh, Ramzi Yousef, Richard Johnson, Theodore K.

And John Freeman Dantes.

Reaching automatically into the pocket of her briefcase, she pulled out a cigarette, squeezing it gently between plain fingers, sliding the filter between her lips. Waiting for the lighter to heat, she cracked the window as a concession to the Hertz no-smoking policy. The lighter finally popped, and she held the hot red coil to tobacco, inhaling greedily. The smoke seared her throat, felt dense in her lungs. Trapping the nicotine, she picked a speck of tobacco off her lip, flicked nonexistent ashes out the window, then finally exhaled the cancerous air.

John Dantes . . . the man who wrote the book *Dantes' Inferno: City of Angels in the 21st Century.* Chapter one: "The Boy Who Was Raised by Wolves in the City."

Sylvia inhaled smoke again. In his *Inferno*, Dantes had dissected the yin and yang of LA: the male represented by technology imposed as superstructure over the female, the natural and functional evolution of village to postmodern megalopolis. For Dantes, it all added up to greed, ambition, and fantasy destroying the heart of the true Los Angeles, the city that belonged to the people.

She glanced at her wristwatch, and the silvery face finally came into focus: one minute before eight. Trapped in an endlessly looping countdown, the tiny black hand clicked off intervals. She was late, getting later with each breath, and traffic was at a standstill.

Shouldn't be a problem, she thought. Dr. Strange, student of dark and disordered moods, knew how to use reverse psychology. Over the past five years, working in prisons and hospitals, she'd come face-to-face with some of the world's worst criminals. She'd earned a reputation among her colleagues as a forensic psychologist with a knack for connecting with the hardest of the hard cases. Exactly the reason she'd been summoned to LA.

Behind the wheel of the Lincoln, she settled into calfskin upholstery that was soft as butter. Her shoes rested beside her on the passenger seat and her coral-painted toenails encased in slippery hose hugged the brake pedal. She eased the seam of her panty hose from her crotch; as soon as the job was completed, she'd burn the torturous garment and fly back home to New Mexico, where a person could walk barefoot on desert earth and watch cumulus clouds form over the Sangre de Cristo mountain range—

Before the first sharp ring faded, Sylvia had her cell phone cradled to her ear. The call jarred her back in time, and for the hundredth time she heard the echo of the words that had split her world down the middle just four weeks ago.

Dr. Strange? This is Mona Carpenter. I called to say good-bye.

A real voice asked, "Sylvia, are you there?"

"Leo?"

"Metro just went under lockdown," psychiatrist Leo Carreras announced. His voice was clouded with concern.

"Bomb threat?"

"The official line is 'heightened security.'"

"My session with Dantes is still on"—half statement, half question.

"So far, so good. Nervous, Dr. Strange?"

"You jumped through hoops to get my security clearance," she said quickly.

Leo had brought her in as the psychometric expert—a fancy way of saying she would administer the psychological tests, the inventories, the batteries. Even though she had all the proper credentials, the profiling project was as political as any primary. Leo and UCLA were one faction, the Feds were another, and so was the LAPD; Rand had its own agenda. But the truth was, final approval belonged to John Dantes. He had agreed to cooperate with Dr. Strange on the tests.

Celebrity inmates with the visibility of John Dantes carried their clout like a big stick.

"You'll have all day to administer tests," Leo said. "Unless you get interrupted by security—so keep the initial interview short . . . "

Barely listening, Sylvia sighed. Just six weeks ago, she'd leapt at this chance to work on such a high-profile project. She had been certain she could snag Dantes where others had failed. But that was before her client killed herself.

Dr. Strange, there will be a board inquiry, of course.

"Sylvia? Are you all right?"

She came to suddenly, knowing Leo had asked something. She nudged her sunglasses to the bridge of her nose.

"I'm here." She found the bottle in record time—cap off—and tossed a tiny blue pellet into her mouth. The tablet stuck to the back of her throat.

" . . . go with a projective warm-up to establish rapport," Leo was saying. "*Then* the MMPI."

"I'm more comfortable starting with the objective inventories," Sylvia said. What was she doing in this city of noise, glare, smog, and concrete? "The MMPI first, then the Millon."

"I know it's time-consuming, but the Rorschach will give us a wealth of information." After a brief silence, Leo said, "Just consider my suggestion."

"Of course."

"Extend today's session," Leo added. "Push for whatever you can get. You may not have another opportunity."

"Yes, Mother." The jocularity fell flat.

"Dantes's oppositional as hell—don't think he'll give you any breaks just because he likes the way you look. He'll take control, try to bait you or just shut down altogether."

"I'll bait him back. Piece of cake."

"Remember, I want all the dirty details. Dinner at the Lobster, Santa Monica Pier. By the way, how was your flight?"

Mona—is the baby there with you? Is Nathan with you?

"The Lobster. I'll call you when I'm finished," she managed. "The flight was turbulent."

"Sylvia, I know I got you into this—I have no doubts you're the one for the job." Leo's tone sobered abruptly. "Just don't forget who you're dealing with; Dantes is dangerous."

She disconnected, nosing the Lincoln toward the right lane. Pressing down on the pedal, she gave its powerful engine gas. Horns blared, but she was already tearing east on the fourth street off-ramp.

I'll be back in New Mexico in four days, five at the most, she reminded herself—just do the work and get out. But no one had forced her to come to Los Angeles. No one had twisted her arm.

Leo Carreras had offered her the job because he needed her expertise; he was counting on her to connect with the world's most oppositional client. And she was here, even though she was off balance emotionally and professionally. She'd accepted because somewhere, buried beneath all the turbulent emotions, she felt the lure of the "important" profiling project—not to mention the draw of John Dantes.

Obsessions are enduring and deep rooted.

His centered on avenging the crimes of the powerful as perpetrated on the postmodern city and its less sophisticated inhabitants.

Hers happened to be a seemingly endless fascination with a brilliant mind turned pathological.

"Made for each other," she mumbled as she released the brake, shifting gears.

The Lincoln covered ground, catching green lights all the way to Broadway. She turned north, then east again.

Passing an entrance to U.S. 101 south, Sylvia turned the wheel so sharply files flew off the passenger seat onto the floor, and the Lincoln left a black stripe of rubber along the curb.

As she passed MDC, the federal detention center that bordered the north edge of LA's Civic Center complex, a stat crossed her mind: downtown LA is home to twenty-five thousand inmates, the largest population behind bars in any American city.

You'd never know it. To the passerby, MDC's ten-story Hyatt facade, with its postmodern steel trellises and bridge-ways casting shadows over Immigration and Naturalization, could easily be mistaken for a resort hotel instead of the largest prison to be built in any major urban center in recent history.

Beyond MDC, in the distance, City Hall's ziggurat trapped the sun, and just for an instant the pyramidal tower glowed like a sparking match before its flame dies out.

Civilization gone in a flash.

Sylvia turned under a twenty-foot painted sign—PAR-QUEO—into the gaping mouth of the subterranean garage that serviced visitors to the detention center and the LAPD, as well as the adjacent Roybal Federal Building. After the vast spaces of New Mexico, she couldn't get used to this urban landscape where each vertical universe was perched over a massive burrow. Too much light, too much darkness.

Guiding the Lincoln through a fluorescent maze of parked vehicles and concrete pillars, she remembered a child's sneaker. Neon green. Ridiculously small. A tiny lizard crest on the tongue.

Jason Redding had been ten and a half years old when he died.

The week following the Getty bombing, a photograph of that shoe had made the cover of *Time* and *Newsweek;* the haunting image had played on CNN around the world.

Molly Redding had delivered a message to her son's convicted murderer as he left the courtroom—

Sylvia pulled into a slot, set the brake, and switched off the ignition. The engine in the sea green Lincoln quieted with an almost imperceptible sigh that matched her own.

"—John Dantes, I'll wait for you in hell."

8:23 A.M. Sylvia pushed her sunglasses back on her head and entered MDC's air-conditioned glass and steel lobby, where the illusion of a resort hotel was maintained with the help of potted palms and soft lighting. Was it the subtly armored environment that made her feel more secure? Was it simply the familiarity of a prison work environment? She suspected something different—she felt safer locked up with the inmates than she did out in the urban canyons of LA.

At capacity, MDC held nine-hundred-plus prisoners, for the most part federal detainees awaiting trial: drug dealers, kidnappers, extortionists, counterfeit-change artists, terrorists. With that many bad guys in the neighborhood, it might be reassuring to find the U.S. marshals quartered right next door and LAPD across the street. Sylvia couldn't seem to give a damn one way or the other.

Today, due to bomb threats and the fact they were eight days away from the one-year anniversary of the Getty bombing, security was heavy; at the control desk she passed through a metal detector while a female security officer urged an eighty-pound shepherd to stay cool. He growled anyway.

Can't fool a smart dog, Sylvia thought, smiling coldly.

She took the elevator. Embedded somewhere in the shaft, gears groaned. At the fourth floor, the doors opened to reveal two shackled prisoners waiting in the hallway; their eyes slid back and forth between the nervous officer who was their escort and Sylvia.

She found herself at yet another security checkpoint: *Look, Ma, no pipe bombs.*

The Bureau of Prisons security officer pulled a tape recorder from Sylvia's briefcase. He swabbed the palm-sized machine with a cotton ball, screening for any chemical reaction with explosive material residue. He examined the thick stack of test booklets, her personal items, then moved on to her spare tape cassettes, going through cotton balls left and right.

Just let me do my job, she thought impatiently. Over several days, that job would consist of the most systematic of tasks, administering the objective psychometric inventories—the MMPI-2, the MCMI-3, the WAIS-3, the Bender, the Halstead-Rëitan, or the Luria-Nebraska Neuropsychological Battery. Each test booklet was several inches thick. Some contained endless questions: Do you . . . If you . . . Have you ever . . . Would you . . . ? Some were multiple choice, or true or false, or tell a story, or finish the sentence. Some were visual—put the puzzle together, match the shapes, fit the round peg in the square hole.

And then they could be scored. There were scales to measure depression, hysteria, psychopathology, mania, hypochondriasis, schizophrenia, psychasthenia.

She was here precisely because psychological testing was the most analytical, standardized, measurable, and emotionally detached portion of the profiling project.

I can't offer judgment calls, intuition, or emotion. Not this month.

No clinical interviews, no therapy, no need for empathic connection.

No trespassing on the dangerous terrain of soul or psyche. Thanks anyway.

Electronic clamor caught her attention, cuffing it on the ear. The officer was nodding her through the yawning jaws of security.

She tripped on a fraying edge of rubber matting, abruptly unsteady, reminding herself she was about to be forty minutes late for a meeting with a killer named John Dantes.

8:41 A.M. "You made it past the hounds of hell," he said softly. At the moment, he was a disembodied presence, his face lost in shadow.

But Sylvia felt the sting of his eyes on her skin.

Fluorescent light abruptly flooded the small square room.

She blinked, off balance, only to find she was staring directly into his face.

It was heart shaped, capped with light brown hair gone prematurely gray at the temples and knotted into a rough ponytail. His cheekbones were prominent, his mouth wide, his chiseled features drawn together by a small, almost pointed chin. Fatigue and prison life had dulled his complexion, and it had been at least two days since his last shave. The fresh bruise bluing the skin of his left cheek added to the overall effect of eighteenth-century castaway mixed with contemporary street fighter.

But it was his eyes that threatened to penetrate her emotional perimeter; behind wire rims, they were green—no, gray—flecked with sparks of white and yellow, fringed with thick lashes. They were the eyes of a visionary. Or a psychopath.

She looked away, belatedly, hearing the echoing hiss of whispered words: "—*last time*—*I can't*—" She registered another presence in the room: a female correctional officer. The Bureau of Prisons employee was young, lost inside a tan uniform with epaulettes and a black and white name tag identifying her as D. FLORETTE.

Sylvia had the feeling she'd interrupted some heated exchange between the guard and Dantes; her curiosity was aroused, but left unsatisfied when CO Florette ducked her head and launched into a seemingly endless rote speech covering rules and regulations.

While Florette droned on, Sylvia had the chance to study the man who—at age twenty-four—had been teaching postgraduate urban structural sociology at one of southern California's most prestigious universities when he wasn't busy blowing up the California aqueduct in retribution for historic sins. Now, at thirty-seven, he was serving his first year of a life sentence—for the Getty, the *one* bombing he claimed he didn't commit.

Over the course of his outlaw career, the media had alternately exhibited Dantes as a mysterious and clever fugitive, an impassioned charismatic defendant, a stridently political prisoner. Sylvia thought he looked less functional than any of his public personas.

"Dr. Strange?" Florette's hard, unwelcoming voice snagged Sylvia's attention. "You can see for yourself he's manacled, ankles only—we freed his hands per your request. I'll step outside, that's regulation—and I'll do my visuals at random."

"Thank you, Deborah," Dantes said politely.

"Please remember to avoid all physical contact with the prisoner. Excuse me, ma'am." Ignoring Dantes, she brushed past Sylvia; the door slammed shut behind her back.

The sound bounced around the angular space before it died at the feet of an artificial silence broken only by the ticking of a clock mounted on the wall.

"She's jealous." John Dantes was the first to speak. "Even prisons have their stars."

Sylvia didn't move. The air pumped into this concrete box tasted stale and delivered a federally mandated chill. "Are you proud of your celebrity status?"

"It offers some advantages."

She gestured to a bruise near his left eye. "One of the perks?"

"You're not what I imagined." He studied her intently for several moments, then said, "You're not one of Leo's *suits*. And you're not a Fed . . . or I'd have smelled you a mile away." But suspicion etched his face.

"I'm Dr. Strange, Mr. Dantes. I work with Dr. Carreras, who arranged this meeting to conduct some psychological inventories. As part of this criminal profiling project, all participants undergo a standard evaluation."

She shifted her briefcase from right hand to left before adding quietly, "But I think you're aware of why I'm here, because you and I have already spoken by telephone—and you also signed a release form."

The echo of a slamming door intruded faintly into the room.

Dantes' eyes cut toward the security window, which offered a view of the hallway, where the top of CO Florette's dark head was just visible. "Standard evaluation . . . that makes the project sound very common, doesn't it?"

"I don't think so, no."

"But it's a bombers' profiling project."

"It's classified as a *criminal* profiling project," she said flatly. Although, like Dantes, the participants were certain to speculate, they would not be given confirmation that the profiling project was limited to bombers; that knowledge would only serve to puff up their egos and skew their responses.

"Sit down, Dr. Strange. You're making me nervous. I'm beginning to regret the fact I agreed to *this*."

She lurched into motion, crossing the room, placing her briefcase next to the chair. Sliding her sunglasses from her hair, she caught the faint scent of him—a basic blend of soap and sweat.

As she placed her tape recorder on the table—pressing *record*—he studied her openly. She had the sensation of being touched.

"Look at you." Dantes' eyes slid from her head to her toes. "All dressed up in your Sunday best." His voice had softened, and his lips curled in an expectant smile.

She didn't react.

This seemed to bother him, and he said, "Before we

begin this common criminal's *standard* evaluation, tell me something about Dr. Strange. You're a forensic psychologist, licensed to practice in New Mexico and California—

"You're board certified, you have a Ph.D., and a diplomate in forensic psychology. University of New Mexico, Case Western Reserve, not to mention UCLA—our shared alma mater."

"You did your research," she said, moving slowly.

"I know some facts about your life—my attorney provides me with résumés—but that's not the same as hearing your side of the story." He appeared as internally contained as the dark eye at the center of a raging hurricane. "I even managed to read a dozen of your published papers." He studied her. "Don't look now but your clinical bias is showing. You might even believe in redemption."

She shifted in the hard chair, and its metal legs scraped loudly over the concrete floor.

"All the way from New Mexico," he said, dismissing her effortlessly. "Did you travel such a distance for the honor of sharing a few hours with me?"

"I often travel for my work," she said, not quite biting back her own impatience. Now she retrieved a packet of pencils from one pocket of her briefcase. She ran her thumbnail along the plastic wrapping without making a dent.

"But it's not every day you travel for the FBI, ATF, all those VIP Feds."

"I already told you, I'm working with Dr. Carreras." The plastic wrap suddenly split, spilling pencils onto Formica; one rolled off the edge and Dantes caught it in midair.

"Just like your predecessors?" He shrugged. "You're not the first to arrive with your psychometric inventories."

"That's irrelevant."

"Is it?" He laced his fingers across his chest, glancing again briefly at the room's only window, a twelve-by-twelve-inch square cut in the door. "Have you seen the new exhibit at the County?" he asked, slowly returning his focus to her face.

She shook her head, letting him lead the dance, feeling she'd missed a step.

"Francisco Goya, the eyes of the Enlightenment," Dantes prodded. His long, wiry body overwhelmed the pitted plastic chair, and yet he wore the state-issue jumpsuit, bullet-proof vest, and ankle manacles like a three-piece suit.

"I've seen his work in other museums." She snapped open the center compartment of her briefcase.

"A true democrat. Equally offended by corruption in state or church." Glancing toward the door for the third time in minutes, Dantes carried on his conversation as if he were hosting a social occasion. "And like Dürer and Dante Alighieri, Goya refused to keep his eyes or his mouth shut. Always a dangerous choice. He was betrayed by spies, by cowards."

Sylvia set the first booklet on the table, adjusting the corners, setting one pencil on top. "Are you comparing yourself to Dürer, or Dante, or both?"

"Are you pissed you aren't the first to offer me your *standard measurements?*" he countered. "Isn't that what they're called in the deconstructing biz?"

"Whether I'm first or tenth, the important thing is to complete the standardized inventories." Her throat felt so dry she could barely swallow. "My participation in the profiling project is highly circumscribed."

He raised an eyebrow. "You don't strike me as the type."

"What type is that?"

"The highly circumscribed type."

They were leading each other in circles, like dogs guarding a bone.

"The FBI sent a tedious suit," Dantes said. His fingers

drummed the table: *a-rat-a-tat-a-rat-a-tat*. "Rand sent a redhead with a bad attitude."

"Do you have any intention of completing the inventories with me?" She shifted in the chair, and the thick test booklet slid from the table, hitting the floor with a *slap*.

"Which of Goya's images stayed with you?" Dantes asked.

Without breathing, she stared back at him, lured by his intensity. "The devils."

"Not the lunatics?" He tipped his head forward, eyelids lowering, as if without looking he clearly sensed her vulnerability. "Oh, c'mon, admit it, Dr. Strange. You feel a kinship with the lunatics."

Dark lashes fringed her deep-set eyes, shading a restless acuity, lending her face an ordinary prettiness. She almost shook her head—this was what she wanted, wasn't it, to maintain contact, to keep him engaged? She flashed on an image: her father and a young girl fishing from a dinghy in Heron Lake. *You've got to give the fish some slack, Sylvie. Play out the line until it's time to set the hook.*

She said, "Goya was chronicling the bigotry and superstition of his time."

"Goya chronicles *our* time." Dantes tapped out a few more hyperkinetic beats, marking double time on the fake wood grain. His gaze was arrogant and cold, but the ember of some passion was sparking deep in those eyes.

Rage, hatred . . . fear? She couldn't quite catch it.

He frowned, the muscles around his bruised eye ticcing ever so faintly. "Those in power, the members of the privileged class, should not abuse their position or their duties of stewardship, neither by commission or omission. If they do, they're common criminals—or worse, they're cowards." He pulled back suddenly, shrugging off the brief excursion into rhetoric.

"You don't think much of cowards."

"Do you?"

"You've made reference to them twice in a matter of minutes."

"I don't like psychoanalysis, either." He smiled.

Sylvia reached out, her fingers sliding over molded plastic, to tear open the seal on the test booklet. The first two inventories she planned to administer—the Millon Clinical Multiaxial and the Minnesota Multiphasic—would total at least five hours.

She glanced at her watch.

"Hot date?"

She met his eyes, saw the mockery there, and reached for her briefcase. "Mr. Dantes, either I'm not doing any better than my colleagues or you're not interested in completing these inventories or both." She stood. "Let's not waste any more time."

Immediately, he held his palms out; it was a gesture of surrender, the action of a lonely man. "You win," he said, reaching for the booklet, sliding it to his side of the table. He picked up the pencil, gesturing for her to be seated again.

She blinked as if coming from dark to light, disoriented, mustering herself. Her head ached, her deltoids were so tight they burned, she had to pee—but the last thing she'd do was take a break now and end up with nothing.

Outside, in the hallway, heavy footsteps sounded. The urgent tones of an argument penetrated the walls of the room.

Taking her seat opposite him for the second time, she said, "This conversation—and the test results—will not be confidential, but the project's coordinators will make every attempt to keep transcripts secure and available only to participants—"

She stiffened when Dantes' hand suddenly covered her own.

"Lunatics and inmates. We're not so bad, are we?" he whispered.

Wrenching her hand away, Sylvia felt Dantes watching her, felt the hunger of his curiosity.

"You can't save them all, can you, Sylvia?" Dantes' voice was soft, seductive.

Sylvia stared at him, blinking, hearing another voice internally. *Dr. Strange, although the committee finds no grounds to cite you with an ethical violation in the death of Mona Carpenter, we do have concerns. It seems you did comply with the standards of your profession regarding safeguards against suicide, but when it came to the use of your judgment you could've gone the extra mile, relying less on intuition and luck, more on solid follow-up.*

Dantes gazed back at her, his face a study in compassion, his voice soothing, as he said, "Tell me about Mona Carpenter."

The shock registered. She said nothing. She focused on a single thought: I know how to handle this—it comes with the job.

Dantes said, "Pills *and* cutting—isn't that overkill?" With each word his breath quickened as if he was aroused. If he had assaulted her physically, it couldn't have been worse. But he wasn't finished yet.

"What did it feel like to actually *hear* her death?" he asked.

Sylvia gathered together the tests and the tape recorder, sweeping them into her briefcase. She watched her sunglasses skid to the floor. Her heart was racing.

Dantes rose straight up from his chair, his presence filling the room as he whispered his last question. "What's it like to know you could've saved her?"

For an instant Sylvia believed he would go further than verbal assault—but he'd already drawn blood. He stood rooted, burning her with his stare.

She knew the protocol for threatening or aggressive patients: remain calm, maintain distance, keep a barrier between you—always know where to find the panic button. She'd been here before—she'd be here again. None of that seemed to matter. She felt the rush of adrenaline, every synapse trapped in looping panic.

"You pathetic son of a bitch," she hissed, suddenly coming to life. "Do you really believe you're any better than a common sociopath?" She turned and took four steps to the door, her fist hitting metal.

The door swung wide. A uniformed guard blinked at the sight of Sylvia. "Done already?"

She left Dantes behind as the door slammed shut.

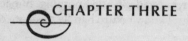

CHAPTER THREE

> Man is a rope, fastened between animal and Superman—a rope over an abyss. A dangerous going-across, a dangerous wayfaring, a dangerous looking-back, a dangerous shuddering and staying still.
>
> Nietzsche

9:55 A.M. From an office in his Hollywood Hills home, Professor Edmond Sweetheart watched as the female psychologist unceremoniously exited the private visiting room at MDC.

As an image captured by the hidden video camera and

transmitted via a live satellite feed, Dr. Sylvia Strange appeared shaken and disturbed by Dantes' verbally aggressive assault; but Sweetheart thought the woman possessed her own raw energy, her own dangerous edge, visible even on the small screen. And when she whispered some inaudible but clearly intense farewell, he was disappointed that the camera angle didn't allow him to read her lips.

He still wasn't sure about her; she was an unknown element—a positive or negative charge—introduced into this particular chemical equation. She was a catalyst—and when it came to John Dantes, a catalyst was exactly what they needed.

Strange walked into the hall, her screen image disappearing as the door closed behind her back. Sweetheart was left to study the prisoner, John Freeman Dantes. In turn, Dantes studied Sweetheart. He did this by facing the eye of the camera hidden in the wall-mounted clock.

Dantes stood without moving, without blinking as the seconds passed, adding up to one minute, then two. He stared through the lens, the wall, seemingly straight across the city into Sweetheart's ebony eyes. Finally, his mouth took a slow turn, curling into a smile. He raised his right hand, middle finger extended.

Sweetheart's eyes didn't waver. He didn't shift his posture on the tatami. His mouth was set in a rigid line, every muscle in his 280-pound frame was firing, but his breathing stayed slow and steady. Each inhalation, each exhalation helped still his violent thoughts.

Nor did Dantes break concentration—or the level of threat in his stance—not even when the prison door swung wide and three BOP officers entered the room. The door slammed and locked as the first officer shoved Dantes off balance. The prisoner resisted against the odds, refusing to relinquish power, even when the second officer raised a rubber baton. With one practiced blow, the guard barely grazed Dantes' ribs as a warning.

The inmate dropped to his knees, apparently compliant.

Watching the show from his war room, Sweetheart didn't bat an eye. His expression was as calm as the faces of the sumo wrestlers whose portraits decorated his walls. His gaze never strayed from the scene taking place on the monitor. The hum of computers, the distant buzz of traffic from Sunset Boulevard, the rustle of bamboo in the garden, the rhythm of his own breathing melded into white noise undisturbed even by the audio transmission coming from MDC. Thanks to the miracle of technology, the live feed could just as easily be originating from four thousand miles away instead of four.

Now the audio transmission was filled with the sounds of physical exertion and pain—grunts, groans. Sweetheart watched calmly, perhaps inclining his body just a fraction of an inch. No one in that small prison room was lifting an aggressive finger. The noise was coming from John Dantes as he collapsed to the floor apparently ill and retching violently.

Sweetheart studied the kinetic reactions of the prisoner. (That's how he usually thought of Dantes these days—in the abstract. It was safer that way.) There was an abnormal spastic quality to those movements, as if they were the result of seizure activity. But Sweetheart had read the most recent physical and neurological reports on the prisoner, who despite institutional life was in near perfect health. The professor stored this latest bit in his own organic information processing system for later retrieval and evaluation.

As suddenly as it had begun, the apparent seizure ended. Dantes stood with the aid of the officers. As the inmate was led from the visiting room—and out of camera range—Sweetheart shifted on the tatami, relaxing almost imperceptibly. He took a sip of green tea from a raku cup before punching a button on a tiny keyboard.

The monitor responded with a new image, which was provided by a second camera at MDC. Sweetheart was now watching the Bureau of Prisons correctional officer Deborah Florette, hunched despondently in a chair inside a security office located in Metropolitan Detention Center's administrative wing.

As the professor adjusted the volume of the audio feed, a disembodied male voice became distinguishable: "Who gave you the money, Florette?"

"I don't know who he was," Florette mumbled, shifting uncomfortably. "I never saw him."

"But you were paid to courier contraband to Dantes. What'd you take him?"

Florette's mouth set in a obstinate line. She shook her head, crossing her arms, every inch of her body language screaming emotional lockdown.

"How are your math skills, Florette?" A red-haired man stepped into the range of the camera's lens, half filling the monitor. LAPD detective Red Church settled on the corner of a desk. "You're looking at twenty years, two decades, ten-and-ten behind bars."

Mutely, CO Florette shook her head.

"C'mon, Deb." Church sighed, his eyes sad. "A smart, pretty woman like yourself, two little ones, it's a damn shame and a waste. You want to let the state raise your kids?"

"They were pictures," Florette whispered. She dropped her chin, shielding herself from view, surrendering. "That's all." She looked up, dark eyes flashing. "Like baseball cards, *that's all*. He's a celebrity, right? Dantes is on those serial

killer baseball cards. And this guy just wanted autographs."
Florette's voice rose to the edge of hysteria. "This is *Holly-wood*, right? Listen, if you want to go after somebody, go after the guys who make those cards in the first place!"

"Yeah," Red Church said quietly. "We found it when we shook down his cell. And damn it, Florette, I'm giving you the benefit of the doubt." Church leaned in close to the woman. "Tell me you didn't know you were carrying a message."

"I swear it—you've got my word of honor—I didn't know."

Sweetheart gazed down at the words transmitted and printed out from his computer twenty minutes earlier—a copy of the communication discovered in Dantes' cell while Dr. Strange kept him busy.

> dear friend
> thru me the way into the woeful city
> thru me the way to eternal pain
> sacrifice the children of heathens
> until no innocents lay claim
> first circle broken
> 8 circles remain
> I do your bidding faithfully
> M—

A cold rage slowed Sweetheart's blood. The second and third lines—the beginning of Dante Alighieri's third canto of the *Commedia*—took him back to the Getty bombing and the obscure scratches on the end cap of pipe bomb. A child dead, his own flesh and blood—"*sacrifice the children of heathens.*" Eight days to the anniversary of the bombing—"*8 circles remain.*"

After the Getty, he'd led the pursuit to track down

Dantes. The evidence had been good—a detonating chip traced to a single manufacturer, a transport trail that led straight to Dantes.

Had it been too good? Had his lust to bring in Dantes blinded him to the possibility of a collaborator? If a collaborator existed, Sweetheart wanted his head.

The FBI would be monitoring the movements of the psychologist, Dr. Strange. She'd passed the profiling project's security protocol, her credentials seemed clean enough, but the timing of her visit to Dantes was going to interest them keenly. He imagined they would keep an agent on her for the next twenty-four hours.

Sweetheart had his own way of tracking human subjects.

He shifted his body to face another monitor, this one a flat screen mounted directly on the white wall. He typed in a search string for Strange, Sylvia.

The computer fluttered its eyelashes—flirting with offers of infinite data—the blink-blink of information flashing across the screen. Within forty-five seconds he was looking at Multiplex prOfiles Systems AnalysIs Kit data.

MOSAIK was his baby; her specialty was agent-based, multitiered profiling.

Quickly, he screened past the basic (and now familiar) biographical data, which included medical, academic, professional and legal records, as well as geographic and personal history. Bits of information registered:

> Ht: 5 feet, 9 inches; Wt: 141; eyes: brown; hair: brown; skin: olive; scars: left eye, left hand; tattoos: NA; moles: right shoulder, right breast
> Profession: psychologist, forensic
> Marriage status: divorced
>> LINKS: relationships, personal
>> LINKS: history, sexual

Heritage: Irish, Italian

    hospitalizations, general: tonsillectomy, 1977
    hospitalizations, psychiatric: 1981, Los Angeles, CA
       LINKS: evaluations, psychiatric.

The data flow was never-ending; it documented her extensive research on prisons, on attachment disorders, on psychopathy; the foster daughter who had been rescued from a barrio on the border of Mexico and Texas; the love affair with a psychiatrist now dead of cancer; her engagement to an investigator with the New Mexico State Police; a long-ago marriage so brief it hardly registered; the tentative relationship with her mother; the father who had deserted his wife and daughter many years ago.

Sweetheart gave MOSAIK a verbal command and a new screen appeared:

    Father: Strange, Daniel, Danny; born 1940, CO,
      Colorado Springs
    REMARKS: missing person
       LINKS: Strange, D, military; Army service
      record
       LINKS: training record CLASSIFIED
       LINKS: Vietnam; Cambodia
       LINKS: Strange, D, POW
       LINKS: covert operations; special ops
       LINKS: CIA
       LINKS: Strange, D, missing person
       LINKS: global tracking, current status
         CLASSIFIED

He was fishing.
As he stared at the screen, he calculated which pieces

of information would provide him with the most leverage.

Sweetheart knew Strange was investigating her father's
whereabouts—she'd hired a private investigator named
Joshua Harold. She'd even visited morgues to eliminate the
possibility that Daniel Strange was a John Doe. With one
command, Sweetheart could pull up the entire file . . .

He scrolled past screen after screen, ignoring data on
DNA and voiceprint and fingerprints, momentarily exclud-
ing the photo library, video storage, linguistic samples, GIS
mapping of mobility.

He reached into a glazed ceramic bowl and selected a
salted plum candy. The soft tech hum provided background
for his thoughts.

Sweetheart typed in a new name: *Carpenter, Mona
Suzanne*.

He added relationship modifiers: client; deceased.

He gave a verbal command.

As new information filled the screen, Sweetheart
thought of Dr. Sylvia Strange, the catalyst. It interested
him . . . this connection between Strange and Dantes had
just taken an unexpected turn: suicide; two women separated by three decades; each had taken her own life.
Dantes' mother. The doctor's client.

This morbid connection between Dantes and Strange
made her valuable—it also made her vulnerable. Especially
if another bomber was loose in LA.

10:09 A.M.   Sylvia hunched inside the leathery cave of the
Lincoln nursing the last of a cigarette.

Ten minutes earlier, she'd stepped out of MDC's artificial womb into searing Los Angeles sunlight. Half blind
and conscious only of the sign for the car park on the side
of the large concrete structure ahead, she'd stumbled across

Alameda, a wide downtown boulevard surprisingly free of traffic. The sun had assaulted eyes already glazed and heavy lidded from stress and chemicals. And fear. Dantes had made her afraid.

It almost felt good—that forced exile from a deadened world.

She exhaled smoke, studying the cigarette she gripped between taut fingers. The ragged, charred edge of tobacco had almost burned down to the yellowed filter. She opened the door of the Lincoln just long enough to jab the cigarette butt on the pavement, then she jerked the door shut and set the locks. Shaking off the fear and a fleeting sense of doom, she turned the key in the ignition. The engine awoke with a powerful growl.

She followed the I-10 west until it slapped smack up against ocean. The Pacific shone with the watery blue of ink. It stretched and rolled and heaved its weight against the wide lip of sand. With Missy Elliott singing about D.C., Atlanta, and LA from the radio (volume cranked), Sylvia watched lunar magnetism muscling the tides.

Traffic was backed up two blocks in front of the neon entrance to Santa Monica Pier. Inching toward the intersection, and finally turning north onto Ocean Avenue, she caught a catty-corner view of the restaurant where she was due to meet Leo for dinner. The Lobster, a glaringly white beach-box structure, stuck out like a swollen jaw on a neck of stilts. A banner advertised Thursday evening concerts on the pier; next week, oldies by the Velvet Underground.

Joggers, sunbathers, tourists, and street people shared the slice of green known as Palisades Park. As she drove past the looming, funky deco prow of the Shangri La Hotel, she tried to reach her fiancé in New Mexico by cell phone. Matt England didn't answer but his machine managed to cut her off just as she told him she loved him. She left a message for Leo Carreras—moving their meeting up to three o'clock. She tossed the phone onto the passenger seat as she drove past Wilshire and Montana, finally turning right onto Marguerita Avenue.

She parked the Lincoln in front of the property owned by Leo, and she stepped out into a balmy ocean breeze. Carrying her briefcase, garment bag, and overnight case, she crossed manicured grass skirting lemony tufts of daffodils until she reached the tiny yellow thirties-style bungalow that was one of a quartet. Leo's stark and glassy condominium occupied the south end of the large lot. He rented the cottages to various LA standards: a television writer, a character actor with a fondness for Irish whiskey, a waiter/singer. The last bungalow, Numero Quatro, was reserved for Leo's visiting colleagues. Over the past two years, Sylvia had stayed here on consulting trips. The key was under the familiar ceramic pot that overflowed with night-blooming jasmine.

Inside, the house smelled of old wood, salt, the faintest hint of ocean mildew, and perfume. She located the source of the sweet fragrance immediately, a fat ocher-tinted porcelain vase filled with white, yellow, and lavender orchids, gracing an antique writing desk. She experienced a moment of pleasure tinged with uneasiness knowing Leo had chosen the flowers especially for her; breaking off one delicate blossom, she pressed it to her cheek. The petals felt silky against her skin.

The bungalow had been built around a simple rectangular floor plan: kitchen and dining nook, living room, bedroom, bath—and tiny sitting room, which functioned as an office—all connecting around a compact central hall.

After cracking louver blinds in the living room, she moved to the bedroom, where she tossed her bag on the nubby white spread. Pulling out shorts, T-shirt, cross-trainers, and her blue Dodgers cap, she stripped off her work clothes—she'd been wearing them since 4 A.M. in New Mexico—and quickly changed into running gear. In the kitchen she poured herself a tall glass of tap water, draining it in seconds. Then she was out the door.

In the middle of the concrete overpass that traversed Highway 1 and allowed access from the cliff park to the beach, she missed her sunglasses. She'd left them on the floor of the visiting room at MDC.

Fine, she thought harshly—let Dantes add another item to his trophy collection; he was eating up shrinks left and right.

She ran for several miles, heading north, parallel with the shore, barely evading the foamy salt water as it licked creamy sand beneath her feet. Here and there she passed other runners, beachcombers, and the yellow all-terrain trucks owned by the state of California.

A hundred yards offshore, surfers bobbed with seals, both species catching modest waves. After the first few miles her muscles loosened up; by the fourth mile she felt herself sprint clear of the chemical cloud induced by the morning's dose of benzodiazepine. She quickened her pace, sweating, breath fast but regular. The sun warmed her skin, and she knew she'd end up with a slight golden hue to her olive complexion. She set her sights on a small but rugged peninsula ahead—her turnaround point. Time evaporated beneath her legs, and it seemed she reached those volcanic rocks in one minute instead of thirty. She cut to a fast walk, working out a cramp in her left calf, opting for an interval of cooldown before her return. The geologic evidence reminded her she was standing on the continental shelf, on a young and tumultuous formation. This was the meeting place of two tectonic plates; grinding and chewing into the earth beneath her feet, they were ripping fault lines all across California.

Pacing herself as she retraced her own trail back toward the pier, she let her thoughts flow in tandem with her legs. Her encounter with John Dantes had been a failure—no tests, no results, nothing to score or evaluate.

Tomorrow she would flee to the desert—she could catch the early flight on Southwest, go standby if they were booked. She wanted out of LA.

The sprawling metropolis represented her past. The city never failed to catch her in its grip when she returned; it stirred memories of another time, another life, when she was raw, a dangerous shadow of herself.

LA, City of Id, jarred; it seduced in the most threatening ways.

It fueled her drive, heightened her appetites, revved her ambition. It reawakened fantasies and revived nightmares.

She stumbled on a strand of dried seaweed. Catching her balance, she pushed hard for the final sprint.

Fuck it anyway. This morning's little dance with John Dantes had thrown cold water on her big-city career goals. He'd trespassed psychologically; she'd done no better than her predecessors. So much for tagging along with the Bombers' Profiling Project.

She cut her stride into a fast, leggy walk, breathing deeply. Her lungs reminded her she'd been smoking too much. The stitch of pain satisfied in a perverse way. Glancing at her watch, she saw she had ninety minutes to walk back to the bungalow, make a few phone calls, shower, dress, and get to the restaurant.

3:20 P.M. "Three strikes you're out . . ." Sylvia stabbed the fat green olive that was magnified in the bottom of her martini glass, then stuffed it between her lips. Finally, she looked up to focus on Leo Carreras, struck by his tall, slender elegance, his darkly handsome face. *There should be a law* . . .

He was watching her closely, attentive, trying to read her mood. He slid into the booth, facing her from across the small table.

"Sorry I'm late," he said, checking the Rolex on his wrist, then scanning the Santa Monica Pier restaurant; the noise level had reached a beehive hum. "Last-minute consult—big-time extortion—Kraill Medical's the target. Forgive me?"

"No way."

Leo gently fingered the tape cassette that occupied the center of the table. "I gather the session with Dantes wasn't entirely successful."

Sylvia snorted. "It sucked. But you be the judge; I recorded everything but the last sixty seconds."

"That was the good part, right?"

Sylvia shot him a funny look. "Right." With unsteady hands she pulled a cigarette from her pocket.

Immediately, he whisked it from between her fingers. "You'll get us arrested if you try to smoke in here."

"Major felony," Sylvia said with no venom.

Slipping the tape into his shirt pocket, Leo addressed the waiter who had appeared at the table. "We need a large bowl of your chowder, the tuna very rare, a house salad with the balsamic, some of your sourdough, and a large bottle of sparkling water." He glanced at Sylvia. "Tomato juice?"

She already felt the buzz from the martini, yet she couldn't resist the chance to be obstinate. She tapped the stem of the martini glass. "I'll have another one of these."

Leo shook his head at the waiter, nixing the second cocktail. "Make that one mineral water, one tomato juice." He drank a sip from Sylvia's water glass, stalling until the aspiring actor in the crisp white apron was out of earshot.

He said, "Syl . . . talk to me."

She set her chin in her hands, elbows resting on the table. "Why did you ask me to be part of the project, Leo? You wasted my time and your resources."

He eyed her suspiciously, crossing his arms high on his chest, leaning back in the booth. "Okay, let's have it."

"I hear Peter Marshall's an excellent psychologist." She brushed dense dark hair away from her shoulder, tucking the same loose strands behind her ear; they refused to stay put. "So is Christine Tanner."

"What's your point?"

"My point . . ." Sylvia spread her hands wide, palms up, almost knocking the water glass to the floor. She sighed, lowering her voice. "I did some homework this afternoon." She sat back in the booth, crossing her long legs. "Peter Marshall and Christine Tanner both tried to administer the tests to Dantes. Marshall was ridiculed, verbally assaulted, threatened. Tanner lasted two minutes, then walked."

"That's correct," Leo said, looking unnervingly calm and cool in his gray summer suit. "You knew you wouldn't be the only evaluator." He shrugged. "Christine works for Rand; she's competent, but she's too straitlaced, too rigid for Dantes' taste. Peter Marshall actually lives most of the year in Virginia, close to Quantico."

"That's all you have to say?"

"No. I want to know all about Dantes—your impressions." He slid her empty martini glass to the center of the white tablecloth; the stem looked fragile caught between his slim tanned fingers. "Behavioral observations, affect, responses, and presentation—was he initially cooperative?

Functional? Oppositional? What, if anything, set him off? It's all relevant to the profiling project. I need your hit on all this."

"I'll fax you my written summary from Santa Fe." She shrugged, spinning one finger around the funneled rim of the martini glass. "I don't do *hits*."

"You don't do *what*?" Leo repeated dumbly, struggling to keep his tone intimate. "Listen, you were the right choice for Dantes. I truly believed you'd pull it off where Tanner and Marshall failed. That didn't happen. Too bad. Now I just need you to talk to me. All information is still relevant."

"You want my professional *hit* on Dantes." Her voice shook when she spoke. "He's a manipulative, arrogant, coldblooded asshole, so, basically, I told him to go to hell." She pulled herself up stiffly, shrugging. "That part isn't on the tape."

Leo opened his mouth, closing it again when the waiter appeared with soup.

"Eat," Leo said quietly.

"Let's get out of here."

"After you get something in your stomach."

Sylvia started to protest, but Leo ignored her, and eventually she acquiesced. While he sat, watching, fingers in constant motion, she forced herself to swallow a few spoonfuls of soup. She knew it was good—but the flavors hardly registered. It was the same with the tuna; for all the delicate spices, the skill of the chef, she might as well have been eating paper.

But Leo had been correct—she'd needed food. After ten minutes, she felt full, and more clearheaded. She finished the last of her water and caught Leo's eye. "Can we go now?"

Leo left a fifty-dollar bill on the table, neatly pocketing a wad of cash between the jaws of a sterling money clip as he stood to leave. He draped his coat over one shoulder; the creamy raw silk made a soft sound.

Sylvia followed, gathering her baseball cap, reaching for her jacket at the last minute.

Leo pressed his index finger firmly against her spine, trying to guide her toward the exit. When she didn't budge, he eyed her curiously, and said, "Help me out here. What do you think is going on?"

"Six weeks ago, you called to ask me if I'd test Dantes. You said you had a hunch he'd respond to me."

"That's right." Nodding slowly, Leo donned gold-rimmed sunglasses. He pushed the door wide, and ocean air rushed in like a wave. "What are you getting at?"

"You also told me Dantes didn't agree to my involvement at first—he kept stalling—until one day he changed his mind, just like that." Sylvia followed Leo outside.

"It took him about two weeks to decide. Why does it matter?"

"It matters." Sylvia touched Leo's arm. "I looked up my notes, Leo. Dantes changed his mind three days after my client's suicide."

"What did he say to you today?" Leo's eyes were hard.

"He knew the details—he knew about the board of inquiry—the phone call, the method." Sylvia struggled to control her voice. "I called his lawyer this afternoon. I managed to learn something from one of the paralegals—she investigates prospective shrinks." Sylvia shook her head. "Leo, Dantes ran a fucking background check on me. He was looking for my jugular."

"I'm sorry, Sylvia. I didn't know."

"Hey, it's not your fault," Sylvia said. "You warned me Dantes was good." She took off, striding ahead.

Leo let her go, following, picking up his pace to close

the distance. With twenty feet separating them, they passed the merry-go-round and curio shops. The arcade was filled with tourists, drifters and grifters, and guys with military crew cuts. The pier had been attracting a diverse assortment of visitors ever since the first decade of 1900, when gambling ships anchored offshore and the wealthy couldn't wait to be ferried out past the legal line to lose a bundle of moola.

Sylvia cut across the flow of pedestrians and stopped to lean against the railing. Fifty feet below, the surf snuggled frantically around the massive barnacle-encrusted pilings. She watched while a leathery man pulled a skate up from the tidal zone. The animal's angel wings drooped pathetically.

Leo found her just beyond the amusement rides in the middle of the pier. There was something so weary about her posture; her voice was barely audible above the sound of the waves.

"Come on in, the water's fine." She was peering down into the roiling waters of the Pacific, and her hair swirled around her face. "Just me, the seals, and the sharks."

For almost a minute Leo stood next to her without speaking. Then he said, "You're scaring me."

"I'm scaring myself."

"Syl . . ." He reached out to touch her, but she pulled away as if his skin scalded, walking rapidly toward the far corner of the pier.

When Leo caught up with her again, she was another woman—composed, withdrawn, tensely contained. She'd rested her forearms on the railing, and with the wind blowing her hair away from her face she looked more like a troubled adolescent than a woman in her mid-thirties.

She said, "I'm going to catch a flight back to Santa Fe as soon as I can shift my reservations."

"How's Serena doing these days?" He kept his voice neutral. "And how's Matt?"

"Good. They're both fine," she said too sharply.

"You don't have to run away from me." Leo's gaze was steady, unblinking. "I've seen you like this before."

"You've seen me like *what*? Out of control? Is that what you've seen?" She shook her head. "I can't trust myself," she whispered. "I don't know what to say to my clients, my patients. I'm running back to New Mexico, but that's the last place I want to be." Her shoulders hunched forward and she took a deep, shuddering breath. "I can't trust my instincts."

Leo gripped her shoulders. "This has got to be about more than losing a client."

Sylvia wheeled around, her eyes black with barely controlled rage. "You make it sound like she went on vacation or switched therapists. But she killed herself, Leo. On my watch. It was my call, and I let her check out of the hospital. You can't prescribe meds and make all that disappear."

"It wasn't your fault."

"Tell that to her baby." Sylvia turned away, walking fast.

Leo followed until she came to a stop in the middle of the promenade. People were passing them on either side, part of a steady stream of foot traffic. Music blared from the Ferris wheel. The sun peeked around a gray cloud and warmth flooded the pier.

"You want my *hit* on Dantes?" she asked, turning. "He's playing with the Feds, with you, with me—he's never going to take those fucking tests. And you're right, Leo. This *is* about more than losing a client. It's about being in this city. It's filled with ghosts."

She began walking backward, pointing a finger at her own heart. "Today, in that room with John Dantes, I felt *nothing*. No connection whatsoever. As far as I'm concerned, he might as well be the living dead." She pivoted, disappearing into the crowd.

The lie worked all the way back to the bungalow. Letting herself inside, she climbed straight up the narrow wooden stairway to the rooftop, where she could catch the last glimpse of sun over the Pacific Ocean. Stretched out in a green-and-white striped chaise, she closed her eyes.

She *had* felt a connection with John Dantes. They were connected through death, through loss, through desertion. She'd also felt his voyeuristic hunger.

She fell almost instantly into a deep, uneasy sleep. Softly clacking palm fronds marked the passing time. The dense ocean air enveloped her in its clammy arms.

Hours later she awoke, chilled and haunted by dreams: floating images of suicides, of a ghost with a sad smile. As Sylvia stumbled downstairs toward the bedroom, she stopped suddenly. A fragment of the dream came into clear focus: the face of the dead woman hadn't belonged to Mona Carpenter. The face had been her own.

She detoured into the bathroom, unzipped her cosmetic case with trembling hands, and downed another blue pill.

As she turned to leave, she caught a flash of argentine light coming from one clawed foot of the bathtub. She bent down, fingers closing around a single silver bangle; delicate crosses were etched in the precious metal. A talisman. There was comfort in the thought of magic. She slipped it over her wrist.

Waiting for sleep, she toyed with the idea of working up her report on Dantes for the BPP; but she'd left her laptop in the trunk of the Lincoln. So instead, she went to bed with *Dantes' Inferno: City of Angels in the 21st Century*.

Her eyes closed and her mind jumped frequencies to a telephone conversation two weeks earlier.

"This is John Dantes."

A perfect end to the first day of April.

"You're calling from Terminal Island?" But Sylvia asked the question only to break the silence; she knew Dantes was locked inside the federal facility on that windswept rock in the Los Angeles Harbor. Even if she'd somehow forgotten, a recorded monotone had reminded her the instant she answered the telephone. She'd had no doubt she would refuse the call—except her finger had pressed one. To accept.

She'd carried the portable handset and her very full glass of wine outside her house into the darkness of that early spring night in Santa Fe. There must have been a million stars scattered over the velvet blanket of sky; the breeze was unseasonably warm and carried the distinct scent of desert rain.

Barefoot, she walked to the edge of the redwood deck. Although her eyes scanned the shadowy ridge that marked the northern boundary of her acreage, her thoughts were traveling a thousand miles due west.

"How did you get my number?"

"My lawyer."

She'd been warned: it was Dantes' habit to make preliminary contact with all visitors. She said, "I only have a few minutes—"

"And you can't discuss testing procedure," he finished. "I won't keep you long."

She didn't respond; she was considering a call to Leo, to refuse the job, to change her mind. She was still in shock after her client's suicide. Maybe a thousand miles was as close as she wanted to get to John Dantes.

A harsh edge suddenly energized his words. "We may be disconnected. The tone is the thirty-second warning."

"I know the drill," Sylvia said. She spilled some wine down her chin.

"Good." He took a breath, releasing emotion with the exhalation. He had already learned what humans learn when they are monitored twenty-four hours a day: how to communicate in subtext, how to speak beneath the words. It was the responsibility of the listener to learn to translate this secret language.

"They're transferring me downtown," Dantes said. "It's all very hush-hush, but I'm guessing they'll roust me at two A.M. for the helicopter." His voice was laced with mockery.

She knew she should hang up. Instead, she swallowed more wine and said, "I'm not going anywhere."

And he laughed.

In the silence that followed, she plunked her butt on the edge of the deck, pressing her bare toes into the moist garden soil below. Inside the house, through the kitchen window, she could see her lover, Matt England, and her eleven-year-old foster daughter, Serena, preparing dinner. The ripple of soft laughter and the scent of savory spices drifted across the dark currents of night. Sylvia felt abruptly grateful for her freedom. And she felt very lonely.

A month ago—if this phone conversation ended back then, she would have walked inside her house to enjoy a good meal; she would've joined in the laughter, and after Serena went to sleep, she would've made love with Matt.

But that was before Mona Carpenter's death.

"Do you know the city?" he asked.

Of course, he meant Los Angeles.

"Some," she said, cautiously. She was aware the sound of her voice was traveling to a man encased in a concrete prison. Maximum security. Lockdown twenty-three hours a day. Maybe a narrow window overlooking ocean, more likely a view of the asphalt prison yard. Plenty of time to think about his most recent crimes, his latest victims: a young woman—a gifted teacher—and a child both killed. Jason Redding had been Serena's age.

He said, "Dantes' Inferno is required reading."

He was living up to his reputation for manipulation. She told him the truth: "I read it when it came out." She downed the last of her wine. For a moment, she felt dizzy. "I have a question for you."

"Fine." But he'd hesitated.

"Your mother's death was obviously traumatic—and you mention she was a powerful influence in your life—but you didn't write about—"

"I was nine," Dantes interrupted. "I watched her swim out past the Santa Monica breakwater. She never came back. End of story."

In the background, an angry, authoritarian voice was ordering an inmate: "Hands behind your back. Hands behind your back. Put your hands behind your back."

"Now I have a question for you," Dantes said. "The day she left me, I replaced my mother. With who, Dr. Strange? With what?"

A series of electronic clicks interrupted the transmission. It took Sylvia a moment to register the thirty-second warning. Unconsciously she tightened her grip on the handset as if muscles and tendons might prevent disconnection.

"—you might be surprised by the changes in LA—all the renovation. I call it 'quakification.'" Dantes changed tone, leavening his farewell with irony. "The interview is still on. By the way, happy April Fool's Day."

And then he was gone, leaving behind the ghostly whispers of dead women and children. She'd remained on the redwood deck, shivering in the desert night until a touch brought her back. As if awakened from a deep sleep, she'd gazed up into the beautiful face of her foster daughter, Serena.

She'd heard a sweet voice asking, "Why are you sad?"

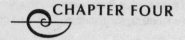

CHAPTER FOUR

So I descended from first to second circle—
Which girdles a smaller space and greater pain,
Which spurs more lamentation. Minos the dreadful

Snarls at the gate. He examines each one's sin,
Judging and disposing as he curls his tail:
That is, when an ill-begotten soul comes down,

It comes before him, and confesses all;
Minos, great connoisseur of sin, discerns
For every spirit its proper place in Hell. . . .

The Inferno of Dante, translated by Robert Pinsky

11:35 P.M. In this hellish subterranean maze he hears the primitive language of forgotten men. Here, the earth smells damp and metallic like blood, and the heat oppresses, sneaking down through vents and plates and cracks in the surface of the world. There is a strange humidity, the product of steam and the relentless seepage of a thousand rusting arteries. There is cancer inside this body, beneath the skin of this schizoid, voluptuous city named for angels.

He stands some fifteen feet below ground, below downtown; beneath three inches of asphalt, almost a foot of coarse concrete, and a layer of chemical-soaked soil; beneath a zone of seemingly infinite casings packed with wires feeding telephones, electricity, streetlights, cable televisions, fire alarms.

On the skid row street above him a barrel bonfire glows;

its luminescence falls down through a grate and dances skittishly across the muck beneath his feet. Voices, ghostly and laced with hysteria and fortified wine, follow the light down to keep him company. He is trapped here in the dark, in this ten-by-twelve tunnel, in the midst of a vast subterranean network of urban arteries and bones. He is imprisoned in the strata of gas lines, water lines and mains, steam pipes. Below him the massive sewer system angles down into the netherworld, the subway vaults and tunnels traverse hundreds of square miles, the old water tunnels leak their precious cargo into ancient culverts.

Only the devil knows what other treasures and evils have been buried during the life span of the city.

Ah, but he is here to find a tall, skinny ferret of a man, a homeless creature known in this underworld as "the Pope" because of a shadowy former existence as a priest. By day, the Pope panhandles above ground; at night, he preaches in this dark, dank cathedral to a congregation of the lost, the maimed, the damned. His knowledge of corners and hidden rooms and tunnels is rumored to be extraordinary. Over the past months, all through the detailed preparation, the Pope's knowledge has proved worrisome. It must be dealt with immediately.

I am a mole, blindly nosing my way through hell.

I am M.

The thought tears through his consciousness.

It is the dark that he seeks—no, *craves*—and the dark that he fears.

It is the haunted whispers, the company of men like himself, men who have crossed the line.

Surely this place is as torturous as any hell he has ever imagined?

M stares down at a half-dead man splayed on the tunnel floor, spent needle still growing from a bruised and scabbed arm. Squatting down, he whispers, "Are you dead yet?" Although he receives no answer, expects none, he sees the man's chest expand ever so faintly. This one will live at least for tonight.

He does not hunger for the sting of needles. His own madness is a poison recently swallowed. When he gazes into the mirror he has begun to notice a darkening of his reflection, as if his blood is stagnating, as if he is rotting just like the men he stumbles upon in this underbelly of the city—the transients, the hoboes, the lunatics, the criminals. He hasn't lost all glimmers of his sanity, but this ability to see his own psychic fault lines, these remnants of rational thought processes, only irritates.

And so he acts.

This city is under siege. Blood will spill and the innocent will die. The ruin cannot be stopped.

Can't stop, can't stop, can't stop—the sound of dripping water seems to taunt him.

He's spent sleepless nights haunting these vaults, drains, pipelines, subway tunnels, until he is a ghostly legend to the transients and indigents who come here to hide or to die.

He steps over the comatose junkie, wading through fetid water, trash, human waste. Somehow, he will find his way. The maps are inside his head. They make his brow burn and his skull ache.

Quick, light footsteps! Is that a shadow? Does he see the peculiar humped silhouette of the Pope?

M follows, picking up speed, ducking through the wide passageway into a narrower pipe. Here, he can't stand straight but must hunch like an ape, loping on bent knees. He hears the fast tap of feet running forty or fifty feet ahead.

He calls out, "Wait!"

The runner picks up speed, splashing through puddles,

tripping over piles of rubble. The rasp of labored breath scrapes the walls.

When he aims his flashlight ahead, the beam bounces off cylindrical, ridged metal. He is breathing heavily now, too, still moving quickly when he almost collides with a low-hanging pipe, almost takes his own head off at the neck. He's come to a fork in the underground road. Which way did his quarry go?

Clicking off his light, he forces himself to stand in blackness, straining to hear. Beneath the ragged sound of his own breathing he detects the suppressed breath of another living creature.

To his own surprise, he whispers, "Help me, please."

The words echo in the tunnel, finally fading away. Apparently he is alone with the stench, the warm unnatural drafts, the ghostly voices.

M turns left, walking another thirty feet to yet another bend in the tunnel. His light illuminates unspeakable things. How can human beings choose to live this way?

It happens so fast. Suddenly, he is face-to-face with the Pope, who asks, "Are you all right?"

"I've been looking for you," M whispers.

The Pope is frightened but manages to speak. "I found out what you wanted. I've seen the monster. Its tentacles are growing. They're swollen as malignant vessels and they're spreading out all around us. The end is near . . . so very near." He speaks with the urgent flowery tones of a street prophet. His breath carries the sickening stench of disease. His eyes are rimmed with circles. He, too, is going dark with his own blood.

"You say you've seen it, then?" M asks slowly.

"In the tunnels, yes." The Pope nods, pointing up, then down dramatically. "It's spreading, Satan's pollution. It lusts for our souls. It is consumed with lust for our goodness."

"And what do you lust for, holy man? What brought you to the second circle of hell?"

The Pope meets his gaze, unflinching. "In my life, above, out in the world of air and light, I lusted for women . . . and money . . . and the power over men's souls. I dwelled in the fallen cities of Sodom, Gomorrah, and Babylon." The Pope blinks, swallowing painfully, aching with this confession. "But my true sin . . . what drove me down into this hell was my lust for righteousness." A bony hand reaches out. "Forgive me." He sighs. "I'm hungry."

"Hungry." For a long time M stares at the Pope; then he slowly pulls a brown square from his back pocket.

Waiting, the Pope is caught between fear and need. He is afraid of this man—this devilish apparition who wanders the tunnels each night—in the same way he is afraid of plague or murder or the big hungry rats. But he is hungry, too. And he needs money to buy food, maybe a little something to take his mind away from these sewers. He gazes down, expecting to see a few coins or a dollar bill in the other man's hand.

But in reality, he sees a Mylar bag.

The Pope looks up puzzled, "Who are you?"

"I'm Minos, judge of the dead." With a wistful smile, M grabs the Pope by his grimy hair, slamming his head into the hard-packed earthen wall, sliding Mylar over skin and skull. Fits like a glove. Made to order, it tightens around the base when he tugs—creating a vacuum effect, molding to the suffocating man's face.

As the Pope loses consciousness, as he flails, as his eyes go red, he sees a vision: Los Angeles is a burning hell, the sky turns black, the city falls in upon herself, and only dust is left.

"I'm sorry," M apologizes to the corpse as he lets it sink to earth. Then he whispers to himself: "The city is so beautiful by daylight. It's only the night that makes her ugly."

He turns his back and slowly begins his ascent to the world.

Tonight, his job is finished—the second circle is complete.

Tomorrow he has a big day ahead. Tomorrow he will work in daylight.

He is used to destructive premonition. He can see the future as clearly as if it is stretching behind him, a trailing past, already written, book closed. A cataclysm will strike this city. Fire will sear her skin and engulf her features; the force of two atomic bombs will rip out her bones and sever her limbs. She will go blind and deaf and dumb, and her breathing will cease. She will be the sacrifice.

Tomorrow they will all face the third circle.

The Pope was right, a monster is on the loose.

The monster is John Freeman Dantes.

Or is it me? he wonders.

It is us.

Yes.

We are the monster.

3rd Circle . . .

The Three-Headed Hound and a Prophecy

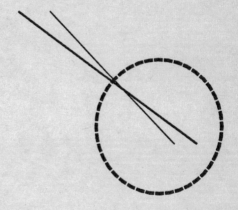

CHAPTER FIVE

Most of the bombcops I know, they answer the door,
open every package with the thought, Shit, this could
be it—kaboom.

Edward "Boomer" Toms, Folsom Prison inmate

Tuesday—5:00 A.M. The knock was loud.

Groggy, and emotionally and chemically hungover, Sylvia
peered through the peephole in the front door of the bungalow to find herself eye to eye with law enforcement insignia.

"Dr. Strange?" There was some shuffling on the outside
stoop; two faces appeared—one, then the other—in front
of the peephole.

Groaning, Sylvia cracked the door, safety chain still fas-
tened, taking a closer look: badges advertised the Federal
Bureau of Investigation and the Los Angeles Police
Department. They were shiny, and they looked real.

"I'm Special Agent Purcell." The woman wore her hair
buzzed, her milk chocolate face squeaky clean, and her
affect flat. She looked so buff she'd bounce.

Next to the woman, the man loomed. In order to meet his
dead-on gaze, Sylvia had to raise her chin, an action that
only made her headache worse. When he introduced himself
as Detective Church, LAPD, the words rumbled in his

throat. "Yesterday you were at Metro Detention Center," he told her, voice stalling out on the final syllable.

Sylvia flicked her hair from her face. Her heartbeat slowed a tad—this didn't concern New Mexico or her family, *thank God.* She croaked out the beginning of a question: "What's this a—"

"You had an interview with John Dantes," Church finished. He smiled without showing teeth; his eyes were sharp. "Do you mind if we step inside?"

"I do mind," she said slowly. For fifteen seconds, she stood unrelenting. Nobody budged, nobody spoke. Then Sylvia blinked, and they won the first round.

Reluctantly, she released the security chain, watching as they entered; first the agent, then the detective. They couldn't be more different: Mutt and Jeff. Only their grave expressions were congruent. She was flanked by law enforcement—one five foot five, the other six foot two.

"Dr. Strange, what exactly did you want with John Dantes?" The LAPD detective's gaze, openly assessing, stayed pinned to her face.

"You just told me what I wanted," Sylvia answered quietly. She felt as if the detective could see straight through her. "An interview."

She tightened the belt of her terry robe until her stomach ached. She knew she looked wild; her mouth tasted of sand. "I met with Dantes to complete a series of psychometric inventories—*tests*—for a federal profiling project."

"And did you complete the inventories?" Purcell asked.

"No."

"Did you complete *any* tests?"

"No."

"Not even one?" Church crossed his arms, eyebrows raised. Without appearing to do so, he was scoping out the interior of the bungalow.

"Not even one, Detective." Sylvia was beginning to regain enough sense to feel annoyed. "Maybe that omission is unfortunate, but as far as I know, it's not a crime."

"You need to come with us," Purcell stated firmly.

"Oh, *no*." Sylvia raised her index finger and squared her shoulders. "There's been some mistake—my work in LA is finished." When neither agent looked convinced, she expelled air in a huff, adding, "I don't know what's going on, but I've got a plane to catch." As if on cue, the alarm clock in the bedroom began to shriek.

"Sorry, Doc," Detective Church drawled. "Your country needs you."

Eight minutes later Sylvia slid into the back of the dark unmarked Ford while the two investigators took the good seats for the drive over to the FBI's Wilshire offices.

She still felt like hell—probably *looked* almost as bad as she felt—but at least her teeth were brushed and she was fully dressed. She tucked her white shirt deeper into the waistband of her jeans. The smell of coffee, the two Starbucks cups on the dash, made her nose itch. No one offered her a sip.

During the drive, she had the opportunity to study her escorts. Behind the wheel, Purcell was doing a passable imitation of a tough guy. The special agent might qualify for that category of female cop obsessed with keeping up with the boys. If Purcell was out to cut some notches on her belt, Sylvia didn't plan to be one of them.

Filling the passenger seat with a cell phone in his lap, Detective Church was large and rangy, and he had the air of the chronically rumpled; his shiny suit clung to his body like a hungry orphan. His hat, a molded fedora, seemed to have taken root over a thatch of red hair. Freckles dotted his thick nose, turmeric sprinkled on a carrot. If he detoured to central casting they'd hand him a Scottish kilt and bagpipes.

Something had hold of Sylvia thoughts, tugging like a small dog on a sleeve: *an LAPD detective who worked on the Getty investigation . . .*

"Oh, come on," Sylvia protested, coming back to reality. Purcell had just cruised past the Westside offices of the Federal Bureau of Investigation, and they were still headed east on Wilshire Boulevard. "Where the hell are we going now?"

Church answered. "Roybal Federal."

Sylvia plunked back in the seat, arms crossed. Staring out the window, she felt LA's international airport growing more distant by the mile. "Roybal Federal—that's right next door to MDC."

"Right next door," Purcell said, eyes reflected in the rearview mirror.

"So, what am I doing here? How long will this take?" Sylvia shot out questions, rat-a-tat. "Am I under arrest?"

"For what?"

"You tell me. Jaywalking? If not, I've got a ticket back to New Mexico, and I'd like to use it today." For an instant, she thought Church was going to apologize.

Instead, he said, "We need input on your interview with Dantes."

"Why didn't you just say so in the first place?" She ran the back of her hand across her mouth. Her stomach rumbled from hunger, her headache was worsening, and she wished she had her sunglasses to ease the glare. "We could've covered this back in Santa Monica. The entire session is on tape if you can straighten out jurisdiction. The profiling project is federal anyway—" She was cut off by the bleat of a cell phone.

Church answered, shifting into listening mode for thirty

seconds. He hung up with a casual, "Okay, Sweetheart."

Sylvia rolled her eyes. "Can't your girlfriend wait until you're off the clock?"

Purcell snorted, and Church shot her a dirty look before he returned his attention to Sylvia. "How did you feel about your meeting with Dantes?"

"I wasn't prepared for him." Sylvia felt the energy coming from Church—the detective had eyes that penetrated like sharp blue darts. She watched his mind work; he was putting together pieces of a puzzle, matching color, texture, pattern, nuance.

Well, so was she.

"So . . . you've got another bomb, right?" she asked slowly.

Church didn't move a muscle. "What are you, bomb squad?"

"I'm not stupid." Sylvia felt herself mirroring the investigator's tension, told herself to breathe. Inside the vehicle, the level of mistrust was palpable. She stared back at Church. "You were part of the Calbomb Task Force. Detective Red Church. You helped track down Dantes." Her eyebrows arched. "You even made *Vanity Fair*. Not a very good picture."

"Nobody said you were stupid," Church said finally.

She glanced at her wristwatch, then the sky, depressed by the sight of a distant metal bird climbing toward the clouds.

Church followed her gaze. "They all look alike."

"Fuck," she whispered.

6:05 A.M. Flanked by Purcell and Church, Sylvia crossed the already warm asphalt of Alameda Street. The route was becoming familiar. She couldn't resist looking up as they passed by the Metropolitan Detention Center. The narrow vertical windows caught the sun's rays, measuring the hour with light. Dantes was there somewhere. She shuddered at the thought of him.

Just fifty feet beyond MDC, they entered the dimly lit, almost deserted lobby of Roybal Federal Building, passing quickly through the security checkpoint.

On the fourth floor, Sylvia followed the investigators through a maze of hallways lined with glass cubicles. It was too early for most employees to be at work, but computer monitors glowed green, and the clatter of fingers across a keyboard echoed across the floor.

Sylvia felt comforted by the human sound. Her stomach hurt, her hands were shaking from caffeine withdrawal; when she glanced down she noticed one shoelace was untied.

The investigators led the way into a long, narrow conference room. A wall of tinted windows offered a view of downtown. A twelve-foot-by-six-foot aerial map of LA covered the opposite wall. The air was too cold, the overhead lights had been dimmed. At the far end of the room, light emanated from a suspended white screen. Sylvia heard the hum of a projector but couldn't locate the source; her eyes were still adjusting to artificial twilight.

There was a soft *whir* followed by a *click*.

An image appeared—two paragraphs of enlarged black type projected starkly against the white screen.

"Yesterday while you were with Dantes," Detective Church began, "a CO discovered a threat communication in his cell. Look at the paragraph on the left."

Sylvia studied the message:

> dear friend
> thru me the way into the woeful city
> thru me the way to eternal pain
> sacrifice the children of heathens

until no innocents lay claim
first circle broken
8 circles remain
I do your bidding faithfully
M—

Church cleared his throat and said, "A second communication—apparently written by the same individual—arrived at FBI offices with yesterday's mail."

dear feds
babbel, babbel, babbel
no more Limbo
2nd circle soon complete
release yr prisoner DaNTes, prophet apocryphal
or hungry for next
Vvv
M—

"You were close to the money when you said we've got ourselves another bomb," Church said. "We've had initial contact from a possible bomber-extortionist."

"And his name is M," Sylvia said quietly. She almost asked what Quantico's psycholinguistic experts had to say about the content of the extortion notes: the literary and religious references.

But she stopped herself.

Her entire body was mobilized for fight or flight; she ignored the juvenile urge to cover her ears with her hands. "Why are you showing me this?"

"Your credentials checked out for BPP, or, trust me, you wouldn't be sitting here," Purcell said.

"That still doesn't answer my question," Sylvia said warily. "I'm not FBI or behavioral sciences, not ATF or bomb squad. And you guys don't hand out information freebies." She slowed her speech as if she was addressing someone who barely spoke English. "So why am I here?"

When no one answered, she stood, abruptly claustrophobic.

"Sit down," Purcell ordered.

"Not until you give me some kind of explanation." Sylvia remained standing.

"Sit down," Purcell repeated, enunciating for a disobedient child.

"No."

As threat posture stiffened Purcell's compact body, Church thrust an arm between the women. "Hey, come on, let's all chill out."

He leaned toward Sylvia. "Thirsty?" Without waiting for a response, he walked over to a small table that had been equipped with pitcher and plastic cups. He was whistling.

Reluctantly, Sylvia acquiesced, sinking into a chair. She could feel the first scratchy symptoms of a sore throat; even with full climate control, her skin had broken a sweat. Church set a full cup in front of her on the table. The water soothed her throat, and she finished it in two gulps.

Now Detective Church perched on the table's edge, staking out the high ground. "You big on anniversaries, Doc?" he asked quietly.

"What?"

"One week and we all get to celebrate the anniversary of the Getty bombing," Church said. "We'd love to skip the fireworks display."

Frustrated, Sylvia shook her head. "The timing of my visit to MDC is based on the fact Dantes is about to ship out of state, and because my security clearance was held up by desk jockeys." Classified at level six—the Feds' highest security level—Dantes was en route to Colorado's Supermax.

After three beats, Church dipped the small black remote he held in his right hand.

While the screen went to white, Purcell said, "The information we're about to share with you is extremely sensitive. The Behavioral Science Unit at Quantico is convinced the threat is real. We're talking about a volatile situation with an extremely high possibility for loss of life." Underneath her carefully mowed speech slunk the faintest of Southern accents.

Nobody said a word. The only sound was the projector. *Click, whir.* A second slide, this one an enlarged photograph.

"This Polaroid arrived with the second threat communication," Purcell said.

Sylvia was staring at a close-up of an improvised explosive device. A time bomb. But not just a utilitarian construction of timer, fuse, primer, and main charge.

The casing was elaborate: a wooden chest, carved and inlaid with metal and stones. Handles on both ends seemed to be brass or a similar metal. In stark contrast to the ornate container, the wired time-delay device appeared to consist of an ordinary alarm clock with a fat, white face, black numerals, and black hands; these were set at eighteen minutes, thirty seconds past one o'clock.

It was not unlike bombs attributed to John Dantes.

"Does anyone know if that's timed to blow today?" Sylvia asked.

"You want to stake any money it's *not?*" Church snorted. "Then you got bigger balls than me."

"You must have hundreds of bomb threats every day. What makes this one real?"

"Obviously the references can be connected to Dantes," Purcell said slowly. "Less obviously . . . when the paper is exposed to light, a series of figures, possibly numerical, become visible on the page."

Whir, click. The third slide revealed a series of small wedge-shaped forms: two angled left to right, nine stacked in horizontal rows of three.

"We've developed several possible theories regarding their significance, but more pertinent to this discussion, we've seen something similar on another bomb," Purcell said.

"The Getty?" Sylvia asked.

"On remains of the bomb that blew up the museum twelve months ago." Purcell nodded. "That information is not public."

"So only Dantes should know," Sylvia said slowly. "And he's serving a life sentence."

"This UNSUB—we're calling him M," Purcell said. "We're dealing with a copycat, a wannabe. Or we're dealing with a collaborator."

"Apparently he's a fan of Dantes—and *Dante*." Sylvia stared at the slide.

"Whatever the perp's profile, we're under the gun," Detective Church's deep voice rumbled. "We *need* information, and Dantes isn't cooperating. The bastard's telling us to pound sand."

Sylvia felt cold, slightly dizzy, as she stood. She began walking toward the door, hungry for air that wasn't pumped through ducts, recycled, sanitized.

None of this has anything to do with me, she thought.

Behind her, she heard the faint and indecipherable voices of the two investigators. She kept going.

When she heard the third voice, she stopped in her tracks. John Dantes. It took her a moment to realize the deep, resonant sound was a high-quality recording issuing from wall speakers.

Addressing unknown inquisitors, Dantes said, "You want a conversation, you listen to this: I'll talk to one person. You get her back in here, you treat her respectfully, and you negotiate through her. Her name is Sylvia Strange. *Dr.* Strange to you." The low rumble of his laughter vibrated through the speakers. "We made it easy for you—she's even got clearance."

The sound cut abruptly, but Sylvia took her time. When she turned to face the investigators her true voice got lost. A hoarse impostor said, "He's crazy."

"Crazy or not, you're going in," Church said.

"If I don't?"

"Your life will become unpleasant. Your professional conduct has been questioned recently in New Mexico. If you refuse to cooperate with us, we'll be wondering why, and we'll be paying close attention to your every move. We'll be deciding Dantes must have a special relationship with Sylvia Strange—maybe *you* belong to his fan club."

Church dropped a shiny black object on the table: a pair of sunglasses. "Dantes said these are yours. Armani. You should be more careful where you leave your things."

While the silence settled, he looked at her, his expression oddly sympathetic. His posture—broad shoulders inclined in her direction—expressed a certain intimacy.

He said, "You'd go in without threats. We've got a bomber out there. If he means business—and we think he does—you're in a position to save lives, Dr. Strange."

His fingers were on a file about an inch thick, and he opened the cover to reveal a stack of documents and photographs. He held them out—an offering. "Anything and everything about John Dantes."

She ran her tongue over parched lips. Seconds ticked away along with the opportunity to turn tail. Finally, she nodded, accepting the file in hands that were less than steady. "What exactly do you need me to do?"

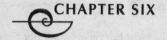

CHAPTER SIX

> City—as Sodom, Babylon, Athens, New York, or Los Angeles—represents the gravest sins of humanity, the transgressions of man against God. The city Dis must pay for its sins. Boo-hoo.
>
> *Mole's Manifesto* (unpublished)

Tuesday—7:20 A.M. Welcome to LA, city of his childhood daze.

Welcome to Los Angeles, where Fat Cats feed off the city, gorging themselves until they swell to bursting.

Welcome, all ye gluttons for punishment.

Last night's haze has cleared; his hunt was successful. He enjoyed his requisite three hours sleep, and now he is alive and well along with the half dozen other working stiffs exiting the Red Line car with the blessings of Ram'khastra, Angel of Rarefied Air, Sui'el, Angel of Earthquakes, and Sut, Angel of Lies.

Lucky duck; he thinks of his very own Angel Face and how good she made him feel when he returned home early this morning. Summoned from sleep by her lover, she smiled from her dreams, reaching out to caress him . . . skin golden in moonlight off the ocean. Honey-colored hair in wisps around her sweet face; she reminds him of a child except for the delicate breasts, the slim waist, the gently flaring hips, and golden fleece between her thighs—the proof she is no child but woman.

His woman. *His Angel Face.*

Riding the escalator, he rises from the depths of the subway tunnel at Union Station. A leather backpack is slung over his left shoulder; although it's heavy, it's nothing a workingman from San Pedro wouldn't carry for a long hot day in the city.

A pretty redhead passing in the other direction on the escalator turns to send him a mischievous wink. As she moves, her red skirt billows around her long slender legs and a speculative smile plays over her unnaturally scarlet lips. She sees a healthy, attractive male in his late thirties. A man she wishes would stop to talk, flirt a minute, perhaps agree to meet for dinner . . . and rescue her from her humdrum life, because she fears she's suffocating.

But he is already out of reach . . . and anyway, he has his own Angel Face; this very moment she's hard at work in San Pedro: order up, three eggs, sunny-side, whole wheat, a cup of joe.

As the escalator reaches bunker level a glittering ribbon of reflected light snakes yellow and red across his slightly dilated black pupils: he catches the subliminal image of Marilyn Monroe. Tarzan's jungle call of the wild sounds above him, echoing down from the tiled domes of high-tech movie star heaven, Mecca of the urban artist.

Ah yes, LA, village of angels. Perhaps until this moment, he hasn't realized how much he's always missed his home. Doesn't every man have a soft spot for the city of his lost innocence? It was here on these streets that he grew to manhood. Here, he discovered his reason to exist. Found his cause, his driving force.

Found his one and only hero. And lost . . .

But he's not a bitter man. Not one to hold a grudge.

Smiling at yet another pretty woman—they sprout like weeds in LA—he strides casually through the long cool tunnel. Passengers from the train platforms above merge down a dozen ramps. Subway, bus, train—this station is the transportation hub of downtown.

Easily, he hefts the backpack, redistributing the weight across his shoulder. Inside the pack, the nine-by-nine-inch metal case is aluminum. It weighs less than thirty pounds. The system works on VHF or UHF radio communications.

Seven miles as the crow flies.

That's how far away a man can stand and still arm and fire, still detonate a bomb.

A couple of pounds of ammonium nitrate; three or four sticks of commercial dynamite; a few sheets of PETN or RDX; a handful of C-4.

Choose your recipe, choose your poison.

Explosive ingredients that will destroy buildings and send wood, metal, and glass shrapnel spiraling into space, start fires, and sever local utility and communication feeds.

Explosives designed to extinguish civilian targets and to bring a city to its knees.

In M's case, all in the name of his compatriot, his *brother*, John Freeman Dantes.

Boom.

Remote control blasting. It used to be a product of fertile imaginations. In the past decade it has become as real as the sturdy aluminum he totes in his leather backpack. It is his genius to understand each job—parameters and goal—and how to accomplish it with 1.5 million or twenty-five bucks.

If you think he's some blue-collar grunt, some hick from the hills, you got another *think* coming.

Abreast with fellow commuters, going with the flow, he recognizes snatches of Lebanese, Spanish, Arabic, and even understands a bit of the discussion about an elder son from Peking who wishes to marry a doctor, and the furious rantings of a Russian who owes money to gangsters. He blends into the growing crowd. Who besides the redhead will remember the clean-cut, athletically built man with the puckish features and clipped salty brown hair who wears a light jacket, blue shirt, khaki slacks, loafers? And sunglasses.

God help him if he neglects to wear sunglasses in Los Angeles.

Past the restricted entry to transportation, passengers find themselves in the cool, vast, vaulted dome of Union Station. A few dine on croissants or sip lattes from a vendor. Fewer still read newspapers and consume burritos at Velarde's.

It's too early to find customers at the bar, a dark and frosted deco set from the 1930s. If all goes as planned, he will be in another world by the time commuters, couples, and business types are nursing martinis and old-fashioneds, posturing Bogart and Bacall—and discussing the explosion that will make CNN headlines.

Bombs are all the rage.

Although the original ticket counter has long been closed, the polished wooden ledge still stretches the length of one room just as it did sixty years earlier, when it was part of a more civilized era. An era, he reminds himself, when the city's oldest Chinatown neighborhood was razed to build this Spanish-colonial-revival-marries-art-deco romance.

He passes a uniformed police officer and nods politely, stepping beneath one of several arched doorways. Slipping out of darkness into the hard white heat of concrete days, he breathes deeply, relishing the faint scent of chlorine. His nose is damn good; it has saved his skin more than once. He's managed to scent his own death in the air when the mix of chemicals turned deadly. Today he is just breathing LA's distinct perfume, a poison all its own.

Crossing the parking lot that fronts Union Station, he picks his way past construction detour signs and turns onto Los Angeles Street. He has a vehicle parked just three blocks north. At the moment, he is a foot soldier.

With care, he shifts his leather backpack to his other arm. The weight hangs more heavily now, but he doesn't slow, continuing his even stride, crossing over Highway 101. Below him, a river of cars and trucks form a solid south-flowing current that threatens to flood Anaheim. He catches sight of a child whose face is pressed to the dusty rear window of a station wagon. He waves; the child sticks its tongue out.

At this more human level, along the rail of the on ramp, transients have cast their blankets, marking their territory with cardboard, old rags, piss, and sweat. The freeway squatters' village reminds him of nomadic encampments he has encountered deep in forsaken deserts. For an instant, he imagines tasseled camels, veiled women, and tents billowing like the sails of vessels beached in the Taklimakan, the Sahara, the Nubian, the Libyan, the Kyzyl Kum, and the Kara-Kum.

He's seen a bit of the world.

Shaking off the memory, and slowing pace in a city of baking asphalt, steel, and glass, he turns in a direction that will take him past the transients. Going by several, he scatters coins toward their extended arms. When he walks in front of a thin, bleary-eyed man sitting cross-legged like any holy beggar in any holy city, he tosses a larger, shinier coin into the air.

The Kennedy half-dollar falls, spiraling, reflecting sharp, fast splinters of light.

It lands in the transient's lap. *For luck*.

He moves faster now, past a row of about-to-be-gentrified brick buildings. Here, in this concrete forest primeval, there isn't much pedestrian traffic because of the heat; the few people he passes, eyes cast downward according to urban etiquette and for protection from the glare, don't dare look up.

But he does. The green-blue walls of Metro Detention Center rise above him. Hotel Metro. He smiles up at his old friend.

Can you feel me? Because I feel you, Dantes.

I feel your every breath. Hey, I promised, didn't I?

I'm Ulysses. Or is that you?

Both of us pilgrims, you and me together again in Babylon.

Ashes to ashes, dust to dust.

Time to settle a very old score.

Smiling, still moving, continuing westward toward a dusty park and a street of buildings awaiting renovation. While he walks, he tastes the exhaust from car engines and the heat of cooked earth. He absorbs the hum of traffic, the rumble of jets high over his head, the vibration of transformers and underground trains. All these things form the pulse of the city.

Dantes' City of Angels with her pure-sex curves, her dazzling smile, her leggy nonchalance. She even wears the priceless jewels of powerful men: a gleaming ziggurat, a pyramid-shaped Tower of Babel. Dantes' girl . . .

As he stares out at this world, he pulls a carved bone figurine from his pocket; it is the size of a child's thumb, and like a child, he rubs its smooth skin between his fingers: Enkidu, companion of the hero Gilgamesh, who journeyed up from the Assyro-Babylonian underworld to tell his friend the sad story of the regions of eternal darkness.

> In the house of dust
> Live lord and priest.
> Live the wizard and the prophet . . .
> Live those whom the great gods

Have anointed in the abyss.
Dusk is their nourishment
And their food is mud.

Welcome to LA, where innocence can't survive.
Welcome to Operation Inferno.

CHAPTER SEVEN

Systematically and with an outlaw brilliance, John Freeman Dantes took on the powers that were and the powers that be by targeting water, oil, boosters, regulators, and planners, and the political machinery that created mythic Los Angeles. The two innocent victims of the aqueduct bombing were victims of war. It was only when he bombed the Getty that Dantes faltered on his course, crossing over the line from prophetic anarchist to coldblooded assassin. I for one mourned his fall from grace.

Letter to the editor, *LA Weekly*, December 1, 2001

7:55 A.M. Purcell and Church finished briefing Sylvia in the empty corridor as they waited for the elevator.

"We'll keep you under audio surveillance as long as you're in there," Purcell explained. "Dantes will expect that. He won't try anything. He *can't* try anything."

"Take your time, be direct, let him set the pace," Church said, coaching. "You'd better give me that." He held out his hand for the file on Dantes.

Sylvia relinquished it willingly. She'd just finished skimming the three hundred pages; much of the material was familiar from her previous research in preparation for the BPP, but some of it was new—for instance, the lab reports of the forensic evidence left at each bomb scene, and the postmortem photographs of the surveyor and the security guard killed when a section of the California aqueduct exploded. The photographs were full color and very graphic—insurance she'd never forget John Dantes was a murderer.

She leaned wearily against the wall, sipping burnt coffee from a Styrofoam cup; the fluorescent lights in the corridor made her eyes sting.

Purcell pressed the *down* button for the third time. Nothing happened. She pressed it again, mumbling, "Damn elevators are slower than molasses."

"Doc?" Church tapped the side of his head. "Use whatever it takes to build up your connection with him, but don't try to outfox the fox." He shifted his weight from foot to foot. "Scared?"

"Yes."

"Good. You should be . . ." Abruptly, his voice died away as if he'd been cut off. But he was simply changing cognitive lanes. He studied Sylvia's face and asked, "Do you know why Dantes asked for you?"

"I'm outside the system. He's planning to use me, manipulate me—maybe he even thinks he can *turn* me. I become his ally." She shrugged grimly. "But those are the obvious reasons."

"What's not obvious?"

"Don't know yet. If yesterday was the test—somehow I passed. Take into consideration it was our first meeting face-to-face—there are issues of *transference*." She paused, glancing speculatively at Church.

"As in, you remind him of his mother, his lover, whatever," the detective said. "I took Psych 101, Doc."

"Close enough," Sylvia said. "Psychologically, Dantes needs my help."

"Therapy?" Purcell spit out the word just as the elevator rumbled to a stop.

Eyeing the FBI agent, Church snorted. "Fucker's bombs are a cry for help."

The elevator doors opened silently.

"I thought you took Psych 101," Sylvia said dryly, following the investigators into the small metal box. She closed her dark eyes for a moment. "Dantes thinks I'm vulnerable." Opening her eyes wide, she added, "That's crucial to him."

Church kept his voice even. "You feeling vulnerable?"

"Oh, yeah," she answered softly.

As if on cue, Purcell punched a button and the elevator descended, picking up speed, passing ground level and two lower floors, to brake smoothly on a third subterranean level.

"Dantes isn't at MDC?" Sylvia asked, fighting back panic. It frightened her to think he wasn't locked inside a cell.

"We've transported him over here for security considerations," Purcell said.

"Mine or his?" Sylvia asked. She swallowed coffee, spilling some from the Styrofoam cup; a blue pill nestled secretly in the palm of her hand.

"Ours," Purcell said flatly.

The elevator doors glided open, admitting stale, warm air. Followed closely by both investigators, Sylvia stepped out into a dimly lit concrete garage. "What is this place?" she asked.

"A basement, with utility access, and tunnel access to MDC," Purcell said, moving forward briskly. She nodded toward a double door marked *No Entry*. "The U.S. marshals use it for prisoner transport, which is why it's equipped with a cage."

"Terrific." Sylvia took another sip of coffee and tipped her head back slightly, ready to catch the blue pill in her mouth.

A wide hand gripped her wrist, fingers clamped tight around the tendons in her arm. Slowly—involuntarily—her muscles let go and the pill slipped away.

"You always eat the breakfast of champions?" Church asked in a very quiet voice. His mouth was almost pressed against her ear, and he hadn't released her yet.

She stared up at him. "Only when I'm having a breakdown."

"Welcome to LA," he said sharply, with a quick dip of his red head.

She didn't answer; instead she took two steps toward the double doors where Purcell and a U.S. marshall waited stiffly.

"Hey, Doc?"

She turned to glance back at Church, catching the faintest wink. He said, "Don't fumble." He tossed something in the air—a pack of cigarettes—and she caught them automatically, neatly.

She opened her mouth to reply, but nothing came out. The palms of her hands hit the cold metal doors of the transport cage. She was pushing a glacier uphill.

8:13 A.M.   The room—about fifteen by twenty—was windowless, hot, designed to hold a dozen maximum security inmates. It could best be described as a mesh-lined metal bunker with built-in benches.

John Dantes was still wearing his prison colors, still sporting his bullet-proof vest. A chain bracelet courtesy of the state linked arms, waist, ankles—the chains also kept him from straying more than a few inches from the mesh wall. He was seated behind a narrow table, but his fingers barely reached the edge.

Sylvia stood in place, conscious of adrenaline, dread, and flowing underneath, a strong current of expectation. She waited, unwilling to be the first to speak.

"Dr. Strange. I want to thank you," he said, oddly formal in speech and posture. His face showed deeper strain than it had twenty-four hours earlier. "I wasn't sure you'd accept my invitation."

"That's what this is? An invitation?" she asked softly. "It feels like a summons."

"Then I apologize." His eyes narrowed, jaw tensing abruptly. "Did they give you a bad time?"

"I'm fine." She was in motion, crossing the cage, dropping the pack of cigarettes on the table. She sat on a metal folding chair. "I'm here."

With careful movements, she tapped the pack until a cigarette protruded from the opening. She held it out, and he strained forward to reach it with his lips. She pulled a lighter from her jacket pocket. Leaning toward him across the table, she flicked the metal lip, extending the flame.

He drew on the cigarette until the tip flared orange. As he exhaled, smoke hovered on the air around his mouth. "Why not ask the question?"

She nodded, placing the lighter on the table. Her fingers found the cigarette pack, and she worried the cellophane. "Why me?"

"We both know you've run through the various possibilities," he said softly. "Can we just say you're a free agent?"

"I'm still on their side," she answered, stretching to pick up an improvised ashtray someone had left on the floor.

"I'm betting you're on the side of justice and equity."

"I'm listening."

"It's not that simple."

"Yes, it is," she said sharply. "You have information they need—"

"My hands are tied." He shifted his arms until the chains pulled taut. His smile was mean.

Sylvia stood, walking away from the table to come to a standstill by the mesh-lined wall. She gripped metal. "They need to know about the extortion letters."

"I only know about my private correspondence."

"Bullshit." She pivoted to face him.

"No," he said sharply. "We do it *my* way."

"Of course we do." She didn't try to mask her derision.

Dantes dipped his head, his face unreadable while he finished his cigarette. "Do you miss Santa Fe, Dr. Strange? Your friends, your family?"

When Sylvia didn't answer, he looked up. "A thousand miles is no distance at all."

She placed the palms of her hands on the table and leaned toward Dantes. Conscious of audio surveillance, she mouthed four words—*Don't fuck with me*.

They locked eyes. Sylvia didn't look away. Not even when she felt him read her mind; he seemed to possess that ability.

"You misunderstand me," Dantes said.

"No, I don't. You just threatened my family. Do it again, I'm out of here. Do you understand *me*?"

He let the smoldering cigarette fall from his lips to land on the concrete floor; he ground it out with the heel of his shoe. "When they shook down my cell, they stole *one* card," he said. "I don't know about anything else."

"The FBI received another written communication yesterday."

"Through the mail?"

"Yes."

"Content?"

"It was a threat." She'd rehearsed the script with Church and Purcell; so far they hadn't veered off track. "But that doesn't surprise you."

"No." He slumped back in his chair. "That doesn't surprise me."

"The message was inscribed on the back of a photograph—a Polaroid of a bomb," Sylvia said. "Who is he? What does he want?"

Dantes smiled complacently. "I could use another cigarette."

"Is he your partner? A fan?" She sat down again, reaching for the pack, tapping on plastic. "A copycat, or a sycophant?"

"Don't be petty."

She held a cigarette to her lips. "The Feds will lose patience before I do." She clipped the lighter, sparking a blue flame, tipping the cigarette to heat. She inhaled smoke—"Give them something to work with"—then exhaled.

When he didn't respond, she extended her arm, offering the lighted cigarette and intimacy with that one gesture.

He accepted. "I used to dream about my victims," he whispered. "The surveyor killed in the aqueduct bombing. He had a two-year-old, another baby on the way. The job wasn't scheduled for Thursday; he came early because his wife wanted him to take a long weekend. And the security guard? She was only forty-one." His face sharpened, and he leaned forward. "I used to dream about them, but I stopped right after the Getty. Why do you think I stopped, Dr. Strange?"

"Because you had new nightmares—new victims." Anger sparked Sylvia's eyes. "The Getty bombing killed a child, his teacher—"

"I'm not responsible."

"The evidence—"

"—was circumstantial. You talk to the bomb boys and everything changes. You've switched sides on me."

"I was never on your side."

"Oh, but I think you were, Dr. Strange. You just don't want to admit it." He sighed. "You and I are very much alike. We both want to play God—we both stretch beyond our reach. People get hurt."

"You're a murderer."

"You're right," Dantes whispered. He gazed up at her, that intense sadness—manufactured or real—in his eyes again. He took a breath, physically releasing emotional weight.

He said, "We never really answered the question, Dr. Strange—why *you?* But you've guessed, haven't you?" He smiled. "Let's talk about Mona Carpenter."

Sylvia stood.

"Her husband must hate you," he said slowly. Slumping back in the hard chair with a smoky exhale, he shifted his gaze to follow wafting tendrils of smoke. "Mona had a child, a son, didn't she? Nathan? Little Nate?"

She turned, walking straight to the door.

"We both know what it's like to witness the death of someone who counted on you to make the world safe." Urgency broke through Dantes' words. "My mother counted on me. Mona Carpenter counted on you."

Sylvia reached her hand up to tap on metal: the signal for release.

Dantes didn't take his eyes from her back. "Have you ever seen what happens when a bomb explodes, the range of destruction?" he asked. "Walk away now, and more innocent people will die—children, mothers, grandmothers."

Sylvia froze. She didn't trust herself to move. Finally, she turned to face him. "That's why you became a bomber? To hurt innocent **people**?" She asked. "I thought John Dantes wanted to save the world."

"There was a time he believed he could do that . . . save the world."

"I'm glad you believed in something," Sylvia said. She walked back to the table.

"My targets were selected to contain damage, to avoid casualties. Obviously that's not always possible. I had a story to tell. I had to make people listen."

"You actually believe they heard your message?" Sylvia asked harshly. "They've labeled you schizophrenic, psychotic, deranged." She spit out the words. "You should hear them on the talk shows. It's fifty-fifty—they want to marry you or murder you. That's your legacy." She leaned in closer, her voice dropping to insinuate. "Nobody's listening to John Dantes. They call you a coward."

"They'll listen," he said coldly. "Before it's all over, they'll listen."

She fixed her gaze on him, as if by simply staring long enough, stubbornly enough, she might penetrate his mind.

Instead she found herself absorbed by his energy, stung by his intensity. Abruptly, she turned her head away. "We need your help." Once again she was aware of Purcell and Church. Her body betrayed her internal shift; she felt the rift in her concentration, like an actor who breaks the fourth wall.

Dantes didn't miss the trick. "Hello, Church," he said cordially, tracking her thoughts. He shifted in the chair, an arrow primed. "Is the lovely Ms. Purcell with you today? Please forgive my rudeness, Dr. Strange, but I'm talking to my old pals from the task force." Dantes' smile was secretive. "My friends are very worried, aren't they?"

He swung his head left, right. His demeanor altered, his calm veneer slipping away. Anxiety had begun to show through like something raw beneath the skin. Struggling to maintain control, he kept his attention focused on Sylvia. "What's got them worried?"

"Take a wild guess," she said harshly.

"A bomber? I don't think so." He straightened in the chair, tensing visibly. "They're worried they fucked up the Getty investigation. They convicted the wrong man." He tipped his head. "Do you really want help from me? The inmate?" He smiled, those electric eyes reaching their point of convergence. "The lunatic?"

She tried to read the fleeting emotions revealed on his pale face, but he retreated internally.

"Question, Dr. Strange," he said sharply. "What does it feel like when you create a device, place it in a predetermined spot, detonate it—with the knowledge you will destroy property, perhaps human lives?"

"You tell me, you're the bomb expert," Sylvia said.

"You're the psychologist. What does the profile suggest?"

"There's no solid profile for bombers—the data from the nineteen ninety-two study is filled with variables," she said. "You're aware of that fact."

"But the FBI's working on another little study," he said. "Like it or not, you're part of the team. You wrote your own book on attachment disorders. It must be psychologically cool to reveal yourself these days. Shrink as confessor. Your missing father was the centerpiece of your literary effort. He walked away, didn't he, Sylvia? You still don't know if he's dead or alive." He shrugged. "But that's all in the past. Let's look at the present. Over the last eighteen months, you've published papers in *Homicide Studies*, in the APA journal, in the *Journal of Behavioral Sciences*. You authored a chapter on pathological attachment for your imaginary friend, Leo Carreras. You made sense, he was full of shit."

Dantes thrust his jaw forward like a man begging for a punch, and said, "You're a sucker for a hard case. Rapist, psycho, terrorist—Dr. Strange doesn't walk away. Not like Daddy. Give the pretty lady a shiny quarter." His mouth was a flat line. "For another twenty-five cents, what is Sinai and Olivet?"

"I don't know." She shook her head, frustrated and frightened; her gaze slid past the clock; they were out of time; he was playing games. "Mount Sinai?"

"Moses, the ascension, and funny cars at Angels Flight. My mother introduced me to that funicular railway when I was five and the fare was a nickel. Perfect synchrony."

"You wrote about her—"

"Last ride, ten o'clock," he cut her off. "The chance to see Bunker Hill in all its glory. Have I told you the story of Prudent Beaudry? Five hundred bucks bought him that chunk of land, and he named it after the battle." He strained against the chains.

"If you want to know me, go see my city of fallen angels. What have I written about this place?" His smile was humorless. "Do your homework—I did mine." His body hunched inside the protective vest, and his voice dropped to a whisper. "I don't envy you your job."

She opened her mouth, but nothing came out.

"You'll use up precious moments of your life *absorbing* John Freeman Dantes. How he thinks and feels, what he loves, what he hates. You'll try to fit his crimes in a context that not only makes sense but also explains the motives, the methods of future bombers. If Dantes bombed the Getty, why did he work so hard to avoid taking lives for fifteen years? Why does he target the city he worships? Why doesn't it all add up into a neat package?"

He shook his head. "You'll strive to find earthshaking truths, but in the end—"

"Please help us," she pleaded, exhausted and disappointed by impending failure. "There's a bomb out there. We don't have time—"

He interrupted harshly—"We have too much time."

Sylvia pushed herself away from the table in disgust. "You claim to care about this city, but you won't stop a bomber who's threatening to kill and maim innocent people?"

"They don't have a clue. They don't know who they're dealing with." Dantes glared past her, through walls, as if he could see his enemies on the other side. Arrogance altered his posture, lengthening his muscles. He shook his head. "Not a fucking clue."

"Then help them—*help us*—instead of playing some private game."

He turned his febrile gaze on Sylvia, staring at her for a moment, as if memorizing her features. He spoke in a tired voice. "The interview's over."

"I'm not leaving." She stood, both hands gripping the edge of the table, knuckles gone white. She spoke in a low voice. "You write about justice, you speak of compassion— is it all a lie?"

"Did Mona Carpenter promise you she wouldn't kill herself?"

Sylvia closed her eyes. "Yes."

"Did she lie to you?" Dantes leaned forward, straining against his bonds, until the tendons in his throat were taut. "Or did she lie to herself?"

"I don't know."

"In your heart—*not your mind*—in your heart do you believe you should have saved her?"

"*Yes.*"

"You're right," he whispered. His gaze lingered on her face—forever—until, finally, he closed his eyes. "She needed you."

Sylvia had the sensation of falling, as if physically he'd released her.

He said, "I don't have the information you need."

"Goddamn you. I'll tell you why you asked for me—you're afraid. You're human, not a god—you asked for me because you need my help—"

"'He that violates his oath profanes the divinity of faith itself,'" Dantes intoned, drowning out her words. "It's written in stone, at the source."

"You can't sleep at night because the nightmares never went away," she said. "You want absolution."

"Tell the bomb boys I can't help them."

"You're *lying*."

For the first time in this room, this hour, he allowed the depth of his rage to break the surface. A shadow transformed his features, turning his face raw and ugly.

He bolted against the chains and they clanged against the mesh wall. "Don't you fucking tell me what's truth!" As his words echoed in the room, the primordial creature dove again, disappearing deep into a murky psychic sea. Tremors wracked his body.

And then it hit Sylvia—however fleeting and archaic the thought, she was watching a man falling into madness.

What would bring him back?

His muscles were so taut his hands trembled. "Welcome to my humble hell," he whispered.

9:09 A.M. Sylvia walked away from the meeting with Dantes knowing he'd lied, knowing he'd told some truths—lie and truth each obscured by the shadow of the other.

The recirculated oxygen she breathed was the same O_2 that had entered the lungs of John Dantes. The intimate exchange of molecules had allowed no access into a bomber's mind, his thoughts, into what was fact and what was fabrication.

She stepped from the transport cage just as the U.S. marshal entered; the door clanged shut behind his back. She found herself alone in the dimly lit basement; no sign of Purcell or Church. She stood for a few moments while she regained her bearings.

She hated not having answers—when it came to people and their behavior, the need to know *why* and *how* was embedded deep in her psyche; that need had driven her to become a psychologist. When she was very young she'd believed answers could change the world. Now she accepted the fact that small glimmers of truth were often exceptional.

But even a little bit of truth could save a life.

Sylvia walked quickly to the elevators, rode up to the ground floor of Roybal Federal, and stepped out into what should have been the lobby. Instead, she found herself in a glaringly fluorescent hallway. The service route was unfamiliar—she was trespassing through areas not usually seen by civilians. Passing two U.S. marshals, she pushed open a heavily reinforced door and stepped into the world of bureaucrats. Industrial-weave carpet the color of new grass muted each footfall. The narrow halls were painted blue-green instead of beige, and work by neighboring inmates was framed and carefully displayed.

She collided with Special Agent Purcell as the smaller woman suddenly rounded a hallway corner.

"Follow me," Purcell ordered.

"Where's Church?" Sylvia kept pace stride for stride.

"Manning the command post." Purcell pushed open an exit door, stepping out into hot air and blinding sunlight.

"What command post?"

Purcell said, "Thanks to Dantes we've got ourselves a bomb."

CHAPTER EIGHT

> A bomb has a heart. If you doubt me just hold a ticking
> bundle in your arms and see if you don't feel the thrill
> of new life.
>
> *Mole's Manifesto*

9:11 A.M. The lure of danger is exerting its influence like gravitational pull.

Uncomfortable in the hot bright air, M approaches the shadow of the building on Spring Street just as the first wave of law enforcement and public safety officials arrive. A quartet of men, focused and deadly serious, flow from their vehicles; they are dealing with a bomb threat. He recognizes Detective Church, LAPD, in the process of establishing a command post.

M has reason to be here, too. Credentials.

His pulse doesn't even jump when a fast-moving cop crosses his path, almost shoving him out of the way. Around him, employees, tourists, and city residents populating courtyards and sidewalks are still unaware of atmospheric changes. Not for long.

Keeping pace with his neighbors, he observes an unmarked sedan as it pulls around the corner of Spring toward Temple. In the distance, a fire truck rumbles. Too soon for sirens. Official emergency schematics will focus on maintaining order, preserving crowd control, avoiding panic, averting chaos.

M has always found social psychology—behavior of the

masses—entertaining. The collective consciousness of fear follows a surprisingly predictable course. At this very moment, he feels the first shift, subtle, fast moving. Expressions alter—pedestrian faces registering surprise, then concern. They glance at each other but nobody is totally spooked. Not yet.

Within minutes, a state-of-siege mentality will override the normal bureaucratic pace of everyday city business.

Danger is something he knows well—it comes with the tools of his trade.

Ammonium nitrate. Acetic anhydride. Paraformaldehyde. PETN. Acetone. Mineral oil.

Datasheet. M-118. M-186.

Recipes for mass destruction.

M is the cook, and his expert hands—with almost delicate bones—always find their mark. The hands of a bomber scarred by experience. Hands of a collaborative artist. Of an extremely careful man.

Always cut a perfect fuse.

Always double prime.

Always wear cotton, silk, or wool; man-made fibers melt.

Never allow yourself to become insolent or brazen unless you've grown weary of this world.

Never turn your back on the beast.

Golden rules for the art of improvised death. There are many more. Rules for the kitchen. Rules for the field. M's learned them over the years. He's learned the hard way.

Like Dantes . . . who knows the rules of safety, too.

He smiles hesitantly at a passing woman, asking, "What's going on?"

He sees her double take, the look of concern. He hears her fading response, "Maybe a fire?" as she breaks stride, then continues on.

Ah, yes. Now, he can feel them reacting; the faint seepage of panic is like blood as it dissipates in calm ocean waters.

He is guessing here—officials will cave in and decide to evacuate. The extortion note implies a connection to Dantes; the location, the importance of the building's occupants, and its symbolic weight for LA all tip the scales in favor of extra precautionary measures.

Your average bomb search in a large building is best carried out by informed employees and public safety officials without full evacuation. It's cheaper and more efficient to allow building security to patrol familiar territory, with the backup of fire department and bomb squad personnel who will deal with suspicious objects or possible devices.

Usually it all comes to naught.

Most bomb threats are hoaxes.

But this isn't your *average* bomb scare.

It's all part of the big plan. Project Inferno. Carefully orchestrated, already embedded in the very heart of the city, its veins and arteries, its central nervous system. He has spent months laying out a fastidious grid of destruction. Now hell is just a hop and a skip away. He watches the FBI and ATF agents—chests puffed, ready to piss on their territory—pulling up in their respective bureau vehicles.

He is careful not to laugh out loud. But damn, he feels good.

Always—it never fails—there comes a time when the poetry, the artistry takes over, and then the technique, the anal precision, the pain fades away underneath a pure and rarefied hum. He is humming now.

M is invisible—blending in with purpose—walking past the perimeter, flashing his credentials. Not one eyebrow raised.

He is a man who creates his own history. Months earlier,

he decided upon a position at a consulting firm. With his résumé, how could they refuse to hire him?

It is his job to track earthquake damage, to map underground systems, to know the city's infrastructure and how it works—under normal conditions and in crisis. He shares responsibility for public safety.

He nods when he hears, "No radio communication, and check in at the command post."

"Right."

He scans the crowd for eyes that flicker with recognition, for faces that sign their own death warrants because he cannot afford to be recognized.

He is less than fifteen hundred meters from Metro Detention and the Roybal Federal Building. The hair on his arms stands erect. Dantes is so close he should be able to read M's mind.

I'm thinking of our years together—especially that day when I died and you went on to become the esteemed professor, the underground outlaw bomber, the famed author and idolized cult hero.

If your public had known the truth they would've slapped you from your pedestal sooner, Dantes.

I know damn well what you're thinking, friend.

You're faced with the coward's dilemma.

You've lived a lie. Isn't it better to take it to the grave?

You're trapped in a coward's nightmare—and the only way out is down to hell.

I never took the coward's path. I took my punishment like a man. And I've nursed my grudge until it's burnt a sweet hole in my brain.

I died. His smile faded. And you stood me up at my funeral, Dantes.

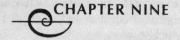

CHAPTER NINE

> In contemporary terrorism, criminalists must focus on the political bomber, the man who believes the urgency of his cause justifies the death of innocent people.
>
> Leo Carreras, M.D., Ph.D., and Sylvia Strange, Ph.D.,
> *Profiles in 21st Century Terrorism*

9:21 A.M. "Move away from the barricades!"

Sylvia stayed close to Special Agent Purcell.

They were just outside the federal building—at the corner of Temple and Los Angeles Streets—and an LAPD uniformed cop worked hard to stay cool while he maneuvered a DPS sawbuck, inching it toward a growing crowd of onlookers.

"The hell's going on?" a large, bombastic woman draped under a bright red muumuu challenged the officer. "I have files for the mayor's office."

"No deliveries, ma'am. Step away from the barricade."

"The hell I'm not, and don't you 'ma'am' me—"

With fleeting pity for the beleaguered cop, Sylvia tuned out the exchange and focused on Purcell, who was moving very fast. They traveled west on Temple toward Main Street. Between snatches of the agent's terse cellular exchanges and a monosyllabic Q&A session, Sylvia was getting a rough picture of the situation.

City officials had agreed to cordon off a five-block perimeter between First and Temple from Hill to San Pedro;

motorized traffic already snaked around the crowds of curious spectators. Under the direction of uniformed officers, a steady stream of pedestrians had just begun to flow from the fortified area. Law enforcement, the fire department, and emergency personnel were working with somber efficiency. They'd hit the street, code 2, urgent, no sirens.

The bomb squad was on the way to look for a bomb—that search would be based upon information that had come from Sylvia's interview with John Dantes.

But which information?

Purcell refused to comment on that subject; she was too busy with her cell phone.

The federal agent flashed her credentials at the jittery LASO deputy manning yet another barricade, this one at the corner of Main Street. They turned south.

Sylvia thought the Civic Center complex, with its various plazas, was beginning to take on the surreal look of an abandoned city. As she followed Purcell gratefully into shade cast by a tall building, she heard music blasting from someone's radio, a fluid male voice urging the listener, "Live and die in LA." The sound faded and exploded again: "I love Cali like I love women—"

The rest of the song's lyrics were lost as Purcell gestured down the block. "Church wants to talk to you."

Sylvia could see the detective conferring with two other men and a woman; they were roughly 150 feet away, at the opposite end of the block. Apparently, the command post consisted of two unmarked sedans angled together, a bomb squad van parked in between, roughly three hundred feet from City Hall's south entrance.

"Our supervisory agent should be here any minute," Purcell continued. "The chief of police is on his way in from Westwood." The federal agent exhaled a soft stream of air. "The evacuation started with the mayor's office."

"The bomb's at City Hall?"

Purcell answered the phone instead of the question.

Sylvia walked away from the agent, calling over her shoulder, "I didn't ask to be part of this—you demanded my help."

"Where are you going?" Purcell called, hand over mouthpiece.

Without slowing, Sylvia pointed toward Church.

In his suit and gray fedora, LAPD badge clipped to belt, the detective paced from van to cars. He shot her a look, raising one finger in acknowledgment as he simultaneously barked into a telephone. Because of the danger of accidental detonation of a possible improvised explosive device, handheld radio communication would be kept at a minimum.

Sylvia glanced back over her shoulder and caught sight of two ATF agents—identifiable by their jackets—jogging across the street. Then she saw Special Agent Purcell moving forward to head them off. The top of Purcell's dark curls would barely tickle the ATF agents' formidable chins, but she had puffed up her chest, ready to do battle in the agency turf wars.

If the situation ran true to form, the LAPD and the fire department and the various SOs would join in the fray—all jockeying to be top dog. Questions of agency jurisdiction weren't easily settled, especially in dense urban areas, where indelible boundaries could never be drawn.

Sylvia skirted the vehicles and the command post, continuing another twenty feet to the corner of First Street. She stopped near the perimeter barricades.

She heard a baby crying, she saw the faces of curious spectators, but she wasn't aware of individual features. Bodies and buildings seemed to melt together, glazed by heat, stress, and optical illusion.

The previous ninety minutes had taken their toll, and the tension she'd managed to dance with all morning had broken through her defenses to step hard on her toes. She felt weary, inadequate, *frightened*—and that was the good news.

M was watching. He had to be. He'd arranged a spectacular show—and bought himself a front row seat.

Snatching a cigarette from her pocket, she looked out at the expanse of concrete, focusing on City Hall, her gaze drawn up the twenty-eight-story tower. LA's ziggurat.

HE THAT VIOLATES HIS OATH PROFANES THE DIVINITY OF FAITH ITSELF.

The oversized letters were carved over the south entrance to City Hall.

Sylvia felt a hollow space open up behind her solar plexus.

"Don't feel bad, Doc. Dantes lobbed it *way* over your head and straight into my mitt." The rust-and-gravel voice belonged to Detective Church. He saw her expression; his own eyes held a cold, hard glint. "Shit, I must've walked under that quote a thousand times. I used to do liaison work with the mayor's office. Dantes knows that."

"You got it right away?" Sylvia asked, stung, and feeling angry—with herself, with Church, especially with Dantes.

"Marcus Tullius Cicero," Church said. "Rome's greatest orator. I'm one of those guys who reads the writing on the wall. History repeats itself: Dantes left a bomb here in nineteen eighty-eight."

"A hoax bomb," Sylvia said, remembering the file she'd examined hours earlier.

"Turned out to be a hoax, yeah."

"So you've got a bomb inside City Hall," she whispered. She was staring at countless tons of concrete and marble and steel, and she was remembering Oklahoma City. Her stomach fluttered uneasily. Reflexively, she took a step backward. "Or you've got another hoax."

"Never bet on a hoax," Church said, his voice a soft rumble. He was sweating, red blotches appearing on his skin. "There's a bomb until we prove otherwise. And never—as me dear old ma told me more than once—*never* try to outsmart a smart guy."

"Your ma was right." With shaky hands, Sylvia lit up her cigarette, inhaling, perversely grateful for hot smoke in her lungs.

As cigarette smoke wafted past his freckled nose, Church said, "I could arrest you for that."

Sylvia held out one wrist. "Go for it. I keep trying to quit."

Church snorted. "You weren't around for the triple play last week," he drawled. Once again, his voice held a note of commiseration. "MDC came *this* close to evacuating three times in twenty-four—assholes screwed my code seven."

"Missed that one." Code 7 was cop talk for mealtime; she'd learned to translate ten code. "Too bad about your doughnuts."

Detective Church shot her a sideways look, one eyebrow trying to jump over the moon. "C'mon, I'll fill you in," he said, already headed back toward the command post. As he walked, he pulled out his cell phone, responding to its inaudible vibration. "This is Church."

Sylvia glanced back at City Hall as the detective updated the caller: "Last of the civilians are out. Our guys already checked parking and street levels. They're on two and three. We get the news floor by floor."

Church went silent, then he grunted several times. Holding the phone in hand, he considered Sylvia. "Back there at Roybal, we skipped a step."

"The debriefing."

"Right." He tugged on the brim of his fedora. "When you were with Dantes, you saw what we only heard. You think we're on the right track with this? Gut feeling."

Eye level with Church, Sylvia found herself staring into two black holes, the opaque lenses of his sunglasses; the freckles on his middle-aged nose stood out in relief against pink skin. In the back of her mind she heard the low drone of a jet, but her thoughts centered on *Dantes' Inferno: City of Angels in the 21st Century*.

A week ago, she'd lost the damn book—she would never have admitted it, she was enough of a Freudian. But she'd replaced it with a second copy.

Dantes had omitted the revelations of his secret life as a bomber, instead focusing on the city's history, physical form, ecology, sociology. With an intimacy, a yearning, he'd written about a lover: City of Angels as mythical mate, LA as anima.

It was fitting that Dantes was being held in the geographic center of his obsession, where physical and mental boundaries merged. Where the world was turned upside down by the threat of explosive destruction.

Fitting that he would use the language of architecture— the syntactical structure of *his* city—to speak to the forces of authority he despised.

Sylvia's eyes widened as she refocused. She ran her tongue across dry lips. "When I was in there, when I called him a liar, his rage broke through, he went into meltdown. Disintegration." She nodded. "Gut feeling—he sent us to find a bomb. But whether he's working with the extortionist—or just taking advantage of an opportunity—I don't know."

Church spoke into the cell phone, "You hear that, Sweetheart?"

Sweetheart . . .

Now the *click:* by reputation Sylvia knew of a Professor Edmond Sweetheart, a psycholinguist—an antiterrorist analyst—who was a minor legend in intelligence circles. He'd played a role in the Ben Black-Abu Mohammed investigation in the Middle East. Ultimately, the FBI's number one fugitive explosives specialist, Black, was killed when an American Tomahawk took a nosedive into a North African terrorist training camp—

Wasn't Edmond Sweetheart related to one of the victims of the Getty bombing?

"I'm sorry?" she said, abruptly aware of Church.

"I said, don't take this wrong. Back there, with Dantes, you *missed* the message. You missed it because he pulled you in. If he gets to you—innocent people die."

His voice faded as he caught sight of a black armored truck—LAPD bomb squad—pulling up beside the blue-and-whites. He started to walk away. But instead, he turned toward the growing crowd of spectators. "I don't want LA to pay for Dantes' bullshit. Got that?" He kept his voice low. "Don't go anywhere yet, Doc—we're gonna need you."

Sylvia stubbed out her cigarette on the metal trunk of a street lamp and trailed the detective to the command post.

9:47 A.M.   Sylvia stayed out of everybody's way—investigators, emergency personnel, and city officials. Their squabbles, their tension, their efforts registered subliminally; her attention was constantly drawn to isolated energetic moments—a loud voice in the crowd, a siren, a flash of light, the smell of smoke, sweat, and exhaust.

She could feel M's presence. The agents and investigators around her felt it, too.

Suddenly, the city seemed to close in around the ziggurat—the modern high-rises known as City Hall East, City Hall West, the LAPD Center, the *Times* building one block to the south, Spring Street, Main Street, the Harbor and the Hollywood Freeways.

Here, this one square mile contained five levels of government, from federal and state down to county, city, and even utility districts. Thousands of people came and went each day.

Walking toward the perimeter and the spectators, she reached for the slender gold chain around her neck. Her fingers closed round something small and solid—a gift from Serena. She gripped the tiny icon of the Virgin of Guadalupe, picturing her foster daughter's angelic face, those rich umber eyes, skin the color of toffee.

The sound of sharp metal jarred her back to the moment. She saw a shape emerge from the armored truck. An LAPD bomb tech in full protective gear. He moonwalked a small circle, testing his mobility. She held her breath until he disappeared ponderously back inside the air-conditioned truck.

Sylvia scanned faces—fire chief, cops, maintenance people, city safety engineers—each marked by fear and hypervigilance.

Waiting for the green light on code 10.

M was waiting, too.

10:33 A.M. Less than an hour had passed before they all knew they weren't going to find a bomb.

By then the temperature had risen to the low nineties, and every temper was short fused. The barricaded streets were eerily deserted except for emergency vehicles—beyond the barricades, the lingering spectators were too quiet. A hush had fallen.

A few blocks away on Broadway, the sidewalks would be

overflowing with pedestrians, the air filled with city music: the noise of hawkers, amplified songs, voices, traffic. The sound would echo up the steep sides of the urban canyons—fissures made of concrete and steel—where raptors shared rooftops with pigeons, rats, and cockroaches. Evolutionary winners . . . unaware that death was only a block or two away.

Sylvia pressed her palm against the back of her neck; her skin felt hot. The sky was an angular scrim, bruised a bluish yellow, suspended between bleached white buildings. The late-morning sun beat down on the concrete desert, creating an opiate shimmer.

A shrill ring sounded, and from the corner of her eye, she barely noticed Church answer the phone. She caught the edge of her thumbnail between slightly crooked front teeth. M—who the hell was he? And how did his life intersect with the bizarre tale of John Freeman Dantes?

"Bombers fit no definitive profile; like other criminals, like other human beings, they are motivated by greed, faith, politics, envy, pathology, need, fear, anger, revenge. Perhaps what makes them exceptional is their resistance to classification.

"And their willingness to kill indiscriminately."

She felt the tight ball of fear in her belly—the inevitable tension of waiting for the other shoe to drop.

"He that violates his oath profanes the divinity of faith itself."

A quote about betrayal . . .

Abruptly she sought the self-medication of another cigarette to keep her hands busy and her chemistry sedated. Seen through the tinted lenses of her sunglasses, the golden head of City Hall reflected light, shimmering like a gaudy jewel. From this distance, there was no apparent danger; the building appeared normal. But in her imagination it shattered suddenly, collapsing in on itself, showering deadly debris in all directions.

Dantes' words raced through her mind: *Last ride, ten o'clock . . . Bunker Hill in all its glory . . . go see my city of fallen angels.*

Dantes isn't finished with us yet.

She turned, moving restlessly across concrete.

"Where do you think you're going?"

For the second time that day, Sylvia collided with Special Agent Purcell. The woman held a palm-sized tape recorder. "This call just came in."

Sylvia set the speaker to her ear.

She heard an oddly artificial voice, a man enjoying his own joke. "I see that John shared our little secret of Babel. His bombs were meant to punish infidels and gluttons. But your greedy city fathers didn't listen. Now it's my turn. No bombs today—but we'll be back tomorrow."

And then he laughed. "Welcome to the third circle of hell."

CHAPTER TEN

The man in the Mousehole, I am gazing up at the world from a warm, dark nest lined with twigs and fur. All I see is an empty sky where God should live. I am a 21st Century Man. Or am I a mouse?

Mole's Manifesto

10:38 A.M. M presses *end* on the cellular phone.

Good-bye. Ciao. Sayonara.

The call cannot be traced—child's play—unless the Feds look up. In which case he will wave.

He is beginning to know the players. The FBI and ATF agents, LAPD, and others. He is beginning to feel a kinship. He makes a move, they make a move. What a perfect synergy. This is a true symbiotic relationship.

Now, with his binoculars, he can see them clearly from his eagle nest atop the *Los Angeles Times* building. His vantage point was chosen in honor of Dantes' *LA Times* bomb. What a fiasco that had been—as if John's bourgeois anarchy would actually affect the course of history.

It is M who will affect history.

The Feds are in such a tizzy, buzzing like insects, disappointed their plans have come to naught.

He understands. He feels let down, too. Always his metabolism drops—a chemical shift—after he has made a delivery. It's as if he's physically lighter inside. A hole gapes. Some part of him has been left behind.

He is in limbo. Floating until detonation, explosion.

At which point, he recharges.

After decades, he believes this is an integral part of his being. He lives inside the space of tension between action and reaction.

His actions: Choosing a target. Constructing a bomb. Hearing it come to life. Watching it die as it lives.

For a moment the LA sun is eclipsed by a very recent memory, and he is transported by neurons to his underground workshop, his own private bunker, where he creates his weapons of destruction.

"My old flame, I can't even think of his name," his parrot, Nietzsche (an African gray), joins in, hitting the last note of the song, his voice wavering like a nightclub crooner with a megaphone. The bird fluffs both wings and dips his head, taking the customary bow for an audience of one. A single blue tail feather drifts past his perch, glancing off one of a dozen bags of Kitty Litter, to land on an otherwise bare basement floor.

"I can't applaud you now." At the moment, the cook's gloved hands are busy funneling sulfuric acid into a small glass bottle.

Gently. With care, he supervises the birth of a capillary fuse. Slowly, the clear and corrosive oil of vitriol nears midpoint.

Some of these materials date back more than fifteen years; he and Dantes bought this off an old man in Pomona. Such good friends, they even shared their chips, their circuits, their clips . . .

Smiling beneath his hood, the cook raises the bottle for Nietzsche's benefit. "Is the glass half full, or half empty, my friend?"

The parrot flexes and contracts one claw. "Empty, my friend," he echoes harshly.

"Nietzsche the pessimist," the cook whispers, capping the bottle with a single-holed wax-coated rubber stopper. He is not a large man—without the modified welder's hood and the heavy sleeved apron, he barely breaks 165 pounds—but he always feels oversized in the close room. It is furnished as sparely as possible to his specifications: two worktables, industrial quantities of highly absorbent Kitty Litter and baking soda, his simple glass and plastic mixing tools—and only those chemicals essential for a particular operation. He installed the fume hood and flue because both are absolutely necessary to draw off the fumes he creates on certain days. But not this particular night. Nietzsche never keeps him company when he is working with noxious chemical exhaust.

M sets the bottle of acid on the smaller table and takes four steps across the room to reach the larger work area. His supplies are neatly arranged. Plastic bag. Brand new jar of Vaseline. Sugar. Potassium chlorate. Mixing bowl and spatula. The jointed pipe. Caps.

The beauty of the pipe bomb is containment. The pipe functions as a metal womb where superheated gases (created from explosive powder, in this case a low explosive) expand until they generate enough pressure to go boom.

The cook is using one of his favorite recipes as filler: sodium chlorate and sugar, which—like ammonium nitrate and charcoal—is highly hygroscopic, attracting moisture like a sponge.

All in all, it is simpler than baking cookies.

As long as no trace of filler carelessly contaminates the space between threads and cap. Vaseline helps grease the turn of the screw.

Others besides M admire the utilitarian efficiency of pipe bombs. George Metesky—the Mad Bomber of New York—included them in his repertoire now and again. Tom Mooney and Warren Billings spent more than two decades in prison for the 1916 Market Street pipe bombing that left ten San Franciscans dead and forty injured. The Unabomber added nails to fill his PVC.

M snaps a Polaroid of the bomb—a gift for his special friends at the Federal Bureau of Investigation.

Nietzsche sings louder, with more heart, when the recipe du jour is pipe bomb. This bomb—like any other of his creations—has a destination: downtown Los Angeles. A special hiding place—

A voice breaks M from his reverie.

"How come they're going?" somebody whines.

Someone else whispers a novena.

The usual letdown after the show.

Relief and disappointment: we were going to see some frigging fireworks, weren't we?

They move as a herd.

M finds himself on street level, lost in the throng of spectators, in the midst of anticlimax. The bomb squad is packing up: body armor, dogs, remote devices, collective intelligence, and fear—all gathered in this square block to combat his evil.

He knows what it will be like when they finally face his device.

The sweating hands, the tremors, the racing heartbeat. The macabre jokes, false bravado, gallows humor. The personification of a killing machine.

Like him, they work with bare hands because gloves are clumsy. The fused plastic shields covering their faces will fog up; most bomb squad survivors dance on the edge of death every time they're invited to a party. It's easy to nurture a death wish. After a while, the proximity of death brings comfort. Every man needs to hold hands with death from time to time. And bomb squad men are no different. Too bad, he thinks. After all those chemicals, all that fear, the adrenaline kick . . . and now they're acting like children at a birthday party with no gift.

Ah, but he and Nietzsche, the parrot, *have* left the Feds a gift: a temple snake protecting the sacred.

Under his careful fingers, the trip wire lay down and rolled over.

Seven feet long, the color of wood, it did not resist the master's touch. It did not bite or sting, did not release its poison as he trained it to follow the flooring seam.

Using bare fingers, he anchored the tail; the mouth feeds on a metal spring, extended and expanded under pressure. Between these two stations, the wire remains taut. Until resistance is applied. The lightest footfall, for instance. Enough to free the safety insulator—the end of a paper match inserted between spring and nail—enough to complete the circuit when the wire is rereleased.

When the "human element" takes one more step.

The military calls this an expedient firing device system.

M has added his own embellishments—for some serious fun.

Delivery made in the name of Operation Inferno. Yes, he still believes he will recapture the glory days when he and Dantes lived as one.

Now he will wait; the next speech belongs to Dantes—this one will be about trust, betrayal, sacrifice in honor of the Fat Cats. They must begin to understand how serious he is about revenge.

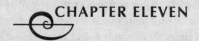

CHAPTER ELEVEN

Every civilization ends. It's only a tragedy when the dust settles in our lifetime.

Mole's Manifesto

10:37 A.M. "Dantes isn't finished with me yet," Sylvia whispered.

Special Agent Purcell shook her head, looking dyspeptic, looking just plain grumpy.

Church took three steps toward Sylvia, flexing his fingers in a backward wave. "So talk to us, what's he want?"

"You heard the interview. All that talk about Bunker Hill, his mother, the railroad—he's sending me to Angels Flight."

"Why?"

"To see if I'll play. To see if *you'll* play."

"We don't do scavenger hunts." Detective Church was chewing gum with such manic energy the ligaments in his jaw looked as if they'd snap.

"What if I come back for more?" Sylvia kept moving, kept talking. "He's parsing out information, running a subtext between the lines. Inmates do it all the time." She spun around, backpeddling across hot concrete. "The quote from Cicero—and Angels Flight."

She turned again just as Church stepped in her path,

arms crossed like a fence over his wide chest. "If you're right, has it occurred to you he and his asshole buddy are sending you out to find the *real* bomb?"

Silent for a moment, Sylvia slowed. "That's why you're coming, too," she said finally.

Church exchanged a look with Purcell.

Sylvia said, "Look, I'm going to Angels Flight—it's worth a gamble—and I need to talk to Dantes when I get there."

"We can put Dantes on the secure line," Church said. "Maybe he'll hang himself."

Purcell flipped open her tiny phone and pressed one button. Her speech was clipped: "We've got Strange—she says she can get more from Dantes."

Sylvia's eyes widened.

"Let's boogie." Detective Church was already moving toward the perimeter barrier and the street.

Sylvia started to follow, but Purcell held out the phone. "For you."

Sylvia heard an unfamiliar voice.

"Dr. Strange, forgive the theatrics"—transmission cut out for an instant, then—"look forward to meeting you."

"Who *is* this?"

"—Sweetheart," the voice stammered in, "—second opinion on terrorists—"

Out.

And in. "—psycholinguistics, encryption. My friends at the FBI have asked for my cooperation."

"I've heard of you," Sylvia said. She deliberately inclined her head toward the phone, as if a miniature of the man lived inside the tiny plastic handset, as if she might lure him out.

"Looks like your friend put you in a tight spot," the voice said, startling her, so that she pulled back physically. "I'll try to stay in contact." The satellite transmission was faint but steady.

"The caller mentioned the third circle," she said. "And the previous message—"

"*No more Limbo*," Sweetheart interrupted. "How well do you remember the *Inferno?* Dante Alighieri envisioned a hierarchical hell. Nine circles." Sweetheart paused as a background hum grew increasingly loud. "The poet Virgil guides the pilgrim through outer hell to the first circle, or limbo—where the heathens exist in a state of nothingness. The second circle belongs to those guilty of lust. Basically, the higher the numerical value of the circle, the more grievous the sin. *Capisce?*"

"He's escalating."

"They'll keep Dantes by the phone," Sweetheart said. "You handle the call—*only you*. Don't make him wait. Don't hide your feelings. If you're scared, show him you're scared."

"I can do that," she said softly, "Hey—what's *three?*"

"I'm sorry?"

"Third circle; what's the third sin?"

"A ravenous appetite for any number of things," he said briskly.

After a second's hesitation, she guessed, "Gluttony?"

"Exactly. Dr. Strange—looks like we've got one bomber behind bars but the other's out there on the streets. Please watch your back."

"Fine," she snapped, clicking off. Fear made her cranky.

10:52 A.M. Once they escaped the mare's nest of the Civic Center, Church burned rubber. Sylvia watched the blur of passing street scenes as the detective guided the town car south on Hill. Yellow tape and red cones marked the road where crews had torn up asphalt for subway improvements or utility repairs; the car slalomed around these and other obstacles, including the rare pedestrian who had ventured out from the shadows cast by the narrow multistoried buildings, the museums, the billboards.

She shivered at the shrill, slicing cry of sirens. Leo Carreras had edited a book on criminal profiling. Sylvia's contribution had been a chapter on narcissism and attachment disorders. Leo's chapter had focused on bombers; according to his data, a small percentage of them registered as polar opposites on the trait spectrum. Nihilist versus moralist, in opposition, yet sharing the tension of absolutes.

Dantes qualified as the moralist.

Sylvia had the feeling they were just beginning to search for missing pieces of the theoretical puzzle.

"Bombers tend to be Caucasian, male, single, or married only for the sake of convenience—but most crime is committed by men, and most males in the U.S. are white. And the bomber's life—concocting deadly explosives—doesn't lend itself easily to a social context. So, how to narrow the profiling field?

"In the late 1970s, Macdonald divided the profile six non-mutually exclusive ways: the compulsive bomber, the psychotic bomber, the sociopathic bomber, the political bomber, the Mafia bomber, and the military bomber."

As Detective Church braked in a no-parking zone, quiet chatter from the radio filled the unmarked car.

"Let's go call your boyfriend."

Angels Flight, the world's shortest funicular railroad, ran east-west, traversing a small hill. On their frequent runs, the two identical red passenger cars were polarized, passing side by side only briefly where the zipper of the track opened for roughly thirty feet.

While Church escorted Sylvia across the street, Purcell stayed put at the base of the hill to monitor the cell transmission—and to keep an eye out for stray bombers.

The car named Olivet, empty and at rest on Hill St.,

met the sidewalk at a forty-five-degree angle. Followed by Church, Sylvia stepped under the distinctive fire-engine archway, passing through the small turnstile to board. She chose a seat from tiny benches reminiscent of an old schoolhouse. Church doubled over to fit his rangy frame inside the small car. They had the Olivet to themselves.

Almost instantly, the ride began with a lurch.

"Two decades after Macdonald, the political bomber and the compulsive bomber seem the most relevant. The political bomber has a cause in need of attention—and he truly believes any method is justifiable in the quest for ideological change. The compulsive bomber is the man who nurtures a lifelong obsession with, and commitment to, explosives, perhaps even deriving— although it has always been a point of controversy—sexual gratification from explosive initiation.

"Again, the categories are not mutually exclusive. The anarchist bomber Ravachol was known for his political extremism, his antisocial personality, and his sexual eccentricities; he wore rouge and carried lipstick and explosives in his purse."

About fifteen seconds into the ascent, Sylvia noticed the second car, Sinai, passing downhill on the northern zipper. As far as she could see, it held one passenger.

"He's one of ours," Church murmured.

The Olivet came to rest with a clank and a jolt. Sylvia debarked, accompanied by Church, ready to hand her fare to the girl inside the ticket booth. History for a quarter. Five rides for a buck. Inflation on hiatus.

But Church flashed his credential at the attendant and she waved them on with a startled look.

"Hey, two bits is two bits," Church drawled.

At first glance, the Water Court was deserted; then Sylvia noticed the other couple. She guessed they were cops.

She picked up speed, crossing to the far edge of the viewing patio.

"*Various and sundry theories factor in personality variables such as the death wish, suicidal tendencies, a low arousal threshold. It is called a 'coward's crime,' but the bomber's life offers the barest apportionment for cowardice. The risk of injury and/or death is extremely high. The overwhelming majority of bombing victims are the bombers themselves, killed in the act of construction or transportation.*"

Brilliant perps aren't the norm, she thought.

"I'm going to call Roybal. Get the transmission set up with Dantes," Church said, joining Sylvia.

"Give me two more minutes," she said, not taking her eyes from the surrounding cityscape. She pushed away the unpleasant thought that she'd better produce results—pray this is a wild goose chase and we can all go home safe and sound.

She imagined Dantes standing in her place. Los Angeles was more than his home, it was his ego, and he'd written about its nooks and crannies, its noir secrets, in detail. The result was a tome—part urban history, part ecosociology—an architecture-as-destiny treatise, with a healthy dose of social psychology by a man who claimed no use for psychologists. Meanwhile, he'd lived a double life as an outlaw, an anarchist.

John Dantes' infernal machines—his bombs—were special. His creations brought destruction—to a small section of the aqueduct, to a Water & Power building, to an oil derrick. But he had no one signature—no definitive method of construction—that he left on each and every device. Some were utilitarian, designed to provide the most bang for the buck. Some were duds—hoax devices. And some were beautiful—created especially to attract the curious.

Not unlike the bomb that killed ten-year-old Jason Redding.

"One man's revolutionary is another man's coldblooded killer. At the turn of the twentieth century, the political bomber is the most dangerous animal in the pack—his psychopathology, hence his motivation, still maintains a hiding place, a safe house deep in the recesses of ideology."

Dantes was sending her on errands. First, to the top of Angels Flight. And she had taken the damn choo-choo because—

In the distance, light fired up the glass and metallic surface of the Bonaventure Hotel. Her heart caught, but it was just the glare of the sun.

No explosions. Not yet.

The sun burned one shoulder, the side of her face. When she looked over at Church, light stung her eyes. A sliver of fractured memory jabbed at her for an instant.

"Call him now," she told the detective with a sharp nod.

Church placed the call.

Less than thirty seconds later, Dantes was on the phone.

"Dr. Strange. How's the view from Angels Flight?"

"Your friend called the FBI," Sylvia said. "He mentioned the third circle."

"Where a cold rain falls, and the three-headed hound of hell guards the damned."

"Is he punishing LA, the city fathers, for the sin of gluttony?"

"Only Ciacco knows the future of the city," Dantes cut her off, "and he's in hell. You'll have to do this all by yourself, Dr. Strange. Tell me what you see."

"A city under siege," she answered quietly.

"I want details, not melodrama," he said. "Grand Central Market to the east. Pershing Square. The Metropolitan Water District, a Wells Fargo bank, a bar, those old hotels from the Chandler days." He paused. "What's behind you?"

"More city," she said, adrenaline level rising like an

internal tide. She reached automatically for her pills, but found her pockets empty.

"Facing north, talk to me."

"Wilshire Boulevard. Olympic, Pico."

"North, not west."

She turned slowly. Three-dimensional Monopoly. She could see half the damn city, including the traffic-clogged recesses of the Civic Center. The Hollywood Freeway. The Harbor interchange. Millions of people traveling along the massive concrete river every day. Such easy victims.

"Why am I here, Dantes? I put my ass on the line for you."

"Be patient," he said.

"While you're getting off on some power games? You against the FBI?"

"They can't give you the answers," he snapped. "*I can.*"

"Maybe. Or maybe you're just playing with innocent lives."

Silence. Was he gone? This was a five-way transmission: in addition to Sylvia and Dantes, Detective Church, SA Purcell, and the U.S. marshals at Roybal were all monitoring the call. The Feds' party line.

"*Hello?*" Sylvia breathed. "Shit."

"Don't jump to stupid conclusions," he said sharply. "You're in way over your head, so listen very carefully. Did you follow my trial before they so rudely and unconstitutionally *gagged* me?"

"Yes—I—"

"Do you remember Judge Heron's response to my final refusal to undergo a psychiatric evaluation?"

"He used your own statement." Caught off guard, she stalled. "About society labeling radicals as criminal or mental misfits . . ."

"Wrong."

"Remind me."

"Pay attention to detail. Otherwise, you're just April's fool."

"I remember reading about—" She broke off. "Dantes?"

"He hung up?" Church asked, mouth gone slack with alarm, earpiece protruding like some black insect. "What did he mean? Shit, *fuck*."

Sylvia shook her head, warding off the sensation of sinking underwater. Her eyes were glued to the coffee stain on the detective's shirt as she said, "The trial transcripts fill entire rooms. Leo Carreras did one evaluation; a state psychiatrist did another. What about the judge—"

"This is fucking useless," Church groaned.

"Back off, leave me the hell alone."

Church did.

"What did he just say? 'Pay attention to detail. Otherwise, you're just April's fool.'" She stared up at Church, but she wasn't seeing him. "That's when Dantes called me—on April first." She closed her eyes, traveling back in time. "I was at my house, on the deck; it was late. I asked him about . . . *what*?"

"What?" Church prodded.

"Object-relations theory," Sylvia blurted out, as a mental light snapped on.

The detective watched her blankly.

"Dantes never knew his father. He lived with his grandparents, but he never bonded with them. His mother was a suicide," she said, frustrated by the need to explain, fighting the urge to bolt. "Dantes asked me what he'd replaced her with, and I didn't make the connection until now."

As Sylvia's delivery picked up speed, she used gestures for emphasis. "She used to take him all over the city, day and night, a sort of constant pilgrimage."

"So we're supposed to wander the damn streets?" Church exploded in exasperation.

"Shut up, Detective." Sylvia pressed redial on the phone—it rang too many times. Just when she was about to panic, Dantes answered.

"During the trial, you told Dr. Carreras that a *place*—instead of a person—could be a child's primary attachment object. You said that had happened for you."

"And then he and Judge Heron used it against me. Bravo, Dr. Strange."

"The city is what you love most. *She's* your primary attachment. She made you feel safe, she made you belong." Sylvia stood stock-still, holding her breath, then quietly asking: "What place in LA are we talking about, John?"

She heard the relief in his voice as he recited three words like a small prayer: "Home sweet home."

CHAPTER TWELVE

Too often, the system devours its most gifted and creative children. Dostoyevsky wrote about such cannibalism, so did Conrad. At the turning of each century, the faults of humanity's social systems are highlighted. The *clues* to the imminent death of a particular civilization are revealed, but only to those who have the courage to seek out the truth, and to read the signs.

Dantes' Inferno

11:20 a.m. Home sweet home was a three-story clapboard Victorian, now boarded up and surrounded by chainlink.

She'd looked up the passage from *Dantes' Inferno*: "*I was raised downtown. My blood is city blood. My skin filters the same urban smog that used to diffuse the air around the white Victorian at the corner of Beaudry and Temple. As a boy I was a knock-kneed ruffian who loved his home sweet home."*

Pale and austere, the house stood alone, waiting to be razed or moved like some Hollywood back-lot prop. The lot was large, at least a half acre, and barren except for the house and a half dozen tall old trees—palm, olive, evergreen. A narrow walkway, overgrown with weeds, still marked the path to the front door.

At some point the neighborhood had been residential, but zoning changes and city expansion were rapidly altering the landscape. On bordering streets, small shops still advertised their trades, but high-rise office buildings, those vertical neighborhoods that were clearly the next wave, loomed over the modest businesses.

Detective Church parked on Temple, catty-corner to the house. He gazed out at the property, his eyes obscured by the black sunglasses. He was still chewing gum. He said, "I remember when we made the search."

"Right after the arrest?" Sylvia asked.

"He was still on the lam. We cornered him at Llano del Rio about two weeks later," Church said. "Forensics went through it again before the trial. They catalogued half a ton of evidence—most of it useless."

Sylvia pushed open her car door and climbed out, saying, "So who's got the wire cutters?"

The trio walked the hundred feet to the street boundary of the property, where weeds sprouted at the base of the fence, clumping between metal links. As they followed the perimeter, Sylvia could hear the *shush-shush* of traffic on the Hollywood Freeway although she couldn't actually see vehicles. The air was heavy with pollutants, heat, humidity. The sky was an unnatural gray-blue.

They passed a photography shop that looked as if it had gone out of business a decade earlier. The storefront had faded, the painted sign was curling at the edges, the gray-tinted plate window was protected by wrought iron bars.

Someone had spray-painted nihilistic graffiti over the billboard that marked the back end of the property: FUCK US ALL. Others had left gang symbols, black and angular. An urban dissident with a juvenile sense of humor had blacked out one of the model's eyes.

The metal fence was solid, formidable; ditto the gate. Fortunately, the padlock was fastened to a wimpy chain. Church got it with one snip.

The investigators had been given the official go-ahead to enter the property. With extreme caution. They'd lost their backup; the other agents had taken off from Angels Flight, headed for MDC. Bomb threats were keeping the Feds very busy.

"How do you want to do this?" Purcell asked calmly.

"Very slowly."

"In the mood for booby traps?"

Church shrugged away the tension, saying, "You first."

"Great," Sylvia murmured. It had crossed her mind that tripping into a serial bomber's former residence—even a childhood residence—wasn't such a great idea. Even the most rabid tourists had stayed on the other side of the fence.

The rear of the house was shaded by two tall and spindly palms and an olive tree. With the aid of Purcell's skill with locks, the door opened smoothly, allowing access to an ample kitchen now dimly lit by daylight seeping through the papered windows. Church entered first, executing a careful visual search. Sylvia started to follow, but Purcell held her back.

"Let's make the call," Purcell said.

The line had been secured for only one purpose, and Dantes answered on the first ring. "What took you so long?"

"We had to find a way through the fence," Sylvia said. Her first objective was survival—her second, to keep Dantes happy. "Home sweet home . . . I'm at the back door. I'm going inside now."

She peered into the gloom. The house was dark and musty smelling, occupied by ghosts. It was almost a shotgun design, one narrow room set after the other, organized around a simple living room and dining room. She could hear footsteps, Detective Church returning from the pantry and laundry room area. A faint, light film of dust coated the kitchen floor.

"What should I focus on?" she asked.

"The Feds took most of my toys away," Dantes said softly. "But maybe they missed something? Why don't we start at the bottom and work our way up? The basement door's at the end of the hall."

He heard her speculative silence. "Tell me something, Dr. Strange. If you don't trust me enough to take the first step, why are we doing this?"

Church was picking up the conversation simultaneously, and he gestured with two fingers—*I'll go down*—moving cautiously across the kitchen. Purcell remained at the kitchen door; Sylvia followed the detective.

She passed bathroom and bedroom and started down a narrow hallway. Church had the door to the basement open, and he flashed a light down the stairs. "It's dusty as hell," he whispered.

"Where are you now, Sylvia?" Dantes asked.

Sylvia shivered; his presence was uncanny. It spooked her, as if his childhood essence had permeated these old walls. "At the basement door," she said.

"I've got another idea."

But Church was already starting down the steps—very gingerly—a barefoot man stepping on cut glass.

"The library's behind you," Dantes said, enticing with his voice. "It used to be my bedroom. Are the bookshelves empty?"

She turned, saw the shelves, which were oak, solidly built into the wall. "Yes."

"There's a credenza to the left of the shelves," he said. "You'll find something carved in the wood—a message from a twelve-year-old." He laughed. "Boys will be boys."

Sylvia heard Church hesitating on the stairs, but she'd already entered the room, with its Victorian window seat, glass panes now shaded. Phone cupped to ear, she approached the empty shelves and the floor-to-ceiling credenza. She didn't see any carving on the wood.

"Dantes, you still there?" she asked quietly.

No answer.

The fucker had a bad habit of—

She didn't finish the thought because at that instant she heard a loud, resonant *click*. At the same time, she felt pressure under her right foot.

Automatically, she switched off the cell phone as she looked down and saw the hole in the floor where boards had been torn away.

That's where she found the bomb.

It crouched like an animal in its lair, deep between loose floorboards, tentacled like a landed sea creature, displaying a tangle of appendages and a limber tail. She could swear she heard it breathing. A harsh, strangled cry escaped her throat. Even as her brain was registering the bomb, she was shrinking away, plotting escape.

But almost instantly, an icy calm took her over, a calm belied only by a soft ripple of fear. She had stepped on the tail of the beast.

She didn't move. Instead, without turning, she called out. "Purcell?" Her voice sounded rusty. "Tell the bomb squad we found our IED."

It was Detective Church who answered. "Make your moves, Doc, but take it slow and easy."

"I think I'm standing on the trip wire." Indeed, a line was attached from the bomb to the wall; the wire was taut, remaining so even after she'd tread upon it.

"Shit." Not very reassuring. The detective asked, "Is your phone turned off?"

"Yes." She gripped the handset, aware that an active electronic frequency could detonate a proximate explosive. "Are you just going to stand there?"

"Yeah," Church said, faking amazingly good cheer. "Hold on to your hat." He was breathing harder than she was. "Purcell will have them here in five minutes."

"Five would be good." *If I get out of here alive, Church, I'll love you for life.*

"Hey, Sylvia?" Now it was Special Agent Purcell, sounding rehearsed, apologetic but firm. "Can you describe it?"

She opened her mouth and a wave of anxiety almost sent her spinning. Her chest constricted, her hands tingled as she stared down at the bomb.

Oh shit. She hadn't anticipated the exotic beauty of it . . . or the violent ugliness.

"Come on, Doc," Church encouraged. "I'm going to stay back here so I don't set anything off. But I'm not leaving, okay?" The bastard was being way too nice for LAPD. "So talk to me, tell me what an asshole I am, tell me about the device," he encouraged.

"It's set below the floorboards." Where was her real voice? "Wires everywhere. The container looks old. Polished hardwood. I think it's the bomb in the Polaroid M sent. A construction. I don't know if that's a working timer—but it's definitely a big clock face."

"You're doing fine, Doc," Church said.

"Tell them it's beautiful. A work of art. Like a sculpture by Picasso or Man Ray." Her voice rose. "And it's *big*."

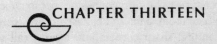

CHAPTER THIRTEEN

Lust and fear, attraction and aversion, love and hate—
these are the basic elements of physical energy.
Everything may be explained within these simple
opposites, which are actually one and the same.

Anonymous

11:50 A.M.   Church and Purcell lied—five minutes passed and the bomb squad was nowhere to be seen.

Sylvia experienced the passage of time as a blur of mutable emotions—fear laced with panic slowly dulled until she was left numb, both physically and mentally. Her foot tingled on the trip wire; she didn't move.

The bomb was situated roughly four feet from where she stood, the trip wire intentionally extended to catch a trespasser unaware. If she flexed her right toe, the wire would rise through tension, to a height of half an inch or less from the wooden floor. If she released her toe—and the wire—she would be blown to bits.

She believed that. Her heart jumped, literally throbbing in her chest, until she calmed herself with ragged breaths.

From the size of the wooden box, she was guessing pipe bomb. It is the contained tension within such a bomb, the increasing pressure during initiation, and the ability to effectively destroy human and material targets that make this type of infernal device a favorite of historic and contemporary bombers, including militia members, the IRA, the West German RAF, and Metesky, the Mad Bomber.

Dantes had used pipe bombs before.

But according to his own confession, not to target people.

In the bare room, a fat and clumsy buzzing insect tossed its body around sharp corners and against tall shuttered windows, occasionally bouncing off her head. Her hair stuck to her skin and her muscles began to ache; she had to pee. A vague and persistent itch roamed her body like a small animal.

A pale diminished anger surfaced at odd moments—she couldn't afford to feel it fully. But John Dantes had sent her to find a bomb. He'd sent her to die.

She could see the watch on her wrist. She'd been standing, basically frozen in place—trapped—for nine minutes. Where were Purcell and Church?

Where the hell were the bomb boys? What was taking so long? Sure, most of the city's police force—and all of its bomb squad—had been drawn to City Hall to defuse a nonexistent bomb, but that was hours ago.

And she'd found their infernal device for them in the parlor of John Dantes' childhood home—just as she'd been sent to do.

In limbo between fear and inertia, lulled by the hush of her less than steady breathing, the buzzing of the insect, distant city noises, she studied the bomb and its surroundings. Both put her in mind of an earlier era, of drawing rooms and gaslights and centuries turning over like slow, ponderous wheels—the room because of its Victorian origins, the bomb by design.

It was the bomb she'd seen hours earlier, as icon, projected on screen.

M had delivered after all.

The wooden box was the color of dark cherries and rectangular in shape. The polished wood was covered with dust, adding to the general impression of abandonment. Candles would have been an appropriate incendiary feature; instead, the attached wires and the large white alarm clock were a messy and modern intrusion of electricity, positive and negative ions, physics.

The black hands of the clock face were set at 1:18:30—just like the photograph.

Thank God they weren't moving.

A bookmark—or scrap of paper—was wedged between two of the wooden knobs. A message from Dantes or M? In dim light she could barely make out individual words in a formal script—Italian:

> . . . quel cattivo coro
> de li angeli che non furon ribelli
> né fur fedeli a Dio, ma per sé fuoro.

Forget the first line, then take a guess: Angels who were not . . . ribelli . . . not faithful to God . . .

No way to know how long the bomb had remained hidden in its nest, just waiting for someone to step on its tail.

The itch—more intense than ever—settled in the soft dip of her throat, then rode a bead of sweat down her sternum between the flesh of her breasts. Her white cotton shirt was plastered to her body, her Levi's had wedged themselves uncomfortably between the cheeks of her butt. Time to bargain with the gods.

Sylvia flinched at the sound of a voice. Church. Asking if she was doing okay.

"Fabulous," she said, taking a deep breath. "Are they coming soon?" Her watch showed 11:59.

"I think I hear the truck. Hang in there, Doc," he lied. "If I could get a better look at the setup, I might be able to get you out of here sooner, but I don't want to take chances."

"Don't take chances," Sylvia said quickly. She could tell he was scared.

Which is what any sane person should be when they encounter a bomb. But he kept talking—even whistled a few bars of "Irish Eyes."

At 12:03, she thought she heard the truck, too. Maybe. Pulling up in front of the house. But she wasn't aware of the uniformed cops or the bomb squad techs setting about their respective jobs or the soft voice of Special Agent Purcell. It was all a blur of background static. Her head was throbbing, perspiration slicked her skin, and oxygen came in shallow panting breaths.

"We've got to stop meeting like this," Church said very quietly. "The boys from the squad have got some things to do here before you can head home." He took another audible breath. "So, tell me, Doc, why'd you decide to play with bombs?"

Oh, God, she knew what he was trying to do—take her mind off this moment of hell. She grasped desperately at the line he threw out. "I took lessons from a pro named One-Shot Mahoney."

"Yeah? Where was that? Socorro Tech?"

"Not EMERTC." She knew he meant the Energetic Materials Researching Testing Center—at New Mexico's

Institute of Technology, where the big boys from Sandia, LANL, the FBI, and ATF came to play. She'd been there to watch a lump of PETN demolish a small house. "Not the first time."

"So tell me about the first time." He must've been smiling. "That's always the sweetest."

"It was three miles outside Golden, New Mexico," she mumbled, her mind resisting focus.

"Golden, huh? Sounds nice."

The view of the basin near San Felipe Pueblo had made Sylvia's heart catch.

"Fire in the hole!" Mahoney's voice rang out over the piñon-studded hillside where five hundred pounds of ANFO was primed and ready to blow. The blasting contractor followed his warning with three pumps on a fist-sized blow horn.

"Doc?" Church prodded.

"He let me prime sixty-one shots with sticks of Magnum 75."

"That's good stuff. Emulsion. What'd you load for shot?"

"ANFO."

"Right. Then you stemmed the shots . . ."

"With crushed rock." She'd watched Mahoney connect each of the yellow shock tubes in a complex pattern factored to create a constantly moving intermittent free face—to redesign nine hundred tons of solid rock—in the span of one second.

"It's a thrill, isn't it?" Church asked.

"Yeah. A thrill."

Especially as she twisted the last four wires into pairs, goose bumps raised her flesh—she was standing ten feet away from the blast site, where they were about to screw with Mother Nature and create a twenty-five-foot mountain.

There are times when denial is a good thing.

In what felt like slow motion, Sylvia followed Mahoney away from ground zero, hiking the two-tenths of a mile to the

powder truck where the shot line originated. There was still an-
other fifty feet of orange lead wire on the wheel.

"Fire in the hole!" *The voice rose up from the road, where*
Mahoney's driller was stationed to prohibit vehicles from entering
the fly rock zone. Catapulted through the air at 120 miles per
hour, even a two-pound chunk of rock could pose health haz-
ards.

Mahoney echoed the warning cry as he finished testing the
wire with the galvanometer; he was looking for a short or a break
but found none.

"We got a circuit," *he said, voice gruff.*

Following final orders, Sylvia connected the shot wire to the
black, palm-sized blasting machine. Her pulse quickened.

"It's just like that old cliché," Church said quietly, in real
time. "Makes you feel alive."

"Oh, yeah . . . alive," Sylvia whispered. Her mouth was
so dry her tongue felt swollen.

"So you got to blow the shot?" Church prodded gently.

The nipple on the side of the blasting machine was soft under
her thumb. It was her job to press the button, make the shot. She
heard Mahoney's countdown, took a breath, and upshifted her
thumb.

Nothing happened.

Then she saw a brown cloud of earth and rock rise above the
tree line. Almost instantly, the cloud was accompanied by a
round of deep staccato booms, the music of five-hundred-
millisecond and twenty-five-millisecond explosive delays.

She felt herself shoved from behind—Mahoney yelled—and
she was under the nose of the Ford as chunks of fly rock pelted
the battered hood. A faint acrid smell followed the blast. From
the edge of the powder truck's bumper, Sylvia gazed up at One-
Shot Mahoney. Her hair was matted with limestone dust, hard
hat tipped at an angle; her back ached, and she knew she wore a
stupid grin.

Mahoney's smile was wicked as he growled, "Hot damn, I love the smell of ANFO in the morning."

The high-pitched electronic whine scared Sylvia all over again. Disorientation kept her from recognizing the mechanical noise. Before she could react, a new and reassuring male voice called out, requesting that she keep calm and, "Just listen, don't move now. And hang in there, Sylvia. It's Sylvia, right? Shorty's got to check things out—we're right behind him."

The vibration was faint, but she felt it travel up her legs from her feet. Her first thought was that the bomb had been triggered. Then she realized she wasn't alone.

Sylvia caught sight of the robot—*must be Shorty*—as it rolled to a stop very near her left foot. In other circumstances, she might have likened the robot to a dog. Actually, it resembled a power lawn mower or a tiny tank. Propelled by ribbon tread, reaching knee height, the squat body was topped by a long neck, lightbulb eyes, antennas, and swiveling cameras. Fearless, purposeful, curious, Shorty had been designed to investigate a possible bomb situation via remote commands; with a computerized chip for a brain, the machine could enter a minefield to collect visual, aural, even olfactory information—it could retrieve a device and transport it from location A to location B.

About the only thing Shorty could *not* do was disarm an explosive device. That remained the bare-handed job of men and women.

She heard Church's quiet reassurance: "You're in good hands now, Doc."

Another voice—*something familiar about its soothing tones*—suggested she continue taking in oxygen, they were almost done, they'd have her out of there in a New York minute.

Yes, please, and thank you.

Perhaps the robot's specific vibration had traveled through the floorboards with enough force to affect physics. Or maybe the arrival of Shorty initiated the slightest shift in Sylvia's body—with the same result.

Whatever. The bomb's metal heart began to tick.

Sylvia's eyes grew wide. Had she imagined a soft voice somewhere in the world murmuring, *Oh shit*?

Shorty's neck lengthened by six inches. One camera eye tipped toward the floor, the other swung around on the smoothest hydraulics to stare down the bomb.

The truth was unavoidable, the hand on the clock face was clicking off seconds: *forty-eight, forty-seven*—

"Help," she called out.

Thirty-one, thirty, twenty-nine—

From somewhere in the house a muffled male voice responded, "We hear you, Sylvia. Hang on, don't move, we're coming in."

Eighteen, seventeen, sixteen—

She groaned, her body tensing so hard her muscles cramped.

"Get ready to roll!" Someone barked out the command.

Seven, six, five, four—

It all happened in an adrenaline haze. Responding to instinct she crouched, Shorty reversed direction, and a heavily muscled person in a space suit and helmet tackled her, knocking the air from her lungs. She felt herself flying backward, hitting the floor—she was crushed beneath two hundred pounds of armor and a bomb shield. She squeezed her eyes shut, waiting for the explosion.

The shrill sound of an alarm filled her ears—

The sound ran down to a bleating whine.

Then a hiccup. Another.

No explosion.

Just silence—and the breakneck beating of her heart.

She caught the harsh ventilated breathing of her savior, tasted the metallic bite of body armor, but all she could see was a blurry face behind a plastic helmet. A disembodied voice said, "We're still here."

After an interminable time, she heard footsteps, careful and light, someone tiptoeing across the floor.

"Kudos, Dr. Strange."

Sylvia pushed, and the saint in the bomb suit rolled to the side, releasing her from imminent asphyxiation. She sat up, instinctively pulling herself together; she shook dust from her hair, brushed dirt from her shirt. No bones broken, definitely dazed. She was still alive.

She saw something flash—again and again—and she shuddered, gazing up at the man she knew only as a distinctive voice: Professor Edmond Sweetheart.

"The bomb?" Her throat was so tight she had to repeat the words twice.

"First, let's get you out of here," Sweetheart said, shaking his head as he pocketed a tiny digital camera. "I'm feeling vulnerable, even though . . ." His eyes were on the explosive device as he reached out, offering her a smooth hand. She accepted and felt herself lifted to her feet.

She whispered, "A hoax?" Then louder. "A goddamned fucking hoax bomb?"

"Maybe a goddamned fucking hoax bomb. *Maybe*. It won't be Dantes' first." Still he stared at the bomb nesting between floorboards, but he nodded, echoing her words with his rich dark baritone. "They've got to make sure the area's clear. They can't do that with us standing here." He rubbed something white between his fingers. *Dust.* The house seemed to be coated with fine powder, as if someone had split open a bag of Betty Crocker flour.

She swayed, bouncing against Sweetheart, feeling his arm steady as a ballast. "Shit."

He gripped her firmly—but not roughly—bringing her to ground. When both her feet were rooted, she took him in: he was somewhere between thirty and forty-five, some strong mix that included Polynesian ancestry, medium height, gleaming blue-black hair pulled from high cheekbones, incredibly smooth skin, dark brows, and fiercely probing eyes. She focused on his mouth, which was generous even when he wasn't smiling, and he *wasn't* smiling. He looked angry—as angry as she felt. Oddly, his size registered last.

Sweetheart weighed at least 250 pounds.

Their eyes met, held; hard to say who would've looked away first.

Simultaneously, they both turned their heads, drawn by the strident tones of a man wearing a dark FBI jacket and cap. The Fed addressed the space between Sylvia's eyes where executioners aim their weapons: "Evacuate the premises. *Immediately.* This area has not been cleared."

Sweetheart loosened his grip on Sylvia's shoulder, asking, "Ready for this?" She nodded, following him across the room without delay. She couldn't wait to evacuate the damn premises.

The federal agent, walking with a heavy stride, stayed directly behind her; Sweetheart took the lead.

Retracing earlier steps, she exited the house through the back door. Searing midafternoon sunlight slapped her face. Squinting into the glare, she saw a scene transformed. Two fire trucks, a squared-off bomb squad truck, LAPD squad cars, obtrusively neutral federal vehicles—and corresponding personnel—occupied the previously semideserted street. The asphalt had been turned into a temporary parking lot; the vehicles partially blocked the view of the several dozen residents who had gathered on the lawns of their sixty-year-old homes. Another hundred feet along the street, at the intersection, sawhorses barred access to curious pedestrians. As Sylvia scanned the scene, a TV news crew pulled up in a van, the logo advertising the network affiliate.

A day for crowds and live broadcast news coverage.

She took a slow, deep breath, simultaneously lifting her thick auburn mane of hair from her neck. Using her right hand, she fanned her face; the cooling effect was minimal, but the physical action helped ward off the shakes.

Apparently she'd walked right into a hoax—literally— but officials were taking no unnecessary chances on what was turning out to be a busy bomb day. A tech strode past, carrying what she thought might be disrupter—either that or some missile-type projectile. Another fully suited bomb squad member followed with a leashed and hyperalert shepherd.

Someone, a passing human shape—*Agent Purcell*— handed her a cup of coffee. She clutched the disposable cup, unaware that her fingernails were digging crescents into Styrofoam. "Thanks." She was grateful her teeth didn't chatter. The aftershocks were beginning to register. The beverage was bitter, sickly sweet, lukewarm—the best thing she'd ever tasted.

Sweetheart covered the seventy feet from house to chain-link fence and reached the gate first. His physical effect was overwhelming, but oddly comforting. He stepped aside, ushering her through the opening. Detective Church appeared from nowhere.

Without thinking, Sylvia walked up to the man and gave him a hug; a soft white powder rubbed off him, dusting her skin. "Thanks," she whispered.

Church made some embarrassed noises, then asked, "You all right?"

"Yeah. You?"

"Getting there." Detective Church nodded toward Sweetheart. "Keep an eye on this guy—he's predictable as nitro—a free agent—one of those smart SOBs who answers questions for Quantico. When he's not basking in his ivory tower, that is."

Sweetheart's eyebrows tilted sharply.

"And obviously," Church added, straight faced, "since he's worked in the Middle East, he must have connections in the CIA—*and* the NSA. Without Sweetheart's profiling system, that asshole Ben Black would still be blowing shit up."

"—the hell did you think you were doing—" A male voice rose and fell, and Sylvia looked over in time to see Special Agent Purcell in the process of being dressed down by a superior. She felt a tinge of sympathy. From the corner of her eye, she noticed Detective Church backing away too casually, moving toward the house.

"Where are you going?" Sweetheart asked.

"Got a hunch to check out," Church called over his shoulder.

"*Funkspiele,*" Sweetheart said, now that he and Sylvia were alone.

"I'm sorry?" Sylvia returned her attention to the professor.

"Funkspiele—German for 'radio games.' Dantes likes to play." Sweetheart's eyes didn't flinch under the glare of the sun. "So do terrorists in the Middle East. They use false signals to throw intelligence off track."

"So, the question: is he messing with us, or with M?" Sylvia's dark brows disappeared under wild strands of hair. Her eyes widened, monopolizing her face. "Maybe both." Her cheeks had lost all color except for the smudges of dirt and dust.

"Either way, he wins." The professor was studying her. "He gets attention, and he feels he's in control."

"When I was in the house, I noticed something on the

device." Sylvia frowned. "Some message on a small piece of paper—in Italian"

"I saw it. From Dante Alighieri's *Inferno*. The theme continues." He pulled something from his pocket—a fold of paper—and offered it to Sylvia.

She opened the quartered page to find a carefully rendered map. It consisted of concentric circles, descending in size, and numbered consecutively from one to nine. Points of interest had been labeled: Dark Wood; River Acheron; Limbo; Gates of Dis; River Styx.

"The original map of hell. It's yours to keep. It might come in handy." Sweetheart extended his index finger and tapped the third circle. "We are here," he added, dryly. He glanced back toward the house. "That quote you saw—it's from the third canto."

Sylvia followed his gaze, then refocused on him, on eyebrows that could belong to the devil. "Can you translate the Italian?"

His eyes traveled her way, absorbing, registering, as if she weren't quite human. "A group of angels rebelled—and were cast out—"

"They fell past earth, into hell," she said impatiently. "I know the story."

"Then you also know they were banned from heaven in order not to tarnish its perfection. And some were not admitted to hell, so that hell could not claim victory over their souls. So they remained in limbo—lost, wandering."

"And the quote?" Sylvia asked, gazing at the map of hell.

"' . . . with the caitiff choir of the angels, who were not rebellious, nor were faithful to God; but were for themselves.'"

"The faithless," Sylvia murmured.

Before either of them could add anything, the house exploded.

CHAPTER FOURTEEN

Cockie Lockie the sky is falling.
Nursery tale

12:36 P.M.   Initiation sent out shock waves like a violently blossoming flower whose roots extended through the main charge, rupturing molecules and causing a chain reaction that ended with mass explosion. As an encore, shaped charges directed secondary shock waves from basement to attic. Their impact was amplified by the gases that had extruded from the stacked bags of plain white flour below ground.

At that instant of detonation, it seemed as if the entire city had exploded into the stratosphere, only to fall to earth again like hard rain. There was a deafening blast, followed immediately by a lesser boom and a quaking rumble. The ground shook, small suns imploded around a black hole, a searing wind sent the world spinning.

Wood is organic, as easy to mutilate as human flesh. The metal shrapnel from the pipes and additional hardware splintered, descending with shards of wood and glass to penetrate matter and inflict damage.

The explosion—the shrapnel—sent everyone instinctively diving for cover. It bombarded Professor Edmond Sweetheart with small branches from the olive tree. It peppered Sylvia Strange with bullet-sized gravel. It smacked a chunk of plaster into the forehead of Special Agent Purcell.

All hell broke loose.

Emergency personnel raced into action; a reporter got the story of her life when her network's well-placed television minicam captured the bomb and its aftermath for live feed and replay; rescue workers scanned the scene, accounting for the living, searching for the dead.

12:41 P.M.   From the corner of his eye, Sweetheart saw Sylvia Strange where she'd hit the ground fifteen feet away. She struggled to her feet and moved unsteadily toward the ruined house.

He covered the distance, blocking her way. She stared at him as if he were a massive tree; he registered the look of numb disbelief on her face.

"Where are you going?" he asked, already steering her toward a clear space on the curb.

"People might be hurt." She swiped at a burning scrap of wallpaper as it drifted to earth. The air was dense with particles—wood, plastic, ash. "I feel sick."

"You're in shock, Dr. Strange. Let the emergency response team do their jobs."

All around them, fire, medical, and law enforcement personnel were coordinating their actions. Two EMTs had unloaded gurneys from the ambulance; the four-inch tires spun across asphalt, metal ball bearings clacking.

Hoses fed from the fire trucks toward the remains of the house now in flames; a firefighter shouted orders to his crew. Twenty feet away, a uniformed street cop tended to several casualties. Sweetheart saw Special Agent Purcell following an EMT toward the bomb site.

Sweetheart heard Sylvia's question, "Do you see Purcell and Church?" through the din of voices, sirens.

"Purcell just walked by—uninjured."

As he let go of Sylvia's arm, she swayed, reaching for solid ground. "I need a ride back to MDC, to Roybal," she told him slowly. She was obviously straining to regain her concentration. Sweetheart imagined she was troubled by the same high-pitched tone that was ringing inside his head. His ears ached, his skull felt as if it had contracted against his brain, but he knew the unpleasant symptoms were transient. He and Strange had been extremely lucky—luckier than some of the others.

He started toward the cluster of LAPD and federal agents just as Sylvia said, "I've got to talk to Dantes."

"Bad timing." Sweetheart pivoted with a shake of his head. "I told you, you're in shock." He pressed his fingers lightly to her forehead as she sank down on the curb. She opened her mouth, closed it again. Her skin was freckled with red welts left by gravel.

Sweetheart studied her, taking in the intelligent eyes with their dark yellow fireflies, infinitesimal and prehistoric, trapped deep in amber. The stubborn set of her jaw. The wide mouth.

She hadn't made the connection yet. Dantes had played her perfectly. He'd used her to hurt other people—and through that dark bond, therapist and inmate were joined in an unstable synergetic relationship. She was no longer just the catalyst, she was part of the formula. And this was only the beginning.

"I need to talk to Dantes," she repeated.

He said, "Dantes may not *need* to talk to you. For the moment, you've served your purpose. You found a bomb."

Sweetheart saw the stricken expression on her face. He looked away. Already he could smell the scent of charred flesh on the air.

She clutched her knees, and whispered, "He'll talk to me."

"The FBI won't let you see him. Not until they've had their go." Sweetheart stood over her like a massive cloud blocking the sun. His face was smudged with dirt; one cheek was beginning to show the first signs of bruising; a sprig of an olive branch extended from his muddled hair. Behind him smoke billowed from the ruin of the Beaudry Street house.

"Look what's gone down during the past six hours," he said sharply. "At the moment, the Feds are rethinking your involvement. At any level." He was silent for a moment before he added, "Dantes used you, Dr. Strange."

"Something went wrong," she said, shaking her head sharply. "It wasn't supposed to happen this way."

The professor closed his eyes; his voice held a brutal edge. "How was it supposed to happen?"

She swallowed, tasting faintly metallic dust. "I need to know if Dantes set me up."

"Set *you* up?" Sweetheart's tone was harsh, and his mouth turned down in distaste. "This isn't about you. It isn't about Dr. Strange. Leo Carreras wanted you as an opening act, a warm-up for Dantes. You had the right credentials. And I'll hand it to Leo—he was right about you. But the stakes just got a whole lot bigger—and they got bigger according to John Dantes' plan."

"I can't believe he planned *this*—" She broke off, silenced by the deafening drone of a low-flying LAPD helicopter. A small plane passed over in the wake of the chopper. Sirens were almost drowned out by the sounds of engines.

"You thought he wouldn't betray you?" Sweetheart cut in, shouting to be heard as the helicopter circled away toward the freeway. "You believe you're immune to his lies?"

"*No.*"

But he knew she did believe that. She'd been seduced by the aura of the big case and by the fantasy—however subliminal—that she would be able to connect with John Dantes in a way that no one else could. Sweetheart understood that kind of vulnerability.

Reaching out slowly, he offered his hand. As he helped her to her feet, his fingers registered the cool smoothness of her skin.

"Beware of Dantes," he said. Antipathy hovered around him like a menacing shadow.

"How can you be so certain there isn't another bomber with his own agenda?" she asked. "What if Dantes took no part in the Getty bombing?"

"M and Dantes are conspirators." Sweetheart's voice was brittle, the richness burned away like singed velvet. "The link is in the data. It will be in the forensic comparisons, in the explosive agents, or the mass spec readings, or the linguistic analysis. It's already in their shared cosmology—Dante Alighieri's hell."

Sweetheart's smile was hard and cold. "I'll find our mad bomber—our obsessive, middle-aged fuckup with the double-breasted suit buttoned at the collar. And he'll be best friends with John Dantes. This is Dantes' work—the fact he's behind bars means absolutely nothing."

Sylvia knew men ran drug empires from inside; they "walked the man," ordering executions; they directed coups d'état—

"Dantes sent you here to die, Dr. Strange."

The voice belonged to Special Agent Purcell. She was trembling, and her eyes were dark and accusing. She seemed to struggle for breath. "Church was inside with two other guys from the bomb squad when it blew. They're going to airlift him to UCLA."

Purcell gazed out at the approaching helicopter. "For his sake, pray he dies before he gets there."

CHAPTER FIFTEEN

I live each day knowing I've caused suffering. I understand I will be called on to rectify my actions.

John Dantes to *LA Weekly*

12:41 P.M. The tunnel shook.

The bomb had exploded. Dantes' first reaction was excitement—his second, regret. He noted these feelings, surprised; but emotions are fleeting and his determinism, his fatalism, quickly monopolized the moment. This was all part of the schema—the scenario set in motion years ago. Now it must be played out to its final act.

He felt the CO eyeing him darkly. Why weren't the guards reacting to the explosion? Why were they moving with icy efficiency thirty feet below ground, where quakes and tremors should be cause for alarm?

The tunnel shook again, tilting, shimmering. Dantes stumbled, gasping.

The guards were staring at him, their faces filled with suspicion.

The lights were humming, fed by a steady flow of power. Perspiration beaded on Dantes' skin, cast green by fluorescence in the subterranean tunnel that fed like a conduit between the federal building and the detention center. Abruptly, the U.S. marshals had decided to escort him from Roybal back to MDC. That was after he lost connection with Sylvia Strange.

"Fuck you," he whispered. The whole thing enraged him—the marshals had told him he'd hung up on the psychologist and the bomb squad. They never stopped lying. God, they loved messing with the minds of prisoners, especially the smart ones, and the toughest inmates, the ones who were harder to break.

Dantes took a deep breath, pulling *chi* from the ground, letting it surge through his body to his brain, to his groin, to his feet. If the earth shook again, he would be ready.

He was no stranger in this underground hell. To get through UCLA, he'd worked as a sandhog. He'd drilled and pumped, he'd packed and trucked. He'd breathed the foul air of dark spaces.

"If a man wants to understand real wealth, true power, he needs to hold the earth's resources in his hands, at least long enough to feel their weight," Dantes muttered to himself. If a man craved the trebuchet of physical labor, sweat was the perfect complement to academia; and academia, with its gossip, its backbiting, its tenure, was the hardest and bloodiest labor of them all.

In his sandhog days, his underground work had included a piece of the current subway system, a share in the sewage system, and even a cut of Water & Power.

From fifty feet under, he'd seen the earth quake; the view was different when you were holding a thousand tons of earth and rock on your shoulders.

In answer to his thoughts, the earth moved again.

But this time, he registered the spasm as *internal*.

That explained the guard's behavior.

Yes, this must be some kind of sympathetic reaction, he thought, as he dug his fingernails into his palms. Control was everything. The energy came like a wave, cresting, finally receding. But it left fear in its wake.

Dantes took a deep breath, orienting himself in space.

Black holes in the mind were a bad thing. That's what the state did to those too quick to speak up. That was the *stately* tradition—cull out your dissidents, your radicals, your desperately poor, torture them, and label them mad like Goya's lunatics.

Lunacy was something that happened to the *misfits* of any society. They did not *fit in*, hence they were labeled as *unfit*. If the label is repeated enough times, a man will come to believe it as truth.

I do not fit, he thought. I have never fit.

Instantly, his thoughts jumped, and he pictured the doctor's face.

Someone prodded him from behind and the picture evaporated.

A voice asked why he walked with his hands out, as if he might stumble? He gave the guards some of their own medicine: he stared at them as if *they* were crazy.

Gulag, gulag, gulag . . . the word tumbled through his mind like a runaway hub.

His shackles, binding ankles and wrists together at his waist, made a dull, repetitive scuffling sound and gave him the look of a medieval prisoner wearing some inquisitional contraption. But he needed no bindings to remind him he was a hostage. He tried to stave off the rage. The passive aggression of the martyr was breaking through. He was being driven to this.

Dantes' eyes held a crazy glitter, partly the result of the lights, partly the result of a blinding headache, which had stayed with him for days on end.

Flanked by U.S. marshals, he followed the course of the tunnel. Two guards met them at the heavy steel door that offered access to Metro. One of them whispered news of a bomb—an explosion.

I knew it, Dantes thought, beginning to laugh.

He stumbled when a CO brought a baton down sharply against his back.

The masters were displeased with their servant.

The pounding behind his skull increased in intensity as he rode the elevator to the Siberian world of his pod. A condemned man, he walked the antiseptic hall to his cell. The door slid open, manipulated electronically; when he passed the threshold, it clanged shut again. He slid his fingers through the steel mouth in the door, staring out at bare walls. The silence was eerie. He was alone in an area equipped to hold twenty-eight men.

All this security, money spent, measures taken, for one solitary man.

Federal tax dollars at work.

All this fuss for the Calbomber, the Getty bomber, the History bomber.

The Feds were stupid. They'd proven their inadequacy time and time again: Ruby Ridge, Waco, Heatherwade. They didn't have a clue.

Which meant he had to take measures, he had to find his own way out of this mess. Well, he was working on it. He sat down on the bed, running his fingers along the hairline fracture between mattress and wall. He felt nothing but rough plaster.

No new deliveries.

Dantes paced, acutely aware of the sound of water dripping across the pod in the tiny shower stall. It stood open, without curtain or door. Just in case he decided to drown himself, hang himself, cut himself. As if suicide was his style.

He heard heavy footsteps, listened to insults bounce around this steel and concrete world. A correctional officer came into view. The man he recognized—and had nicknamed Ciacco, the Glutton—for his thick, muscle-bound neck and the flaccid rolls around his waist, his bird head, the nasty glint in his dumb eyes, the cloud of garlic and grease that always hovered around his fleshy lips.

Ciacco, Dante Alighieri's disfigured and ravenous friend; a companion of childhood and youth, who foresaw the violent future of a city corrupted by gluttony, by hunger, by the depravity of unrestrained appetite for the fat of the land, and for power, always for power. It is those "men of good reason" who fall deepest in hell when the sins are judged and the punishments meted out, Dantes thought.

"Who are the 'men of good reason' today?" Dantes called out to the guard. "Do they recognize themselves?"

"Asshole murderer." Ciacco made a show of strolling back and forth in front of Dantes' cell, freely showing off the spectacle of his stupidity. He was unusually dumb for a federal CO. Resentment smoldered in the man like a punk. Dantes provided focus for that emotion.

"What you looking at, Dantes?" Ciacco growled. "You expecting somebody else? Florette maybe?" The CO's lips curled up. "Don't hold your breath."

But eventually, Ciacco bored himself. After he'd gone, voices colored red by frustration rolled down the hallway into the pod.

Dantes moved carefully to the sink. Lowering his head, he splashed water on his face—at the same time he moved a stealthy hand under the sink along the wall. His fingers encountered the rough edge of paper. He was just able to grip the card, freeing it from its hiding place. Making a fist, he crushed the paper.

The television set—mounted on the wall opposite the cell—jerked to life. Dantes cringed. The artificial sounds and sights drove him crazy. Yet he craved news of the outside world, of *his* city.

She was his city, after all. He'd touched every part of her—even here, locked away in hell.

He began to shake. At first it was a tremor, but it built uncontrollably.

On screen, the picture changed manically, the work of the COs. A news flash, via remote. An explosion at Beaudry Street. Several victims critically injured, one dead.

An LAPD detective.

Again and again the news footage was replayed: his childhood home shattering into fragments. Home sweet home.

He saw nothing else but the house as it splintered, exploding into a million pieces.

The faces of the dead and the injured merged: he couldn't escape the wide, innocent gaze of Jason Redding's ghost.

He knew he would meet these phantoms in hell.

Dantes took a shuddering breath, and the electricity shot through his body.

He cried out in pain. His eyes rolled back in his head, his body began to shake violently as one thought streaked through his brain.

The doctor . . . she'd found the messenger.

Horrible, high-pitched laughter bounced off the concrete walls of the prison pod. The sound curled and jumped and rode to hysterical heights. Who could make such an awful noise?

That is the noise that lunatics make.

His body contracted, his muscles shortened spastically. He fell stiffly to the concrete floor of his cell, where he trembled and vibrated as violently as an epileptic wracked by seizure.

"It's me," he screeched again and again. "I'm the lunatic."

And then his tongue, swollen and filling the back of his throat, shut off the words as he began to choke.

CHAPTER SIXTEEN

Are you naïve and cocky and grandiose enough to believe you'll return from the devil's lair with a neat package: WAIS-R, MMPI-2R, inventories and interview tapes, hell, even a Rorschach? Pencil and paper answers. Psychometric scales. Intuitive connections. All adding up to that elusive, intangible key to unlock a man's psyche, his very soul. You think you'll find truth? Don't bet on it.

Letter from John Dantes to court-appointed psychiatrist

1:19 P.M.   The helicopter had barely touched down while Church and the other bomb victims were loaded on board. Now Sylvia watched as the craft took off again, veering toward west Los Angeles and the hospital at UCLA. The rotors cut the air with an urgent *thwack-thwack*.

On a very different frequency, she heard the shrill voice of a female reporter. She turned away from Sweetheart—away from the sight of the bombed-out house—to stare at a slender woman in a gray three-piece suit; the reporter was speaking quickly into a camera: "—at least three injured, all critically, and authorities are obviously concerned about additional booby trap devices—although, as of yet, the FBI has offered no official cause for this explosion—"

Sylvia wasn't listening. Her attention had been drawn to a man, maybe eighty feet away, who was crossing the yard of a one-story yellow house on the other side of Beaudry. He had a baseball cap riding low over his face, his eyes were hidden behind sunglasses, he moved with an easy stride, dodging around curious spectators. The fingers of his left hand were looped around the strap of a leather backpack.

As he turned his head to look her way, sun glinted off the metal frames of his glasses. He raised one finger in salute.

"It's him," she said, as the man disappeared behind the house. She took off, ignoring Sweetheart's protests. She dodged a woman stepping off one of the fire trucks and hopped a low fence, crossing the front yard of the yellow house, where weeds flourished in clumps. A flash of white streaked her way, and she yelled at the furious poodle, but she didn't stop.

She could hear footsteps behind her; glancing back she saw Sweetheart keeping pace, neck in neck with a uni-formed LAPD cop. The dog turned its fury on the new intruders, but Sylvia didn't see what happened because she was already rounding the back of the house, moving rapidly now, propelled by adrenaline.

The yard was fenced, but the one-by-fours had listed, allowing trespass in several places. From the corner of her eye she noticed a weathered doghouse, socks dangling from the line, a storage shed, but the clatter of metal cans drew her attention toward the far boundary. Catching her sleeve on wooden splinters, she squeezed through an opening where two boards were missing. The next yard was a clone of its neighbor except the wooden fence had been replaced with a four-foot-high block wall.

The wall wasn't stopping the man as he vaulted into the air, landing easily on the other side. The back of his head, the baseball cap, seemed to taunt. Without looking back, Sylvia called out to Sweetheart. She thought she heard him reply.

By the time she reached the wall her quarry had disappeared. She plunked her butt down and swung her legs across rough cinder block. She was no longer within the residential neighborhood, but instead she found herself in a culvert; wide enough for two vehicles, it ran for a long block, then cut beneath an old, abandoned overpass. Here, the noise of traffic on the Hollywood Freeway had the liquid pulse of blood sluicing through a vital artery.

A chain-link fence marked the opposite side of the culvert.

Two choices: over the fence, or jog toward the underpass. She chose the latter, moving slowly, scanning the area for any sign of the man with the backpack—hoping Sweetheart and the officer were hot on her trail.

She found an open trench located between orange hazard cones, yellow construction signs, and lifeless earthmoving equipment. A hydraulic drill had devoured huge mouthfuls of hard, rocky earth to a depth of ten or twelve feet below street level. Deep in the hole, the exposed end of a massive drainpipe, which was at least six feet in diameter, protruded from the debris. The connecting joint (if it existed) was still buried, providing one way in, perhaps one way out.

"It's part of the old drainage system from the teens or the twenties." Sweetheart came to a halt by her side, lifting his face, reminding her of a hound tasting the air for a scent. He was breathing easily in contrast to the uniformed cop hard on his heels.

Instead of retreating, Sweetheart braced himself between barricades and swung his body out and over the opening. He released his grip, dropping to land feetfirst in a half inch of brackish water.

"Throw down your flashlight," he called to the cop who now stood on the edge of the ditch, shoulder to shoulder with Sylvia. When the cop complied, Sweetheart caught the flashlight with one hand, switching on the powerful beam so that light flooded the obscure concrete tunnel. He stepped inside, disappearing quickly—like a very large rabbit down a hole.

On impulse Sylvia followed. She landed off-center, stumbled, then regained her balance. Pain fired nerves. Drawn by the light of the flashlight, now roughly ten feet inside the drainage pipe, she moved forward. The toxic smell hit like a door in the face.

Sweetheart, lost in shadow, turned as she approached.

"Watch your back," he whispered.

The massive, crumbling pipe was perfect for an ambush. It appeared to contract and expand as light bounced off its surface, twisting planes and angles, distorting distance. With each meter traveled, the stench—chemicals and human waste—became increasingly unbearable.

Their progress was further hindered by man-made debris, protruding branches, skull-sized rocks. Where water had seeped through cracks, the ground turned to mud.

They traveled deep into the pipe—fifty feet, sixty-five, seventy—until any remnant of daylight from the opening no longer penetrated.

A sharp sound echoed from somewhere ahead.

Sweetheart picked up speed.

Sylvia had to stay close to the light to avoid tripping over obstacles. Here the noise of the city's surface had disappeared; the earth enclosing this pipe was absorbing all traces of civilization.

She began to break a sweat, heartbeat picking up pace. She almost plowed headfirst into Sweetheart. He'd come to a sudden stop. There was a click, and the world went black.

A familiar scuttling sound.

"A rat," he whispered hoarsely.

Still he didn't move.

They stood in silence, close together, and Sylvia strained to hear what he heard. The faintest sound tugged at her consciousness, audible the way a blinking light was visible—at intervals. This noise was stealthy, soft, indistinct.

As if someone was trying not to breathe.

The hair on the back of her neck stood at attention. She shuddered, glad for Sweetheart's company in this claustrophobic world. Now, the odd pungent smell of molding earth was strongest, and the air was thick with dust.

Was that the faint breath of eucalyptus?

Another sound. Muffled, eerily indistinct.

A footstep?

Followed by a sharp cracking noise.

Sweetheart snapped on the torch—the pipe flooded with light. Sylvia squinted into the sudden, blinding brightness, barely able to make out the professor as he lunged forward.

She pressed back against the wall of the pipe.

That's when she saw the shadow moving just ahead of Sweetheart.

There. Gone.

Sweetheart pursued. She followed, crouching down where the space narrowed to half its size. She fought back the fear of this claustrophobic space—and the fear of the man they pursued.

For several seconds, she lost Sweetheart as he turned out of sight; then she reached the same angle of pipe—and turned—to collide with him.

"Dead end," he growled. "Where the hell did he go?"

He shone the light on their surroundings, letting the beam play slowly over roots that reached through cracks in concrete like dark fingers. Here, the pipe had been intentionally widened until it reached an area of roughly twelve feet square.

Abruptly Sweetheart seemed to realize he wasn't alone; he gripped Sylvia's arm, and the strength of his fingers worked as a ground.

"I'm okay," Sylvia breathed. She was aware of water, dripping steadily, like a heartbeat in the earth. "How far did these pipes go?" she whispered, brushing cobwebs from her face. "Where does it come out?"

"It used to connect to a water shed, but the system's long dead. What you're hearing is just surface runoff—sprinklers, gutters, seeping down."

As Sweetheart aimed the beam of light, searching for the gleam of water, the source of the sound—a space opened up, high in the pipe. The remnants of an old ceramic neck—a way to the surface.

Cautiously, Sweetheart moved closer; as the light found a clear trajectory, he grunted. "That's how he got out."

"Can we get up—and follow?"

"He's long gone. And it would be a dangerous climb; it's ready to collapse."

They focused again on the subterranean cul-de-sac. On the ground at their feet a filthy pile of rags resembled a dead body. Where a candle had burned down, dirty wax covered a crate. Junk was scattered everywhere—old appliances, trash, scavenged food. The stench was thick and ripe.

"Mole people. This is their trash. They live down here."

"In a burrow," Sylvia whispered. "What an awful home."

"'Ma quando tu sarai nel dolce mondo, priego ti ch'a la mente altrui mi rechi.'"

"Translate."

"'Pray . . . when you return to earth's sweet light,

remember me to humanity.'" He took a breath. "We'll get forensics down here. Our bomber's a very bright boy, doing his homework: establishing our routines, our schematics for emergency response."

She turned toward Sweetheart just as he gripped her arm. His fingers dug into her flesh; pain shot along her nerves.

"Are you working with Dantes?" he demanded.

"No."

"He asked for you—you led us to the bomb."

"I could've been killed."

"But you weren't." The professor's dark eyes trapped the light; it flickered like a dangerous flame in both pupils.

"What about you?" she asked. "You're obsessed with Dantes. This isn't just an investigation, it's a vendetta." He was standing so close, Sylvia could feel his breath on her skin.

"You're right," he said softly. Abruptly, he pushed past her, thrusting the flashlight like a knife—

He stopped in his tracks.

Sylvia stared up at the message painted on the wall.

4TH CIRCLE

Sweetheart said, "It seems we've just entered the next level of hell."

For Sylvia, the rest of Tuesday passed in a blur . . .

An interminable debriefing session at FBI offices before she was finally released.

Leo driving her back to the bungalow—the exits rolling by while vivid pictures in her mind evaporated and reformed much like the freeway landscape.

The realization that there was only one connection between John Dantes, Sylvia Strange, and the bombings: LA, City of Id, where the shadow thrives.

Leo doctoring her: with chicken soup, with a hot bath, with an offer to sleep on the couch; a vague recollection of the alarm system arming itself for battle, and exhaustion winning out over fear.

Serena's e-mail:

> Dear Sylvie: Matt told me you're helping the FBI catch a bad man. He said I might see some bombs on the news, but I should know you are safe. I'm saying special prayers to St. Christopher and St. Michael. Te amo mucho!!! Come home soon. xoxox, Starfish

Falling into bed with her lover in New Mexico—thanks to AT&T. Finally drifting out of consciousness while Matt was still on the phone, promising he would take the next flight to Los Angeles.

Sleep was no refuge.

Nightmarish images formed, dissolved—twisting reality or diverging from it completely.

Stepping on the trip wire—the bomb exploding beneath her feet.

Detective Church covered with blood, mangled, smiling ghoulishly, repeating, "Tick-tock, dickity-doc."

M laughing, chasing Serena in circles.

Matt introducing Mona Carpenter's parents—"They want to know why you killed their daughter."

Special Agent Purcell looming close, cackling like a witch: "He used Betty Crocker to intensify the blast—he used *flour*. Think of a silo accident when grain explodes."

And deep in the tunnel, Sweetheart pulling off his face to become John Dantes.

As Dantes' arms tightened around her body, she pulled away, trying to scream. But his mouth found her lips, covering her mouth.

And he sucked poison from her body so that she felt hard pieces of something pulled from belly to throat.

Little stones, she thought. I'm filled with toxic stones.

But when Dantes broke away to spit the poison, tiny plastic bits of a toy city—people and buildings—spewed from his mouth.

4th Circle . . .

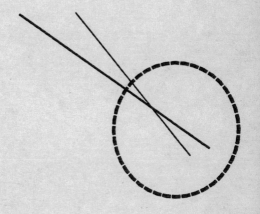

CHAPTER SEVENTEEN

> Call me nihilistic, but I enthusiastically embrace the annihilation that has come part and parcel with urban pathology since the first gatherings known as civilization. Be they tent cities in the barren deserts or steel and concrete bastions, eventually they must fall to ruin.
>
> Mole's Manifesto

11:53 P.M.   His mind goes in circles like a dog lying down.

M knows he's dreaming, but still the images blur with disturbingly fluid realism. A few minutes before midnight. He lies on a double bed next to a woman—at the same time he watches the house on Beaudry Street explode.

In his dream he watches as they—*his old friends, his new friends*—are thrown or drop to the ground, then pick themselves up, dazed. Some begin to run, some are yelling, others crying.

He has exposed himself to sunlight with reluctance. He hates the heat, which brings the red scars of old burns to welt on the surface of his skin.

But as always he must witness the punishment. To be a voyeur is the only way of sharing that he has left.

M watches with deference. This explosion—*any* explosion—is the prodigy of Byzantine alchemists and their two-thousand-year-old invention, Greek fire. He has never lost his appreciation for the beauty of the holy triad: initiation, oxygen, fuel. In this regard he is a satisfied voyeur. But something is definitely absent—his sense of awe. Certainly the knowledge of his power, his omnipotence, remains. But it is an empty awareness. A dead place. Devoid of desire, devoid of love or hunger or even suffering.

He's not dreaming; he's a lost man wandering the dark empty tunnels of his waking nightmare. What fills the space? Nothingness. Is there anything more awful in the universe? In contrast, suffering must be divine and death a pleasure.

After all, he deals in death. By inference, he is a pleasure broker.

Gunpowder, nitroglycerin, trinitrotoluene, ammonium nitrate, C-4, PETN and RDX, Tovex, Semtex—these labels represent his personal history and the tools of his trade, his particular science of destruction.

He has the knack for choosing what will hurt most. He understands the pain of others. There was even a time he felt pain himself. He misses that pain the way most men miss love. He knows how to create the perfect hell for others because he's been there so many times.

The earthen walls, the fetid water, the stinking gruel; oh yes, he knows about hell, where men are chained like beasts, left to sleep in their own excrement, to beg for the scraps of rotting meat, the slop that comes spiced with maggots.

We'll shit in your food. We'll piss in your drink. Soon you'll be grateful we give you shit and piss. Learn quickly.

In the empty space of his soul, there is a single need that keeps him alive—a man, as he is, clinging to his last breath. That need is revenge.

Only then will this waking nightmare truly end.

His eyes fly open—this time he's *awake*—and he is stretched next to the woman on the bed. She is snoring softly, evenly. Sleep releases her from the agony of her daily existence. Moonlight paints her skin milky white. Her lips are parted, tiny breaths warm his arm. Each inhalation is to choose life, each exhalation a flirtation with death. Every breath a human takes is a decision to go on living.

He stretches, elbows back, yawns, then runs his fingers through his light brown bristle. His scalp feels tight, itchy, with scars rising to his touch like topographic landmarks of past misery.

He doesn't find refuge anywhere—not even in dreams. To him, sleep is simply practice for death; he needs few hours, two or three. Insomnia is a habit he learned in the long winter's night known as prison.

He turns toward the red gleaming numbers on the digital clock: three minutes to midnight.

The fourth circle promises new levels of commitment. Theirs. His.

Dantes is acting his part to perfection. Yes, this partnership has survived the years, the distance, the agony of betrayal.

M slides his naked body from between cotton sheets that are the color of fresh limes. Rise and shine, there's work to be done. Shower in the tiny tiled bathroom. Select clothes for the new day—khakis, short-sleeved blue-and-white cotton shirt, work boots. Make coffee.

Say good morning to Nietzsche, who offers love bites from a yellowed beak.

Before he leaves, he always fills Einstein's bowl with kibble. The cat switches her tail. She is ridiculous with her crazy-quilt fur, a cacophony of dark and light spots and stripes. Why is a female cat named Einstein? Ah, yes, the boy named her—children do things like that, he reminds himself.

Once more he sits quietly on the edge of the double bed,

sipping coffee, watching the woman's body sprawled between tangled sheets. Her skin glows with a soft sheen.

She tells him daily that he is bringing her back to life. He is teaching her to touch and be touched again. Each time she cries out in love, tears streaking her face, she is bewildered by the fact he can bring her to climax even in the midst of her grief.

She would kill him if she knew the truth.

Perversely, the fact he represents both death and life to her excites him sexually. He has never had problems servicing women, but this time there is a special ease created by the give-and-take of survival.

In turn, she stirs the faintest longing inside him, a longing for passion, for love, but most of all for the capacity to feel remorse. He believes these twinges are like the pains of a phantom limb—or perhaps more accurately, the vestiges of a primitive tail, because a phantom limb implies that he was once capable of loving.

M strokes the back of her neck, lifts the tawny hair from her nape.

Ah, but that much is true, he reminds himself. John Dantes robbed him of his capacity for pain and love. Paradoxically, it was also Dantes who made him strong.

He whispers the boy's name to himself, as if he's testing the shape of the word on his tongue. But thoughts of the dead child leave him as empty as everything else in his world. He has practiced the pretense of what it means to live with a heart behind his ribs. He can recite a small list of those who have died for him—women and children who became his *family*, at least for a matter of months.

I touch others through death, he thinks. It is a fact, not good or bad. At all times, he is alone, even when he's surrounded by a hundred, a thousand of his species, even when he's lying next to one.

Solitude is the only state he can tolerate. Solitude is killing him.

But he cannot falter. Not from this precise moment . . . not until he and Dantes have played their parts to the hilt.

Again, he whispers, "Jason." Although the ghost of the child wakes nothing inside M, it pulls Molly from sleep. She reaches out her arms to him, soft gold hairs shiny against skin.

"Hold me," she whispers; her cheeks are wet with fresh tears.

He wraps his arms around her. "You dreamed again?"

She nods, gulping back a sob. "Bad dreams."

"Tell me." He kisses her lips, her cheeks, her eyelids. "It's okay, Angel Face."

"No, no," she says, unconsciously refusing his reassurances. She gazes up at him, visions of her dead child fresh in her eyes. "Jason told me in the dream . . . there's a monster buried beneath this city."

"Go back to sleep," he whispers. He runs his fingers along the nape of her neck. With these same bare hands, he has murdered his lovers. This is unusual for bombers, he knows, this ability to dole out proximate death. Blood has soiled his hands; he doesn't mind the stains. It is part of his business, tying up loose ends.

"Sleep, Angel Face," he soothes. "I'll keep you safe."

Amazingly, she does. Her breathing deepens, and she hardly stirs when he leaves her bed.

Eyeing him warily, the woman's improbably calico cat now occupies a windowsill. The two-bedroom apartment offers views of San Pedro's harbor. Freighters, their lights glowing yellow in the misty night air, line the loading docks. When he is restless, he can use the shipyard scenes as a tranquilizer. Even the salty smell of ocean helps to ease him down a notch. He has always been driven at a higher speed than most of his fellowmen, but lately, the constant fast idle of his internal engine seems more intense than usual. He hungers for stimuli, for his daily fix of chaos, for destruction.

In the shoe-box kitchen, his fingers fly over the keys of his laptop. He has trained himself to record each detail of every operation. Always, he does his homework. Standard procedure. Although he no longer feels elation when a job is well done, he still gleans satisfaction. Any fucking fool can blow a federal building to hell and back. But only a master of his trade can neatly collapse twenty-five hundred tons of steel using a mere handful of explosives. And only a genius can bring a city to its knees.

He pulls up digital images on-screen: bomb squad, investigators, explosions, played and replayed. He settles on one—a head shot of the woman, Dr. Strange. For his own amusement, he adds a label: *Miss Los Angeles*.

Enlarge. Crop. Print.

M needs a good photograph of Dantes' girl; he has a date to keep with the good doctor in Santa Monica.

He checks his watch: 1:09. It is Wednesday.

He spends exactly twenty-one minutes entering data into his system—which is extensive—on the response to the bomb threat at City Hall. He does the same with the Beaudry Street scenario. He was there to observe both operations in their entirety: response time, arrival of personnel and equipment, choices, strategies, and final results.

In preparation to leave, he gathers his laptop, his jacket, the keys to the truck.

On the freeway, he heads north, then west, toward the ocean.

They are sloppy, he thinks. Out of practice. Well, he will give them more practice.

CHAPTER EIGHTEEN

The psychopathologizing of radical dissent was never limited to the gulags and mental asylums of the Soviet Union; although I have not yet been forced to inscribe these words on a bar of soap, I am an anarchist labeled alternately as a paranoid schizophrenic, bipolar, psychotic—a man made invisible by the title of *lunatic*.

Trial transcript, John Dantes addressing Judge Heron

Wednesday, 4:34 A.M. The telephone wrenched Sylvia from sleep. Her arm flew out, knocking the alarm clock to the floor. After three electronic bleats, she connected with the receiver. She pressed the cool plastic to her ear and rolled off the bed—one action, the kinesthetic memory of so many crisis calls over the years.

The first word out of her mouth was her foster daughter's name. "Serena?"

"You have thirty minutes to find your way downtown to the Los Angeles City Hospital—south-side loading door."

"Purcell."

"This is your chance to see your friend, Dr. Strange." The silky contralto was raw around the edges.

Instantly alert, Sylvia kicked at the clock with her bare toe—the illuminated dial showed 4:35 A.M.

"South-side door. I'll be there," she breathed, tossing the telephone handset onto the bed. Already moving, she grabbed bra and T-shirt from the shoulders of a squat armchair, Levi's from the floor; the clothes smelled faintly of her perfume.

No time for a shower. Ducking her head through the neck of her T-shirt, she glanced around for her lightest silk jacket, which was in a soft heap behind the armchair. Sneakers untied, she strode out the door, across the lawn. She moved quickly; the shadows made her edgy.

She started the Lincoln after smearing salty dew from the windshield with her sleeve. While the engine idled, she took mental inventory: her laptop was in the trunk, where she'd left it thirty-six hours earlier, but Purcell had her briefcase, which contained necessities: cell phone, recorder, lipstick, sunscreen, cigarettes, a credit card, miscellaneous cash, stress vitamins, candy bars.

She left Leo Carreras presumably still asleep in his condo. If the situation had been reversed (which it truly should have been because Leo was the one who worked with the Feds on a regular basis), if he'd left her out of the loop, she'd be pissed. But she had to admit it—the idea of role reversal gave her a little rush.

By the time she passed the Fairfax exit doing eighty-five on the Santa Monica Freeway, any whisper of ocean mist had burned away; the air radiated stale heat like an empty oven. A three-quarter moon illuminated the endless urban ocean that flowed in all directions beneath the freeway, lending it the filtered quality of cinematic night. Warm winds skimmed off the desert. Palm trees swayed like land-locked sirens, their fronds rustling against the concrete ramparts, tapping out a haunting song.

In counterpoint, Miles Davis and "All Blues" drifted from the radio's speakers. The melancholy jazz tune ended, and a Cognac voice announced, "It's four fifty-nine in the city of your dreams, mellow LA. We're with you all the way, all night, all day, from Compton . . ."

The Lincoln ate road, sliding effortlessly onto the Harbor Freeway, the 110 north, retracing the now familiar route.

She caught a glimpse of her face in the mirror. Déjà vu. Same dark circles beneath black-brown eyes, same haunted face.

Just do the work. Stay focused. This might be her only opportunity to see Dantes—she wasn't going to ask herself why the FBI needed to roust her from her bed before dawn. Questions would wait until she found Purcell. She had minutes to make it to the LA City Hospital.

With one hand, she riffled through her pockets, searching for cigarettes. She'd given up smoking in the past three months. Several times.

After two hits of nicotine, she pinched the tip of the cigarette and tossed it out the window. She knew City Hospital was located on Sixth Street. She took the next exit.

Her internal engine was speeding faster than the machine she navigated through the unsettling urban landscape. Steel and glass high-rises shimmered with ghostly light. Blinking traffic signals lent the impression of an abandoned city. Like the devil's breath, steam fumed from gutter vents.

An absurd snatch of dream floated to consciousness: a young woman standing on the crest of a white dome, staring up at huge cutout stars suspended in a painted pitch black sky; a godlike voice commanding, *Come back when you've lost your mind.*

Sylvia in Griffith Park . . . God, she'd been a miserable lost child, a runaway in Los Angeles. A girl searching for a father, searching for herself . . . back in time when the craziness of the city matched the mania of her psyche. Back when she believed she'd die if she didn't escape.

Why did LA always mirror the more psychotic moments in her life?

Sylvia accelerated along the overpass, noticing distant head lamps in her rearview mirror. She kept tracking the other vehicle. It trailed her for two blocks before it turned into an alley. She was aware that Dantes—this case—had left her vulnerable. She was wide open in more ways than one.

On the west side of the freeway, the neighborhood changed; the buildings, less structurally imposing, seemed diminished.

A man wearing slacks—no shirt, no shoes—darted across the intersection of Lucas and Fifth; a woman in a skin-tight dress and stiletto heels followed, her movement more indolent sax riff than walk.

Sylvia guided the Lincoln past the crumbling facade of City Hospital, circling the block. When she was back where she'd started, she slowed to a stop.

She heard the shrill and plaintive whistle of a freight train in the distance. No sign of Purcell, but high beams flashing briefly in her rearview mirror caused a burst of adrenaline. The truck raced past, and she watched the red taillights until they disappeared.

Sylvia turned down a narrow alley, cruising slowly, scanning the dark building for another loading area. Nothing. No one. Had she been hallucinating? Purcell had called, hadn't she?

Once more around the block.

This time, when she passed the south-side dock, she caught the angry red flare of a cigarette. It illuminated the ghostly shape of the federal agent stepping out of shadow.

She parked, locked the car, and covered the shadowy distance at a walk-run. The night had her spooked.

"Where's Dantes?" she started to ask Purcell.

"Cream, no sugar." The special agent greeted her with one hand thrust out, offering coffee in Styrofoam. "I didn't know how you take it." Her voice was slow and Southern as molasses. "I've still got your briefcase, by the way."

Thrown by the sudden downshift, Sylvia said, "I got over here as fast as I could." She accepted the cup, took a sip, and lukewarm coffee dribbled down her chin. Restlessly, she pressed the heel of her hand to mouth and chin, then she returned her full attention to Purcell, and asked, "Where the hell are we?"

"Knocking at the back door."

Sylvia thought the special agent looked awful. Even by the glow of cigarette and distant streetlights, she had the stunned look of an injured animal. The woman was ten years older than yesterday. Then there was the curious lethargy—what had happened to the urgent command to show up within minutes?

"Hurry up and wait," drawled Purcell, the mind reader. "We should get the go-ahead anytime."

"Is this an authorized visit?"

"You'll only have a few minutes with him."

"Sure." Sylvia nodded, wary, feeling her pulse flip-flop, allowing the night air to slow her down. Purcell wouldn't, or couldn't, meet her eye.

Sylvia took a few moments to study their surroundings. They were sheltered in a loading area behind the old brick hospital. The faint stink of trash hovered in the warm air; the temperature was the coolest it would be for the next twenty-four hours.

She kept expecting the big red-haired LAPD detective to appear from the shadows. Disbelief, outrage, grief were all part of the emotional package he'd left behind; and this for a man she'd known less than eight hours.

Sylvia said, "I'm sorry about Detective Church."

Purcell shook her head, closing dark, velvety eyes. She held her body stiff and still, as if something dangerous passing in the night might be blind to her presence.

She took a labored breath, turning to Sylvia. "Do you

believe in fate—" Her words died away, punctuated by the abrupt, birdlike twill of an electronic pager. The agent tossed her Styrofoam cup into an open Dumpster. "Follow me."

Sylvia did. Right down the throat of the subterranean corridor to the basement of City Hospital. Fluorescent lights flickered, footsteps echoed on tile, the faint stench of mildew reached her nostrils. She was actually stepping on the soft debris of peeling paint, the tunnel sloughing off its own skin.

Where were the Feds keeping Dantes? Where the hell were she and Purcell, underneath how many tons of earth and concrete? Uneasily, she quashed thoughts of restless geologic faults—the discovery of hundreds of new and unsteady seams below the city, the fact that the LA basin experienced thousands of invisible shocks each and every day.

The passage ended at a heavy steel-lined door. Using her muscled weight for leverage, Purcell crossed the threshold, guiding the way into yet another corridor, a near replica of the previous one, except the angle of trajectory was up, not down.

This subterranean section of the old hospital had probably been condemned after the most recent quake. Twice, Sylvia was certain she felt the ground vibrate; overactive imagination, she told herself.

They stepped through another door, this time entering an institutional-looking hallway.

When someone gripped her arm, Sylvia jumped.

"Sorry," Dr. Mendoza murmured, her name tag prominently displayed over her left breast pocket. She was a plump, dusky woman with pert features that sharply contrasted with melancholy wide-set eyes. "Dr. Strange?" Mendoza caught Purcell's confirmation—a quick nod of the head. She said, "Dantes has been asking for you."

"I was told he's here for security—" Sylvia stopped

speaking when she saw Mendoza emphatically shaking her head. She turned to confront Purcell, but the special agent had evaporated. The halls were deserted.

Mendoza handed her a white hospital coat complete with identification tag.

As Sylvia shrugged into the coat, she asked, "Where are all the guards? LAPD, FBI?"

"There's LAPD outside that corridor—there's one officer in the room with Dantes—and you've already seen Agent Purcell. Normally, this wing of the hospital is completely closed off," Mendoza added quickly.

The doctor blinked her stubby lashes nervously. "I want this clear, I had nothing to do with his current condition."

"What condition?"

"Orders came down the pike—and I've only been on since midnight—"

"Who authorized . . . ?" Sylvia let her voice fade, stopping short of asking this beleaguered doctor questions best answered by the FBI. "Take me to him," she said.

Mendoza pointed toward swinging doors, presumably leading to working areas of the hospital. She touched her finger to her thin lips, stepping around a corner, out of view of anyone who happened to glance through the small windows.

She said, "For your information, you came down a supply tunnel that's been closed for years." The doctor shook her head, looking puzzled and disturbed. "Somebody doesn't want you attracting attention."

A hard knot was forming in Sylvia's stomach as she moved around the corner with the other woman. Mendoza said, "You'll see—his body sustained minimal trauma during the seizure."

"*What* seizure?"

"I thought . . . didn't Agent Purcell tell you?" Mendoza

shot Sylvia a quizzical look. "Apparently, when Dantes heard about the bombing, he became—upset."

"Upset can mean worried; it can also mean psychotic," Sylvia said, trying to contain her impatience. "It doesn't usually mean *seizure*."

Dr. Mendoza paused, mouth drawn into a moue, as if she were tasting words. "We got the neurologist's preliminary report," she volunteered finally. She saw the question in Sylvia's eyes. "He's exhibiting symptoms inconsistent with his physical condition—symptoms with no obvious organic basis, no evident neurological explanation."

"I need to see him."

"Follow me." As Mendoza walked, she lobbed questions at Sylvia: "Yesterday, did you notice problems with his vision? Photophobia?" Her hand sliced from the tip of her nose toward the wall. "Diplopia—double vision?"

Holding back her stride to stay even with the doctor, Sylvia caught a loose strand of hair and tugged it behind one ear. She fingered the bracelet on her wrist nervously. "Maybe light sensitivity—but he seemed to be focusing. You said minimal trauma."

"As far as we can tell, he *mimicked* an epileptic seizure." Dr. Mendoza lifted her hands, palms to the ceiling. "No sign of spinal or cerebral trauma. No evidence of organic defect: A clean E.E.G. He's exhibiting some symptoms, including paralysis of the limbs." Mendoza tipped her head, her eyes growing round. "I read about it in medical school."

"Read about *what*?" Sylvia pressed tensely.

"Conversion disorder."

Unconsciously, Sylvia shook her head. Conversion disorder was one of the somatoform disorders, a controversial diagnosis formerly known as conversion hysteria. The appearance of physical neurological symptoms unexplainable by any known medical condition. The diagnosis made some psychiatrists and psychologists very nervous—in part because it harkened back to the end of the nineteenth century, to Freud and Charcot.

In plain speak—it was what happened when the body exposed the secrets of the mind.

Both women had come to a standstill in front of a metal door that was coated with eroding white paint: B-103. Dr. Mendoza gestured toward a small window. "See for yourself."

Sylvia peered through dull glass. The room was square and plain, and its institutional paint was faded with age and grime. The one chair was currently occupied by a uniformed LAPD officer, who stared back at Sylvia without blinking.

She had a pretty good idea that Purcell hadn't gone through normal channels to arrange this visit.

"That's Officer Jones," Mendoza said under her breath. "Stay out of his way, we'll be fine."

Dr. Mendoza stepped forward wielding an O-ring crammed with innumerable keys. The lock turned with a groan. Sylvia entered the room—and stopped in her tracks.

The overhead fluorescent lights were off, and the only illumination (other than the television) was provided by moon and street lamps, a milky wash spilling through a high, narrow window.

The TV was mounted on the wall, and it cast out a flickering seasick haze. Two security cameras suspended on either side of the TV recorded activity around the center of the room.

There was no bed; instead a gurney—raised to a forty-five-degree angle—faced away from the window.

She heard Mendoza greeting the cop—careful, casual chatter about early-morning rounds and a change of shift. Sylvia approached the gurney just as the overheads flickered on.

Oh, dear God . . .

John Dantes was strapped down, immobilized, his arms and legs clamped tight with leather braces. Thick gauze covered his eyes. But the most bizarre element of the tableau was the rigid arch of his body as it strained against the gurney like a tautly strung bow. The man looked as if an electric current was shooting from his head to his toes, forcing extreme muscle contraction.

Conscious of the cameras, Sylvia stepped forward, softly calling his name.

He shuddered.

"Dantes," she repeated. She touched his arm, feeling the feverish heat of his skin through cotton.

"Doctor Strange," he whispered through parched lips. His attempt to speak again failed.

Sylvia felt a firm hand on her shoulder. When she looked up, Mendoza was eyeing her warily. "Be careful of the patient, Doctor," Mendoza cautioned slowly. "Let's avoid security issues."

Sylvia nodded. "Can we do something about the bandages?" she asked quietly.

Mendoza glanced back at the officer, then said, "You're right; we should remove the gauze to check pupil responses." Quickly, she pulled away the sterile dressing.

Dantes' skin was pale, only slightly bruised. There were no obvious signs of injury or trauma. Nevertheless, he presented a disturbing image.

As much as his bizarre physical pose, it was his eyes that caught Sylvia's attention; they stared out at the world unseeing; they might have been empty holes.

She held two fingers in front of his pupils. Dantes didn't blink, nor did he focus or exhibit any motor response whatsoever. He stared straight ahead, his gaze fixed high on the barren wall.

He whispered, "Water."

Mendoza raised a plastic cup to his lips. Most of the liquid dribbled down his chin, but he managed to swallow a few sips.

His body went slack abruptly; he seemed to be coming out of a state of extreme disorientation. Mendoza stepped away from the gurney, returning her attention to Officer Jones, engaging him in conversation; she complained mildly about long nights and sore feet.

Keeping her back to Jones and Mendoza, Sylvia leaned closer to Dantes. For a moment, she was mentally transported back inside the house, staring at the bomb in the floor, the handwritten Italian scorched across wood.

"I found your message," she said, reciting the verse in an undertone: "' . . . angels who were not rebellious, nor were faithful to God; but were for themselves.'"

Abruptly, Dantes went rigid again; his fingers clamped metal, his veins stood out like ropes against his skin—but the spasms were fleeting. "Not my message!" he hissed.

"You sent me to find the bomb."

"You're stupid," he whispered. "So was Church." He took a deep, shuddering breath. "Why should I trust you?"

Sylvia didn't move. She had to work to control the anger. She said, "Because I'm here."

She wasn't ready for his response.

He said, "Karen knows." His voice dropped so low it was barely audible. "Ask the master."

The convulsion hit him like electricity. His eyes rolled back in his head, he gagged, and his body stiffened, bowing upward in a rigid arc.

Mendoza reached the gurney in three strides. "I need to get him sedated," she said sharply. Pressing the panic button on her pager, she signaled for assistance. Under her breath, she whispered, "Leave. Now."

When Sylvia didn't move, Mendoza said, "*Now*, get out of here."

With a last look at Dantes, Sylvia left the room, running head-on into Purcell.

The agent gripped her by the arm, leading her forcefully around the corner. "He didn't give you a damn thing but gibberish."

Sylvia leaned heavily against the cold cement wall. She felt a gulf opening up in front of her, as if Dantes had separated her from the rest of the world.

She shook off the eerie sensation, focusing on the federal agent. "You force me to work with you, but you don't tell me what's going on—you feed me bullshit—you disappear so you can listen in—"

"The bastard forgot to mention this." Purcell thrust out her hand.

Sylvia took the single sheet of paper, scanning the message.

> dear john, prodigal son . . .
> message received
> will follow orders to the letter
> on our journey to 4th
> they shall be punishd for sins of other
> sacred city seen sacifice
> remember our relentless thoughts bk 9, M

The words blurred on paper. "Your threat communication analysts—"

"They're working on it now," Purcell said. "We got it from Dantes—the COs found it in his hand when he had the seizure."

Footsteps sounded from around the corner; Sylvia heard

voices speaking in low, urgent tones; she heard the door to room B-103 close and lock.

But her attention was on the page. The visual pattern encasing the message took shape: it was an irregular rectangle, traversed by a faint and flowing linear delta, and marked in several places with small triangles.

"What are those lines, those marks?" she asked Purcell hoarsely. "Some kind of crude map?"

Nodding warily, the agent said, "They may be coordinates."

Moving fast, Sylvia retraced her steps toward Dantes' room. Her fingers closed around the handle; she looked through the small window in time to see Mendoza plunge a needle into Dantes' arm.

"Oh, no . . .," she whispered.

But the drug Mendoza had given him was already flowing in his veins. He was beyond reach. His head lolled back, his body became deadweight, the living image of one of Francisco Goya's doomed lunatics.

CHAPTER NINETEEN

And so, in the end, ladies and gentlemen, it's best to do nothing at all! Conscious inertia is the best! A toast to my hole under the floor!

Dostoyevsky, *Notes from Underground*

6:33 A.M.   M is psychic.

As he watches the psychologist leave LA City Hospital,

he knows that she is upset, angry, and afraid. She's in way over her head. Pulled one way by the Feds, pulled another way by Dantes.

M predicts the future.

He's not worried about losing track of Dr. Strange. He knows exactly where she came from—he's quite familiar with Leo Carreras and the bungalow in Santa Monica.

He can also tell you in a heartbeat where she's headed: to Edmond Sweetheart's lair. No denying the professor took a shine to Miss LA yesterday at Beaudry Street. That much was clear, even from a distance.

M knows where Sweetheart lives.

He's put in the tedious hours of surveillance—the very best way to get to know a human target, its habits and tastes, its likes and dislikes, its natural habitat, its world.

In his line of business, he depends upon his predictions. He has to know what a target is thinking *before* the target knows.

In order to successfully complete a mission, he has to prepare, do the legwork, set contingencies—

Set the trap.

First things first. M must check in on Dantes. Just a visual. To see where he and his old friend stand.

M tips his hat to the good doctor as she disappears from view. He'll catch up with her again very soon.

Already, she has given him valuable information: she's guided him straight to Dantes.

Granted, this relocation caught M off guard; he would've put his money on the nearby detention center.

But this works. With his credentials, no one will question his authority to check out reports of power surges, water leaks, or tunnel erosion in the old hospital building.

"No rest for the wicked," he jokes with Thomas, the head janitor, when the man asks him why he's working so early in the morning. It is Thomas—an elderly man with elegant white hair—who tells him that the cops are making life difficult, messing with his crew and his schedule. He is grateful when M courteously agrees to return next week for a look at the basement, the only area strictly off-limits.

It is also Thomas who adds, quite casually, that judging from all the tests, the fuss, the hubbub, "This celebrity outlaw patient must be stone cold crazy."

CHAPTER TWENTY

> . . . to the extent an offender's schema is well developed and stable, a profiler will be able to isolate discriminating, stable characteristics of the offender.
>
> D. A. Berkerian and J. L. Jackson, *Critical Issues in Offender Profiling*

6:43 A.M. *Relentless thoughts . . .*

Those two words from M looped like a mantra in Sylvia's mind as she followed Purcell's vehicle west along Melrose Avenue, red light after red light: Cahuenga, La Brea, Fairfax. The sun touched her shoulder blades, warm fingers of a downtown dawn reaching out through the mesh of haze and smog.

Karen knows . . . ask the master . . .

Sylvia didn't have a clue what Dantes meant, and she wasn't likely to learn any more from him, at least not for the next few hours.

Before she'd left the hospital, she'd managed to extract a

last bit of information from Dr. Mendoza: Dantes now had thirty milligrams of Novodipam flowing through his system. Enough to sedate a patient who suffers from convulsive disorders or status epilepticus. Within five minutes of the injection, Mendoza predicted he would be unlikely to communicate—probably would not open his eyes—for the next twelve to eighteen hours.

Dantes was the obvious link to M.

A lot could happen in eighteen hours. The city could explode, for example.

The sight of Dantes, his physical and mental deterioration, had left her shaken. Was he seriously ill—or was he a consummate actor?

And did she actually believe she might find a fallen hero hidden inside the violent criminal? If so, she was harboring a dangerous illusion.

Sylvia almost missed the turn, cutting too close to the curb as she followed Purcell's town car north onto Crescent Heights.

John Dantes is exhibiting signs of visual disturbance and paralysis.

Detective Red Church had been killed and a bomb squad tech had been blinded by the blast, his arm torn off.

Dantes shows no evidence of organic defect . . .

Somatic symptoms with no obvious organic neurological justification . . .

Sylvia pulled a cigarette from behind her ear and stuck it unceremoniously and unlit between her lips. Bright sunlight glinted off the single silver bangle on her left wrist.

Dr. Mendoza had opened the door to one of the more colorful psychoanalytic explanations for his symptoms: 300.11 conversion disorder. That diagnosis—and its requisites—could be found in the DSM-IV, the diagnostic bible of mental health professionals.

" . . . *presence of symptoms or deficits affecting voluntary motor or sensory function that suggest a neurological or other general medical condition (Criterion A). Psychological factors are judged to be associated with the symptom or deficit. . . ."*

Conversion disorder, a subset of the somatoform disorders, the fucking black hole of diagnoses.

She shook her head, warning herself, Don't even go there.

But she would; she always did. Like a moth drawn to light, her intellect could never resist the attraction of perplexity, the psychological enigma, that one piece of the puzzle that defied logic.

Swerving around a protruding manhole cover, she stabbed out the still-unlit cigarette in the ashtray of the Lincoln. This particular disorder was the stuff of nineteenth-century drawing rooms, crinolines, the vapors. The domain of Charcot and Freud and nineteenth-century hysteria. In ancient times, the Greeks had blamed its manifestation in females on a wandering uterus; hysterical men were just plain loony.

Times hadn't changed all that much.

Wedging the cell phone between chin and shoulder, she pressed the first button on auto dial. The more likely scenario: this was about factitious disorder and secondary gain. In other words, Dantes was preconsciously manufacturing his symptoms to gain some advantage. It was a step up from malingering, or pure fakery. *Maybe.*

Accelerating through a yellow light, she flicked another cigarette from the pack. Preoccupied, she tried to draw air through the unlit cigarette, succeeding only in dampening the filter.

The damn phone wasn't ringing. She punched in the number manually.

If you followed classic Freudian reasoning—*for half a*

moment—you ended up with someone experiencing extreme conflict as in shame or guilt, repressing ineffectively, and acting out, or physicalizing the anxiety via the body—somatic expression, as in paralysis and blindness . . .

Still no answer.

Bumper to bumper with Purcell, Sylvia ran a red light, bracing for the next. She tossed the damp, otherwise untouched cigarette onto the floor of the Lincoln. "Leo?"

"Where have you been?" His overly precise enunciation revealed his level of frustration and concern.

"I had to leave in a hurry," she said apologetically. "I didn't have time to explain."

"Explain now. I was worried."

"I've been to see our mutual acquaintance." She wasn't going to mention John Dantes by name on an open transmission. Leo would fill in the blanks.

She was relieved to hear his voice; she'd needed a sounding board—correction, she needed a *friend*. She felt an abrupt pang of longing for Matt, Serena, and her friends in New Mexico—she craved bare earth beneath her feet.

"How did it go?" Leo was asking slowly.

"Interesting . . . uh, pretty bizarre. . . . we should talk about it." She flipped on the car's air-conditioning, tilting her face toward a vent. "Leo, when you did the pretrial evaluation, didn't you come up with a V-profile on the MMPI?" She'd read Leo's report a half dozen times, but she wanted to make sure she wasn't hallucinating; if MMPI scales one and three were elevated, and the depressive scale (two) was low, the visual was literally a V—hence the name. A V-profile could confirm a tendency toward hysteria, hypochondriasis . . . toward conversion tendencies in general.

"Meet me in thirty minutes," Leo said. "We'll go over that information."

"Not possible. A *yes* or *no* will do."

"It was a mild V-profile, yes." Leo was silent for a moment, before adding, "I'm concerned about your role in all this."

"Me, too. We'll talk. I promise."

She followed Purcell past Laurel Canyon, then east, onto Selma, a small, tree-lined street at the very base of the Hollywood Hills. At the end of the second short block, the agent turned into a driveway, stopping short of an eight-foot-high grilled fence.

Sylvia pulled up alongside Purcell's vehicle to exchange final notes. "You're not coming inside?"

"No need." Purcell glanced at her wristwatch. "Go talk your shrink talk with the professor—but make sure you conjugate for me in layman's terms."

"Where will I find you?"

"I'll find you." Without ceremony, Purcell shifted into reverse, turning in the direction of Sunset Boulevard.

Sylvia pulled the Lincoln forward; she spoke into a metal speaker set in a post.

"This is Dr. Strange."

Five seconds later the gate rolled open, allowing access to the inner circle; she guided the Lincoln to a stop behind a minivan and a Harley.

The stepping-stone walkway was protected by a canopy of flame trees. The lawn—a smooth green sea—surged gently upward to meet a reef of bonsai pines, azaleas, bird-of-paradise, day lilies, and ginger.

It was all a far cry from the Xeriscape gardens of New Mexico, with their delicate, hardscrabble cholla, echinacea, and chamiza.

The Craftsman-style house was large, low, and elegant, with distinct California–Pacific Rim accents.

She passed under a simple wooden arch into a Japanese-

style garden. Surrounding the granite path, perfectly raked
river stones supported a glassine reflecting pool.

Her gaze was arrested by a life-sized gleaming bronze
sculpture of a flight-helmeted, harnessed fat man with a
wing—*one* feathered angel wing—looking heavenward,
poised in midstep, already committed to venturing off the
edge of the precipice. She was studying the work when the
front door opened after the staccato click of at least three
dead bolts.

"*Fallen Angel*," a voice announced.

Sylvia turned to see a man, late twenties, standing in the
doorway. He was handsome in his white tank tee that
exposed a tattoo of a flying fish on his right biceps, tight
paint-spattered jeans, broken-down biker boots.

"The fallen angel's about to take the plunge all over
again," she said softly.

"Ain't that the way," he agreed with a nod. "Michael
Bergt's the artist—actually, he lives in Santa Fe like you.
Great guy. The professor collects his work—incredible
paintings, sculpture."

He smiled, letting the words roll on the waves of his soft,
deep voice. "Dr. Sylvia Strange. We've been expecting you.
I'm Luke."

"Nice Harley," she said.

"Thanks, but I don't get to play with it as much as I'd
like. When I'm not slaving over my dissertation, I'm the
professor's slave." He winked. "I loved your paper on narcissism, by the way."

Hollywood.

"Thanks. Nice to meet you, Luke." On second glance,
he might be just over thirty. Her hand slid from the cool
bronze of the sculpture to touch his, and then she stepped
over the threshold into Sweetheart's domain.

Inside the foyer, two dogs scampered around her legs—a

miniature bulldog and a Jack Russell terrier—and she stooped to scratch soft ears. When she stood again, she took in the crisp paper lanterns (Isamu Noguchi, no doubt), and the polished wooden stairs that curved so gently upward. A massive yellow, blue, and white abstract painting—reminiscent of de Kooning—filled much of the wall next to the staircase.

The interior decor was more than tasteful; it was impressively simple, maintaining the Asian flavor of the garden.

Three arched doorways opened off the foyer; Luke turned left, leading Sylvia into what looked like a formal dining room, except for the fact it was lined with work stations.

A strapping woman greeted Sylvia with a loopy smile and a myopic gaze framed by horned-rimmed glasses. "I'm Gretchen. Welcome to antiterrorist command central. I love going after the *bad guys*." A definite Scandinavian accent. "That's why I came to America—to study under the professor."

"We have more bad guys?" Sylvia asked.

"America, the FBI—you are the world's rottweiler." Gretchen caught her lip between her teeth and considered Sylvia from head to toe. "I feel as if I know you."

"Really?" Sylvia smiled uneasily.

"MOSAIK's profile works like a primer, synthesizing all this," Gretchen said vaguely, nodding toward a green-glazed, very modern dining table in the center of the room; it was littered with books, manuscripts, pages, graphs, maps. Food had been strategically interspersed with work product.

"What profile?"

"*Yours*." Gretchen gave a casual shrug. "Paternal desertion—uprooted by the move to California as an adolescent—UCLA, the episode of your mini marriage—then back to New Mexico to buy your father's home, your foster daughter—the prison work."

With barely a breath, Gretchen extended her arms like a game show model now advertising the prizes behind door number two: "Grapes, cheese, green tea, miso . . . the peaches are organic. So is the seaweed. *Ooh*, and organic Belgian chocolate."

She winked. "I have a wicked sweet tooth, too."

"Oops." Luke flashed Sylvia a sympathetic smile. "None of us are thrilled when we find out our lives are in the database, but it's a damn good way to acquaint yourself with the possibilities of our system."

"Really." Sylvia met his smile with a flat stare. "Then I'll start with Sweetheart's profile."

Luke turned his back to attend to a computer, but his laugh was quick and deep.

No less than three printers were feeding out data; the hum of computers filled the room. Chopin didn't stand a chance, although Sylvia thought she recognized faint musical strains in the background.

On one wall, she noticed a five-foot-square version of the map of Dante's hell that Sweetheart had given her; red pushpins marked the first four circles.

She veered toward framed degrees on the opposite wall—gilded letters advertised various universities, including Yale, University of Hawaii, Penn State, and Cambridge—all for Edmond Holomalia Sweetheart.

A photograph caught her eye; muscled wrestlers captured in midbout.

"The professor's into sumo," Luke said. "Hey, really, you'd better eat something," he added. "It's going to be a long day."

"I need *coffee*, very strong coffee." She grabbed a peach and bit in. "Where the hell am I?"

"Died and gone to heaven, Dr. Strange," Luke said. "MOSAIK—Multiplex prOfiles Systems AnalysIs Kit—is multitiered and agent based. The profiling program is geared for terrorist analysis, and she digests all data typology: linguistic, forensic, geographic. She works from the bottom up. We begin with scaled-down basics, avoiding pitfalls of the top-down model, which failed to take every variable into consideration."

Excitement lit up his pretty face. "MOSAIK *links* so we can search historical *and* predictive data, mapping patterns, all depending on the level or tier you're after. At the moment, we're tracking a dozen terrorists around the globe—linking crimes, methodology, and suspects."

Sylvia's eyebrows arched. "Is that how you tracked Ben Black?"

"MOSAIK was the key to the Black–Abu Mohammed investigation," Luke said, nodding.

Gretchen ran her fingers over a keyboard. "MOSAIK's sortable by linguistic venue: verbal, written—extortion, threat, confession, suicide. The program matches syntactic similarities, speech patterns, grammatical errors—for example, who is Shakespeare?"

"And mapping shows us geographic patterns," Luke interjected, "as the perpetrator expands his home range, his sources, enhances his signatures—even seasonal or temporal data."

"Well, shit," was all she could think of to say.

At which point she heard that distinctive voice: "Didn't I tell you the doctor has a way with words?" A thick, carved door swung wide, and Sweetheart stepped into the room. This morning he was wearing a charcoal-toned linen suit over a pale yellow shirt. Seen in the shadows, his expression was pensive, almost brooding, but he smiled at Sylvia. She was struck again by the handsome planes of his face, the almond eyes, the rich gleam of his skin, the power of his massive body. He looked good in his home.

He said, "MOSAIK . . . think of it as the gestalt of computer-based profiling. I know it's a bit overwhelming."

"Gestalt." Sylvia tested the psych term in a computer context. "So spatial, forensic, psycholinguistic information is combined—"

"In an effort to glean the larger pattern or patterns." He offered his hand, maintaining contact well beyond the brief seconds allowed for social convention; it was one of those moments when a connection is made, no telling, no use analyzing, whether the live current is chemistry or alchemy.

He said, "The program was developed by Nightsky in Santa Fe—your home town. Nightsky was started by members of the Santa Fe Institute. The company specializes in data-mining, or 'info-harvesting.' We're linked to Quantico. Gretchen is our linguistics expert; she's handling M's extortion communications. Luke is our geographic-spatial man; he's working on the crude map we pulled from Dantes."

"So it really is a map?" Sylvia asked.

"I'm still trying to extract coordinates." Luke offered a rueful smile as he gathered discs and walked away from his desk. "Ask me again in an hour," he said over his shoulder, disappearing through the carved door; Gretchen followed.

Sylvia found herself alone with the professor.

"What did Dantes have to say for himself?" Sweetheart asked abruptly.

"You tell me."

Sweetheart didn't evade her question. "It's true we monitored the live feed." He watched her with interest, as if she were some unknown substance smeared on a slide. "But I'm asking for your analysis."

Sylvia kept her voice carefully neutral: "How do you feel about conversion disorder?"

"Bullshit diagnosis." He caught his lips between very white teeth. "Psychology is already a soft science—please don't turn it into cotton candy. Dantes is playing crazy. He likes games. Don't believe me, just look at his infernal boxes."

"I thought you'd say that."

"Don't tell me you actually buy his hysterical symptoms? He's a good actor—he's doing Anna O."

"All right, so it's the wrong century for hysteria," Sylvia said, shrugging. Josef Breuer, Sigmund Freud's mentor, had made a splash in the 1880s with an unusual case: Anna O. exhibited dramatic but fleeting hysterical symptoms. "But Breuer's hypnosis worked."

"His talking cure?" Sweetheart snorted.

"The symptoms abated."

"Then they got worse," Sweetheart said, with an impatient wave. "Phantom pregnancy, hysterical childbirth—which probably wouldn't be an issue with John Dantes. Forget hypnosis, catharsis—we could try voodoo."

"You think this is funny?"

"No." Sweetheart's gaze was direct. "I think too many people have died because of this man."

His straight, dark brows accented piercing eyes. "I prefer hard, clean, clinical data to your moth-eaten Freudian repression. Give me an MRI, even a PET scan; give me Planck's neuron transistors, and the latest superresolution scans of interneuronal connections, synapses, neurotransmitter concentrations—show me where these repressed emotions light up the brain, give me fingerprints on the cortex, and then maybe I'll begin to listen to your theories."

"That's your bailiwick," Sylvia said, gesturing toward humming computers and scanners.

"Agent-based data-mining is the foundation of my specific profiling analysis, *yes*." Sweetheart's eyelids creased at the outer corners. "We've developed MOSAIK, building on what the Feds accomplished, capable of comparing collateral data, behavioral scripts—"

"Whoa." Sylvia held up both palms, planting her feet. "You're losing me."

"Simply put, MOSAIK makes it possible to sort through gigabytes without losing data through the cracks—the problem with Unabom. We've taken the crucial step in data-based profiling."

Sylvia selected a strand of grapes from the table; she pulled the fruits off, one by one, adding punctuation to her words. "You can play with the FBI, CRI, Holmes, and Catchem databases until the cows come home; you can search for linking information; map, chart, and play with patterns; your analysis is based on national data sets to ensure statistical validity; you can infer, enhance, hell, you can even intuit . . . but *only* if the offender makes you a *gift* of his signature."

"M exists, he *lives*, in our data—I guarantee it. We *will* extract him—and more important, we will link him to John Dantes."

"Great. If you're so perfect, why am I here?"

He eyed her quizzically for a moment; long enough to make her uncomfortable. Then he offered a half smile. "You're my wild card, Dr. Strange." His brows rose, lending him a rueful air. "Cognitively, you leap crevasses." He shrugged. "Although I have great faith in MOSAIK, that's still a very human trait."

"It really puzzles you, doesn't it? The idea that the human mind is capable of something the computer can't achieve?"

"AI will catch up tomorrow—the day after tomorrow, humans will be left in the dust." He smiled. "But for the moment, you have a knack for creative links; it was evident in your recent paper on psychopathy, child abuse, and object-relations theory. I may disagree with your means and methods—but I'm intrigued by your end results." He moved toward the door. "Shall we?"

Following him into the inner sanctum, Sylvia felt like a child in a fun-house maze, traveling deeper, each threshold adding another layer of complexity to the issue of escape.

She found herself inside a large office crammed with books, files, and two additional computers. Sweetheart closed the door, shutting out the noise from other rooms. The lighting was dim, the space close, and the computers glowed amber like cybercoals.

"Take another look at the data we've extracted from M's written communications. Gretchen's been playing for the past twenty-four hours." Sweetheart's fingers skimmed over the keyboard. "Our first step is to analyze each communication, extracting salient details; second step, search for similarities, mirrors, and matches in the existing database; third step, develop our profile." He scowled. "Something beyond the obvious—white male, loner, antisocial, paranoid ideation."

Sylvia moved to Sweetheart's side, noticing the rather delicate shape of his hands as she gazed down at the messages displayed, enlarged—and variously highlighted—on screen.

> dear feds
> babbel, babbel, babbel
> no more Limbo
> 2nd circle soon complete
> release yr prisoner DaNTes, prophet apocryphal
> or hungry for next
> Vvv
> M—

dear john, prodigal son . . .
message received
will follow orders to the letter
on our journey to 4th circle
they shall be punishd for sins of other
sacred city seen sacifice
remember our relentless thoughts bk 9, M

The professor clicked a key and flipped screens. He said, "Sort, associations, three-level," and a series of word associations began to race across the monitor face in endless loops like cyberized tickertape.

babbel = [error, grammatical] = ?words = gibberish = ?Dantes' Inferno

babbel = babble = babel = Babylon = tower = tower built to heaven

Dantes = prophet apocryphal = false prophet = fallen angel = apocalypse = ancient seer

yr = ?your [repetitive error] = you are = you're = lexicon = query

yr = you are = form of address = Dantes addressee = relationship = query

yr = ?year abbreviation = error punctuation = lexical error = data search in

yr = yur = ?Ur = city of Sumer, ancient Mesopotamia = trading city = height of

yr = Ur = city fell to Babylon = city under rule of Nebuchadnezzar = query

yr = Ur = code of Ur-Nammu, world's oldest code of law = older than Hammura

Vvv = [numerical] = Roman = 15/5 = ?cuneiform = ?four = ?4 = [alphabetical]

prodigal = wasteful = lavish = spendthrift = prodigy
= child marvel = monster

punishd = [error, grammatical] = ?punished = puni-
tive = vengeful = revenge

Limbo = outside gates of hell = Divine Comedy =
Dante, Alighieri = Inferno

sacifice = [error, grammatical] = ?sacrifice = sacred =
sacrilegious

sacred city = holy city = angels = Los Angeles =
scared city = cite = Ur = Babylon

seen = experienced = map = known = map =
revealed = scene

M = maker = maestro = master = god = ?God = ?ini-
tial, surname = query

relentless thoughts = anger = unbearable = unmerci-
ful = obsessive

As Sweetheart bit into an apple, the fruit's sharp scent
was released into the air. Between bites, he asked, "Care to
leap?"

"My mother told me to look first," Sylvia answered.
"Babel, as in tower, as in the hubris of humankind to
believe they could reach heaven. God's punishment in
the form of language reduced to *babble,* or gibberish,
which isn't that far removed from schizophrenic word
salad."

"Not to mention the myth of the Tower of Babel,"
Sweetheart interjected.

"The skewing of language as punishment." Sylvia was
enjoying the riff. "For that matter, M definitely babbles."

The professor examined the now exposed apple core in
his palm. "Ur . . . if it *is* Ur . . . fallen cities."

"Babylon—fallen civilizations. Los Angeles—fallen
city."

"I've given some thought to M's Polaroid of the bomb—the timing device, the setting on the clock face," Sweetheart said. "Eighteen minutes, thirty seconds past one."

"There was no explosion at one eighteen."

"I believe the numbers pertain to *where*, not *when*. One eighteen point thirty is the latitude of Los Angeles. M's got big plans for the City of Angels."

"Isn't that obvious?"

Ignoring her testy reply, Sweetheart said, "The triangles embossed on the threat note . . . they're sexagesimal symbols, the oldest example of place value numeration, predating the Sumerian-Akkadian system—"

"Sumerian as in Mesopotamia?"

"As in Babylon, the ruin, nothing but sand, rock, wind. I've *been* there."

"So you're saying our guy wants to facilitate the fall of *New* Babylon, bring it to rubble."

"It's a thought—which begs another question." Sweetheart watched her closely. "Suicidal ideation?"

Sylvia frowned; her delivery was suddenly hesitant. "Dantes equals false prophet and his work equals gibberish." She kneaded the muscles in her neck. "If *God* equals M, and *fallen angel* equals Dantes, then this story is about envy and narcissistic rage."

"Narcissistic rage?"

"As in, rip their balls off." She shrugged. "As in projection defense."

"Rage," Sweetheart confirmed. "Aggression turned *outward*."

"But that doesn't eliminate the possibility of suicide-slash-homicide." Sylvia's mouth formed a tight line, and she picked up a pen and twiddled it between thumb and forefinger. She was silent for more than a minute. Sweetheart just waited.

Finally, she said, "I'll give you a leap—hell, I'll leap the Grand Canyon."

She squeezed her eyelids shut; excitement fired her up. "The second message begins with an implication," she said, catching her lip between her teeth. "'Dear John, *I* will follow *your* orders to the letter.'"

She gripped the pen tightly, oblivious to the ink staining her fingers. "Or . . . 'John will follow *my* orders to the letter.'" She stared up at Sweetheart. "And . . . 'they shall be punished for sins of *other*.'" She dropped the pen on the table. "What if John Dantes equals M's *other?*"

"Then Dantes and M are enemies," Sweetheart said, cool and matter-of-fact.

"That's not all they are." Sylvia stood abruptly, scattering books and papers. "M is holding Los Angeles *hostage*—the city is the victim in this scenario." She kept her eyes on the professor. "John Dantes isn't our perpetrator, he's M's puppet."

"I don't buy it," Sweetheart said sharply, dismissing her speculation.

Sylvia pulled back as if she'd been slapped.

8:44 A.M. Luke and Gretchen stared at a monitor while a series of maps flashed lightning-fast across its face.

Without looking up, Luke said, "I've been running M's spatial pattern against the obvious base map—"

"LA," Sylvia finished. She noticed a series of flashing neon orange dots overlaid on the screen. They looked like large grains of red pepper scattered at random: five spread out like petals, and a faint linear series.

"Right. But it's needle-in-the haystack stuff because we've got no idea of scale . . . whether it predates nineteen twenty-seven's standardization ratios or whether—"

But Sylvia was focusing on Gretchen. "You're the linguistics tech . . . your program obviously came up with

Dante Alighieri and the *Inferno* for the reference to *Limbo*. Are they mentioned in *Dantes' Inferno*? As in *John*?"

"Give me a nanosecond." Gretchen moved to her computer and plopped down, fingers already flying across the keyboard. "MOSAIK already devoured the entire text of *Dantes' Inferno*, along with Dantes' thesis, his student papers, the trial transcripts, the psychological files, just about everything and anything." She held up a well-thumbed copy of John Dantes' book as the computer purred into action, too high-tech for lights, bells, or whistles.

Sylvia took the book from Gretchen, then leaned over the other woman's shoulder. "At the hospital, Dantes said something like *Karen knows . . . ask the master*."

Gretchen frowned. "In verbal communications, it's important to consider the influence—"

"Fallen civilizations—and lessons in literature," Sylvia murmured, her mind booting up and zigzagging at hyper speed. Silently, she turned over phrases: *ask the master . . . the one who has mastered the field . . . ask the master, ask the teacher*.

Line up the elements: guilt, repression, stress, conversion . . .

Gretchen began to patter in Swedish but caught herself.

Thumbing through *Dantes' Inferno*, Sylvia found herself gazing down at the dedication: "*This is for my mother, Bella Dantes, who said good-bye much too soon . . . and for James Healey, Head Master, Oxford Academy . . . two who introduced me to Dante Alighieri, his Heaven and Hell, his Paradise and Purgatory.*"

"Ask the master. Take a lesson in lit," Sylvia whispered. "*Master* James Healey."

9:27 A.M. As Sylvia splashed water on her face in the small copper-and-bamboo bathroom, she thought about the interaction with Sweetheart. He was rude, arrogant, aggravating. He was also very smart. She muttered to herself as she peed—muttered to herself as she dug through her briefcase. Lipstick and a comb made her feel better.

In the dining room, waiting for her host, she downed a cup of dense black coffee. By degrees, her cloudy mood was lifting. She left a message for Matt asking him to cancel his flight from New Mexico; she wanted him to stay very close to Serena until this mess was over. She was about to boot up her laptop to send e-mail and to review her notes on Dantes when Sweetheart appeared.

He signaled he was ready to move. Downing the last of the coffee, she gathered briefcase and computer, and she followed him along a corridor to a heavily secured garage. A dark green Mercedes purred in response to an electronic greeting.

As the professor revved the car's engine—and the garage door lifted smoothly—Sylvia said, "Before we go any further, I want to clear something up. You were an asshole back there. You owe me an apology."

"You're right."

"I know I'm right." She waited.

"I apologize."

She was silent for a moment before she nodded. "You asked for my intuition. Here goes: For all intents and purposes, Dantes is sick. He's withdrawn himself from the game, he's a passive participant."

Sweetheart was listening carefully.

Sylvia continued, "Either Dantes is faking conversion disorder—and it's part of the plan with M. Or he's not faking, in which case M will blame us for taking Dantes out of circulation." Sylvia pushed black sunglasses over her eyes.

"Here's my prediction: M is going to strike closer to home now. He'll go after one of us."

CHAPTER TWENTY-ONE

"The sun gave me a frightful headache and I have to wear smoked glasses all the time. In other words, phooey on Cal. . . ."

Nathanael West

10:13 A.M. On the winding canyon road, M tracks the green Mercedes from a distance.

Sweetheart's baby is a beauty—and she's custom fit for an antiterrorist cowboy: fast, fully loaded, 350 horses; vibration sensors, ultrasensitive radio alarm and paging system, bullet-proof glass, sheet-metal chassis undercoat, locking hood, locking wheel covers, locking gas tank, exhaust barrier.

If you sneeze within thirty feet of baby, she'll start bawling.

She needs a gentle touch.

M, a connoisseur of sophisticated technology and machinery, strokes his fingers lightly over the steering wheel of his truck.

Patience . . .

In this business, a man who wants to survive bides his time.

He also knows enough to remember those who were less than patient in the annals of explosive history . . .

1605: Guy Fawkes—arrested for hiding copious amounts of gunpowder under the House of Lords, London.

1886: Four anarchists—hanged for the deaths of seven officers in Haymarket Square.

1903: Lieutenant Joseph Petrosino, New York City, director of the first official bomb squad, which focused on fighting the Mano Nera, or Black Hand—assassinated in Italy.

1922: Bomber John Magnusson—identified and captured through handwriting analysis and comparison.

A moment of silence, please . . .

M has no intention of joining the ranks of the impetuous, the foolish, the dead.

He's not about to mess with Sweetheart's fully armored baby.

And he doesn't have to.

Because the work is done—the bomb is in place, the timer is set, the clock is already ticking.

⟡ CHAPTER TWENTY-TWO

> Many of the "estates" up along Outpost Drive belonged to people who conceived of themselves as homesteaders who happened to have six-figure incomes. . . .
>
> Randall Sullivan, *The Price of Experience*

10:33 A.M. Just a stone's throw from the *other* bastion of southern California preppy WASP elitism, Oxford Academy had hosted the sons of LA's finest for a century.

Sweetheart guided the Mercedes off Mulholland onto Coldwater, and the shape of the landscape shifted markedly, as if the groomed trees, the acres of manicured lawns, the gardens—exotic even by LA's standards—

belonged to another, more civilized stratum of the urban ecosystem.

When he turned again onto a long, winding drive shaded by jacaranda, gnarled olive trees, and scarlet flame trees, Sylvia gazed out the open window, absorbing a retinal montage of wild color splashed against turquoise sky.

Here, they had risen above the layer of smog blanketing the Valley and nuzzling the flanks of the Santa Monica Mountains.

Here (one could easily come to believe) life for the chosen few was elevated to an entirely new and splendid level of entitlement.

They passed under an arched gate where a life-sized stone statue seemed to note their progress with fierce disapproval.

"Plutus makes an appropriate guardian for Oxford Academy," Sweetheart commented dryly.

"Wasn't he the Greek god of wealth?" Sylvia asked.

"He was Demeter's son. He was also the challenger in Dante Alighieri's fourth circle of hell, which was reserved especially for the greedy."

"Terrific."

"Lambs to the slaughter?" Sweetheart finished.

The road continued for more than a mile, past an unmanned security station, past a cluster of single-story buildings, past several discreet student parking areas filled with showcase automobiles: Corvettes, Porsches, Rollses, Bentleys.

Neither Sylvia nor Sweetheart spoke as the Mercedes crept another hundred feet to come to a standstill in front of a Spanish-style administration building. Two willow trees framed the sloping red-tiled roof. A gleaming path led from the parking lot to the building. Date palms flanked the walkway. Clusters of hot orange ginger blossomed around each whitewashed tree trunk. Cruising his domain—three acres of lawn—a small man in safari gear, respiratory mask, and goggles straddled a sleek mower, leaving behind the faint scent of gasoline and a trail of perfectly cut quarter-inch blades of grass.

Sweetheart made no move.

Sylvia glanced at him sideways as she climbed out of the Mercedes. She leaned against warm steel. "You ran a profile on me?"

"Mmm." The low vibrato was affirmative. He opened his door slowly, stepping out as a group of students, all male, all white, all dressed in suits and ties according to dress code, approached. Two of the younger boys glanced surreptitiously at Sylvia; one stumbled, the other punched him lightly.

After the group had passed, Sylvia said, "I'm wondering if I should feel insulted, or violated. Oh, hell, why not both?" She stooped to collect a long, dark seed pod from the manicured grass. "When did you decide you needed to treat me as one of your subjects?"

"When you agreed to participate in the evaluation of Dantes." Sweetheart didn't look at her, but his voice held impatience. "I make it my business to know everyone in the world of terrorism. More important, I need to know who I'm working with, whether I can trust them under pressure."

"What's the verdict?"

"You're here.

"Fair is fair," she said slowly. "When do I see *your* profile? Because you know what? I need to know who I'm working with, too."

He had a way of *looking*—more tactile than visual—that felt invasive.

She turned her head away. "Did you guess Dantes would connect with me?"

"Leo Carreras guessed for me. He's a very intelligent psychiatrist, a good member of the team. I respect his judgment."

Sweetheart held out a hand for the seed pod; his fingers closed around the mahogany-toned bud. "But it's gone much further than anyone could have foreseen, Dr. Strange. You've been chosen to serve as Dantes' confessor. M won't like that."

"No," she agreed softly. For a moment her eyelids hooded the energy contained in her dark golden irises. Her head dipped, her mouth relaxed. She was traveling to other worlds, her thoughts caught in the past.

Then—blink, blink—she was back, looking directly at Sweetheart.

She stepped away from the Mercedes. "Master Healey should be expecting us right about now. I told him we'd make it by eleven thirty."

Sweetheart pointed to a neatly painted sign set a few feet above the grass: *Davis Avery Gymnasium*. An arrow directed pedestrians toward a large white structure about a quarter mile in the distance.

Sylvia started forward, but she swung around when Sweetheart made no move to follow. "Waiting for an invitation?"

"Oh, I'm perfectly happy to accompany you while you talk to the former headmaster." His smile was cold. "Or I could stay right here in case M decides to drop by."

Her eyes widened. "Doesn't this car have an alarm system?"

"A very sensitive system. In fact, it's designed to detonate IEDs within a range of thirty to fifty—"

"*Stay*."

* * *

11:26 A.M. Avery Gymnasium was as humid as a hot-house.

The two boys locked in physical combat in the center of the wrestling mats were sweating heavily. Master Healey Sr., with his whistle and his gray workout suit, looked just as overheated as the boys.

"Don't let Underwood up, Findlay—don't let him up!" A strapping, big-boned man, Healey was pacing the mats, watching his fighters.

Just when Sylvia had decided he was going to ignore her presence, he signaled for her to approach. "You're the one who called about John?"

"I'm Dr. Strange."

"Why talk to me?"

"I thought you could answer that question. Dantes sent me to see the *master*." She squared her shoulders, demanding the man's attention. "Have you followed his career?"

"You mean the Calbomber's career?" Healey grunted. "I've spent too many years with Milton and Dante not to believe arrogance and hubris are real sins. John was the brightest student I've ever encountered. He was a star athlete, a golden boy—he was also egotistical and self-righteous. He still is."

Suddenly changing focus, he barked with surprising strength, "Findlay, what did I tell you, damn it! You should be able to take Underwood down in fifteen seconds!"

Sylvia watched the struggle, a primitive face-off based on strength, aggression, cunning, and heart. Underwood was being held down by Findlay, who was at least fifteen pounds heavier. Their raspy labored breath echoed almost painfully in the cavernous room.

Master Healey took four strides along the edge of the mat; he was watching his fighters, but addressing Sylvia. He said, "Dantes overestimates his strength. Something a warrior should never do."

"He said you could tell me about *Karen*. Was she a teacher?"

"*Charon* guards the river Acheron in hell." Healey clapped his hands together. "Pin him! Force his shoulder down to the ground!" He stopped moving abruptly. "What else did Dantes say?"

"*Relentless thoughts—b-k-nine*," she blurted out, thinking of the message from M. "Does that mean anything to you?"

He was quiet for several moments. "How current is your Milton?"

"*Paradise Lost*. High school." Sylvia blinked at the blatant condescension. "Refresh me."

"My students knew the great books, I saw to that." By now his skin had turned an alarming shade of pink. Ignoring the boys, he stopped directly in front of her, his face inches from hers. In round vowels, affecting a light Germanic accent, he intoned, "'For only in destroying I find ease/To my relentless thoughts.'"

His eyes disappeared behind wrinkled lids. "Book *nine* of John Milton's *Paradise Lost*." His chin jutted out as he glared. "As spoken by Satan."

Healey returned his attention to the boys on the mat. "Don't let him step out, Findlay. Don't let him get his other arm free!"

As if on command, Underwood suddenly slid his arm free of the larger boy's grasp and jumped several feet out of the action. He looked toward Healey for approval.

Healey bellowed, "You just gave away two points, Findlay. You just let a guy, a peanut half your size, get away from you, you effing simpleton."

Switching gears, the former headmaster dropped his voice so that it had an edge of intimacy. "John Milton set out to justify a Puritan God who was less than tolerant. In my mind, in the mind of many other scholars, he failed. But Milton succeeded in creating one of the consummate tragic figures in Western literature, the fallen hero."

"Satan."

"A painfully human Satan." Healey glanced over to the mat.

"Why did John Dantes send me to find you, Master Healey?"

"Why don't you ask him?"

"Was there another student?" Sylvia pressed, fishing for connections, for anything that might lead to M. "Someone he was involved with? A teacher?"

Healey kept his back to Sylvia, his focus on his wrestlers. Finally, Sylvia said, "Perhaps Dantes meant another *master*." She covered the twenty feet to the double doors. Her palm touched wood—

"I can tell you who played the unforgiving God to the fallen hero!" Healey called out.

She stopped.

Shoving the whistle in his mouth, Healey blew a sharp command. Findlay, the larger wrestler, now hovered over the smaller. The boys' bodies contracted, their faces grew tight, and their skin began to redden. Round two had begun.

Slowly, Sylvia retraced her steps.

"There was a student," Healey said, ushering her away from the mats. His mouth pursed, as if he'd eaten something sour. He kept his voice low. "Simon Mole. The boys had some bond. I tried to discourage it. It wasn't . . . healthy."

"Was it a homosexual?"

"God, no." A look of disgust crossed Healey's face. "More like hero worship; Simon was always acting the sycophant." Healey frowned. "I spoke to John about the fact this friendship was . . . undesirable. Especially for the school's only scholarship student."

"How did Dantes respond?"

"He ignored my advice." Healey looked as angry as if the episode had occurred yesterday, instead of two decades earlier. "For the honors program, they completed their senior dissertations as a dialogue. Dantes wrote a primitive draft of his *Inferno*—many years later, of course, that became his Ph.D. thesis as well as a best-seller."

"And Simon Mole?"

"Simon responded with a Miltonian treatise: *Mole's Lost Paradise*. It was a campus joke; the other students nicknamed it *Mole's Manifesto*. It was adolescent rivalry at best."

"Did you—"

"You know what to do!" Healey barked toward the center of the room, where the boys were locked in fierce and silent struggle. "So *do* it!"

His cold and cloudy blue eyes refocused on Sylvia. "Just inside the gates of hell, Dante and Virgil see a raging demon rowing across the river, where souls of the damned wait for passage. The demon is Charon, the ferryman. But Charon recognizes that Dante is still alive, and he refuses to let him cross."

"Charon won't take Dantes?"

Master Healey smiled meanly. "Don't you mean *Dante Alighieri*?" Watching her confusion, he mocked her. "But you're right . . . it is *John Dantes'* journey you and I are concerned with. Don't forget the original *Inferno* was an autobiographical work meant to purge Alighieri's own demons."

Sylvia took a deep breath; she found herself staring at the two young wrestlers. "Do you know if the boys maintained contact after they left Oxford?"

"Simon turned down *Yale* to go to UCLA, to be with his hero."

"They were at UCLA together? Did the FBI see the manifesto when they were building the case against Dantes? Did they follow up on Simon Mole?"

"There was no reason to follow up." Healey shook his head. "Before completing his first year at UCLA, Simon Mole died."

Sylvia had covered half the distance to Sweetheart and the Mercedes when she stopped in the middle of the path. She was thinking about a demon, an angry boatman from hell who refused passage to a pilgrim who wasn't really dead. Dantes had sent her to find out about Simon Mole; was Mole the impostor in the land of the dead?

If so, was Simon Mole living as M?

CHAPTER TWENTY-THREE

A whole history remains to be written of spaces—
which would at the same time be the history of powers (both these terms in the plural)—from the great
strategies of geopolitics to the little tactics of the
habitat.

Michel Foucault, *The Eye of Power*

12:19 P.M. Sweetheart guided the convertible to a stop under Plutus' arch. "So much for the fourth circle," he said quietly.

As the Greek god of wealth glared down on a high-tech and highly secure exchange of information unimaginable in his golden age, Luke's voice emerged from the speaker-phone.

He said, "The *Times* morgue has it—" The speaker went dead for a moment, then he was back. "Uh . . . sorry . . . I'm here, I'm scanning. It was a fire—a gas explosion—and it incinerated the family home."

He took an audible breath. "Give me five minutes, I'll put all this in the usual directory. You can—"

"Just give me vitals," Sweetheart said, cutting him off. "We'll do the FTP later."

"It's a Valley Vista Drive address—less than three miles from where you are. April second *Los Angeles Times*—gas line explosion—emergency medical—" He whistled through his teeth. "Okay, okay, his sister, Laura Mole, sixteen, DOA. Simon Mole, nineteen, critical—"

He coughed, paused again, the clicking of computer keys audible. "Two days later, the *Times* ran a short piece—the parents were political fund-raisers—Republicans for Reagan—traveling when the accident occurred. Simon downgraded to serious condition, but he lost an eye—hold on—*Times* again, May twenty-eighth, the explosion ruled accidental by the LA fire and arson unit; opinion affirmed by the utility company and insurance investigations."

"Accidents happen," Sweetheart commented dryly.

A leaf fell from a massive oak and settled on the windshield directly in front of Sylvia. Her laptop rested on her thighs, ready to boot up. She said, "What's the follow-up on Simon?"

"I've got obituaries," Luke said. "Laura Diane Mole—a student at Holyoke." His voice faded as he scanned through data. "No obit for Simon—hold on—*bingo*—but it's almost two years *later*. Simon Eton Mole, both his parents, and thirteen other passengers killed in a train accident in

Milan—sabotage suspected." He blew air between his teeth. "Unlucky kid."

"Go ahead with a kitchen-sink search on our Mole."

"And Luke," Sylvia said, leaning forward slightly. "Haul ass."

She knew that the broad-based search file should eventually include school evaluations, psychological reports, academic records, family background, and credit reports—better yet, gossip and innuendo—both accident reports, medical and pathology sheets, and a death certificate. In short, any possible stat that could be tabulated on this particular human subject, dead or alive, kit and caboodle. All information would be fed into MOSAIK to become part of the intensive and complex process of data-based profiling.

"How's this for a fast ass," Luke said with an audible grin. "I nabbed the assessor's file." He recited the physical address, then added: "The property was never sold; it's in trust—a legal firm in the UK."

"Keep us current," Sweetheart ordered, ready to disconnect. "We'll be back by two—"

"No, you won't," Gretchen's disembodied voice interrupted. "Messages: Dr. Carreras called regarding some evaluations of Dantes at UCLA. If you can make it by one thirty, Carreras will meet you and Dr. Strange at the Bay View on PCH."

"We can make it," Sweetheart confirmed, with a quick glance at Sylvia.

She shrugged. What evaluations had Leo managed to dig up? Why hadn't she seen them before? She wanted to get her hands on them ASAP.

Nodding, she barely registered Gretchen finishing a list of international callers: " . . . and Special Agent Purcell, who said she'll contact you at oh four-thirty hours."

Gretchen hesitated a fraction of a second. "Professor? Your niece called. Molly needs to meet with you—"

But Sweetheart disconnected before she could finish the message.

12:29 P.M. Looking more surly than Plutus, Sweetheart guided the Mercedes from the academy grounds onto Coldwater Canyon Road. At the intersection with Mulholland Drive, he braked, heading toward Vista Valley Drive.

Settled deep in leather upholstery, Sylvia kept her eyes carefully on the roadside scenery, the visually eclectic progression of homes lining this stretch of Mulholland Drive. The side streets were named for artists—Picasso Way, Dali Drive. And indeed, the urban view from the ridge made her think of paintings, the pastel dreams of Monet, the primary nightmares of Brueghel.

She felt her mood spiraling, but she kept silent while she organized her thoughts; she knew stress, exhaustion, and fear could push her past the point of control. Professional boundaries blurred under these circumstances.

Still, she'd been shocked by Sweetheart's crude reaction to mention of his niece.

The road narrowed where Sweetheart guided the convertible around a tight corner, cutting close to the steep drop-off from Mulholland into the San Fernando Valley.

"What?" he asked, finally. "You keep looking at me."

"No, I don't." She fingered her bracelet. "I've made it a point *not* to look at you." After a moment's silence, she said, "It really bothered me the way you reacted to Molly Redding's name."

"That's none of your business."

"Wrong." She snapped down the cover on her laptop. "An hour ago you told me you ran a profile on me. Why? So you'd know who you're dealing with—and more important, whether you could trust me under pressure."

"If you've got trust issues, Dr. Strange, I suggest you deal with them."

"Fine and fuck you." She stared at him, fighting to regain control over her emotions—

The words slipped out: "When we get back to your house, I'll run it through MOSAIK: what's the skinny on Sweetheart's screwed-up relationship with his niece?"

She was sorry as soon as she said it.

But Sweetheart didn't give her time to apologize. He shifted into third gear, his foot riding the gas pedal.

Sylvia was aware of the narrow winding road and the speedometer needle, trembling just above fifty miles per hour—then fifty-five—sixty.

She said, "I'll apologize if you slow down."

He just scowled, mouth set, as the Mercedes picked up speed. Warm wind kicked up dust, spinning tires spit gravel. Trees and shrubs blurred into a tapestry of watery color. The needle on the speedometer jerked upward in small but steady increments.

"Slow down."

He ignored her.

"Slow. Down."

But he didn't, and the greenery melted into one continuous soft hedge bordering the roadside. The verge of Mulholland Road seemed to undulate beneath the Mercedes' tires. She counted to five.

"Pull the fuck over, I'll *fucking* walk!"

He didn't look at her, but his foot eased off the accelerator. The car coasted for a quarter mile, rolling to a stop near a tall stand of eucalyptus. Dust swirled around them, settling reluctantly. With the engine silenced, the cicadas swelled to song. Sylvia sat stiffly.

"You want to talk about it?" she asked finally.

"I don't need a shrink." He snapped the visor up. "There's nothing mysterious about compensatory attachment objects, affiliatory readjustments." His speech was flat and mechanical; he tipped his head every few beats, physically marking criteria off some internalized master list. "These are life's unpleasant but mundane stressors."

"Stop." Sylvia took a deep breath, waiting several seconds before she was able to continue. "Don't call Jason Redding's death *mundane*."

When Sweetheart spoke again, he sounded diminished, worn down like a stone in the tidal zone. "My niece was never stable; she's been troubled all her life; but Jason was bright and gifted. When he died—" His voice broke.

Sylvia closed her eyes; Sweetheart's pain was an invisible presence; it took up space. She felt cornered, she felt crowded.

He tried again: "I never approved of his mother's lifestyle. She is an addict. I paid for treatment, once, twice . . . the statistics on rehab are negatively skewed . . ." He let go of his breath with a sigh. "I did the only logical thing—I distanced myself."

He sat immobile, a palpable tension emanating from his stillness. "Jason no longer exists—neither does his mother."

Sylvia couldn't take her eyes from his face; the lack of expression was more disconcerting than any possible affect.

"I need a focus for my anger," he said, returning her gaze blankly. "I chose John Dantes because he murdered Jason. It's very simple psychology—from the greatest book: an eye for an eye."

He pushed open the car door and climbed out. "I'll see that Dantes goes to hell."

Numbly, Sylvia watched him walk toward the trees and the embankment. He stood silently for long seconds. Then, just when she expected him to return to the car, he stepped off the edge of the road.

She didn't move; she wasn't ready to face him yet. In her years as a psychologist, she'd come across psychopathological attachment countless times—she knew its danger. But it was rare to encounter this level of obsessive pathology in one of the *good guys*—a man she might have to count on to save lives.

She caught up with Sweetheart at the edge of a chain-link fence and the dead, leaf-filled swimming pool that lay beyond. Carefully, as if she might be scalded, she laid a hand on his arm. Beneath the cotton shirtsleeve, his flesh felt pliable and very human.

For a moment, he didn't move; then he pointed down the slope. "That must've been a hell of an explosion."

Measured by the visible foundation, Simon Mole's home had been large, perhaps five-thousand-plus square feet. California Spanish style from the look of the remaining walls, the skeletal fireplaces, and crumbling stucco. A graceful arch still marked the western boundary. Just beyond, wild roses, fruit, bougainvillea, azalea, ice plant—the lushes of this Mediterranean subclimate grew jungle thick.

They walked the perimeter, avoiding bramble growth, wild azaleas, ginger, bird-of-paradise: nature left to take back her own, southern California style. Visible within the foundation of the main living area, a deep crater had further excavated what had already been a basement. Sylvia stepped over the low wall and moved carefully toward the crater; from here she seemed to be staring down into the mouth of a giant burrow. She set her hands on her hips.

"Natural gas blows the hell out of exterior structures," Sweetheart said. "It pops the roof, explodes the walls."

"Since when does it leave a ten-by-fifteen-foot crater?" Sylvia asked.

He moved to her side—they were shoulder to shoulder on the spongy terrain. He said, "The family had money, they were visible, and banking on political futures."

"They would object to an investigation," Sylvia said. "Especially one that would reveal the fact their son was playing with explosives."

"Explosives that blew this hole in the earth and killed their only daughter," Sweetheart said softly. "It's plausible."

Sylvia took one more step toward the crater. Over the years, branches, leaves, and trash had gathered in the deep hole. A gleam of light caught her eye. She moved to the edge, identified the lip of a large corrugated pipe, twisted, torn, and penetrating earth and broken concrete. For an instant, she felt herself sway, unsteady, off balance. Water dripped from the rough metal—a rhythmically hypnotic sound. Part of the city's infrastructure . . . another pipe leading deep underground.

For only in destroying I find ease/To my relentless thoughts.

Abruptly, she cried out as earth gave way and she dropped toward the bottom of the filthy crater. Pain streaked through her muscles, her shoulder burned where her arm was stretched back and up. Sweetheart had caught her, heaved her onto solid ground—all one neat movement. Sylvia stumbled away from the hole.

"Jesus," she murmured when she'd caught her breath. *"Thank you."*

He nodded, remaining silent.

For several minutes they stood at the edge of the lot where the land fell away to blend with the home-studded hillside, the canyons, and the distant—and very vulnerable—city.

Finally, Sylvia said, "Dantes' guilt is one issue; *yours* is another. You're not responsible for Jason's death."

Sweetheart swung his head round to stare at her now.

His eyes, the color of a storm sky, were accusing. But their focus was internal. The professor—for all his intellect and analytic skill—was a man stricken and turned inside out by grief and rage.

A dangerously potent combination—especially under the circumstances.

Sylvia took one more breath, gathering courage as she stepped off the edge of an invisible psychic cliff. "I believe it's possible that Dantes has chosen psychological blindness—perhaps he truly doesn't possess the ego strength to *see* the truth.

"But you, Sweetheart . . . you can't afford *not* to see. Don't confuse revenge with justice. Time is running out."

5th Circle . . .

Two Damned Souls

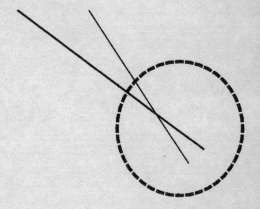

CHAPTER TWENTY-FOUR

Each man is born possessing the map to the Holy
Land, a territory of the body and the soul to call his
own. But oh so quickly heaven turns to hell. I too have
loved and lost.

    Mole's Manifesto

1:01 P.M.   The bomb is set to detonate at 1:18:30.

M's truck is idling in the shade of an old eucalyptus. He
tears the sanitary paper wrapping from the tip of his straw,
and he sips very cold cola. The radio plays oldies.

All morning, he has tagged along with Sweetheart and
Strange.

Now he has managed to get ahead of them for a few
minutes.

Obviously, they have no idea they are carrying death
with them in the green Mercedes. After their detour to
Valley Vista Drive, Sweetheart went over his baby with
great care; he found no IEDs attached like barnacles; no
one had tampered with gas tank or hood; nothing had triggered the silent alarm.

But the truth is, M has been ahead of them since the
beginning.

They carry death because Dr. Strange brought it with

her—from the trunk of her rented Lincoln to the house on
Selma, to the armored Mercedes.

M gazes out at the two-lane road for a sign of the green
sedan. Nothing yet.

He spends more time surveying the surroundings. The
hill behind him and the canyon across the road both wear
the scars of recent wildfires. Each burning season, the Santa
Ana winds catch sparks in the California desert, and then
they whip those flames into a molecular frenzy until earth's
very skin is burned away and whatever is left is scorched
and blackened.

M is grateful for the shade. He has inhabited places in
the world where the only relief from the sun is a man's
own shadow; and he has seen grown men—skin blistered,
eyes singed, tongues swollen and black—leaping like joy-
ful toddlers, arms stretched wide, legs hopping as they
chase their own shadows across endless oceans of sand. He
has been among those whose job it is to bury such fools.
Wielding rope and shovel while the sun and the mercury
dance skyward, he has hurled sand over withered bodies,
he has sent souls from this world with curses instead of
prayers.

It is reason that bursts into flames, it is sanity that burns
hottest, and it is the ember of faith that dies last.

Oh yes, it is faith that prolongs the torment and suffering of men.

He folds back the wax paper from his sandwich, and he
carefully removes a thin slice of dill pickle. From his parking place, he has a view of traffic as it traverses the canyon.
For at least five hundred yards each vehicle is in full view,
even spotlighted by dappled sun.

M waits for his inquisitors, taking advantage of this
momentary lull by enjoying a shady lunch hour. This has

also given him time to meditate—on life, on death, past and future. On the imminent future of the man and woman who pursue him.

Sweetheart and Strange. They sound like a vaudeville team. He smiles.

But his smile fades.

They are not so funny after all, he thinks to himself as the green Mercedes crests a small rise to emerge into plain view.

Dantes has grown much too involved with the woman. He is playing with fire.

And Sweetheart. . . .

After all, the fifth circle is reserved for the angry, the wrathful, the sullen.

He turns the key in the ignition. He fastens his seat belt. He adjusts the rearview mirror, even checks his teeth for remnants of food.

The last of his sandwich rests beside him on the seat of his truck. Quickly, neatly, he collects the scraps of lettuce, ham, and bread and the plastic paper wrap, and he deposits it all into a trash bag.

As he releases the brake and allows the truck to roll forward, gauging his entrance into traffic, he checks to make sure his cell phone is handy.

Timing is everything.

CHAPTER TWENTY-FIVE

Accelerating Metal with Explosives: This method is used to predict the velocity to which explosives can accelerate materials placed in contact with them.

Paul W. Cooper and Stanley R. Kurowski, *Technology of Explosives*

1:03 P.M. To quiet the chaos of his mind, Sweetheart kept his eyes on the tumbling view of the canyon as the Mercedes navigated the twists and turns of Topanga. The environment of dense foliage, thick underbrush, and tall tree canopy represented a simple system compared to the complexities of human interaction.

Sylvia seemed content to focus on scenery, too.

Sweetheart took advantage of the mutual silence to let go of his previous mood. Their exchange at the ruins of Simon Mole's old residence had bothered him much more than he liked to admit. He didn't want to think about Jason. Or Molly. He shook off images that threatened to disturb his focus. He concentrated on the mechanics of driving.

The Mercedes was in its element, gliding along, oblivious to the steep drop-offs, the ragged corners, the rock slides of Topanga. For miles, traffic was surprisingly light; they shared the road with a few bikers, assorted commuters, a horse trailer or two. Until they reached the village. As they passed the market, the secondhand store, the restaurant and realty offices, vehicles lined up and the cruising speed slowed to fifteen miles per hour. At this pace it would be *tomorrow* before they reached the coast.

Two miles outside the village, the Mercedes doubled speed again, hitting thirty, then forty. Still, they were a good ten minutes from the junction of Topanga Canyon Boulevard, Pacific Coast Highway, and the restaurant.

1:14 P.M. Sweetheart watched as Sylvia riffled in her briefcase.

He reached across, placing his cell phone in her lap. "Use mine."

She punched in a number—Sweetheart thought it must belong to Leo Carreras—then she hugged the handset to her ear. After thirty seconds, she swore under her breath. "His voice mail picked up."

"In four minutes we'll be at the restaurant—you can talk to Leo in person."

"Why didn't he make it easy and meet us at his house?"

"I'm assuming he had business out this way; a consultation." He glanced at her. "This isn't exactly a major detour."

Sylvia nodded, but Sweetheart saw her jam her hands between her thighs. A sudden awareness, he guessed, that she'd been gnawing on her fingernails for the last five miles. Better fingernails than pills or cigarettes, he thought.

With a big sigh, she closed her eyes and leaned back in the seat. She didn't open them again until Sweetheart slowed around a curve. They were less than a mile from the coastal highway and the Pacific Ocean. Here, small businesses had worked their way up the canyon, and hodge-podge signs and billboards advertised surfboards, flowers, hamburgers, palm readings.

Hot weather had only intensified the usual seaside crowds.

He shifted into second gear, anticipating the intersection, now three quarters of a mile away.

Sylvia jumped in her seat as the cell phone bleated.

When she offered Sweetheart the phone, he barked: "Yes, Luke?"

"Professor?" Something was wrong—Luke's voice was thin and tense. "*He's* on the other line—he says it's an emergency."

"Turn on the recorder, then put him through," Sweetheart said, his voice flat with urgency. He heard several clicks as Luke made the connections; then a new voice addressed him.

"Furious Phlegyas—you're just in time for a lesson in the fifth circle. We both know who falls so low . . ."

"Souls ruled by anger."

"Dantes said you were good, Professor."

"Get to the point."

"Stay away from the temple of the sun god."

"Apollo." Sweetheart was concentrating on aural information—instantly processing M's verbal content, tone and phrasing, references. At the same time, he was scanning traffic, pedestrians, the intersection ahead.

"Who's burning the temple?" Sweetheart caught sight of a low sedan with tinted windows. Then a van parked in the lot of the market across the street caught his eye. He said, "Simon? Is that—"

"Shut up and listen," M ordered. "Your baby is carrying a special package—and she's set to blow in . . . one minute, two seconds."

"What do you—"

"Make that one minute exactly."

Click. Disconnection.

Sweetheart saw his fear mirrored in Sylvia's dark eyes.

"Start timing forty-five seconds," he ordered. "We've got a bomb."

"Oh, shit." But she was already focusing on her watch.

"Give me every five—out loud," he said through gritted teeth.

"*Forty-five.*"

"What did you bring with you in the car?"

"My briefcase—my phone—*forty* seconds—my laptop—"

Sweetheart saw the laminated plastic case beneath Sylvia's feet. "It's in the laptop."

Sylvia pulled back abruptly, and her fingers dug into leather—but she didn't lose focus. "*Thirty-five* seconds," she said. "Can we throw it—"

She broke off, registering cars, pedestrians, the highway traffic signal—now just a hundred feet ahead—turning yellow. "*Thirty!*"

"Hold on!" Sweetheart bellowed, bearing down simultaneously on the horn and the accelerator.

The Mercedes shot forward, weaving past a FedEx truck, a yellow school bus, and an open Jeep filled with teenagers, then dodging a dozen oncoming motorcycles. He barely registered the surprise on the faces of the middle-aged bikers.

"*Twenty-five seconds,*" Sylvia hissed.

"Give me your briefcase!"

She shoved the leather case into his lap.

The Bay View Restaurant, just ahead, was perched on fortified bedrock and pilings, overlooking the Pacific Ocean.

Due to constant shoring of an eroding coast, the parking lot (where it met the cliff edge) was rimmed with a series of five-foot-high metal posts, each embedded in a roughly molded concrete base; orange hazard tape strung from pole to pole was all that alerted drivers of danger—a headfirst dive onto the rocky tidal zone twenty feet below the cliff.

Thank God it was tape instead of the usual seven-foot-high chain-link fence.

Sweetheart downshifted, scanning the area; he saw a young mother pushing a baby in an elaborate stroller. She was midway across the lot.

He prayed the Mercedes had enough metal to contain most of the blast.

"*Twenty* seconds—"

—and a red light.

But Sweetheart kept going—horn blaring as he plowed the Mercedes through the busy intersection. Oncoming cars skidded left and right. A massive tour bus went into a long, harrowing skid across asphalt. The Mercedes scraped bumpers before it bounced over the curb into the crowded parking lot of the restaurant.

They were headed straight for the cliff.

Now he braked, shouting, "Get ready to jump!" From the corner of his eye, he saw Leo Carreras standing near the door of the restaurant.

"*Ten* seconds!"

"Do it, now, Sylvia! Jump!"

She pushed open the door, and he shoved her out with his right arm. He saw a blur of color as she hit the ground.

Just ahead, a narrow parking space with a blue-and-white handicapped insignia would give him access to the ocean—if the Mercedes didn't blow first.

He pushed open the driver-side door.

Please don't detonate—

He jammed Sylvia's briefcase onto the accelerator just as he thrust himself from the vehicle. Pain shot through his body as he collided with earth.

The linen sleeve of his jacket caught on metal as the Mercedes shot forward like a two-ton bullet.

Sweetheart's feet left the ground, his body torqued, and he was dragged ten feet to the edge of the cliff.

When he was inches from air—inches from jagged tidal rocks and roiling ocean waves—the fabric of his suit gave way like a zipper.

The Mercedes lunged, plunging off the side of the cliff in a perfect suicide dive, but Sweetheart, suddenly free of forward thrust, seemed to float in midair.

Abruptly, he fell to the ground, where gravel bit into his skin as his body came to rest halfway off the precipice. He grabbed for a handhold, catching a bit of exposed root, a few strands of yucca.

He heard the booming explosion of the bomb as it drowned out the softer roar of Pacific breakers. He saw flames, and shooting stars.

His Mercedes crumpled, shattered into fiery bits and pieces.

He thought it like a prayer: *Nokotta. You're still in the match.*

You're still alive.

CHAPTER TWENTY-SIX

The disagreements that have arisen over the meaning, significance, and consequences of anarchy—especially with respect to the extent to which the absence of central authority hinders the prospects of inter-state cooperation—is at the center of the latest academic controversy between neorealism and neoliberalism.

Brian C. Schmidt, *The Political Discourse of Anarchy*

M watches as the car explodes into a vortex of mutating metal, glass, plastic, until it is broken down to its basic, primary *car* elements.

He shifts into first gear, merging carefully with southbound traffic on the Pacific Coast Highway.

Time to go. The forces of good will arrive any minute. And he has a long drive ahead of him—and an important stop to make, a crucial job to do—before he can return to the apartment in San Pedro.

He doesn't look back at the scene of most recent destruction. No need to linger. It is nothing special.

His inquisitors won't miss him; they are busy, and it's been a very big day.

They have been searching for truth. Along the way, they have discovered a boy, a house, a school.

In his mind, the boy who lived in that house—the young man who went to Oxford and UCLA, and who died in Europe—was never meant to survive. From the moment of his birth, from the first bawling complaint, that boy had been unfit, a runt earmarked for the drowning sack.

Those without the fiercest will, the *weak*, are culled; that is the brutal truth of the world's order, that is the world of Darwin's hierarchy of evolution, which itself evolved from Christian theology sprung from the deserts of Negev and Kara Kum, inscribed by feverish monks dodging plague and pestilence, embellished by the poetics of Dante and Milton. *That, ladies and gentlemen, is God's fucking truth.*

Dead boy, Simon. Stupid boy who worshiped blindly.

A one-eyed, one-armed fool who lost his way in a world where he never belonged. He was put out of his misery many years ago.

M is another animal altogether. His flesh is encased in

chitin. He was born a beast. One who vicariously tasted innocence, found it to his liking, and feasted. His sins are too many to mention, but don't imagine he fears Dante's hell.

The only thing he truly fears is *nothing*. Emptiness. The void of his existence.

What keeps nonexistence at bay? *The anticipation of revenge.*

He chides himself softly. All these archaic games, this schoolboy bluster, *enough*.

Tonight he has work to do close to home.

Last-minute touches for his pièce de résistance have begun.

Tomorrow he will take the first step down to the sixth circle of hell.

Two more lives his soul to take.

CHAPTER TWENTY-SEVEN

But whom thou hatest, I hate, and can put on
Thy terrors, as I put thy mildness on,
Image of thee in all things; and shall soon,
Armed with thy might, rid Heaven of these rebelled;
To their prepared ill mansion driven down,
To chains of darkness, and the undying worm.

Milton, *Paradise Lost*

8:27 P.M. Flanked by Purcell, two other federal agents, and an LAPD investigator, Sylvia covered the last ten meters to room B-103 and John Dantes.

I've come to see a man about a bomb.

But this time, there were more shields than civilians.

And Leo Carreras was by her side.

They'd spent the last seven hours dealing with the aftermath of the latest improvised explosive device. That would teach her not to leave her laptop laying around—not even in the locked trunk of a car.

As designed, the Mercedes had contained much of the blast. No one had died. Bruises and abrasions, yes, but no one had been seriously injured. Not even Edmond Sweetheart. But his rage had been fueled.

For that reason, Sylvia was relieved Sweetheart had chosen to monitor this interview with surveillance agents in the room that adjoined B-103. He needed to keep his distance from Dantes. Sylvia wished she could be sure of her ability to contain her own anger.

She came to an abrupt standstill in front of the door.

"Hey, champ," Leo said softly, capturing her attention. "Are you ready for this?"

Purcell and the other investigators drifted away just enough to offer the illusion of privacy.

Sylvia waited one second too long before she responded to Leo's question.

"Because if you're not—" Leo frowned. "Let's not lose our best shot—"

"I'm ready."

But Leo wasn't convinced; he seemed to sense she needed a few moments to calm herself, to prepare. Gesturing for her to follow, he moved a short distance down the hall. "Keep in mind he's still under the influence of the sedative."

"They gave him enough diazepam to take down a wild horse." Her muscles ached. The abrasion on her elbow was beginning to burn.

"Are you planning on using the UCLA psych report?"

"Any objections?" She paced, too keyed up to land in one spot for any length of time.

Leo had already briefed her on the basic contents of the fifteen-year-old psychological evaluation; it dated back to Dantes' first year at UCLA—and a visit to a student health clinic. He'd suffered a series of epileptic seizures. No-brainer diagnosis: epilepsy. Except there was a problem: the electroencephalograms revealed no organic pathology.

Leo's touch brought her back. He began to gently massage her shoulders, speaking in a low voice. "From the description of the presenting problem, Dantes has been through this before—seizures, paralysis, other somatic symptomology—which provides support for a diagnosis of conversion disorder."

"Dantes went to the clinic—he sought treatment—less than six weeks after Simon Mole's house exploded," Sylvia said, lowering her chin to her chest. Her neck muscles were painfully bound. "If it was conversion disorder, what was the stimulus?"

"Guilt?"

"It's possible." She raised her head, nodding. "Dantes felt responsible for the death of a young girl, and the near death of his best friend."

"Maybe he *was* responsible," Leo said.

"It's provocative, but it proves nothing." Sylvia side-stepped away from Leo. It was taking too much effort to keep herself in physical and emotional check. She said, "This could be *faking*—plain and simple." Her voice revealed her frustration.

"You've spent the most time with him," Leo said. "Do you believe it's that clear-cut?"

She dug her hands deep into empty pockets. "No. We're surrounded by smoke and mirrors."

She covered the distance back to the room; through a small mesh observation window, she saw a familiar face just inside B-103: Officer Jones. Beyond Jones, Dantes was stretched on a seclusion bed, his features obscured by shadow.

She backed away, focusing again on Leo. "I should be dead. Today, in that Mercedes, Sweetheart and I *were* dead."

Her fingers worked the threads of her jacket. "But M still wants to play." She pressed her palms to her temples, easing a headache. She was bruised and battered. "Very soon, he'll get tired of the game—tired of cat and mouse. We're left with one alternative: get him—before he gets us."

Leo nodded grimly. "If you need me—"

"I need a cigarette."

"—I'll be right here."

But Sylvia had already turned to Purcell. "Let's do it."

Inside the hospital room, shapes were blunted by shadow.

Officer Jones sat stiffly in a wooden chair, reading by the narrow beam of a Tensor. He looked up from his paperback to give her a nod of recognition. She caught the book's title: *The Green Mile*.

Dantes was in full restraints on the seclusion bed. His face still wore the mask of illness—deep furrows marked his brow and the corners of his mouth; his skin held a gray cast; the stubble on his chin marked a rough beard.

Sylvia approached, walking slowly around the end of the bed until she was even with his shoulders. She kept her distance.

"Dantes?" She took a breath, monitoring herself internally; twice, this man had sent her to a close encounter with death. Her emotions would be useful only if they were under her control. So she'd skip the murderous rage for now, she thought, mustering some humor, trying for balance in a very unbalanced situation.

He tilted his head in her direction; his eyes were open, but his focus was *off*. She knew that he'd been complaining of a limited field of vision; hospital staff had noted that the paralysis in his arm was more pronounced than it had been just fifteen hours ago, before the anticonvulsive drugs had been administered.

And she'd been warned, he'd lost some vocal capacity; instead of his deep baritone, he was communicating in whispers.

If he was acting, he was good.

From the corner of her eye, Sylvia noticed Officer Jones observing her; she was grateful for his familiar presence in the room.

She pulled a chair toward the seclusion bed, allowing the wooden legs to scrape the floor. The noise was grating, but Dantes didn't react.

She positioned the chair so that she and Dantes were head to head. She sat.

This time his eyes found her face. She saw him register her presence, but she couldn't read his reaction. Relief, or disbelief?

"Beatrice," he whispered. "'Will you not aid the one whose love for you raised him high above the crowd?'" As he recited the quotation, his speech was sluggish, and tinged with irony. He smiled. "You came back."

"Are you surprised?"

"Less and less, Dr. Strange." He took a deep breath. "What happened to me?"

"You were medicated—you had a reaction."

With effort he raised his head to examine his body; his gaze traveled carefully from arms to legs, as if he were discovering some stranger in his bed. "I can't feel my right arm."

"Two days ago, at Metro, apparently you had some sort of seizure." She paused, assessing. "Do you remember?"

"I think so."

"Have you had seizures before?"

"Doesn't matter." His expression was impassive, indifferent.

"Have you ever blacked out?"

"No."

"The doctors will run more tests—they'll screen for organic—"

"*No*." His hands became fists. "They're liars. I want to talk about *you*. What happened?"

He read through her silence. "You found M," he whispered. When she didn't respond, he said, "I can't help you unless I have information."

"There was another bomb." She kept very still, struggling for internal control.

Surprise altered his features for an instant before he recovered. "But you weren't the target."

"How do you know?"

"'Do your eyes not see death near him?'" He watched her carefully. "My guess would be Sweetheart."

"Why?" When he didn't answer, Sylvia leaned closer. "Is Sweetheart *your* target—or *Mole's*?"

"You found the master after all." A smile played over Dantes' lips. "How is the sadistic bastard?"

"Healey told me about Simon."

"Obviously." He blinked. "Sweetheart blames me for Jason's death."

"Should he blame Mole?"

"He should blame himself." Dantes closed his eyes.

"Why?" Sylvia leaned down, and her fingers tightened

around his sleeve. The institutional cotton scratched her skin. She said, "It's time for this to end."

She was close enough to see the tiny hairs on his neck. She said, "Dantes—I'm asking you, help me before it's too late."

Dantes turned his face toward hers; his eyes struggled to focus. He nodded, running his tongue over pale lips. "I know—"

There was a crash as the door flew open and Sweetheart burst into the room. Officer Jones dropped his book, lunging forward to catch the intruder; he was knocked off balance by Special Agent Purcell as she darted past him.

Leo Carreras and a federal agent entered on Purcell's heels.

But Sweetheart already had his hands around Dantes' throat. He said, "You arrogant, lying son of a bitch. I'll kill you." His voice was cold. His body was immovable—only his hands strained, fingers digging into Dantes' flesh.

"Back off now!" Purcell ordered.

Sweetheart didn't respond.

Sylvia was close enough to see murder in his eyes. She said, "Let him go."

For thirty seconds, they all stayed frozen in violent tableau.

Then, very slowly, Sweetheart released his grip.

Dantes said nothing. But he smiled like a fighter who'd won a round.

9:55 P.M. Sweetheart left the hospital without a word.

Sylvia waited just outside the front doors of the lobby for Leo Carreras. Purcell kept her company. They stood in silence for several minutes, then Purcell tipped her head, making that familiar birdlike gesture, slipping something from behind one ear. There was a small and sudden burst of flame as she lit up a cigarette. She inhaled, handing it to Sylvia. They shared half the smoke in silence.

"You're not going back to Santa Monica tonight," Purcell said, exhaling smoke.

Sylvia shook her head. "We'll stay at a hotel in west LA."

The agent nodded. "I'll follow you over. Use Dr. Carreras' cards. You have a dog?"

Surprised, Sylvia nodded. "Two."

"What are their names?"

"Rocko and Nikki."

"Cute. Tell them you'll accept calls for Mr. Rocko. I'll check in with you in the morning." Purcell was quiet for several seconds. They could see Leo's Lexus turning the corner at the end of the block. "We've got twenty-four-hour surveillance at Sweetheart's, in case M decides to go another round."

"He'll go four more rounds. There are nine circles in Dante's *Inferno*." Sylvia took the cigarette from Purcell. It was almost down to the butt. Silently, she inhaled the last hit. "You dragged me into this investigation—don't leave me out of the loop."

"Like I said, I'll call you tomorrow when I have news."

"What happens between now and then?"

"Simon Mole," Purcell said. "If he's M, he's been up to something for the past fifteen years. We'll pick up his trail somewhere along the way." She walked with Sylvia to the curb as the Lexus slowed to a stop.

"So MOSAIK's job will be to come up with an empirical match," Sylvia said. "Simon equals M."

"Wrong." Purcell held the door open. "Officially, after this mess with Dantes, Sweetheart's out of the game."

"Unofficially?"

"Watch your back."

* * *

11:43 P.M. Edmond Sweetheart felt his soul evaporate. The warm night air brought whispers of bamboo and wind chimes. The paper shades on the open window rustled gently.

He was at home—sitting lotus on the floor of the library, surrounded by bombs.

A plain white board ran the entire breadth of one wall. Photographs, arranged in six clusters, had been tacked neatly in place. Above each grouping, stenciled black letters filled a half dozen paper signs.

Six titles.

The first reading, HOLLYWOOD FREEWAY.

The second, ANARCHY, LA TIMES.

The third, WATER & POWER.

Fourth, SIERRA SUBDIVISION.

Fifth, OIL SWINDLES.

Sixth, GETTY.

A wormwood table ran the length of the bulletin board. On it were the intricate and detailed models of six explosive devices—representing hours of craftsmanship—each beneath its title.

Sweetheart let his eyes linger on the models.

He saw history and civilization. Each one was a historical statement of some injustice committed against the city, against Los Angeles.

Sweetheart stood slowly, finding center on the soft mat. Air filled his lungs; as he exhaled, he let go, crouching into *shiko*.

Moving to a slow rhythm, he lifted one leg high—held it—then he stomped his foot back into the floor, slapping his hands on his knees as he exhaled; the movements flowed, coming full circle to a crouching squat. Two hundred eighty pounds of muscle, intention, focus. He blocked out all physical pain. He ignored the injured muscles, the strained ligaments.

It began again with the opposite leg. Inhale, lift, hold. Exhale, stomp, slap, crouch. Over and over he repeated the *shiko*. It is the sumo wrestler's most basic exercise.

As he worked, he cleared his mind.

Last thought: *I know what drives a man to destroy—all-consuming hatred; I know because Dantes taught me.*

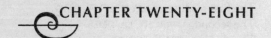

CHAPTER TWENTY-EIGHT

I would give anything to feel pain again. That right was stolen from me. I want it back.

Mole's Manifesto

Thursday—12:13 A.M.   M feels the world accelerating.

Over the next forty-eight hours, his routinely minimal quotient of sleep will drop to mere minutes. Catnaps. That is how he will survive from now until the end.

He is a busy, busy man.

His parrot, Nietzsche, keeps him company. He is below ground in the old shipyards in San Pedro—surrounded by concrete and steel and earth and water. His bunker was once a subterranean storage room in a now derelict factory that dates back to World War II.

It is perfect. The grounds are abandoned. Only a few stray bums come nosing around. Rent is cheap and there's no view.

It is like many other spaces he has known over a lifetime. Dark. Tight. Enclosed. Some he entered voluntarily, others not.

Over the past year, he has spent many nights in this concrete womb. He feels safe here. And productive.

Molly is used to his nocturnal wanderings—"It comes with the job, Angel Face," he says, "and long hours mean more pay, and somewhere down the line a vacation on a perfectly white beach in Tahiti or Belize."

But an entire night away, at this late date, might spook her, might jinx Operation Inferno.

Don't want to do that.

No reason for Angel Face to know he quit the job two months ago. He still leaves for work six days a week.

So he will dutifully return to the stifling apartment, to that shedding cat, and to Molly. In her sleep, she'll find him, wrap her body around his, let her mouth touch his most tender places.

A perk that brings him less and less pleasure.

He sidesteps the corpse at his feet. Through plastic, he can make out the crude details of her face. Just over an hour ago, she was warm, blond, petite, in her twenties. Now she's just a prostitute on ice. He'll move her body tomorrow. She—along with another—will provide the key to the next layer of hell.

Tidying up, M sweeps around the corpse. She has a part to play—a performance of sorts—to be enjoyed by those who believe they are smart.

Nietzsche breaks into the chorus of "My Way."

M hums along.

CHAPTER TWENTY-NINE

Who's the true sinner? Is it the murderer who kills for faith? Or the coward who preaches nonviolence? The nihilist who embraces his barren life with all its horrible emptiness? Or the moralist who finds comfort in righteousness and "belief"?

Anonymous

6:49 A.M. Sylvia sat up abruptly in bed. Bad dream. Underwater, gasping for breath, drowning.

She buried her face in her hands; her cheeks were wet with tears.

Just a bad dream.

She wasn't in New Mexico, and no ocean tsunami had invaded the desert. No current had washed her foster daughter from her arms. She had not dived under the waves to find Molly Redding's bloated body.

Sylvia shuddered. In sleep, she'd confused Molly Redding with Dantes' mother, Bella.

The mother of a murdered child . . . and a mother who had committed suicide and left behind a young son.

Just like Mona Carpenter.

Nightmarish echoes of murder and suicide.

Waking wasn't much better. She was in Los Angeles, at a Hilton in west LA. The day after a narrow escape. Two days since a bomb had killed Detective Church.

Brushing damp hair from her face, she checked the hotel's digital clock. At least she'd slept for eight hours.

She kicked the sheets from her body and made her way

to the bathroom. When she switched on the lights she caught a glimpse of herself in the floor-to-ceiling mirror: wild hair, a wrinkle from the bedding etched along one breast, bruised thigh, painted toenails. She switched the lights off again.

She lingered under a hot shower. While her skin was still damp, she slathered on moisturizer, courtesy of the management. Wrapping herself in the fluffy hotel kimono, feeling half human, she walked back into the room, ready to call Matt and Serena.

Leo was waiting with hot coffee, scones, and orange juice on a silver tray.

"Room service." He smiled, but his eyes were serious. "You look like you got some rest."

"How did you sleep?"

"I didn't," he said, picking the corner off a raisin scone.

She raised her eyebrows. "Did Purcell call?"

"Not yet." Leo opened the blinds, admitting daylight and a view of LA streets.

Sylvia poured herself a cup of coffee to go with breakfast. The orange juice and the pastry calmed her jittery nerves— the caffeine revved her up again.

"I'm not going to sit around waiting for the damn phone to ring," she said, as she plunged the last bite of scone into her coffee. "We've got work to do."

"Somehow I knew you'd say that." Leo nodded, rising from his chair to cross the room. He opened the connecting door that turned their adjoining rooms into a suite, and the click of a computer keyboard was audible.

Sylvia stood, curious, but not surprised to see Luke at work on a laptop in Leo's room.

"We set up about thirty minutes ago," Leo said. "We're tied into MOSAIK's database."

"Nice robe," Luke said, smiling at Sylvia.

Leo picked up a black-and-white striped shopping bag from the bed. "I had them send up a few things in your size. Italian jeans okay?"

"Italian jeans are great," Sylvia said, accepting the package. But her thoughts weren't on fashion. "Where's Sweetheart?"

The two men exchanged a look. "The professor's at home—logged on to MOSAIK—running data batches," Luke said. "He's ignoring the Feds, and he's refusing to give up the search. He left explicit orders not to be disturbed until we get a match on M."

"Fine," Sylvia snapped. "Let's give him one." She picked up a thick stack of pages.

"Everything Gretchen could pull on Simon Mole," Luke said, answering her unspoken query. "Intelligence and aptitude tests, preparatory and college admission applications, letters from teachers and advisers, letters of recommendation, medical reports. . . ."

He gestured with one arm, and the flying fish on his biceps quivered. "Gretchen spent most of last night feeding Simon's text sample—his UCLA application essay—through MOSAIK; she ran a linguistic comparison with the threat communications. She should be just about finished double-checking those results."

He moved his fingers restlessly across the keyboard. "In the meantime, I can search in any direction you want."

Fragments of nightmare imagery took shape in her mind—dead women underwater; murdered children and children abandoned by suicide.

She placed both hands on the table next to the computer and said, "Sweetheart said he wanted intuitive leaps—so let's play wild card. See what you can find on Bella Dantes."

"Dantes' mother?" Luke scratched the top of his head. "You want to get any more specific?"

"Sure. Specifically, I want to know why she killed herself in front of her own child. Call it a *hunch*."

Ignoring their curious stares, she aligned the stack of pages end to end before she carefully divided it, handing Leo his share. She was eager to get at the new information. This was part of *her* data input process—and part of her coping mechanism. *What stress? Who's afraid of the big bad wolf?*

Settled on the cream-colored leather couch, bare feet propped on a glass table, she slipped on her reading glasses and began to study.

Forty-five minutes later—accompanied by the click of Luke's keyboard and the hum of the computer—she and Leo were beginning to glean some sense of the world according to Simon Mole. Chronologically with each page, each report, a profile—a variation on the poor little rich boy—began to take shape. Sylvia scrawled notes on a legal pad. Leo was working his way through another pot of coffee. When they came across items of particular interest, they read aloud.

"It was his kindergarten teacher who had him pegged," Sylvia said dryly, playing with the bangle on her wrist. "*Simon is obviously bright and shows an eagerness to learn, but he is not popular with the other children, on the playground or off. At times, Simon resorts to unpleasant passive-aggressive interactions (and even tantrums!) to get his way. This makes him all the more unpopular, encouraging a vicious cycle. He has managed to make only one or two friends, who seem to respond to his single-minded attentions, although these interactions often turn into rivalries.*"

"As he grew," Leo murmured, "so did his narcissism, his rigid internal schemata, his grandiosity."

Sylvia removed her glasses, running one stem along the page. Sunlight poured through the hotel windows; it bounced off the walls of the room. She spoke softly, to herself—to Leo. "So we've got early childhood experiences defined by paternal puritanism, maternal praise and overprotection . . . desire to maintain that approval. . . . extreme attachment to his younger sister, Laura, and his mother."

"Never bonded with Dad," Leo said.

"But he sure as hell bonded with John Dantes." Sylvia dropped the last report onto plush white carpet. "Do we have the transcript from yesterday's debacle?"

"Dantes?" Luke asked, fingers already signaling new commands across the keyboard. "Give me a minute."

Sylvia stood, moving toward the window. "What did he say about the bombing? *Exact* words."

Luke scrolled, reading.

"*Dantes:* You found M. I can't help you unless I have information.

"*You:* There was another bomb.

"*Dantes:* But you weren't the target.

"*You:* How do you know?

"*Dantes:* 'Do your eyes not see death near him?'"

Luke glanced up from the screen. "That's a reference from the *Inferno*."

He went right back to reading.

"*Dantes:* My guess would be Sweetheart.

"*You:* Why? Is Sweetheart *your* target—or *Mole's*?

"*Dantes:* You found the master after all. How is the sadistic bastard?

"*You:* Healey told me about Simon.

"*Dantes:* Obviously. Sweetheart blames me for Jason's death.

"*You:* Should he blame Mole?

"*Dantes:* He should blame himself."

"*Why?*" Sylvia pushed herself up from the couch, moving restlessly.

"Manipulation," Leo said. "Dantes was going for the closest jugular."

"You think it was diversion?" Sylvia asked. "What if Dantes was on the nose?"

"About?"

Sylvia turned toward Luke. "The Getty bombing—was there ever any evidence that pointed toward Jason Redding as a target?"

"That possibility was certainly considered." Luke shook his head. "But it was ruled out. The school field trip was rescheduled because the teacher was sick. There was no way Dantes could've known about the change."

"What about M?" Sylvia asked. "For all we know he worked at the Getty."

"You're reaching, Sylvia," Leo said. "The Feds were all over that investigation. Anybody at the museum could have found the box, triggered the bomb. Tragically, it happened to be a curious little boy."

"All right," Sylvia said slowly. "Back to Dantes going for the jugular. Why did Sweetheart go berserk? Why is he so close to the edge? What's eating him?"

Luke shook his head warily. "I wouldn't ask him today, if I were you."

"Right. I'll ask his niece. What's Molly Redding's number?"

2:02 P.M.   Beverly Hot Springs was an exotic cave buried deep in Hollywood's seedy heart.

A woman with a pleasant smile admitted Sylvia, leading the way to the wood-finished locker room. The dressing area was empty.

Sylvia left her new clothes in a locker, sliding the key band over her wrist. Draping the thick terry towel over her bare shoulder, she passed through the wooden door. At first she thought she was alone in the baths. In semidarkness steam swirled and settled over a small, free-form swimming pool. Glass doors to private stalls lined one wall.

Then, through the dim light of artificial dusk and mist, Sylvia saw a child.

A ghostly child-woman.

Molly Redding was so delicate she looked prepubescent. Her skin was pale, her hair a dark wispy fringe surrounding her pretty face. She reminded Sylvia of one of Modigliani's nudes: wide eyed; long, slender neck; slight bones; small hips and breasts. She was resting on a towel next to the pool.

But her voice belonged to a woman. It was soft and low. "Sylvia?"

"Thanks for agreeing to see me." Sylvia set her towel down on the warm tiles. She sat easily, sliding her bare legs into warm water that was laced with the scent of minerals. Dark bruises stood out on her knees. "This is one of my favorites places in LA. How do you like it?"

"It's pretty nice." Molly blinked, working her mouth into a small frown. "On the phone, you said you're working for my uncle. I don't really understand why you want to talk to me."

"The work we're doing is—sensitive," Sylvia said. "I think your uncle is under a lot of strain. Maybe you can help me figure out why." In the subdued light, steam beaded on her skin; it ran from her neck and her breasts. A small droplet of water glistened in her belly button; a tiny rivulet disappeared in the dark tuft between her legs.

"What did he tell you about me?" Up close, Molly's expression was serious, her eyes somber.

"Very little," Sylvia answered truthfully. "I know you're estranged."

"You could say that. He stopped returning my calls after Jason."

"But yesterday you tried anyway," Sylvia said.

"It was—I . . ." Molly lay back on the warm stones and closed her eyes. Her ribs were defined by light and shadow; it seemed as if they were all that kept her from disappearing. "It was a spur-of-the-moment thing."

Sylvia lowered her body into the silky mineralized water. Elbows on tile, she rested her head on her arms. The lazy drip of water from the cavelike roof, the hush of their breathing, the faintest strains of violin music were the sounds layered in the steamy air. The silver bangle on her arm bit into her cheek, and she readjusted herself just enough to relax to yet another level. Molly Redding was a bad liar; she was also skittish, and likely to bolt if pushed too far or too fast.

Molly's voice drifted through Sylvia's thoughts. "My uncle and I lost contact long before Jason died."

"Would you mind telling me why?"

"I used to do drugs. At least, that's what he'd say."

"What do you say?" Sylvia asked gently.

Molly sighed. "Have you ever gone crazy?"

"Talking-to-myself crazy, seeing-things-on-the-wall crazy—does that count?"

"Ever wanted to die?"

"I've had my moments." Sylvia studied Molly. "Are you feeling that way now?"

Silently, Molly skimmed her hand across steaming water. She let the liquid dribble through her fingers. Another scoop, and another. "No."

"Are you sure?"

"Did my uncle tell you he was my guardian? My parents

died when I was twelve. But Sweetheart was busy with his terrorists—his *demons*—bin Laden, Ben Black, Abu Mohammed . . ." Molly laughed wearily. "He pretends to be so evolved. Did you know he was born in Hawaii, but he lived in Japan for years? He even studied sumo."

"I didn't know that," Sylvia said. "Does he still—"

"He gave it up to become a *scientist,* so he could measure the world in millimeters or something. Don't let him fool you," Molly said. "I used to be afraid of him, how smart he is; but when it comes to people, he doesn't even understand the basics."

"Maybe he spends too much time with his computers."

"Machines don't ask for love, they don't go crazy or make demands, they don't get strung out on meth, they don't get pregnant."

Molly's face belonged to a guileless child, and her voice was soft. She slid into the water and buoyed herself with gentle strokes. "Do you have children?"

"A foster daughter," Sylvia said. Eyes closed, she found herself absorbing the blue air of the Sangre de Cristo Mountains. Like a marble on a tilted surface, her thoughts kept drifting back to New Mexico. She imagined Serena and her father, Cash Wheeler, doing the simple things of family. At that moment she felt the separation as a physical pain. What would it be like to lose a child forever?

She said, "Serena's eleven."

"Jason's age." Sorrow flooded Molly's face. "You can't hold on to them," she whispered. "No matter how hard you try, how often you check the weather, walk them to school, tuck them into bed. You can't keep them safe."

"No," Sylvia agreed softly.

"I used to think God punished me because I was a bad mother . . . the drugs . . . everything." Molly dipped underwater, returning to the surface to shake water from her head. "But I know that's not true. God is forgiveness."

"Do you blame Sweetheart for Jason's death?"

"No . . ." Molly's voice was barely audible. "Why would I do that?" She shook her head. Then, suddenly, she smiled and a light transformed her features; her face came alive, her eyes took on a glittery spark. "You can tell my uncle I'm healing."

Sylvia was watching the other woman intently—she saw a dangerous edge. This wasn't the slow return to balance after catastrophic grief; this was the manic swing from depression, the hydraulic lift effected by extreme chemistry, natural or otherwise.

"I have a message you can deliver," Molly Redding said, pulling back physically and mentally. "Tell my uncle I'm getting well." She took quick breaths; beneath taut skin her ribs expanded again and again—the rhythm of a desperately wounded creature struggling to maintain a fragile hold on life.

"Tell him I don't need him anymore. I've moved on."

5:21 P.M. Sylvia left the new rental car with the valet, and she entered the lobby of the hotel. It was a busy Thursday afternoon, and a line had formed at the registration desk. She was almost to the elevators when she felt someone grab her arm roughly. She swung around ready to defend herself.

"How dare you talk to my niece without my permission." Sweetheart loomed over her, his face an angry mask, tension emanating from his body like electricity. "What you did was wrong." Abruptly, he released his grip.

"I tried to talk to you," Sylvia said, ignoring the stares of people passing by. "Come up to the room."

"No."

"Look at yourself," Sylvia said sharply. "You're so

invested in the empirical equation, you can't see what's in front of your face. Molly's on the edge. She needs you. If she doesn't get help, she might—"

"Kill herself?" He shook his head. "I know my niece; I've seen her go to the edge a dozen times. Aren't you talking to yourself, Dr. Strange?"

"I'm talking about missing pieces to a puzzle—something's wrong."

"This isn't about Molly. It's Dantes. He's manipulating everyone—you most of all." Sweetheart spun around and disappeared in the crowded lobby.

Sylvia found Leo and Luke spread wearily on the cream-colored couch. Room service trays with half-eaten meals had been left on the floor.

"You just missed Sweetheart," Leo said.

"No, I didn't." Sylvia sighed, glancing at the blinking laptop monitor, where numerical columns lined the screen. "MOSAIK?" she asked, abruptly reenergized.

Leo nodded. "Gretchen sent through her results."

"It's a match?" She looked from Leo to Luke. "C'mon, guys."

"Before you check it out," Luke cautioned, "remember that MOSAIK aims for a profiling gestalt. We input all the data—forensic, geographic mapping, psycholinguistic, archaeological, as in personal history—and we get a numerical score."

Sylvia frowned impatiently. "So, theoretically, the scored profile will be unique to the individual profiled."

"Correct." Luke pressed a key.

The computer chimed in, dropping to a frenzied hum, sending output to the printer. Leo retrieved it from the printer, handing it to Sylvia. "Simon Mole's broad numerical profile."

Sylvia studied the string of more than twenty numbers.

"Now take a look at M's data; it should show a close correlation with Simon Mole—assuming they are one and the same person."

She gazed down to see numerical equations covering both pages.

The lines and graphs were similar—but not identical.

Leo said, "According to MOSAIK, there's a point fifty-seven probability that Simon Mole and M are a match."

"Is that conclusive?"

"On a really good match, we get point sixty-five or higher. But this is enough to go on."

"A *good* match. That's why you don't sound happy." Sylvia closed her eyes. "I think our very own Simon Mole has a unique gift for re-creation; he's restructured himself from the inside out. Psychologically, Simon and M are more like brothers than doubles.

"Be happy, guys." She faced the two men. "It's like I keep trying to tell Sweetheart—the world's not black-and-white."

6th Circle . . .

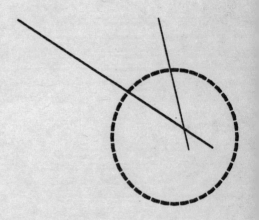

CHAPTER THIRTY

Nothing is more despicable than a coward, except perhaps the man who places his faith in a coward.

Mole's Manifesto

Friday—12:01 A.M. In Pershing Square, the earthquake fault line shimmers in the reflecting pond, the grounded constellations catch the moonlight, and minerals burn with lustrous fire among the orange groves and the palm trees. From a rooftop, the faint and achingly magnificent strains of Verdi dance off metal, stone, and glass surfaces.

Urban landscape, urban wind.

These are the highest artistic achievements, the most impressive aesthetic representations of man's supremacy.

But that is *above*. Fifty feet below Pershing Square, M watches the Thief vomit into an already foul puddle of stagnant water, trash, and ruined cans of corrosive acids dumped illegally.

The Thief. That is a man's name, his identity, here in the bowels of the city.

The Thief is a compact five ten, 170 pounds, dirty blond, and blue eyed.

Both eyes are blue, but that's okay.

He is filthy, and M has already arranged for a bath and a haircut. Nothing fancy, just get the job done.

The Thief hasn't been a mole long enough to have done irreparable damage to his body. And his body is what M needs.

M has selected the Thief just as this pathetic creature begins his long downhill slide into shit. The fall is slippery, steep—it's a long way down—and the fall is forever. No way back.

The Thief crouches like another kind of animal, shivering in the glow of a small fire, his feet slippery on the slick of ash that glazes the ground. Smoke from a thousand fires has blackened these underground girders, these poured concrete pillars that hold up all that beautiful art on the city's surface. But culture has always lived, fed, *thrived* on the broken backs of peons, the expendable people, the untouchables.

Bombay has nothing on Los Angeles.

M smiles sympathetically at the other man. "Why do they call you the Thief?"

"Because I steal," the Thief says harshly. He can't stop the tremors, his teeth chatter.

"What do you steal?" M moves closer, careful not to frighten the other man. They have spoken before. This is not a chance meeting.

"Whatever I can," the Thief says, beginning to laugh. "I'll steal your wallet, your clothes, your girlfriend if she's not half bad." The laugh turns to a hard, hacking cough.

"I'll make you an offer." M shakes his head. "I'll *give* you my clothes—once we get you cleaned up. I'll *pay* you, if you do a job for me."

"I steal better than I work," the Thief says, squinting through smoke suspiciously.

"The job is stealing, my friend," M says. "That *is* the

job." M frowns suddenly. "There's one thing you should know—you can have my clothes, but not my girlfriend."

Both men laugh, enjoying the joke.

M produces a pint of good whiskey from his pocket. "Shall we drink on it?"

"What do you want me to steal?"

"Something holy."

12:59 A.M. Even though it's dark on the street above, the Thief squints as if moonlight can blind. He doesn't say much; he's the quiet type. But he follows M along the dark streets and into the area known as the garment district.

The two men could be brothers—of a pair, as people say. Same height, same build, same coloring.

They pass the street people camped along the sidewalks, the proud owners of cardboard boxes and packing crates. These are the moles who have not yet accepted their fate, who have not surrendered to their *place* below ground.

They'll be there soon enough, M thinks.

They reach their destination, which is the Gentleman's Hotel on Sixth, where M has already arranged the room; by the hour, $11 per. Here, the Thief cleans himself up—a scrub and a shave—using the communal bathroom.

In the dingy, depressing room, the Thief sits on the thin, sagging bed. M cuts his hair, while the Thief is responsible for his own nails. "You sure I don't get to do your girlfriend?" he jokes, wagging his manicured hands.

The extra clothes M has brought fit the Thief to perfection. By the look on the Thief's face, he has suddenly discovered himself in the Ritz. Life is definitely looking up. Prosperity makes him hungry.

They find food at the flower mart, where the workday is in full swing at 1 A.M. Steaming coffee with lots of cream and sugar, pastries, an order of steak and eggs for the Thief.

As they leave, they pass through the huge warehouse where flowers overflow buckets and trays, and the fragrances are both as cloying as drugstore cologne and as delicate as the best French perfume.

The Thief steals a carnation for his boutonniere.

M's truck is parked a block away. Now, he feels that the Thief can sit in his vehicle, on his seats, without permanent damage, without soil and stench. M drives, the Thief whistles. In Chinatown, M parks. They will walk the five long blocks from here.

The Thief balks when they reach the manhole that will provide access to the ladder and their destination. "Can't we stay on top for a while?" he whines. He doesn't want to return to the darkness. Not yet.

"We won't be long," M reassures. He can be unbearably smooth, incredibly soothing when he wants to be.

And so the Thief goes willingly, entering the chimney, descending to a space that is ten feet long by ten feet wide by six feet high. He can stand with the tops of his hairs just brushing the ceiling.

It is a utility station, abandoned these days, where the air is stale but the light is achingly bright. It illuminates the female corpse that is dressed in borrowed clothes, wrapped in plastic, and laid out on the floor.

Blinking and curious, the Thief turns to stare at M. "You want me to steal this?"

M just smiles.

The Thief's mouth drops open, and he spits up on his new clothes when M brings the rubber truncheon down on the back of his skull. The blow is professionally delivered; with perfect force. This is followed by an injection.

M works happily in his hole, forgetting time and space. Deep in the conduits leading from the subterranean room, an echo can be heard by those creatures who thrive in the dark. It is the echo of laughter running like a steady stream beneath the city.

The Thief will sleep—through the night—through the operation.

M reaches into the left pocket of his pants, where he feels the hard round ball. He pulls it out, hefts its weight in his palm. A white marble with a design of blue and black.

He turns back to the Thief and sits, propping the unconscious man's head between his legs. A spoon works well to pop the eyeball—the *right* eyeball—from the socket. There is very little blood.

The marble will fit perfectly in the now empty socket. Of course. It is not a marble; it is a glass eye.

Before M leaves for the night, he binds the Thief's arms and legs simply but securely with duct tape; he tapes his mouth shut.

He props the Thief against one wall.

He places the severed eyeball in the middle of the floor near the corpse.

When the Thief opens his remaining eye—the *left* eye—this is what he will see: his *right* eye returning his horrified stare.

For hours, the Thief will be able to commune with his severed organ.

As for the rest of the operation, that will wait until I return, M thinks.

One thing at a time.

CHAPTER THIRTY-ONE

Judging from the style and content of threat demand, the operational methods of the threat actions, device construction and type, we are looking for a male, mid-twenties to mid-forties, solitary, opportunistic in relationships or friendships, who has a background in electronics or engineering, in a "low" or menial capacity versus a capacity that would demand high functioning or levels of high achievement.

Introduction, FBI profile, UNSUB, alias M

5:14 A.M. Sylvia heard a door slam. She opened her eyes, slowly taking in reality.

Room at the Hilton, seventeenth floor. Underpants and T-shirt instead of pajamas. Her lipstick stain on the wineglass by the bed; dregs of *fumé blanc*. Dimples in her skin where the cell phone had been pressed to her ear. Oh, yeah . . . she'd fallen asleep to the sound of Matt's voice. She experienced a sharp ache at the thought of her lover a thousand miles away. Then the breath of panic—*if I don't get out of here*—

Abruptly, she sat up, stretching her arms overhead. The quarter hour turned on the digital clockface. The sun was definitely awake, light leaking through the window drapes.

Sighing, she pushed away the sheet and stood. She sidestepped the room service tray with its leftover Caesar salad, saltines, oily decaf, and green napkin. On the way to the bathroom, she tapped lightly on the door to Leo's room. He didn't answer, and she remembered he'd stayed up late, too.

Let him sleep a few more minutes while she showered and dressed.

The hot water soothed both muscles and mind, triggering memories of her conversation with Matt.

Sylvia had been startled by the soft ring of her cell phone.

"Hey, baby, I'm sorry it's so late. You all right?"

"I miss you. How's Serena?"

"Better. She's got a rash. The doc thinks it's an allergy— not measles."

"Is she hurting?"

"Not bad. She says it's just *itchy*."

"*Pobrecita*. God, I miss you guys. I miss the dogs."

"They miss you, too."

It had felt great to laugh and to share everyday intimacies. They'd barely talked about business—hers or his. Intentionally avoiding the world of criminals and their victims.

But Matt had eventually touched a nerve: "Sylvia . . . about Mona Carpenter . . . Robert Montoya told me they brought her husband into the DA's office for questioning."

"Mona's husband? Why?"

"I'm going to make a few phone calls tomorrow morning. I'll let you know."

And then she'd drifted off to sleep while Matt described Serena's latest watercolors and an anniversary party for their best friends, Ray and Rosie Sanchez.

Thank God for long distance.

In the misty bathroom, she toweled off, applied moisturizer and sunscreen, and wrapped a towel around wet hair. The new Italian jeans would go another day; she dug in her suitcase for a crisp cotton shirt the color of lime sorbet.

Last night, she and Leo had returned to Santa Monica just long enough to pack suitcases under the watchful eye of two local cops.

Luke had shut down his computer equipment and returned to the house on Selma; she imagined he and Gretchen had worked much of the night.

This time, she rapped with her fist on the connecting door. "Leo? Hey! Lee-oh."

No answer. He was a light sleeper and an early riser. He must be in the shower.

She dialed his room and let the phone ring a dozen times in stereo before she hung up.

She jumped when her cell phone rang seconds later.

Fumbling for the handset, she kicked over the cold coffee on the room service tray.

"This is Purcell, Dr. Strange. I'm at City Hospital. Dr. Carreras is with me. How soon can you make it?"

"I'm leaving now."

7:01 A.M.   In the truth of daylight, LA City Hospital was another sister of mercy altogether. Gone were her mysterious and moody angles, the black and blue shadows of night; the hospital exterior had flattened to a dull, nondescript gray, presenting an uninteresting profile, a dreary facade to the surrounding city.

Sylvia pushed through the main doors and stopped. The vast admissions area felt foreign. Patients, their families, and staff occupied the echoing space. A young boy in a wheelchair pushed by an *abuelita* repeated a plaintive phrase in Spanish.

Sylvia reached the glassed-in reception area and stuttered at a tired clerk, who just stared at her blankly. Then she heard someone call her name and turned to see Purcell, beckoning with a quick jerk of the head.

"Do you know how *old* this is getting?" Sylvia asked.

"I really do."

The special agent guided her quickly down a narrow hallway to a service elevator; they were its only passengers. A mesh grille clanged shut behind thick, pitted doors. The worn metal buttons offered three subterranean destinations, including theirs: B-3.

"Are you going to explain?"

"I'll let Dr. Carreras do that."

The ride was slow, and working parts complained all the way down. When they hit bottom, the fifteen seconds before the door finally clattered open stole Sylvia's breath.

God, don't ever leave me locked in an elevator, she thought. Tight spaces, dark places . . . best left to night's furtive creatures.

"You all right?" Purcell asked.

"No."

Outside the elevator, traversing the mazelike hallways, the area began to look both oddly amorphous and familiar. They stopped outside Dantes' room.

It was empty. The door was locked.

"Where is he?"

"This minute?" Purcell glanced at her watch. "They're just about finished with the sodium amytal interview."

"Sodium amytal?" Sylvia shook her head, her voice flat. "Why wasn't I told?" She knew that sodium amytal, or sodium amobarbital—used in forensic settings—had originally been labeled a truth serum. A misnomer. The drug was mostly effective in reducing substance-induced amnesia. Clinical studies had proven that some subjects could lie very effectively under the drug's influence.

She heard footsteps and pivoted to find herself staring into the familiar face of Dr. Carreras.

In a voice so businesslike it sounded cold, Leo said, "The

FBI asked me to supervise the interview. He's on the IV for another five minutes; they want you there as he comes out."

"Why didn't you just ask for my cooperation?" Sylvia whispered harshly.

"The interview was voluntary." Dr. Carreras swallowed, and his Adam's apple bobbed visibly under taut skin. "You know he'll recover almost as soon as the IV's removed."

"My connection with Dantes is tenuous. It depends on my being around when he's vulnerable." Sylvia felt betrayed and angry. And maybe that was the point of all this manipulation—to keep her off balance.

"It wasn't my procedural call," Leo said.

"Bullshit."

Leo dropped his voice to a level only she could hear. "They called me two hours ago, Sylvia."

She brushed past him, focusing on Purcell. "Where is he?"

"Straight ahead, first door around the corner."

"By the way." She spun around. "How did it go?"

"His symptoms abated," Leo said flatly.

"Which reinforces a diagnosis of conversion disorder," Sylvia said. Under the influence of sodium amytal, true conversion-disordered subjects tended to recover from their symptoms, at least temporarily. Those who were manufacturing symptoms often exaggerated their pain, their afflictions.

"That's right," Leo cut into her thoughts. "The blind man could see again. But don't forget, he's probably read as much of the literature as you or me."

"He probably has." She took two steps toward Leo. "Did the serum work?"

"Yes." His voice dropped, his tone flattened until it was sober and cautionary. "Don't let him make a fool of you. He may not use a knife or a gun, but he's a stone killer." Leo shook his head sharply, and light glinted off the lenses of his gold wire rims. "He sold out Simon Mole, aka M—signed, sealed, delivered. He did it because it serves his purpose. He's trading a bomber for a ticket out of LA with privileges. His lawyer had already drawn up the terms."

Sylvia stared at him, confusion altering her features. "That doesn't make any sense," she whispered. "Why would he give up Simon now? The timing's not right. He has nothing to gain. He doesn't want to leave LA."

"Really?" Leo watched her closely. "The Feds are already on their way to a warehouse in LA Harbor—where, according to Dantes, they'll find M's workshop."

"I hope they find their bomber," she said slowly.

She entered the room by herself. The distant sounds of city, the noises of a working hospital penetrated the walls. Her focus was on Dantes.

She sat next to the seclusion bed, watching him breathe. His skin was achromatic, with the dull sheen of someone suffering a fever. His mouth was chapped, caked at the corners. It was almost as if he was surrounded by a shadowy mist, as if his features had blurred. The last of the amytal dripped from the IV bag into the antecubital vein in his elbow; his brain teetered on the verge of unconsciousness.

Was it a trick of the light, or had his eyes just flickered open, lids closing again? She spoke softly. "Dantes?"

She felt herself pull back, retreating emotionally, refusing to empathize. Jason Redding, Detective Church, and others were dead because of this man. For an instant, she longed to surrender to the simple clarity of black-and-white thinking, the polarity of absolute good and total evil.

But she wasn't made that way. For better or worse, she

saw the world in complex layers, in grays, with the nuance of multiple points of view. That was her weakness—and her strength.

Sylvia took a deep breath, registering the internal shift as she let her prejudices and preconceptions fade, at least temporarily; she blanked out the faces of the victims, she blocked thoughts of the exchange with Leo, thoughts of M. For these moments, she would allow herself to think of Dantes as a man who was a prisoner—of himself *and* the state.

His voice startled her. "I told them about it . . ." He swallowed with difficulty, running his tongue over dry lips. "About Simon."

She recognized the confusion that was caused by the drug and by stress. But there was something else—something underlying the chemically induced disorientation. She couldn't put her finger on what it was; not yet.

"I told them . . . worked together . . . that's what . . . they want."

A nurse was preparing to remove the IV. Sylvia knew she had a very small window with the drug; she wanted to make use of the time, but she could feel the gulf that had opened up between them.

"Why are you lying to them, Dantes?"

"Not up . . . to this one . . . are we, Dr. Strange?"

"The Getty bombing was a calculated massacre—it targeted civilians." She shook her head. "I don't believe you killed those children."

"It went . . . wrong."

"Tell me the truth." She gripped the metal rails of the seclusion bed. "You owe me that."

"Because you kept . . . the faith?" He closed his eyes and took a slow, deep breath. "Nobody listens . . . until children die."

"I know you're lying," Sylvia whispered. The room suddenly felt cold and very dark. "But I don't know why."

His eyes were on her, reading her thoughts—and the eerie sense returned that another animal, calculating and predatory, was hiding inside the skin of this man.

"Dr. Strange . . . wants . . . a fallen . . . hero."

The nurse, who had been hovering nearby, pulled the needle from his arm.

Sylvia leaned toward Dantes, whispering, "What's M got on you?"

He closed his eyes. "It's over."

7:49 A.M. The sharp tang of chemicals permeated the bomber's workshop.

This is the lair of Simon Mole, of M, Sweetheart thought, *but it feels like a prison.*

He stood dead center, still as a tree, while forensics experts worked around him.

He was aware that the choppy gray sea of LA Harbor was lapping at the footings of the factory, perhaps a hundred yards away.

But for all the silence a man could be in the middle of the Sahara.

The fourteen-by-twenty-foot space was neat to the point of sterility; anal retentiveness was a good trait for a bomber who wanted to stay alive.

It occurred to Sweetheart that he was looking at the outer skin of the bomber. Next to a pair of goggles, a heavy welding hood rested on one of two wooden tables. A sleeved apron of thick leather hung from a hook. The rubber boots that fishermen wear were side by side on the floor beneath the apron. Gloves—thick leather gloves; rubber gloves; an unopened box of surgical gloves—lined one small shelf.

This paraphernalia was sized to fit a man of medium height, average weight.

Another shelf was stocked with vials and beakers of various shapes and sizes. When Sweetheart carefully sniffed the top of one, he recognized sulfuric acid.

Bags of Kitty Litter had been stacked along the base of two walls.

Another shelf hosted rolls of string: inflammable fuse cord, detonating cord, nylon and cotton cord. And wire— both insulated and bare—of various thickness.

The contents of drawers could have come from any kitchen: baking soda, baking powder, sugar, potassium chlorate, aluminum wrap, and wax paper, and countless plastic bags. White plastic mixing tools were hung from a rack.

A fume hood and a flue had been installed; the job was carefully executed, by a man who knew what he was doing, a man who knew how to stay alive.

Then there was the hardware: miscellaneous pipes, joints, nails, screws, vises, wrenches, sharp knives, and other tools.

The investigators hadn't been lucky enough to stumble upon bombs in midconstruction. That's because Simon—or M—was smart. He would complete one job and then clean up after himself.

And although there were agents posted surreptitiously outside, Sweetheart doubted M would return—the bomber's instincts were too sharp.

He found himself feeling grudging respect.

He closed his eyes, struggling to catch elusive thoughts darting here and there in his mind. He could feel M's presence—but there was very little of the schoolboy they called Simon in this space.

Sweetheart took the steps up to ground level. At the

edge of the basement door, a flash of color caught his eye. He reached down and captured one blue-green feather.

When he straightened he saw Sylvia standing a few feet away. He wasn't surprised; he felt relief, and perhaps pleasure, at her presence. "What do you think?" he asked, tipping his head toward the room.

"I believe it's M." She frowned. "But he's evolved way beyond Simon Mole."

"This is no *deshi*," Sweetheart said, nodding. "No apprentice. This is the home of a *makuuchi*—a master."

Sylvia nodded toward the feather that Sweetheart held delicately between two fingers. "A master with a parrot."

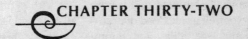

CHAPTER THIRTY-TWO

"There's a speed limit in this state, Mr. Neff. Forty-five miles per hour."
"How fast was I going, Officer?"
"I'd say about ninety."

From the screenplay *Double Indemnity*

7:50 A.M. M is at the wheel of a two-and-a-half-ton bomb.

He maintains a sedate fifty miles per hour in the right lane of I-10, the San Bernardino Freeway. As he drives, he's surrounded by city—the urban she-devil who devours open space the way the tide eats sand.

An hour ago, he'd stopped just east of San Berdu. The flat brown terrain reminded him of other deserts, always at the edge of the world. An apt spot to trade in his loner for this shiny silver food service truck.

He checks his bearings; he's about thirty miles from downtown LA, which is excellent. No time to check on his friends—the Thief and the hooker. Doesn't matter; they'll keep.

He *does* have time to drop off the truck. Later a man who needs a few bucks will drive it to its final destination. *No questions asked.*

Only a fool would want to know that this load of ANFO is primed with commercial-grade explosives that come all the way from New Mexico; a hitch in the state's antiquated blasting laws encourages a healthy trade in stolen explosives. Pick up the right form at your local county office. One page printed up courtesy of the Land of Enchantment. Fill it out, smile at the clerk, banter around a few names of folks in the business, and you walk out with permission to buy yourself a truckload of death—"all nice and legal like."

Exhausted miles and minutes evaporate behind the truck. The landscape fills in like a jigsaw puzzle until the whole board is covered—with urban condensation: malls piled on outlets on industrial parks on condos on apartments on high-rises on barrios.

I-10 pierces downtown LA and then it's a straight shot to the 101 north, the Hollywood Freeway.

M's bright and shiny snack truck will end up parked in the middle of an underground garage, shades of the WTC.

Jesus, those jerk-offs came so close to taking down the Twin Towers, blowing them to kingdom come . . . Piece o' cake and they blew it . . . Guess that's what you get when the blind lead the dumb.

To keep the security guards from getting too nosy, a little paper sign will decorate the truck's windshield: BROKE DOWN, BACK ASAP, MANNY.

Manny, the regular driver of the real lunch truck, will take the day off.

But M is getting ahead of himself.

He changes lanes now to snig-snag onto the Hollywood.

After a mile or so, he takes Echo Park to Sunset—too bad there's no time to cruise Elysian Park and wave to Dodger Stadium; he's an avid baseball fan.

Just across Sunset, he slows, turning left into the parking lot of Ralph's. Grocery shoppers are out in full force, and the lot is full. He parks the truck in a shaded slot. A kid walks by, his radio blasting angry bass: "*Going back to Cali, Cali, Cali, I'm going back to Cali—I don't think so.*"

M walks the two blocks to his own truck.

Once inside, he snaps open his laptop, boots up, types in a brief e-mail message, and sends it off to his sweetheart in cyberspace.

That should whet their appetites.

He's been up all night and he feels great. Primed. Ready.

Soon it will be time to step down to the seventh circle.

To do that, M must shut down operations in one of downtown's busiest buildings.

CHAPTER THIRTY-THREE

At least we know the famous triad—fire setting, bed-wetting, cruelty to animals—doesn't hold up.
Special Agent Mackavoy, FBI Crime Lab

10:03 A.M. It was Gretchen who discovered the cyber-message that had landed on Sweetheart's mainframe.

* * *

lost yr way? new city stnds on ruins old dust to dst 7th
crcle awatz—M

It set in motion a chain of events, which was certainly
what M had anticipated. The Feds were talking to
Sweetheart again; they asked him to focus his team on the
rudimentary map that had shown up in Dantes' cell three
days earlier. The consensus: M's next move—the seventh
circle—would be directly connected to information contained on that single sheet of paper.

Sylvia left her suitcases in one of several guest rooms in
Sweetheart's house. As she retraced her steps along a hall,
the first person she encountered was Gretchen, who
handed her several books; from the titles, histories of Los
Angeles.

"'New city stands on ruins old,'" Gretchen quoted. Behind thick tortoise spectacles, saucer-shaped baby blues
sized up Sylvia. "I almost forgot." She turned to retrieve a
stack of computer printouts from a desk. "Bella Dantes. You
wanted to know about her suicide, so I focused on medical
history, for example, possible psychiatric commitment.
Nothing under Bella Dantes . . . which is why the press
never got wind."

Gretchen tapped her glasses. "So I ran Caldini, her
maiden name." She grinned. "Bingo. Bella Caldini spent
two weeks at County General in the locked ward. And she
was recommitted about six weeks before she drowned herself. The docs thought she was a high-functioning schizophrenic."

"You're a genius," Sylvia said, stacking the pages on top
of the books.

"I know." Gretchen winked. "We've got a desk set up
for you in the office next to the guest room where you'll

be sleeping. Or you're welcome to claim your territory out here. There's a fresh pot of espresso. You know the drill."

In the main work area, Sylvia chose the wide leather armchair that occupied a corner. Opposite her, Gretchen was at work analyzing M's latest message for verbal content, syntax, anomalies, and patterns.

The large room was awash with sunshine. Both the Jack Russell terrier and the English bulldog were stretched blissfully on the rug. Sylvia tried to focus on the history books, but the light was giving her a headache. Thinking a jolt of espresso might help, she poured herself a cup.

While she sipped the coffee, she found herself replaying her brief phone conversation with Leo Carreras: "Why didn't you tell me about the amytal interview? A knock on the door, a phone call? Either would've worked."

Leo hadn't hesitated. "If the FBI wants to keep you informed, that's their job, not mine."

"This isn't about the FBI's conduct. It's about you and me. I trusted you."

"And I'm in love with you. But that's nothing new . . . we've both known how I felt . . . since the day I first saw you. Good old Leo, the fallback guy. Things don't always turn out the way we want."

"Leo . . ."

What had she wanted to say to him?

"Are you sure you aren't trying to save Dantes' soul?" Leo had finally asked. "Good guys and bad. Choose sides, Sylvia."

The memory dissolved; she found herself studying the enlarged map of Dante Alighieri's *Inferno* that still decorated one wall. A red pushpin now occupied the inner edge of the sixth circle, the cusp of the seventh circle, where someone had carefully printed, SINS OF VIOLENCE. From the seventh circle, hell deepened to the eighth—and finally, it fell into the deep pit of the ninth and final circle.

12:39 P.M.   In contrast to blinding daylight, Luke's office was the long polar night. The green-violet glow from a half dozen monitors did little to disturb the cavelike darkness.

He had the glazed expression of a man running on half rations of sleep. His blond hair was sprouting like a new wheat crop. His tattooed flying fish hovered airborne on his buffed biceps. His feet were tapping to an inaudible rhythm.

Sylvia knew just how he felt: frustrated, manic, wired.

At the moment he was staring, transfixed, at a wide computer screen. Over his shoulder she studied the symbols, searching for familiar urban topography, something that resembled Los Angeles.

Without looking up he said, "This is the county's primary maintenance map."

"Then it's underground?"

"LA's *subterranean* infrastructure." Luke offered a weary smile. "*Inferno.*"

She leaned closer, trying to find points of orientation. The bangle on her left wrist trapped a splinter of light, then set it free. "So where's downtown?"

He pointed to an area in the upper right quadrant of the monitor. "Think of it as a skyscraper, only going *down* instead of up. You've got your electric and phone casings a few feet below the pavement. Your utility vaults start at that level, too, and go down about eight feet. Then, on the next level down, you've got your gas lines; then the water lines and mains; then steam; then sewers. The subway vaults could be anywhere from fifteen feet to twenty stories underground; and down below it all run the storm drains, the storm tunnels, which are also the biggest conduits."

"The belly of the city," Sylvia said softly.

"I got sucker-punched in the gut once," Luke said, leaning back in his chair, arms behind his head. He glanced up at Sylvia and grinned. "It was weird. There I was on my back staring up at this biker asshole. I couldn't move, couldn't breathe. I just kept thinking he had a nicer tattoo than me."

"Tattoo of what?" Sylvia smiled back.

"An angel . . ." He mimed generous female curves. "Hey, I was semiconscious."

"So, what if a city gets sucker-punched?"

"Back when we were chasing Ben Black—after he escaped the Iraqis—we got our hands on some intelligence: he'd figured out the schematics to attack New York."

Luke shifted in the chair, making leather stress and give. "We're not just talking the level of the 1993 World Trade Center and Sheik Rahman or Oklahoma City . . . It was going to be a simultaneous hit, multiple targets, enough to shut the city down for days—to impair functioning for months—perhaps to alter economic power structures."

"And?" Sylvia prodded.

"Obviously it never happened," Luke said. "New York still stands. We heard that report two weeks before U.S. missiles destroyed the training camp."

"And if Black hadn't been killed?"

"One of these days a major U.S. city will be hit. A variation on the WTC bomb—or the more likely scenario, biological weapons."

"Would you have caught up with Black without MOSAIK?"

"MOSAIK only took us so far."

"Explain." Sylvia leaned on Luke's desk, inches from his face.

Luke focused in on his screen, shifting images—plunging to an even deeper stratum below Los Angeles. He shook his head, his voice low. "Let's just say *luck* didn't hurt."

4:21 P.M. The sun's heat lidded Los Angeles, agitating molecules, compressing, reacting, tinting the city's sky a dirty white.

Inside the professor's house on Selma it might have been midnight in Anchorage: the lights were achingly bright, the air conditioner iced the atmosphere, computers hummed compulsively.

Sweetheart had disappeared into his inner sanctum.

Sylvia's eyes ached from staring at pages, early maps of the Los Angeles pueblo. She was startled by a hand on her shoulder.

"Time for a break." Luke smiled. "Follow me."

The map man led her into new territory. As they passed through a wide hall where framed monotypes and etchings decorated the walls, she caught glimpses of early rural London, Paris in the 1800s, New York, and Los Angeles at the turn of the last century and back in the days of Spain's rule.

A floor-to-ceiling print of Los Angeles covered one wall. The old was melded with the new, a network of early Spanish aqueducts, crisscrossing railways and streetcars from the booster period, deco to postmodern functionalism. Animistic oil wells, movie billboards, and palm trees grew in place of other vegetation. The impression was of a city of invention instead of history.

Sylvia was studying the image so intently she almost bumped into Luke. He'd come to a standstill. Now, to her right, she noticed a door; at first she thought it must lead to a closet. But he opened it and stepped through.

She followed him up two flights of a narrow twisting stairwell that led to a eight-by-eight widow's walk. Except for a massive evergreen, a magnolia, and an old willow, they were above the tree line. To the west, Los Angeles stretched from hillside to coastline; blocks in miniature were laid out as rough rectangular grids; main thoroughfares crisscrossed the city like ribbons over a package.

"We've all got our reasons for working on this project," Luke said, leaning his hips against the railing. Sylvia turned to study him, and he shrugged. "Gretchen's cousin was one of the demolition experts who helped excavate the network of booby-trapped tunnels left from World War Two. Both sides used tons of mines and other explosives. You know that even today they're disarming those bombs on a daily basis?" He took a deep breath. "Her cousin died last year. Blew up and was buried under a ton of rock. They still can't decide if the bomb was German or English. Does it fucking matter?"

"And you?" Sylvia asked softly. "What's your reason?"

"The way the world is going—with the Internet, the crazies, all the access to materials, all the mean thinking." He shrugged, sorrow aging his face. "I won't forget Jason. I want kids someday. I want them to grow old, have kids of their own."

Sylvia nodded. Then she turned to gaze out at the world.

Soon, dusk would fall over a city where urban prophets abounded—the turn of 2000 had done nothing to dampen predictions of doom. Ruin could come with natural cataclysmic events such as earthquake, fire, drought; it could come through riots and other products of social and economic breakdown; it could come through acts of terrorism. If the opposition was smart enough, powerful enough, rich enough, they might cripple a major urban center. Not *might . . . would*, one of these days. That time was coming, just like Luke had described.

He was on the same train of thought. He said, "Cities are born, they have a life span . . . economic, cultural, social. Cycles of growth and expansion. I think we forget the other side of the cycle. Eventually, they die. They survive for a while, but diminished. Or they blow away with the wind, wash away with the tides."

Sylvia nodded. "We see it in the Southwest—the Anasazi ruins: Chaco Canyon, Mesa Verde, Canyon de Chelly."

"That's right," Luke said softly. "Entire civilizations—with calendars, astronomy, complex trading patterns, religion, and family units. And they disappeared almost overnight. Mexico, South America, Africa, the Middle East—they all claim ghost civilizations, thriving centers of culture turned to dust. I don't mean to sound grim, but even in the twentieth century, hurricanes and earthquakes altered the future of major urban areas. The hurricane that destroyed Galveston created another megahub: Houston–Dallas–Fort Worth." He shrugged. "That's life."

Sylvia rested her elbows on the railing of the widow's walk. All cities die. Urban energy shifts the way blood stops flowing to a dying organ—the brain reroutes it to more productive body parts.

But Los Angeles was a long way from dead.

Unless M had his way.

Light exploded off a strand of silver high-rises lining Sunset Boulevard—the last spark of day giving way to night. Sylvia closed her eyes, seemed to feel the city in every cell of her body. But she was already moving in another world.

New Mexico. A moonlit night in October . . . a walk in Chaco Canyon with Matt. Shadows cast, dark against light, bright as daylight. The cry of coyotes. She had led the way along the trail to Casa Grande. At one point an owl cried out, the primal call cut the dry night air. That's how raw the sound felt . . .

For hundreds of years, generations had been born here.

And then they disappeared, leaving roads, calendars, ways to measure time, meetinghouses, graves. Leaving behind the ghosts of their endeavors for archaeologists to find and puzzle over.

She and Matt had stopped at the ruins of the ancient pueblo. Alone in the desert, they had taken shelter inside a small home, made love in the sand.

That night, back inside their tent, rain had woken her before daylight. For a few hours she thought she'd heard the whispered answers to ancient secrets.

"Sylvia?" Luke's voice tugged her through space and time back to the present, back to urban reality. He appeared to be restless, ready to return to work. "Are you all right?"

"I'm okay," Sylvia said softly. "I'll be down in a minute."

Without a word he left the widow's walk, descending the stairs two at a time.

She gave him ten minutes. In that time, the sun dipped toward the ocean, dimming the sky, until the city was draped in shadow.

Had the Anasazi people felt the end of their world?

M was excavating the past. If he had his way, how long would it be before Hollywood joined Babylon?

Like a sleepwalker retracing her steps along the expansive hallway, catching glimpses of great cities as art, she heard the click of the keyboard as she entered the map room. He had his back to her, and he was typing in commands. The screen flashed color, form, text—after a few minutes it seemed to settle on a solitary image.

"Hollywood-Babylon," Sylvia said. "The map . . . try Babylon."

CHAPTER THIRTY-FOUR

Crimes against society include the acquisition of natural elements by illegitimate means; in such cases the criminals are far worse than common thieves, as their greed affects the future of the city. Forceful means of rectification are not only justified but necessary.

   Dantes' Inferno, excerpt published in the *LA TIMES*,
   November 7, 1999

4:48 P.M.   M stands atop Ishtar's Gate, staring out at the blight known as Western civilization. A shaft to the underworld runs directly beneath his legs. It is through this same hellish passage that the next beast will race—at his command—bringing destruction in its breath of fire.

The beast will travel to the top of this steel and glass tower, this hub of transportation, just as Moses once ascended the mountain of Horeb to touch the hand of God for one stunned moment.

He lifts his head and stares directly into the pulsing orb of the sun.

I'm here. Strike me dead if you exist.

That would be life's great joke.

Of course, nothing happens, except pain as the sun irritates old scars.

False god. Bully.

No divine revelation, which is the penultimate burden after all. He should be grateful he holds no religious delusions. His laughter rings out over the sun-bleached rooftop. He lifts his arms, spinning slowly.

The soul was long ago burned out of his body.

Master of the day of judgment. How often he heard those words. They remind him of the taste of blood. His own. The men who prayed daily on hands and knees were also diligent in their torture. It does not take long to break a man. It can be done quickly, cheaply.

I sold them my soul, he thinks—and they believed they had purchased something of value.

I sold them air. Fucking air.

He walks to the edge of the building, standing so close to the drop he can feel the hot updraft between buildings.

A white bird soars past. A gull, scavenging in an urban sea.

He smiles, turning slowly. His jacket billows out behind him like a fabric wing. If I had a soul, I would fly off this edge right now.

The bird changes course with the swift shift of feathers.

But *his* course is set. He has spent months planning, collecting, preparing.

Just like last's years project at the Getty—when he'd researched every step from conception to the night of the gala opening.

Building by building—grounds surveys and preparation, transportation-access mapping, utility infrastructure, foundation installation, structural erection, landscaping, garden design, and execution.

Along the way—in the company of modernist Richard

Meier and abstract expressionist Robert Irwin—he had left his mark on one of the city's prime cultural landmarks. None of his work was visible to the naked eye—at least not until the final coup de grâce. But whenever urban critics waxed poetic about Euclidean vision, Aristotelian structure, dogmatic unity, and thematic chaos, all at a billion bucks a pop—he had quietly enjoyed the knowledge that his seed had been planted, then nurtured, by corporate complicity. Collaboration was such a lovely thing.

As unwitting as the woman who carries a clumsy satchel on board an international flight after her revolutionary boyfriend sees her off with a kiss: Call me as soon as you get there, love.

This post-postmodern corporate bastion of classicism had been the repository of his artistic creation: concrete blocks stuffed with explosives and imbedded in the environmental control unit; additional sheet explosives lining a duct unit directly above the doctored blocks.

No one questioned a man who wore the uniform.

Finally, the motion-sensitive delay detonator using primary explosives, which were highly reactive even in beauty-mark doses, to initiate the less receptive main explosive. All packaged inside a magic box. A work of art. A bomber's trademark.

Open, and oops. The perfect foreplay, the explosive train.

After many experiments, he had leaned in favor of his booby trap device that would trigger delayed motion initiation. Which meant that Pandora would have to lift the lid. Ah, but then she always did. People died in war.

Boom.

"We'll be signing off by six," a voice yanks him back from the brink of memory.

The beauty of it: while these workers toil to build, he toils to destroy.

On the floor below, a dozen men are at work, finishing on schedule.

But by *his* records, running behind schedule by two days. This building will be shut down over the weekend—a high-rise ghost town. It's official. It's quakification.

He's spoken to the supervisor, Jack, who joins him on the roof to say, "I'm counting on a clean bill of health on this thing. Otherwise . . . well, it could fuck up the next renovation we do."

Jack pulls a pack of cigarettes from his pocket and offers one to M. Both men light up, sending more smoke out over the city.

"I wouldn't anticipate any glitches," M says, smiling. "I got a feeling you'll roll through without a hitch." He shrugs, sympathetic because he knows the drill—city permits, approval, payoffs.

"But hey," he says, "seems like those guys always got to give you some grief or they don't feel like they earned their overtime."

"No shit," Jack agrees with a rough laugh. "Government guys, far as I'm concerned they're no better than getting welfare."

"On the dole," M nods. "Give me private sector any day." Cigarette sending smoke from the corner of his mouth, he squats down and begins to unroll the first of the maps. "So . . . let's just go over this stuff before I put it into our system. All this should've been done back in two thousand." He squints under the bright glare of the sun. "The heating ducts run here . . . the water's draining here . . ."

And so on . . .

After they've done an honest half hour's work and supervisor Jack heads back down to reel in his crew, M stays on the roof thinking about his truckload of ANFO.

The World Trade Center . . . Oklahoma City . . . University of Wisconsin way back in the sixties. Ammonium nitrate—strategically placed near the primary weight-bearing columns—is still the most efficient way to inflict massive structural damage.

The bird emits a demanding screech; it dives close, nagging for scraps.

He sits on the edge of a girder and boots up his laptop. Caressing keys, opening files. The map appears on-screen. Full color. City of cities. Pinnacle of civilization.

Clicking keys, configurations, he begins his calculations. How much destructive power does he possess today? One jigger C-4. Three jiggers ANFO. Two jiggers aviation fuel. A party cocktail. Awaiting *God's* touch: six hundred volts.

He keys in more commands and the screen goes haywire—colors and images flash, driven by a thousand-megahertz processor. A grid appears. A map of Los Angeles—but not your everyday street guide and directory. He's got his hands on the nervous system of the city . . . from LA Harbor and San Pedro, from Inglewood's LAX to Marina Del Rey, where Ballona Creek sends half the urban center's storm runoff to the ocean, to the war room in Alhambra where fifteen dams are coordinated—this is the project that makes blowing up Ishtar's Gate look like child's play.

It's all part of the universal urban karma, he thinks, smiling.

But *first*, life and death in the seventh circle.

7th Circle . . .

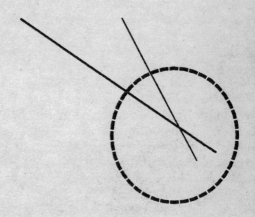

CHAPTER THIRTY-FIVE

Farewell happy Fields
Where Joy for ever dwells, Hail horrors, hail
Infernal world, and thou profoundest Hell
Receive thy new Possessor.

Milton, *Paradise Lost*

Saturday — 12:12 A.M. Luke—sleeves rolled to elbows, hands behind head—was on the floor, staring up at the domed ceiling, which was filled with a city in miniature. He seemed exhausted, intent, and satisfied.

He said, "It looks as if M gave us the major boundaries of ancient Babylon after Koldewey. The expedition was famous—Robert Koldewey excavated between eighteen ninety-nine and nineteen seventeen on behalf of Deutsche Orient-Gesellschaft. The map is a benchmark—cited in all the archaeological references to Babylonian times."

Sylvia swiveled in the leather chair, letting it slowly tip back. While she watched, Babylon came into full relief above her head.

The city was rectangular, defined by walls, and roughly bisected by the Euphrates River. Streets, designed around municipal buildings, fed out of the city through gates. Sylvia saw Nebuchadnezzar's palace, the Temple of Marduk, and the Tower of Babel.

"The map predates NAD-27—" Guessing that he'd lost Sylvia, Luke slowed to translate: "NAD . . . North American Datum . . . international standards were set in nineteen twenty-seven, then revised in nineteen eighty-three, with NAD-83. NAD was created for just this reason—there was no way to work with multiple maps unless you applied universal standards."

"So without it—without, what, NAD—can you still work out the scale?" Sylvia brought the chair back to neutral to sip coffee from the rough-fired clay mug in her hands.

"That's the million-dollar question." From his prone position, Luke manipulated a remote mouse, flexing his left arm so the fish tattoo seemed to fly higher.

Sylvia tipped back again to watch the overhead show. Babylon faded and a red grid map of downtown Los Angeles was instantly splattered across the dome. Key points were delineated with bold geometric shapes. The lines and symbols overhead reminded her of planetarium stars.

Luke played with the images: Babylon; Los Angeles; Babylon. His voice, settled deep in his chest, emerged in a throaty bass. "If I had an array—four or five known points of correlation—I could rubber-sheet the good map—LA—and the bad map—Babylon. Line up the main intersections, main points."

"I get the idea," Sylvia said. "Can you project Los Angeles again?"

She was becoming mesmerized as she watched the changing images. "Since we don't have correlation points, what about matching that general rectangular area?" She extended her fingers in the air, delineating the core of Los Angeles and the center of Babylon.

"Yeah," Luke said, clicking the remote several times until the images lined up, Harbor Freeway to Euphrates River. "Or we can line up the Hollywood with the Euphrates . . . or we can line up the Tower of Babel with City Hall . . . or . . ."

"I get it," Sylvia said, sighing. "We need an array."

"You need to go deeper," Sweetheart said, entering the room slowly. "We're talking *Inferno*."

"We'll get to the underground stuff," Luke said. "But we're left with the same problem of endless possibilities."

He clicked keys, frustrated when his fingers didn't keep up with his mental commands. "The Euphrates could be the Metrolink tunnels, the Red Line, here. And Processional Way that leads to Ishtar's Gate . . . What about this storm drain—it comes off the LA River's downtown drainage system, which could represent the eastern boundary of Babylon."

"Sunset and Hollywood," Sylvia murmured. "That's where D.W. Griffith created a massive set of Babylon back in 1910 or so."

"Sorry, Professor," Luke said. "I'm seeing stars—but no point alignments."

"Don't give me sorry, just give me results." Sweetheart turned and disappeared.

Luke sat up, turning toward Sylvia. "I'm glad to see he's in a good mood."

A few minutes later, Sylvia followed Sweetheart.

The creaks and cracks, the soft complaints of shifting walls and footings reminded her of an old dreaming dog. Like a sleepwalker, she had no conscious cognitive chart to lead her to the narrow teak door at the end of an unfamiliar hallway.

Of course, she entered.

Inside was a war room where the battle had been fought and not necessarily won. It was square, with low ceilings, and an air temperature that literally ran a few degrees colder than the rest of the house.

Her attention was drawn to a large flat screen, where film images moved abstractly in gray, then in color, then black-and-white, and back to gray; brutal explosions of ever-changing targets: embassies, churches, buses, apartments, pubs, schools, factories.

The eerie scenes of destruction had been caught on amateur video, surveillance satellite, security cameras, and they ran now on an endless grainy loop.

She felt his presence: Sweetheart. He was seated lotus style, still as a statue, on a tatami.

For an instant Sylvia thought he was sleeping. But he blinked—and his eyes moved, the whites gleaming in the shadows, tracking her movements.

She didn't switch on the overhead lights, choosing instead to find her way by the low, lemony moonlight that spilled through two high windows.

She seated herself in front of a cold computer monitor, swiveling the chair to face him. When he didn't speak, she turned back toward the desk.

Files—both hard copies and discs—were stacked neatly. She scanned the labels: *Zaire, 1975; Paris, 1983; Kenya, 1990; Nairobi, 1987; London, 1988, 1981; Munich 1999*.

She opened the first manila folder. Names lined a single page: *Ben Black, Benjamin J. Bland, John Blake, Jean Bonai, J. Bonay*—they went on and on, filling two columns.

Aliases of an international terrorist. Aliases of a dead man.

Two words echoed in her mind: *Dead boy*.

A chill ran across her skin like a breeze over water.

"What happened to the investigation?" she asked.

"Ben Black died," Sweetheart said, his voice barely audible.

In this room, just as in others, the walls were lined with the maps, the patterns of Sweetheart's MOSAIK—the gestalt of deciphering information from isolated data, of connecting the dots, of discovering the topography of the bigger picture.

In this case for the purpose of constructing a profile of Ben Black, a man who for decades had disappeared like mist, alternately reported dead, imprisoned, tortured, or working under the shade of Qaddafi's and bin Laden's wing.

Sylvia didn't look at Sweetheart but let her voice fill the space. "If the war is over, why not shut the war room down?"

"Because he was better than me, better than MOSAIK. His forensic signature was almost untraceable . . . he never used the same method twice." Sweetheart sighed. "We didn't stop him."

"What did?"

"Luck."

Sylvia closed her eyes; cold leather pressed against her back; in her monkey mind, restless thoughts chased their tails. Ben Black's death had been an anticlimax for Sweetheart—after all those years of pursuit, they had killed him by chance.

Wasn't it Molly Redding who had talked of her uncle's demons?

And then, soon after Black was gone, Sweetheart had transferred his obsession to John Dantes. The linking event? Jason Redding's death; the child had been a random target, a victim of chance and coincidence.

At least that's what everybody wanted to believe.

"All the terrorists you've pursued," Sylvia whispered.

"What do they mean to you, Sweetheart? Where's the synergy? Is it their twisted ideology? Their nihilism? What do you want them to prove? Or is it just that you look at them and see yourself?"

She caught the rhythm of her own breath, and for an instant that sound was the only thing holding her to earth. She pictured Sweetheart standing outside M's workshop, a feather in his hand: *This is the home of a* makuuchi—*a master.*

The words escaped her lips. "You don't believe Ben Black is dead."

"We had intelligence confirmation." Sweetheart stared back at her, his eyes shining dangerously—and then they went flat and closed, as if the man no longer inhabited his body.

"The final circle of hell is reserved for traitors," he murmured, rocking slightly. His breathing was labored and harsh. "Judas Iscariot, Cassius, Brutus . . . the traitors. Dantes had the intelligence, the charisma, the *gift*; he had the chance to help the world. Instead he chose destruction. I won't let you take away Dantes' sins. Now, get out."

Sylvia stumbled from the house, pushing open French doors, fearing she might break the glass. Outside, she forced herself back to the present. Talking. Walking. Slowly coming down. In truth, she didn't think she could stand to be enclosed inside that house a minute longer.

The walled garden was filled with the fragrance of night-blooming jasmine. Moonlight polished the sculpture of the *Fallen Angel* so its bronze glowed with a milky patina, and the decidedly human seraph calmly surveyed the softening dark.

Faint sounds of traffic drifted up the canyon from Sunset

Boulevard. And then, a distant coyote sent a primal message echoing off the urban mountains behind the house on Selma. Her skin raised goose bumps. For a moment, she tasted New Mexico and its crisp arid spaces.

In the high desert around her home outside Santa Fe, the coyotes went crazy on chosen nights. During a kill, there was a terrible wildness to their cries; she thought it must resemble the manic laughter of African hyenas. Always, the day after these orgiastic deaths, Sylvia would discover on her walks the matted feathers from a blue jay, or the barely bloodied puffs of a rabbit's fur. All that remained of the natural and fatal dance between efficient predator and available prey.

Under the spell of midnight she let the stillness of that remembered desert fill her cells, expand her lungs, lure her thoughts to a higher plane where the air was thin and rarefied.

Now, inside her, she discovered an ache created by absence; she was homesick for damn molecules. For that intangible mixture of tropospheric gases at seven thousand feet. She craved comfort. She was homesick, but she couldn't go home.

Behind longing lay something deeper and much more frightening: the sense that she, Molly Redding, Sweetheart, even M had all been drawn into a vortex—*Dantes' Inferno*.

She squeezed her eyes tight, shivering in warm air.

The demons stirred, raising their grotesque heads, sniffing the air for a scent.

Move. Don't let them take possession.

She heard whispering voices: an *abuelita* who talked to *brujos*, a magical child with uncanny vision, an inmate who flew with the night creatures.

A walk on crazy ground . . .

It took her too long to restore any sense of safety. She found herself pacing, jumping at the slightest sounds of night. Everything was wrong. She was going over the edge. She was missing something. Something very dangerous.

She heard the rustling of branches and she looked up. To see the sky—to look for the stars that weren't there. *An empty celestial ocean . . .*

She took one ragged breath. In New Mexico the stars were so bold and bright a person could safely navigate the deepest, darkest night. Arcturus, Antares, and the Corona Borealis in June; Cassiopeia and Perseus and Polaris in December. Standing out like hot jewels against ebony skin.

Here, in this hellish city, there was nothing to show the way . . . not if you were lost. God help you if you were lost.

CHAPTER THIRTY-SIX

At the turn of the nineteenth century, urban anarchists went on bombing sprees in Paris and New York, claiming hundreds of victims. At a time when the new sciences of psychology and psychiatry were exploding with theories—by James, Wundt, Titchener, Kraeplin, Breuer, Freud, Watson—bombers, free of the stigma of psychopathology and reveling in the heroics of revolution, were exploding their infernal devices.

Leo Carreras, M.D., Ph.D., and Sylvia Strange, Ph.D.,
Terrorism in the 21st Century

* * *

3:33 A.M.   John Dantes woke from a nightmare, and he lashed out, his hands forming fists.

"Take it easy, man," a voice said. "It's tomorrow. You're shipping out."

Dantes shivered, gazing up at Officer Jones—but seeing the ghost of the boy.

"Looks like you're doing better with that arm," Officer Jones said slowly.

Jason Redding had visited again in the dream. Dark holes where his eyes should be. Such sadness in his heart. There were no secrets between child and man.

You're killing yourself with hate, the boy had whispered.

Dantes tried to answer but he couldn't breathe. Disgust lodged in his chest, blocked his throat, until he couldn't suck any air to his lungs.

Dying, he thought. *I'm dying*, he said in the dream. *Dying because I failed them . . . first Bella, then Laura, then Simon, then you.* He gazed at the boy, imploringly.

"C'mon, man, are you okay?" Officer Jones asked.

"No," Dantes whispered.

Coal eyes glowing, Jones stared down at the inmate, who made no attempt to respond.

Dantes remembered a passage from somewhere in the chaos of his feverish brain:

"There are times I believe I'm going mad, not psychotic, not schizophrenic, but mad in some banal way. I have no use for the pseudosciences of the mind; when I touch my madness, I know psychology has failed to explain the darkness of the human spirit, those quiet corners of despair that never see the light of day. That's when I turn to the city, civilization, a maze of streets always leading me somewhere, even when I'm lost, even when I'm blinded by the loss of faith."

He stared up at the white peeling plaster on the ceiling.

No sky, no heaven, no peace. He tried to save what he loves most, but his actions have led to coward's hell.

"Dantes, man, didn't you hear me? You're shipping out. Time to move you to the transfer station. Last stop before Colorado."

It was as if those words finally woke him from the darkness.

He sat up, shaking off the sleep, the dream.

"I hear you," he said, his voice hoarse but audible.

"You can't take much," Officer Jones said, kindly. "But you don't got much anyway. You want to take your books?"

Dantes mustered a smile. "Yes, thank you, Officer Jones. I would like to take my books. You ever been to Colorado?"

"Never have. Heard it's nice, though. Lots of trees and all those mountains."

With no help, Dantes stands. He straightens his clothes, he runs his hands through his hair. He needs a shave. And a bath. He stinks of hospital and sweat.

He wonders if the Feds are satisfied now that he has given them M's cave. He can picture the abandoned warehouse just across the water from Terminal Island. No accident it had been visible from his prison cell; M leaves little to chance.

Mackie's back in town.

"I could use a good meal," he said to Jones. "What day did you say it is?"

"Saturday, by a couple hours."

As the officer gathered together the few possessions in the hospital room, Dantes closed his eyes. He waited to see if he could feel the presence; they've always had that connection; over the years, the miles, they've never lost that.

"I know you're coming," he whispered.

Officer Jones looked up from his work. "You talking to me, Dantes?"

"Yes, Jones," Dantes said, eyes still shut.

"What you say? I couldn't hear you, man."

"I said, 'This time, I'm ready to meet you halfway.'"

CHAPTER THIRTY-SEVEN

> There was nothing to it. The Super Chief was on time,
> as it almost always is, and the subject was as easy to
> spot as a kangaroo in a dinner jacket.
>
> Raymond Chandler, *Playback*

3:43 A.M. M has come to worship darkness.

Only in her soft arms does he find fleeting peace.

Darkness and pain. His life—all that's left.

Dantes has betrayed him, sending the Feds.

And they have done their bootjack swagger, pissing all over his workshop; they have violated his last sanctuary.

He watches bitterly from his truck, which is parked on the hill a half mile from the derelict factory. He sees the two Feds who are waiting for a stupid bomber to show himself. Well, M isn't stupid—*he knows you can't go home again*.

So he sits, tracking images on the monitor of his laptop.

This visual and spatial representation of the world represents more than two decades of work. True, it bears faint resemblance to its schoolboy inspiration, but nevertheless, the seeds that grew this creation were planted when he was a gawky love-struck teenager.

With the press of a key, lines overlay images, layers upon layers, worlds upon worlds.

Map of heaven. Map of earth. Map of hell.

A three-dimensional construct.

The blueprint; his master plan.

It's part of the job of charting geographic information systems, mapping miles of conduit, recording a city's infrastructure, both above and below ground. There is a vault where steel pipes—originating from the transformer station—carry enough volts to blow half a city sky high.

Cables, wrapped in oil paper and lead, and sealed in neoprene, are fed through ducts. Each duct bears electricity produced at major generating plants; the plants supply transformers; the transformers lead to underground rooms.

Tap into the power of a cable and you can connect to a power station, an airport, a harbor, a dam. Let the infrastructure work for you. Stage one: the crucial interconnection of neurons from the spine—the simplest of remote dialing systems. *Phone it in—blow it up.*

He is touching nerves that lead directly to the nerve center, the brain . . .

Bottom line. He has a very simple plan to stop the heartbeat of Dantes' greatest lover: Los Angeles.

Time to move the operation along.

The Thief and a hooker have been prepared to meet their maker.

And the woman—she will serve as the bait.

By possessing her, he will initiate a reaction similar to an explosive chain. Molecules expanding, splitting, combusting. All to end in one big bang.

His fingers work the keys; the screen goes blue, then white again.

M begins to type:

> it is time for the next tier
> we tire of waiting, dont kare if the end
> we sacrifice what false prophet values most
> the "she" he loves
> can be found at the mouth of hell
> already wating

No question they will follow her scent, travel down to *his* burrow, *his* territory, where the world is a quiet, insulated place. Even before Dantes, M craved the comfort of dark hidden spaces. After the accident, he found himself slipping below the surface of the world at any opportunity.

The surgeons in Europe made him whole again—at least skin-deep whole. But the sun irritates his scars, ferreting out memories of pain. And then there is the pain of torture always fresh in his mind.

"Goodbye, LA. Farewell, Angel Face."

He studies the message, finally deciding that it isn't what he wants to say.

Don't give it all away, he thinks with a smile.

He begins again.

> She lives in the red world of death . . .

Nope. Torch song with violins.

> You fucking bastard you didn't even come to our funeral!
> You didn't call, you didn't write.
> I want to rip your head off your neck and stuff it up your asshole.

* * *

Over the top.

> there is a hell for those who ignore the cries of the
> innocent . . .

That's more like it.
Subtle, yet with a hint of gusto.
There's so little time to spend in the seventh circle.
And yet that is where the violent drown in a river of their
own blood and dead men die again and again and again.

CHAPTER THIRTY-EIGHT

George Metesky, the Mad Bomber of New York, had a
seventeen-year career, and signed his work *F.P.*; the
Unabomber maimed and killed for eighteen years, and
marked his bombs *F.C.* John Dantes left poetry. What's
with these assholes?

Officer Robert Macias, LAPD bomb squad

4:07 A.M. "Jase?"
Molly Redding sat up in bed. Confused by sleep, half
blinded by tears, she saw a ghost where white curtains billowed in the fourth-story window; she saw the face of a
small boy instead of the calico cat.
She moaned, catching the damp sheet between her teeth,
rolling over and folding herself into fetal position. If only she
could stay enclosed forever—without moving, without
breathing. It didn't ease the pain, it simply allowed a less ex-
cruciating numbness to tone her existence.

Please, God, bring Jason back and take me.

Stop. The bargaining would kill her; she couldn't let the loop begin to play.

Please, God, torture me, but give me back my son.

Please God, his life is not over—it's just beginning.

A trade: one life for another; my life for my son.

The scale won't tip and no one will be the wiser.

Oh, dear God, please . . .

This small corner of night was the time when dying seemed wise. Death was the cool breeze. Death was the woman with the soft, sweet voice. Death was the straight road to Jason. Death was the ticket.

Molly reached out, fingers sliding into the table drawer beside the bed, encountering cool metal. The sharp edge of the razor gave her a taste of what was to come. She withdrew the blade, holding it to the light, while blood beaded on her injured thumb. Molly felt warmth rush through her muscles as she placed the blade across her pale bluish skin. Her weariness ran so deep she knew she had just enough energy left to strike deep with the blade—once across each wrist.

Metal began to bite . . . she heard Jason cry out . . . and then a white butterfly drew her eye.

Molly turned her head to track the small ivory business card fluttering from the bedside table. Unconsciously she released the pressure on the razor blade against her skin.

A face filled her thoughts: Sylvia Strange. She pictured the warm brown eyes, the kind mouth, the face alive with intelligence. An energy flowed from the woman, and it was Sylvia's strength that Molly needed so desperately at this moment.

She rolled over, clutching the blade in her palm, reaching down for the card—

But this dark night was taking on a different shape.

Molly didn't react when she heard the noise. The swollen heart of her pain told her maybe the universe had finally listened. Perhaps Jason would shuffle in from the kitchen, barefoot, tousled, and smelling of sleep and milk. Her baby would snuggle beside her on the bed. She would press the curls away from his forehead. She would kiss his cheek before he could squirm away.

Another sound. A footfall. It did not belong to a child.

The sound came from the real world, not from one of her nightmares. A presence. Someone in the room with her—not the cat. Not her dead child.

An emergency that demanded her response. In real time. She sat up, completing the action in slow motion. But she had no desire, no fight left in her, no reason to live.

Not until Einstein meowed and propelled herself from the ledge. Not until Jason, her ghostly child, took her by the shoulders and shook her hard. He gripped her hand and refused to let go. Not even when Molly saw who was in the room.

"Michael," she whispered calmly, thinking he'd brought solace, knowing he'd brought evil, all in the same instant.

The pain had not been complete until now. Betrayal cut a heart that Molly had believed was dead. No, there was life there.

Enough to make her want to laugh at her lover. At the hypodermic needle in his hand.

Then she saw that it wasn't Michael—*not her angel*—it wasn't the man she loved. This man had the same blond hair and blue eyes, the same youthful face, the same scar on his arm. But the eyes—one real, one glass—belonged to nobody, to nothing at all.

She lunged from the bed, darting across the room.

Einstein shrieked as Michael caught Molly by the ankle. She fell hard to the floor, bruising bone; Michael huffed, not expecting a fight, and fending off cat claws.

Molly felt a sharp sting in her butt, and she kicked out, arms flailing. Her rage against the world, against a God who had taken everything, finally found a home. A ragged cry tore loose from her throat; she thrust out her legs again and again.

He answered with a hard fist to her face.

As Molly dropped off the ledge of consciousness, falling hard toward a huge, dark hand, she remembered the blade in her fingers. Guided by something much more powerful than self, she mustered her strength and sliced the blade deep across Michael's soft flesh. He cried out, enraged.

Molly felt the fingers of night close around her weary soul; she lay down beside her sleeping son and snuggled close.

CHAPTER THIRTY-NINE

> When the hour is very late, you have to shock people out of their fear, their inertia. Yes, I believe that. History makes that point painfully obvious.
>
> Professor John Dantes, radio interview, 1990

4:37 A.M.   It was Sweetheart who roused Sylvia from half sleep.

"I need you *now*."

"What—"

"*Molly*. Meet me at the car."

And then he'd disappeared from the doorway.

She stumbled into jeans and T-shirt, didn't even stop to pee, just grabbed her high-tops and baseball cap.

Luke was at her side as she half ran down the hall toward the garage. He shoved a page into her hand, relaying news in a breathless, verbal shorthand: "This e-mail came in four minutes ago. Computer's set to alert us. I tried Molly—no answer, no machine. Fifteen minutes to San Pedro if you burn rubber. On orders, the cops are waiting outside her apartment."

Luke already had the passenger door open on the newly leased Mercedes, and he shut it firmly when she was inside. "I've got the maps up—ready to plug in any new coordinates. Purcell will meet you there," he called out, as Sweetheart gunned the engine.

Sylvia didn't read the e-mail until they were pulling out of the iron gates.

> hell 4 thse who ignore cry innocents
> mke best victims
> sweet heart?
> yr niece so luvly
> read yr map well bet. palace and rivr
> we meet agin
> M

5:19 A.M. If Los Angeles was a dreaming woman, San Pedro was the crook of her elbow, where she rested her head on the Pacific. Molly Redding lived on a hill overlooking the docks and the choppy blue-gray waters of the harbor, where tankers were lined up along the landing piers.

A squad car was parked on the street outside the modest

1950s-style building where Sweetheart had just entered the single glass door. He was beginning the ascent by stair to the fourth floor.

Sylvia followed on his heels.

They discovered a uniformed cop rooted just outside Molly Redding's apartment.

Sweetheart flashed his credentials. "Did you go in?" he asked sharply.

"Yes sir, I did. To eliminate the possibility of a 10–45." The cop nodded. "There aren't any bombs."

With a growl, Sweetheart invaded the other man's space. "You did not *locate* an explosive device. Doesn't mean it's not there. You got that?"

"*Sir.*"

"If you moved one molecule of evidence—"

"*No sir.*"

They brushed past the officer into the small apartment, treading very carefully, acutely aware of the possibility of booby-trapped IEDs.

Light was the first thing Sylvia noticed; the small apartment glowed yellow. Dawn's rays turned the painted walls to melted butter.

The second thing she noticed was the *hissing.* She felt the adrenaline rush just as she spotted the cat—*not a bomb.*

It was a fat calico, cornered between stove and cupboard, fur erect, teeth bared round a throaty yowl, eyes psychotic.

"Einstein."

She turned in surprise to see Sweetheart squatting down, hand out.

"I gave her to Jason," Sweetheart said quietly. "C'mon, kitty, c'mon, cat."

Using calming tones and *no* motion, he coaxed the

animal forward. Sylvia watched open mouthed as the cat—Einstein—not only allowed herself to be held but began to purr in the professor's arms.

He stood very still, lost for a moment in the beating heart of this small animal, a simple connection to Jason, to Molly.

Sylvia left him, stepping into the bedroom, to find herself gazing into the skewed Crayola eyes of a jack-o'-lantern, a boy's view of a Halloween hobgoblin.

"Nietzsche rules!" a voice screamed out.

She swung around to defend herself—

"God is dead!"

"Fuck," Sylvia breathed, inches from a parrot in a cage.

"African gray." Sweetheart was beside her, his body rigid; the cat was anchored to his chest, claws extended. "The feather in the workshop."

"He almost—oh, *Jesus*." Abruptly, she'd focused on the surrounding scene. Sheets from the double bed were tangled across the floor. A lamp had been knocked from the bedside table.

She knelt to find her own business card on the floor. A stuffed tiger, threadbare and one-eyed, peered at her from the center of the bed. The note had been pinned to his black button nose.

she knu wy to 7th crcle
whre hrpies fly tres bleed
Beatrice cn't save her
+ sweetie blows it evry tme
2 late
gne to Ishtr gate 2 rest
enemy shl nver pass
u follw to 8th

*   *   *

"He won't kill her right away." Sweetheart showed no expression.

"She's still alive," Sylvia insisted softly.

"For now."

"Sweetheart . . ." For several seconds, her mind went blank. Her throat so dry she could hardly get a word out. She took a breath. "Dante's seventh circle in the *Inferno* . . . the pilgrim and Virgil have almost reached the nadir of hell."

"In the seventh circle, the trees bleed because they entrap the souls of those who have damaged their own bodies."

"Suicides," Sylvia said, dreading the word.

"Gone to Ishtar's Gate," Sweetheart said quietly. "My niece is the sacrifice."

Sylvia ran her hands through tangled hair. The bangle on her arm slipped to her wrist; the red welt embedded around her forearm resembled a shadow bracelet. "You know him, don't you? You know M."

"So it seems," Sweetheart said hoarsely, massaging the cat, unaware of its struggle for release.

"Ben Black? Is that possible?"

"A ghost?" Sweetheart closed his eyes.

She was inches from his face, and she could smell the faint scent of sandalwood. She said, "Black's common-law wife and child, eighty other people were killed by U.S. bombs."

"We had to go on intelligence—reliable intelligence—but we never had his bones—" His voice broke.

"What if he's come back for Dantes—*and* for you?"

"'The enemy shall never pass.'" Sweetheart didn't react when the cat sank her teeth into his wrist. "Those words were carved on Processional Way, in Babylon, near Ishtar's Gate—"

At the sound of footsteps, they both turned to see Purcell standing in the bedroom doorway. "I've got a forensics team on their way up," the agent said grimly.

"He's got my niece."

Purcell had joined them beside the bed. She was silent for thirty seconds as she read the threat message, then she looked up, her dark eyes narrowing. "When I spoke to Luke, he told me he can only guess on coordinates."

"We're going with the obvious," Sweetheart said bluntly. "Which puts Ishtar's Gate somewhere in a half-mile radius between Fort Moore and Union Station. Just so you know, we're forced to guess scale, coordinates, international standards—there's nothing scientific about it, *nothing*."

"M will lead us partway there," Sylvia said slowly, keeping her eyes on Purcell. "He'll let us get close because he's a sadist." She turned toward Sweetheart, but he averted his gaze.

He said, "We'll use Union Station as our locus—we'll work with Luke."

"I'll notify dispatch," Purcell said brusquely. "It's oh five twenty-nine hours. We'll keep you and Luke on the line—and we'll have agents in the area before you get there."

"And *underground*," Sweetheart said. "Alert transit authority and LAPD to possible IEDs."

Purcell was already punching buttons on her phone. "I'm right behind you. Get going."

"So you know, Purcell," Sweetheart said distinctly. "It's possible we're dealing with Ben Black."

CHAPTER FORTY

True faith belongs to the skeptics.

5:29 A.M. Molly is drunk from the chemicals of pain and fear.

Her mind has cut loose, running wild; not just a single crazy horse but an entire herd race through her skull, sharp hooves clipping brain, slicing senses.

Bound—can't move—neck muscles screaming, so tight, hands and feet icy cold. The dark is all around. The air is frighteningly stagnant—and warm. Can't breathe through the gag.

Can't breathe!

She remembers Michael walking toward her. No expression, that's what's odd, nothing at all in his eyes, blank slate for a face. She'd known it was wrong.

Her own eyes go wide. Somewhere in her soul, she'd been praying he would just kill her, put her out of her misery.

Shame—she feels it coursing hot and fast through her veins. Her son saved her, coming to her side, taking her hand. If Jason was alive, he would fight.

Oh, baby, forgive me.

She'll make sure the man she's known as Michael doesn't get the chance to hurt another child, another human being. She will fight, and she will do it for her son.

For the first time in a year, inches from death, Molly Redding has found a reason to live.

She opens her eyes, shuts them, opens them again. Does she see some tiny glimmer of light?

There are smells—sharp and sour. Fuel of some kind? Oil? Also the horrible, sweet scent of organic decay. A dead rat or mouse. *Something dead* . . .

Sounds. The faintest hum. A loud rumble that rattles her bones.

Her heart begins to pound again, threatening to break through her chest.

Keep the heart slow, so I don't waste oxygen.

This box will not be my grave.

Ticking . . . ticking . . . she can hear it now.

And then the slow, shuffling footsteps so terrifying in darkness.

A voice speaks to her; she recognizes the man she's known, the man she's *loved*.

He whispers, "Angel Face . . ."

She whimpers—clamping down on the gag to shut off the panic—then pulls back, shivering at the sting of his fingers on her face.

"Scare you, Angel Face?" He is almost visible now, a charcoal outline against the darker background. "I'm just taking away this nasty thing."

Tape rips skin from her face, tearing bunched fabric from between her teeth. She cries out, then begins to scream. The sound is abruptly severed when he slaps her hard enough to stun.

"No . . . one . . . can . . . hear . . . you . . . Angel Face." He must be repeating the words until she struggles up to the watery surface of consciousness. "We're the dead. The forsaken. *We're the damned, Angel Face.*"

She cries out when blinding sun sears away the darkness; the harsh artificial light burns holes in her retinas. She wants to shield her eyes, but her arms are bound. The numb pain steals her breath.

She can't focus on his familiar face because it continues to disappear behind double suns, the scaled shadow on her optic nerve. "Fuck you."

"Do you know anything about implosion formulas?" He is making polite conversation. "What am I, stupid? I keep forgetting you couldn't even add up your checkbook, Angel Face."

There is a new sound, wet and spongy—and the pungency of something fresh. The first object her eyes discern: an apple. He is slicing through an apple. And he is smiling at her, shaking his head, chiding. "I bet you're thirsty."

Oh, God, the dryness in her throat is torture, but she ignores the pain and finds her voice. "You're sick," she whispers. "You're pathetic."

"Feeling brave, are we?" He is displeased and sarcastic. "Mustering our gumption, by golly."

Molly recognizes familiar notes in his voice. They've shared a bed, shared nights, shared their bodies. Why did she think this was love?

I trusted you, she thinks, I *prayed* to God in gratitude.

"I have to introduce you to a friend," Michael says.

He turns away, turns back, grunting.

She feels the bile turn in her stomach, churning up her throat.

The man is dead, and his eye—

Just like Michael.

And there's another body.

She doesn't try to block out the rage. Let it flood every cell; she'll turn his evil back on him.

"You're going to make a phone call for me, darlin'."

She squeezes her eyes shut, tries to shake her head. "Nnnooo . . ."

But he says something that changes her mind.

He says, "By golly, Miss Molly, if you give me any trouble, I'll blow a hundred Jasons to hell just for the fun of it."

8th Circle . . .

And There Was a Great Earthquake

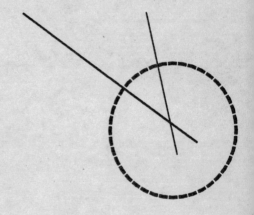

CHAPTER FORTY-ONE

$$W(\text{TNT·equivalent}) = W_{exp}\ (P_{cj}/p_0)_{exp}/(P_{cj}/p_0)_{TNT}$$

Air shock wave equation (Paul Cooper and Stanley
Kurowski, *Technology of Explosives*)

5:57 A.M.   As if they'd heard a subliminal signal, Sylvia and Sweetheart simultaneously stepped out of the Mercedes to gaze up at the creamy Spanish-style facade and red-tiled roof of Union Station.

Impatient pedestrians—early-morning commuters traveling by subway, train, bus, and light rail—passed by. A distant siren filled the air; to an observant eye, law enforcement was more visible than usual.

Sylvia turned to see Leo Carreras jogging across the closest parking lot. He came to a stop at her side. He was slightly out of breath. "Purcell should—*here* she is."

A gray-and-brown car zigzagged through traffic. Special Agent Purcell brought the Lincoln to a stop at the curb. As she exited the vehicle, squinting into the glare of the sun, her sunglasses slid down her chocolate nose.

"We've alerted LAPD and the transit guys; they're prepared to evacuate the station. So far, the search teams haven't turned up a damn thing." She surveyed their immediate surroundings—parking lots already filled with cars, commuters coming and going, a train pulling up on track B just beyond the main terminal. And buildings—everywhere—a million places for a bomber to hide. "We need more than guesswork—" Her phone emitted a sharp bleat, and the air took on an instant electrical charge.

"This is Purcell. Give us ten seconds, then put him through." She eyed Sweetheart. "M. He wants you. Keep him talking, we're running the trace."

At that moment, a gray van pulled up behind the Mercedes, and a man wearing Levi's and a golf shirt stepped out. Purcell—followed closely by Sweetheart, Sylvia, and Leo—sprinted to the open door, motioning them to climb inside. Sylvia went first, then Sweetheart and Leo, and then Purcell joined them, slamming the door. Another agent was already inside; that made five bodies and assorted surveillance equipment encased behind tinted, bullet-proof windows.

The agent was wearing an almost invisible headphone. "The speaker will pick up everything unless I cut off reception," he told them. "Keep your mouths shut unless you want him to hear you. Ready?" He extended an index finger in Sweetheart's direction; with his other hand, he clicked a switch. He nodded—*go*.

Sweetheart identified himself by name.

For a moment, there was nothing.

Then a voice issued from a speaker: "Uncle Sweetheart?"

"I'm here, Molly. Are you all right?"

"He says the missiles killed his family," Molly Redding said softly.

"Let me speak to him," Sweetheart said. "I know he can hear me."

"He killed Jason, and he's going to kill me, too."

"M? Why are you always hiding behind women and children?" Sweetheart asked. "Why do you let them take your bullets for you?"

"Are you talking about me? Or you?" This new voice was male, monotone.

"I'm talking about *you*: Simon Mole—Ben Black—M."

They waited. Sylvia realized she was holding her breath, and she expelled a soft stream of air reluctantly just as she heard the voice again.

"I believe in retribution."

"Let Molly go," Sweetheart said calmly. "You and I can settle our score. I'll meet you anywhere you want—I'll come alone. You have my word."

"This is *my* show," he responded softly through the speaker. "If I say *jump*, then be ready to jump." He was silent for several seconds. "If I say *die* . . . "

"As long as you keep Molly alive, you have my full attention," Sweetheart said. "Isn't that what you want? *Attention?*"

Sylvia bit down on the tip of her thumb—*don't push him too far.*

"I want to talk to Strange," M said impatiently.

All eyes settled on Sylvia—Leo mimed *stretch it out*—she nodded.

"I'm here," she said. "What do I call you?"

"*Simon* works."

"Bear with me, Simon. I missed some of the basics. How many hostages do you have? What do you need so we can end this without anybody getting hurt?"

"It's just me and Molly McGee," Simon said. "Too late for negotiation. I already told you and the Feds what I needed. Nobody pays attention these days."

"I'm paying attention. I want to understand—"

"No, you don't. You're just interested in Dantes."

Purcell was leaning forward, listening intently to

communication from her tiny earphone. She gestured to Sylvia, then she pointed toward the window, toward Union Station, mouthing, *Almost got him.*

"Simon—," Sylvia said, nodding at Purcell. The interruption had thrown her, but she didn't have the time or the room to stumble. "*You've* controlled this show from the beginning."

"Bullshit!" Now he sounded the way she imagined Simon Mole should sound. Whiny, peevish. "Nobody listened! Not you, not Sweetheart, not even Dantes! But I'll *make* you listen."

"Is this about getting back at Dantes?"

"No . . ." His voice broke. "*Yes.* I'm tired of the games."

Sylvia froze when she heard Molly Redding's scream in the background.

"I'm going to die," Molly sobbed. "He's going to blow us up."

"Molly, where are—"

"Shut up or she's dead," Simon said. "It's all over anyway. Tell Dantes I left him behind to rot in hell."

"You can tell him yourself," Sylvia said, desperate to offer bait.

"I'll trust you to give him the message. And while you're at it, tell Sweetheart—no more genetic future."

"Talk to me—," Sweetheart interjected.

"Please—" Through the speaker, Molly Redding's voice cracked with terror. "Don't let him—"

"Molly!"

But the line was dead.

Simultaneously, Agent Purcell made contact with FBI monitors. "We've got him," she said. "Just northeast of Union Station."

But Sweetheart was already out of the van. Sylvia followed.

She scanned the surrounding buildings, her gaze lingering on the low arches and soft angles of Union Station.

Sweetheart stood rooted, eyes closed, face tilted upward. He created a still point in the midst of chaos.

She heard him call to her, and a fragment of refracted light drew her eye skyward to the logo MTA.

Three o'clock. North by northeast. She shifted her body to stare up at the elegant tower with its angles of white and gray and blue, building and sky working together in visual harmony.

Ishtar's Gate. Not Union Station but its closest neighbor, the Metropolitan Transit Authority; MTA. The gateway to a city.

And then Sweetheart stepped forward, just as the molded tower began to crumple in upon itself like wadded paper, echoing the deep reverberating noise of destruction. People screamed, crouching to the ground, their faces turned skyward, displaying astonishment.

Ishtar's Gate—in the process of meltdown—but standing even as glass skin shattered and half its skeleton was exposed to air. A shimmering aura of fragments forming where solid matter had existed. Positive and negative space shifting in an instant. An atomic bomb, a tornado, a black hole—the clouds rising in mushroom curves.

A large chunk of twisted metal landed on the sidewalk not far from where Sylvia leaned into shelter behind the car. The deafening roar, delayed by physical barriers to sound waves, followed. People were thrown off balance.

For an instant, time stopped. Then sirens split the air.

Through it all, Sweetheart stood staring up at Molly Redding's tomb. A great roar escaped his throat, and the sound was swallowed by the echo of the explosion, and then it was lifted into the sky like a horrible bird.

CHAPTER FORTY-TWO

Each human is progeny of environment, be that island, savanna, rain forest, or mountain. Echoing the great Sierra chain, Los Angeles has thrust itself violently upward and outward, indelibly shifting landscape and vista, psyche and soul—shaping, molding, testing its offspring; seducing generation after generation—man, woman, and child—to the promise of its urban bosom, a dry teat of steel and glass.

John Dantes

Sunday—10:10 A.M. Sylvia stared out at the western flank of Los Angeles. Viewed from the fourth floor of the FBI's Los Angeles field office, the city appeared to be functioning as if nothing extraordinary had happened over the past eighteen hours—as if a high-rise in the center of downtown hadn't been ripped in half by a bomb, as if a miracle hadn't kept the casualty rate down to a handful. She touched her fingers to the tempered windowpane; one story below, a man dangled from a harness; while she watched, he scraped a squeegee over glass. Below the window washer, on street level, pedestrians flowed in a light but steady stream to and from the parking area.

The FBI's LA field office (on Wilshire Boulevard) is the third-largest in the nation. With almost six hundred agents, the office handles the work created by an abundance of bank robbers, star stalkers, gangsters—and bombers inspired by the explosive precedent set on October 1, 1910, when activists blew up a corner of the *Los*

Angeles Times building, killing twenty, injuring seventeen.

The same historical crime—unionists versus antiunion forces—motivated the placement of one of John Dantes' bombs almost a century later.

But Sylvia wasn't thinking of Dantes or the questions that remained unanswered. For a few minutes, she was hardly aware of Special Agent Purcell, now carrying on a telephone conversation at her desk. Instead, she thought of Molly Redding and her son, Jason. She pictured the delicate, childlike features of the woman, mirrored in the boy, both dead by the hands of the same bomber.

"We've got the preliminary forensic report," Purcell said, as she hung up the telephone. Slow to start, the federal agent seemed reluctant to speak at all, but she ran fingers through her cropped hair and said, "The remains of at least two adults—one male, one female—have been identified. No positive DNA match yet for Molly Redding, but we did find some personal items still fairly intact. They've been identified by her uncle. The lab is rushing the PCR-DNA, and we should have it within forty-eight hours." Purcell sighed. "If the building hadn't been closed for quake renovation, we'd have a casualty rate in the hundreds."

Sylvia didn't turn away from the window; she could feel the warmth emanating through tinted glass. It was only four o'clock, and the sun wasn't giving the city any breaks when it came to heat. "Did you locate any existing samples to match Simon Mole's DNA?"

"Not yet. Not Simon, not Ben Black." The agent chewed on her lip; fatigue showed around her eyes, evident in the darker shadows above her cheekbones. "But we'll stay on it until we have conclusive evidence—I promise you that."

Sylvia nodded listlessly. She respected Purcell—was

even beginning to like the woman—but she didn't want to be here listening to promises that the FBI had no power to make. She took two steps back toward the window, touched her fingers to glass, but the exterior view didn't distract from the feeling that she was caged, contained inside a small cubicle. Her mind felt imprisoned— her thoughts kept hitting the wall.

Through the room's sole interior pane—narrow and vertical—she'd gleaned a limited view of a long carpeted hallway; she'd seen Sweetheart pass by earlier—he hadn't reacted to her presence.

Sylvia had a pounding headache, but she kept her focus on Purcell; the agent was weighing how much more information her superiors had authorized her to share with a civilian psychologist against what she *felt* she owed Sylvia out of respect. Respect won out over duty. She offered a photograph.

"A digital cam—an experimental street surveillance project, thanks to LAPD—caught this food service truck, which was packed with ANFO, entering the underground parking lot," Purcell said at last. "A variation of the Oklahoma City and WTC bombings. You can just see the face of the driver. The camera was mounted on a pole opposite MTA, about a hundred feet away, but our techs enlarged the picture."

Sylvia stared at the photo. Three quarters of the driver's face was obscured, allowing only a glimpse of profile. "M would hire a driver for delivery. Exposing himself, taking stupid risks, that's not his style." Sylvia shifted, aware of her own uneasiness. "What about the man living with Molly Redding?"

"We're on it." Purcell nodded. "But he didn't leave much of a trail. The neighbors hardly saw him—he came and went at all hours. He drove a truck—it looked like some kind of company truck—but nobody remembers a logo. Everything in the apartment was clean—too *clean*."

"Just like the workshop. *That* sounds like M. An invisible man with an African gray who quotes Nietzsche." Sylvia picked up a pencil from Purcell's desk. When she flipped it nervously through her fingers it slipped to the floor. "Do you believe M is dead?"

"Do you?" Purcell asked.

"No. I believe Simon Mole is dead."

"M and Mole are the same man," Purcell said warily. "We're not talking twins or split personality . . ." There was the slightest lift of inflection punctuating her statement.

"No multiple personalities," Sylvia agreed, pressing her fingers to her aching temples. "But, we *can* talk about splitting. It's almost as if Simon Mole died in the Mulholland explosion—but it was a *psychic* death, not a physical one. That's why the profile match only came up with a midrange probability."

Purcell offered an exaggerated sigh. "Any profiling system has its weaknesses, including the human brain."

Too carefully Sylvia examined the surveillance photographs that decorated the walls. Bank robbers—in the act of threatening, shooting, killing. There were labels attached to various photos: *He's-No-Einstein Bandit, Red-Nosed Bandit, Bully Bandit, Ma and Pa Bandits, Romeo Bandit.* A handwritten standard proclaimed, LA, BANK ROBBERY CAPITAL OF THE WORLD. The impact of the photo collection was a low-grade depression, inspired by the frequency, stupidity, and banality of index crimes.

Sylvia took an unsteady breath. "How is Sweetheart?"

"You haven't talked to him?"

He's ignoring me."

"He's shutting out everyone, if that's any comfort."

"No particular comfort," Sylvia said softly.

Purcell hesitated. Once again, she was weighing need to know against closure. She said, "Dantes will be shipped out to Colorado sometime late tomorrow."

"They're going through with the transfer?"

"It's time to get the Calbomber out of Los Angeles. You didn't hear it from me, but he's been moved to the old holding facility at LA City Detention Facility." She shook her head, touching one finger to her lips. "The U.S. marshals will handle the actual transport."

"Get me in there."

"I can't do that—"

"Purcell."

"I thought you were going back to New Mexico tonight."

"I need to see Dantes one more time." Sylvia kept her voice level. "That's all I ask. I won't be back to bother you."

"Give me an hour to see what I can do," Purcell said finally.

As Sylvia turned to leave, she blinked against a sharp blade of sunlight reflecting off glass and metal. An internal voice whispered: *This isn't over yet.*

1:08 P.M. The Los Angeles City Detention Facility consisted of several large facilities sprawled over dozens of acres. The luckiest inmates in the main facility rated a view of Sunset where the famous boulevard began its eastward journey under the alias of farm labor reformer Cesar Chavez. Beyond the avenue, downtown's skyscrapers formed the sharp peaks and deep valleys of the urban landscape, fed by a river of railroad tracks.

Those same inmates had enjoyed front-row center seats for the bombing of the MTA tower at Union Station. Now they could kill time with a bird's-eye view of investigators as they sifted through rubble and searched for bodies.

But Sylvia wasn't stopping at the jail.

She checked in at the kiosk. While a correctional officer verified her destination via radio, she took in the familiar shape of the fortified landscape: the twelve-foot-high perimeter fence topped with razor ribbon, the security towers, the steel-reinforced walls of the housing units. She'd done more than her share of time in prisons.

The CO waved her through with terse directions to go straight, take the first right, then the second left. So that's what she did.

The jail's old holding facility was a rusting green warehouse. An armed officer manned a second kiosk, where access to the inner perimeter fence was controlled. As she passed through the chain-link gate, she could see the silhouette of another officer inside the double doors twenty feet ahead. John Dantes was well guarded.

A landing strip and heliport outside the old holding facility provided a convenient stopover and transfer point for especially high-risk or high-profile criminals.

Inside, a man with skin the shade of black walnuts announced he would accompany Sylvia down a short flight of stairs to what used to be called the Irons.

"Why *the Irons?*" Sylvia asked CO Henry as the clip of their heels hitting smooth concrete echoed off the bare walls.

"Way back, they used to put the escape artists down here," CO Henry said. "Just to make sure they didn't get itchy feet, they welded them to those old ball and chains."

LAPD's Officer Jones was seated outside cell number nine. His eyes lit up with recognition when he saw Sylvia. Apparently, he was going to deliver Dantes to the door of the transport helicopter and into the custody of U.S. marshals.

"Hello, Jones," Sylvia said.

"Hey, Dr. Strange," the officer said in a soft voice. He stood to unlock the door while CO Henry stood by. Jones asked, "Came back for one last look?"

"When is he shipping out?" she asked. Her question was indiscreet, but Jones didn't hesitate to respond.

"Word is, sometime tomorrow or the day after. But good thing you got here today—tomorrow he'll be restricted." He shifted his feet. "You're not supposed to be in there unless he's cuffed." He rubbed his jaw, shrugging. "You want me inside?"

"Just stay close to the door."

He stood back while she entered John Dantes' temporary home, a windowless ten-by-ten-foot cell.

Dantes was no longer strapped to a gurney. He wore no bandages. No IV fed chemically laced fluid into his veins. His color was good, he looked rested and very healthy. His prison cottons were clean, he was neatly groomed.

At the moment he occupied one of two chairs, both of which were bolted to the floor. A book rested on the table, *The Count of Monte Cristo*.

Dantes' hands were folded in his lap. He said, "Thank you, Jones," but his eyes were on Sylvia. "I was hoping I'd see you again. I'm sorry about Sweetheart's niece."

"I don't think he cares how you feel." The door closed quietly; she was left alone in the cell with Dantes.

"Do *you* care?" he asked.

She didn't answer. The silence lengthened; she sensed his discomfort.

He reached for the book, held it up. "It's quite good," he said. "Wrongful imprisonment, escape, romance, revenge. What else is there?" He half smiled. "Have you read it?"

"I've always meant to." She was driven by restless energy, a dull, free-floating anxiety. She took eight steps, which brought her in a complete circle around Dantes. As she moved, she noted the copy of his own book that rested on the blanket of the jail bed. She caught a quick view of some notes scrawled on a Big Chief pad. She saw the photograph of his mother, taken in the late 1950s, when Bella was a beautiful young woman.

And she read the title on a faded hardcover: *Hysteria: History of a Disease*. The author was Veith; she was familiar with the text, which covered the historical origins and symptoms of what was now known as conversion disorder.

"I'm glad you came," he said, studying her, his voice low and smooth. "On my last day in Babylon, you're the only one I cared about seeing."

"You never know," she said slowly. "I may surprise you and visit Colorado."

She had reached her starting point, and she had a clear view of his features—the secret smile on his lips, the gray-green eyes with their unblinking gaze, the delicate definition of bone beneath the skin of his jaw. They gave away nothing of the man.

"You're feeling better," she said, sitting. Her fingers worried the bangle on her wrist. Now they were no more than four feet from each other.

"Much better."

"No more seizures?"

He shook his head, unclasping his hands, pressing palms to thighs.

"Headaches?"

"My health—"

"Numbness or paralysis?"

"—is good." Dantes smiled slightly; his pupils contracted, revealing color.

Sylvia forced herself not to look away; Dantes seemed

curious, engaged, entertained. He was *waiting* for her next move. She realized he believed himself to be in absolute control—but she knew that his level of somatic dysfunction couldn't be faked. Not completely.

Finally, she said, "I found out something about your mother."

"Really?" Nonchalance was a stretch.

"Did you know she was diagnosed as a schizophrenic?"

"No."

"She was hospitalized more than once. The last time was just a few weeks before she died."

Dantes stared at some point in space; but his thoughts had turned back to the past. "My grandparents never told me," he said finally.

"Some schizophrenics suffer intense mental anguish. Even the people closest to them can't reach through the psychosis."

He closed his eyes, retreating to a private place. Finally, he took a deep breath, mustering himself. "Why is it so hard to accept the fact I couldn't save her?"

"Children often believe they hold the power of life and death in their emotions."

"God's power," he said softly, offering that melancholy smile again. "These days I'm forced to make due with my very temporal powers of manipulation."

"Charcot's most popular hysterics were the pretty young women," Sylvia said, following his lead. "They put on quite a floor show for those neurotic neurologists and surgeons."

"True," Dantes said. "The audience enjoyed the excitement, the titillation; they wanted to be fooled. That's what magic is about—a dance between performer and audience."

"Or between doctor and patient?"

"One can't exist without the other. Charcot, Breuer, and

Freud had their own hysterical reaction to their flamboyant patients. But they documented their case studies; they provided valuable information for the fledgling science of psychology."

"There is such a thing as true suffering."

"We're back to Goya's lunatics," Dantes said.

"Most of Freud's and Breuer's hysterical patients had diagnosable psychopathology."

"I'm not a sideshow, Dr. Strange."

For an instant, Sylvia felt the familiar electricity of his gaze; but just as quickly his green eyes turned cold, and his wildness retreated to some dark, closed corner. "No, you're not," she said softly. "Simon Mole was the sideshow."

"It was a long time ago," he said. "We were going to change the world."

"And Laura?"

"She was in the wrong place at the wrong time."

"What happened?"

"Acetylene becomes unstable at twenty-five pounds; its explosive range is two point six to eighty percent." He recited the facts, his delivery a throwaway. "It's just a little lighter than air. In a closed space, if someone forgot to close a valve on the acetylene tank, a catastrophic explosion would occur." For the first time that hour, Dantes looked away. "I was the only one who escaped the blast. It was a revelatory experience. Until that moment, I actually believed I possessed the courage of my convictions."

"You ran."

"I damned myself."

She stood, and walked to the door, where she stopped for one last look back. "M is alive, isn't he?"

"It's all over, Dr. Strange." Dantes offered her *The Count of Monte Cristo*. "I already know how it comes out," he said. "Read it one of these days."

* * *

3:55 P.M. Behind the wheel of the rental, Sylvia turned west on Sunset.

The famous boulevard ran like a seam through the city. The seedy offices, the fast food mini malls, the restaurants advertising Thai, Korean, Spanish, Indian, sushi, and Kentucky Fried all blurred together into a ribbon of simple commerce that revealed the complex patterns of human migration, cultural exchange, and expansion.

Keep going and narrow high-rises constructed of glass and steel stood shoulder to shoulder, bordering concrete and asphalt. At Doheny, the real estate consisted of trendy shops. Jog west, and the clubs and night joints sat sullen during daylight hours, like floozies waiting to come alive at sunset with that first sip of eighty proof. Traffic formed a constant glimmering ribbon, winding, twisting, mile after mile. The air held the bite of smog.

But she was only aware of the anxious looping thoughts: a boy named Simon Mole was reborn as an international terrorist who called himself Ben Black; when U.S. missiles hit Afghanistan in 2000, Black escaped to reconstruct himself yet again—into M.

A man who had survived bombings, train wrecks, prison, and military attack wasn't going to conveniently commit suicide in downtown LA.

M *doesn't die, he transforms.*

So, where was he? What was he waiting for?

She turned south and east, drawn once again to the heart of the city. Downtown, she followed the seam of Main Street, the zero point, the dividing line between east and west. Shadows were coming to life under the glow of neon.

Fifth, east of Broadway, was no-man's-land: skid row.

It was the barrel bonfires center street and the cop cars

rousting drunks that gave the Nickel away. In Los Angeles, the fifty-block row is centered between Main, Third, Alameda, and Seventh. Liquor stores—windows blocked with cardboard—were plentiful, and the multistoried transient hotels showed depressing, dingy facades.

Driving slowly—not stopping—Sylvia recognized the faces of the mentally ill, the addicted, the homeless. She wasn't sure what she expected to find, but she was left with the hangover of misery and poverty.

She turned west, heading for the ocean and one last night in LA. Early this morning, Leo had flown to Arizona to consult on a case. His condo was dark. Inside bungalow number four, the shades were still drawn.

She made phone calls—and she heard the news from Matt: Mona Carpenter's husband was being held in custody, charges pending. He'd violated a restraining order; he'd seen Mona an hour before her suicide.

"Her parents want him charged with assault and attempted murder," Matt said.

"He didn't force the pills down her throat."

But Sylvia knew the dark power Bob Carpenter had wielded over Mona. The news brought sadness, but also the beginnings of closure.

She showered, lingering under the hot beads of water; her skin was splotched red when she slathered on cream. Crawling naked between clean white sheets, cradling the pillow, she fell into an almost narcotic sleep to wrestle with dreams that were fitful, nightmarish.

It was Molly Redding who smiled at Sylvia from the dream world. She held out one hand, beckoning. Her mouth didn't move, but she spoke: *Is it revenge that counts at the end?*

As Sylvia surfaced to consciousness, the question echoed. She made her way to the window, opening pale yellow blinds. The night was dark, and fog shrouded the streets and the ocean beyond. There were nine circles in Dante Alighieri's *Inferno*. M had taken them through eight. Why would he stop there?

She picked up the copy of *The Count of Monte Cristo*. Thumbing through, she missed it the first time. But the key was there—a half dozen words, almost invisible—traced between the margins.

CHAPTER FORTY-THREE

The world is filled with such joyous noise when one is deaf to the sound of pain.

Mole's Manifesto

Monday—4:12 A.M. Sylvia slammed both fists on Sweetheart's front door.

Molly Redding's message from the dream ran through her head: *Is it revenge that counts at the end?*

She raised her fists to knock again—

The door opened and she stumbled forward, connecting with Luke's chest. Recovering her balance, she caught a quick glimpse of day-old beard and bleary blue eyes.

"Where is he?" She pushed past him, stepping into the foyer. "Where's Sweetheart?"

"Dr. Strange—Sylvia—we're all exhausted," Luke began. He followed the psychologist, watching her nervously, not trusting her manic energy. "Listen, we've all been through—"

He broke off, looking past her toward the private wing of the house.

"You shouldn't have come."

Sylvia swung around at the sound of the deep voice. She found herself within inches of Sweetheart. The sight of him—face blanched ashen, gray circles, disheveled clothes—was frightening. He shook his head, turning to leave.

"I have the coordinates." Sylvia held up the book—*The Count of Monte Cristo*.

Sweetheart stopped.

"The *true* coordinates for Babylon," she said softly. "We were wrong. Ishtar's Gate isn't MTA. I don't believe M was even near the tower when it blew."

"Molly?" Sweetheart whispered. No one said anything for several seconds. Slowly, he held out his hand for the book. His fingers were trembling.

She opened to the page to find the words carved in paper: *brdwy = euphrtes/e wall = 110/pro wy = la st/neb pal = pueb*.

4:25 A.M. Topographic images flashed across the monitor. Magenta, turquoise, ebony, onyx, peach, violet—a blinding swirl of colors delineating contour feet, rivers, zones, erosion and flow patterns, counties, roads, municipalities.

To center on urban Los Angeles.

And Babylon.

The images jumped as the skeleton of the twenty-first-century megalopolis filled the ghostly skin of Babylon, encompassing more than three thousand years of urban history.

Shifting one way—then the other at lightning speed.

Perched restlessly in front of the monitor, Luke spoke

in the clipped sentences of someone short on time. "Four correlation points—should be enough to rubber-sheet—to overlay. Say your prayers—I'm switching overhead."

Sylvia blinked, shielding her eyes. Light from the projecting system illuminated the floral patterns of the antique rug. She saw Sweetheart watching her; she offered him a weak smile. She felt afraid—they were a day late, a dollar short.

This was one last game dreamed up by Dantes, the master manipulator.

Overhead, red, yellow, and pink stars were exploding in infinite space. The lost world of Babylon. Los Angeles, a dying civilization.

"All right," Luke murmured tightly. "I can zero in on the coordinates now. Hollywood-Babylon, here we come." His fingers flew over the keyboard.

Turning away from the light, she looked up. On the dome of the ceiling lost galaxies glowed. Shadows erased the stars and brought the maps into stark relief. Overlapping points burned red.

Suddenly the screen image froze—coordinates aligned and locked in three-dimensional space. She was staring at a web of intersecting lines—at its locus stood the Tower of Babel and LA's ziggurat; north to south the Euphrates melded with Broadway, each a river of transport through an urban center.

North wall of Babylon—the 101 freeway.

East wall of Babylon—the Harbor Freeway.

Euphrates—Broadway.

Processional Way—Los Angeles Street.

Nebuchadnezzar's palace—the historic pueblo Nuestra Señora la Reina de Los Angeles—Our Lady Queen of the Angels.

Sylvia paced nervously. She needed to be in motion. Tension was a palpable presence in the room.

All civilizations come to an end. *Dantes' world*.

Mole's hell. Excavation of the past.

The two had finally met, overlapping to create one doomed city.

"The traitors of the ninth circle," she whispered.

"The deepest level of hell." Sweetheart's delivery was sharp. "Luke—take the picture *down*; show me the lowest level of the grid."

The images began to shift, moving through the city's topography in an ever deepening pattern until infrastructure covered the screen: an intricate web of gas, telephone, cable, electrical conduits, water, sewage, storm drains, subways, manholes, transmitting stations, and subterranean utility vaults.

A subterranean world where a person could get lost.

Or be found.

Luke clicked a mouse and a red light shimmered on the overhead projection.

"Ishtar's Gate," Sweetheart whispered.

"Aligned with the corner of Cesar Chavez and North Vignes," Sylvia said.

As Sweetheart crossed the room, he said, "Allowing a half-kilometer radius for error."

"When I spoke to Pete Carson with county flood control, he said there are condemned utility vaults in that area," Luke said. "And some underground storage areas that belong to the railroad."

"So . . ." Sweetheart glanced away from the screen, closing his almond eyes. Behind him, the first light of dawn leaked through louver shades, outlining his body with a faint golden glow. "John Dantes sends us west from the LA River in an underground drainpipe for three quarters of a mile, to turn north at the lesser drain and head for Sunset, now Cesar Chavez, to keep an eye out for Ishtar's Gate along the way."

"You'll be following the street grid, only *lower*," Luke said, ignoring the professor's caustic tone. "Because that's how the utilities are laid out, although there are exceptions." When he saw their questioning expressions, he said, "We can't plan for all the possibilities: condemned tunnels, old locks, abandoned sewers, oil pipes from the boom days, or train tunnels."

Luke leaned back in his chair, tapping his fingers like a drummer. "Pete Carson says he'll guarantee us old railroad and subway tunnels run through this entire area from Union Station to Roundout Street, which is traversed by tracks."

"Adjust the image to the east."

"Roger that." Luke guided the mouse with his thumb; the subterranean world slid across the ceiling.

"Looks like this flood drain runs just north of Union Station all the way to the old pueblo." He stopped, as if he was registering the immensity of the search, the odds against finding anything at all—alive or dead.

"Purcell says LAPD will send officers along with county maintenance, if we tell them where to go in," Sylvia interjected, trying to pull her mood out of its downward spiral; they couldn't afford to crash, not now. "And you said this guy from county flood control—Pete—will take us in? That gives us two teams."

"Pete's ready to meet you both at the two forty-one maintenance station," Luke said.

"Purcell's contacted LA Detention," Sylvia added. "They're moving Dantes out within the next hour."

"Let's go *down*," Sweetheart said bluntly.

Sylvia stopped in her tracks. "You said Ben Black had a master plan—he was going to destroy New York."

"Detailed plans to attack major infrastructure—water, power, shipping, air transportation." Sweetheart's voice faded, but he recovered. "We found the blueprints after the missile strike. Among other things, Black knew which vault and transformer to blow in order to knock out Wall Street."

"Blow it to hell," Luke said softly, a stricken look on his face.

Sylvia took a quick breath. *How much damage could one man do?*

CHAPTER FORTY-FOUR

When I was a young boy I knew right from wrong,
somewhere 'cross the years I lost my way.
    Jai Uttal, "Conductor"

Monday—4:28 A.M.   In darkness, John Dantes lay on the jail bed, fingers laced behind his head.

It was time.

He stood carefully, stretched, and walked across the small cell to the door. When he angled his neck to get a view through the window, he could just see the back of Officer Jones' head. Tight dark curls bobbed gently. Dantes smiled. His faithful watchdog was asleep at the door.

He walked to the toilet, where he unzipped his pants, slid them down, and sat.

Prisons took away the privilege of privacy. He was used to performing almost every bodily function in front of witnesses. But this time, there were no obvious witnesses, and he wasn't responding to physical demands.

He let his right hand brush the wall. In his palm, he possessed an ordinary penny. He gripped it tightly between close-cut fingernails.

He tapped the penny against the metal pipe of the toilet. Metal was an advantage of an old facility.

None of this had happened by chance. He was pleased with that fact.

Tap, tap, tap.

The sound echoed, then it was still again.

Two young men bound together by idealism, by brotherhood, by loneliness, and finally, by hatred.

Tap, tap, tap.

At the age of eighteen, they had made a pact; they had taken a vow of blood: "If either one of us is ever imprisoned, the other will set him free."

Deliverance. Salvation. The ideals of love before love turned to hate.

Dantes had broken the vow.

Simon Mole had not.

Tap, tap . . .

Finally, at 5 A.M., Dantes heard what he'd been waiting for.

His own signal coming back at him from below.

Tap, tap, tap . . .

Good.

Very soon now it would be time to face his friend, his enemy.

CHAPTER FORTY-FIVE

Pausing in his savage meal, the sinner raised
  His mouth and wiped it clean along the hair
  Left on the head whose back he had laid waste.

> *The Inferno of Dante*, canto XXXIII, translated by Robert
> Pinsky

5:01 A.M. Think of a labyrinth, a dark cloister laid beneath a city of light and air, a conglomeration of cells, a network of arteries, veins, a pathway of neurons, which are the messengers of everything utilitarian in the body of Los Angeles.

Think of gas, electricity, water, oil, steam, fuel and waste, heat and coolant flowing through a maze of conduits and pipes inside tunnels, all laid out beneath the four thousand square miles of the LA basin.

In this way, every building, every high-rise and warehouse, every subway, every airport, every bus station and train station and gas station is interconnected and allowed to breathe, eat, shit.

Welcome to the underground infrastructure of any megalopolis.

Welcome to the belly and the backbone of Los Angeles—the place where she is most vulnerable.

Welcome to the core of urban existence.

M intends to shoot it all to hell.

Not for the last time in his life, he is a dead man. First it was Simon, then Ben Black. What happens from here on out is up to M and Dantes.

M will create change through molecules; they are his god—those invisible jots, those fragments, those bonds to be broken, resulting in explosive reaction.

Dantes will create change by revisiting the past.

M hasn't seen sunlight for almost thirty-six hours. He's been too busy with final touches on Project Inferno to come up for air. That doesn't matter much because his desire for close, dark spaces has turned to a pressing hunger.

M has come to worship darkness.

Only in her soft arms does he find fleeting peace.

Darkness and revenge—sweet, sweet revenge.

Here, beneath the city, the earth surrounds him.

If I was mad, I'd never return to daylight.

But he isn't mad, he thinks, smiling to himself. A lesser man would never have survived the loss, the imprisonment, the torture. He isn't a lesser man; he's just a guy who settles old scores.

One for his sister, Laura's, death.

One for his scars.

One for loss of innocence.

One for disillusionment.

One for his years in that hellhole.

One for the torture.

One for the Tomahawk missiles.

One for the loss of his god and his soul . . .

And who will pay the price?

While he works, he gazes up at the metal racks where two cables join in a lead sleeve. He wraps his hand around the molded sleeve, feels the warmth of a live thing—the heat, the faint vibrations of a heart or a pulsing neuron.

Phase two: a series of explosions will rip open the city's nervous system. He has chosen strategic locations.

One: just beneath the Criminal Courts Building complex, the nerve center of LA's Superior Court.

Two: Los Angeles International Airport with its jet fuel feeder lines.

Three: First Interstate World Center and the Central Library.

Four: Santa Monica–Golden State–Pomona–Hollywood Freeway interchange.

Five: Santa Monica–San Diego Freeway interchange.

Six: Los Angeles Harbor, San Pedro.

Seven: Union Station and the nerve center of the city's transportation (to finish the job he started with the MTA tower).

Eight: the war room at the dams.

Initiation is easily accomplished by a remote dialing system hooked through the city's own communication system. He is pleased with this simple solution. He has spent more than a year infecting this city; like the AIDS virus, he can turn LA's cells against themselves.

The beast is crouching in the bowels of the city.

The monster has spread her tentacles of death and destruction.

And the beast, the monster, goes by the name of technology.

From New York to LA, the phone companies relegated their POTS (that's plain old telephone service) lines obsolete.

All that perfectly good copper conduit crisscrossing the city, laid neatly in place underground and forgotten. It's so much easier to just lay new fiber-optic cable.

Well, *almost* forgotten.

Digital subscriber companies remember that copper conduit; they might even rejuvenate those once-defunct lines for their clients, sending superfast, supercompressed information fifteen hundred feet in less than half a nanosecond.

Ben Black, bomb tech for hire, remembers the copper, too. Miles and miles of it with the power boosters already built into the conduit—the power to do the big jobs.

It's all so simple—it's done with a variation on cluster radioscopes and telescopes—the very large array of explosives. You simply synchronize a dozen smaller scopes to create one massive one.

Simon says, hook up a phone at point A.

Call point B.

After two rings, the call is forwarded to point C.

Ditto, point C to point D.

It's a chain reaction, a party line that stretches from LA Harbor to LAX to Water & Power to the war room at the dam to the flood channel at Ballona Creek to Union Station to the Red Line hubs.

But the best part is the payoff.

At each and every point—A, B, C, D—he's wired a thirty-second delay to a primer charge; the primer connects to the main charge, the main charge is C-4 and PTN.

When the first call goes through, an electrical spark zooms along that good old copper conduit, the phone rings, the delay is triggered by the spark, and the call—hence the charge—is forwarded on to the next daisy in the chain. Meanwhile, the first bomb goes BOOM.

But that's the second phase.

Phase one: a series of explosions will neatly pop gas lines as they cross over and intersect with LA's steam pipes, sewers, and 2,370 miles of storm drains. The gas will do what comes naturally—it will saturate available space, creating one massive bomb just ripe for initiation.

But don't forget what truly matters to M: *phase one* will offer freedom to a prisoner.

John Freeman Dantes will share in the glory with M because Edmond Sweetheart will make that possible. Sweetheart is an honorable man, and he will come after Angel Face.

Now M gazes at the charge that is set in an eight-inch bored hole just above his head. This work was completed last week. The charges must be set close to detonation time because they are sensitive, and like beautiful and restless women, they don't like to be kept waiting.

Just checking. He tamps fixative around the base; he has set each of four charges on a delay. They should be accurate, contained, doing only the damage that he anticipates.

M is directly beneath the LA City Detention Facility.

He closes his eyes, listening very carefully.

Yes, there it is: *tap, tap, tap* . . .

He lifts his wrench.

Tap, tap, tap . . .

9th Circle . . .

The Lair of Traitors' Souls

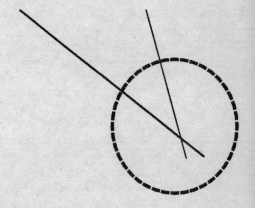

CHAPTER FORTY-SIX

He's the kind of guy who doesn't leave the house without a pair of M26A1 frag grenades in his pocket. A real Boy Scout. Always prepared.

Devil's Hand: The Life and Death of Terrorist Ben Black
(International Press, 1999)

5:39 A.M. Except for headlamps, it was pitch black in the storm drain.

The county flood control truck didn't exactly hurtle. Pete—supervisor with the Army Corps of Engineers' Los Angeles flood control—kept his foot lightly on the accelerator, maintaining an average speed of thirty miles per hour; but navigating a subterranean tunnel—the effect of light curling up this concrete cylinder driven deep through hard rock and earth, light flaring at the edge of total darkness only to die out—made for optical, spatial, and energetic illusions. It made for intense discomfort.

"We've got about twenty-four hundred miles of storm drains under LA," Pete said, tightly. "Flood control can take up to a hundred and forty-six thousand cubic feet of water per second before the LA River overflows. When she does flood, it's a hell of a sight. Bad seasons in thirty-six, sixty-nine, and the nineties."

Sylvia was wedged in the front seat between Pete and Sweetheart. In spite of his size—or perhaps because of it—Sweetheart had an acute self-awareness: he always knew what place his body occupied in space, and his physical boundaries were meticulously maintained. Sylvia thought most babies must take up more space.

"Right now," Pete continued, "I'd say we're under our zero point . . . Main and First Streets."

Which would put them directly beneath downtown Los Angeles; they were approaching the locus point—the intersection of Vignes and Cesar Chavez.

Sylvia bit her lip nervously, staring out at the walls as they drove; although graffiti had become scarce after the first quarter mile or so off the LA River, a few displays—the work of brave and definitely *not* claustrophobic artists—were fleetingly visible. No elegant bison or big cats. Instead, there were skulls, swastikas, gang symbols, gargoyles: guardians of the underworld. Each one a statement: I was here, I existed long enough to leave my mark. A discourse on the human need for procreation, belonging and identity, and the inevitable.

FUCK EVERYTHING

DEVILS RULE

DEATH WINS

Urban cave paintings. LA's new Avignon.

"Who came down to hell to fetch his true love back to earth?" Pete asked in a voice that was too loud for the tight, dark space.

"Orpheus."

"Who fought the Minotaur so he had to follow some string to get out of the maze . . . you know that one?" Pete turned toward Sylvia, his face alive with nervous energy. The truck came perilously close to scraping paint on concrete.

"Theseus," Sylvia said sharply. Sweetheart was too damn quiet.

"I knew that—" Pete braked suddenly. "Hey . . . what the . . .?"

Sylvia peered out into the briefly illuminated subterranean cylinder. Her throat felt uncomfortably tight.

"Somebody's been sleeping in my bed," Pete said quietly. He opened his door, set one leg outside, and flashed his torch on a pile of rags, a rough foam mattress, a few fast food wrappers.

Sylvia peered at the makeshift camp, following the flood control employee. "Have you ever run over anybody?"

"Almost squashed two transients once . . . missed 'em by inch—Jesus H. Christ—" Pete's voice dropped out of sight.

A deep rupture in the belly of the drain had left a jagged concrete gash—roughly three feet across. It was passable on foot, but the truck wasn't going to like the jump.

"What the hell?" Pete asked, shaking his head. "I'm going to send out a marker on this one."

"I want to scout on ahead," Sweetheart said. He squatted down, running his fingers along the edge. He sniffed his hand. "He used RDX tape. All he had to do was run it along the cut he wanted."

"Give me a minute to mark down our bearings," Pete said in a somber voice. He disappeared inside the truck, his mind on his business. By agreement, any transmission would be relayed ASAP to Special Agent Purcell and the LAPD—another search team was active beneath the city—but that meant leaving the deepest and most remote areas of the storm tunnel to find a location with reception to transmit.

The truck's headlamps illuminated a word spray-painted in black: CAINA.

"In the ninth circle, the *Inferno*," Sweetheart said quietly, "Caina represents treachery against family, against a kindred spirit."

Sylvia shivered, suddenly cold in the dank, moldy tunnel. M had marked his trail.

Pete joined them, his features drawn, his voice sharpened by anxiety. "If you want, we can scout ahead a ways."

They left the truck—following headlamps—traversing the drain on foot. The stench of foul water, moldy earth, and things unthinkable caught in their throats. In places, a sharp chemical odor hit as if they were wandering in and out of noxious clouds.

After a long five minutes, the drain had curved just enough to shake off most of the light from the truck's beams. Now their flashlights cut through darkness like three yellow blades; the world was made of instants, abrupt illuminations, inches sliced away from the dark whole. Sweetheart slowed behind the others. From what Sylvia could tell, he was examining the concrete wall where something had snared his curiosity: beneath a metal plate, an electrical conduit—and a neat cluster of wires.

"Sweetheart," she prodded. When he didn't answer, she dragged her heels, then trailed after Pete. Each step was hazardous due to rock, broken glass, sticks, and whatever else the runoff deposited.

"What have we got here?" Pete's question bounced around the tunnel. He flashed his beam ahead on the high curve of the ceiling. Sylvia missed it at first; but when Pete prodded at the wall with his stick, rubble fell clear.

"Is it some kind of drain?"

"Not one of ours."

"What do you mean, not one of yours?"

"Somebody decided to improvise their own . . . and did . . . a pretty sophisticated job of it."

She glanced back for the professor, who was twenty feet behind, the beam of his flashlight darting wildly as he scraped at the wall. "Your average transient wouldn't do that, would he, Pete?"

"Look here . . .," Pete murmured, in a fading tone that said his mind was already following a curious scent. "Somebody carved out some toeholds."

She saw the faint, tight cuts in the wall; they resembled the prehistoric marks she'd seen in the Anasazi cliff ruins of New Mexico; three or four inches across, an inch or so deep. She said, "The ancestors of the Pueblo Indians used them so a person could scale a sheer face and escape enemies."

"Good idea." Pete grunted, already hoisting himself nimbly up the wall. While Sylvia watched, he scrambled through an opening high in the concrete.

Moments later, she followed. Head and shoulders crammed through the opening, she could see by the light of Pete's flashlight. Within a matter of inches, the passage expanded to a width of at least three feet and a height of about five feet. A ripple of emotion washed over her body, carrying with it the ancient fear of cramped dim spaces. She couldn't see where this new tunnel ended; it stretched out like a long, dark throat.

She scrambled the rest of the way in: "What is this, Pete?"

"It's old. Hell, I've never come across it before." He ran workingman's fingers along one wall and dust formed in small clouds. "Old clay . . . so it could've been used for sewage or water." He whistled uneasily. "I've been at this job for so damn long I've heard just about every tall tale."

"About?"

"Old Spanish tunnels."

"Spanish as in seventeen hundreds?"

"Where a guy like Zorro could hide out for years," he said flatly. "I don't like it. You better stay back—this kind of unshored tunnel is what we in the earth business call a very long tomb."

"I'm going to be stupid and follow you." But she was afraid, fearing what she'd always feared most—the loss of bearing, emotional or physical, the failure of her ability to rely on her instincts. That was where Sylvia felt most vulnerable in the world. She imagined it was the way a sailor used to navigating by the stars must feel when clouds obscure the night sky.

She held her breath while the worst of the dust cleared. She was grateful for the hard hat, the leather gloves, the clear goggles. The first aid kit she carried was digging into her hip through the fanny pack. She slipped the eye protectors on now.

Pete's flashlight illuminated earth held in place by a thick weave of roots, rock, clay. Sylvia was afraid to swallow. She dreaded each step that took them deeper into earth. This territory belonged to other creatures, night animals.

Appropriate that a mole would have a lair, she thought.

Pete grunted, coming to a standstill. He had his light directed straight ahead; in front of them, the tunnel had collapsed in upon itself. His light beam began to chip at the dead end tunnel wall. For the thirty or so still-navigable feet in between, three low openings led off the tunnel. But they were crude, cramped, diving even deeper into solid earth.

She just had time to brace herself against the internal recoil when more dirt showered down on them, forcing her to squeeze her mouth shut. As the dust settled, she opened her eyes and wiped the grit from the lenses of the goggles. Pete's flashlight was on the tunnel floor; its yellow, dying beam illuminated the wall and the three letters painted in black: DIS.

Dis, city of nether hell. An invitation to journey deeper into M's world.

"We're going back," Pete said suddenly. "I can't be responsible—have to get help."

Recovering his flashlight, he brushed past Sylvia, with a gruff "C'mon now."

She didn't follow. Behind her, she heard Sweetheart's voice—somehow he'd managed to squeeze through the opening.

"You know exactly where we are—you take the truck, Pete, send help," Sweetheart told the flood control employee. "Sylvia?"

"I'm not going back without you," she said softly.

"I've got all the reason in the world to keep going—even if it means I never come out. You don't have to—"

"Shut up and move."

After a moment, Sweetheart nodded, saying, "Tell them Dr. Strange and I will probably need a rescue."

"This ain't legal," Pete said.

"It is if I pull rank," Sweetheart insisted. "Federal government beats LA County." Sweetheart flattened his mouth into a grim line. "You're wasting time we don't have. On your way out, take a look at the electrical cable in the main flood drain. Our friend seems to have wired your tunnel."

"Wired? As in . . .?" Pete's eyes went wide.

"Explosive capabilities," Sweetheart said. "Make sure Special Agent Purcell gets that information."

"Right." Pete stared at them both, shaking his head at the same time he offered Sweetheart his tool belt. "This might come in handy," he offered. "We'll get back just as soon as we can. I know how to find you." And then he was gone, returning through the mouth of the improvised tunnel to the main flood drain.

Sylvia willed her rapidly beating heart to slow down. She squatted, got down on all fours, and began to crawl through the smallest opening, just below the entrance to nether hell.

No way Sweetheart would make it through—but when she turned, there he was, her substantial shadow.

For a distance of about fifteen feet this new tunnel was narrower than the last—but it widened out abruptly. Fighting off the claustrophobia, and in spite of the dust, Sylvia inhaled deeply. Breathing helped.

Sweetheart took the lead. They traveled in silence. The distance was almost impossible for her to gauge—fifty feet? One hundred?

Abruptly, they heard the dull rumble of dirt giving way; the sound came from behind—a cave-in. The flashlight revealed a wall of earth where a section of the ceiling had collapsed.

Silently they moved forward, only to arrive at another dead end. But this time there was a short chimney overhead, extending to a narrow opening.

Another message on the wall: ANTENORA.

Without waiting for a question, Sweetheart said, "Betrayal of cause or country. If it makes you nervous, turn around."

"It doesn't make you nervous?"

"Scared shitless."

"I feel better," Sylvia managed to whisper. Her throat was aching. The flashlight attached to her hard hat cast eerie shadows. "*Turn around?* Damn you. And go *where?*"

In the semidarkness, she caught Sweetheart's face in the

light beam and saw him crack a smile. Then he leveraged his arms on the sides of the chimney and he hoisted his body upward, barely fitting into the space. He was down again immediately. He said, "Metal door."

"Manhole cover?"

"Probably an entrance to a utility vault."

"Locked?"

"Or sealed."

"Pete's tools."

Sweetheart flashed his light at the tool belt, searching through items and finally selecting a rusty, generic key. "Worth a shot."

Almost instantly, he hoisted himself again, bracing himself with one foot wedged against earth, grunting, groaning. But it wasn't going to happen.

He dropped back down, shining his light along the ground. "Didn't I kick something hard about ten feet back?"

Sylvia followed the light beam as it caught the tail end of a piece of rebar. She retrieved the makeshift prying tool, handing it to Sweetheart.

For the third time he pulled himself into the chimney, forcing the metal tip into a rounded seam of the cover. He leveraged himself again, arms overhead, going for one final effort before his muscles failed.

Five seconds, ten, fifteen—when the cover gave way, it didn't just open; it *broke*.

There was a sharp cracking sound. Warm, stinking air hit their faces. Sylvia gagged.

Sweetheart dropped back to the tunnel floor, whispering what sounded like a curse. Then he scaled the ladder, lifting himself up and into the dark, boxlike space.

Sylvia waited a few seconds, then she gripped the ladder and let her feet take the rungs in small, quick steps.

It was a concrete, rectangular vault, about ten by ten by six. The walls were covered with thick metal sleeves running the length of the room to duct banks. The sleeves probably contained electrical cable or phone lines. In the center of the room, a heavy, rusting ladder hung down from a hinge in the ceiling.

Sweetheart directed his light along the floor, moving clockwise. At first, Sylvia thought he'd discovered a dog lying on a bundle of filthy rags.

Then she saw the pale, lifeless face of Molly Redding.

6:31 A.M. As they crouched over her frail body, Sylvia felt the faintest butterfly breath on her arm, saw the most subtle movement of ribs expanding beneath Molly's worn yellow T-shirt. She was alive—barely.

"She's dehydrated, in shock," Sweetheart said, accepting the first aid kit from Sylvia. He broke it open, scattering contents, extracting a plastic needle, tubing, and a saline bag. His hands were steady while he readied the supplies.

"You'll need to hold the saline bag so we get infusion." He slapped Molly's arm, pinching, looking for a vein to guide the needle, but her skin was so pale it seemed bloodless. Finally, he positioned the tip above a faint and flaccid vessel. "I'm going for it," he said grimly.

The needle nosed its way through surprisingly resistant skin; a small bead of blood welled.

Molly moaned.

Sweetheart repeated her name, tapping her cheeks with his fingers. "Come on, Molly, come on back." He fed the end of the tubing into the needle.

Soft hazel eyes fluttered open. Whimpering in pain, Molly tried to focus.

"It's okay," Sweetheart said gently. He cradled her in his arms, whispering, "I'll make it be okay."

Molly stirred; perhaps she tried to raise a hand, but her muscles refused to function. She opened her mouth. Sylvia leaned close to hear.

"Sweetheart . . ." Molly swallowed, taking a shuddering breath. "I prayed . . ." Her eyes closed again.

He refused to let go of his niece; he ordered Sylvia to direct light at the ladder overhead. It ran from the ceiling to the floor at a slight angle; the metal rungs were heavy and red with rust.

She aimed the beam at the manhole cover just above the ladder. For an instant, they had a way out. The light reflected off heavy security bars—the cover had been intentionally sealed, bolted over with heavy metal panels that crisscrossed the cast iron cover.

"Show me where we are," he ordered.

Sylvia shifted, exposing empty space before light hit the outline of a rough steel plate in the far wall. From what she could make out, it was some kind of exit, similar to the one they had used for entry—perhaps an opening into another passage.

Did it lead deeper into the subterranean network of tunnels, pipes, ducts? Or was it an actual exit to open air and safety?

Sylvia said, "Let's try to carry her out the way we came."

"We'll never make it. You can try—bring back help."

"Are you sure you can't get us out the manhole?" she asked. She flashed the light overhead a second time. The seal looked tight.

"Maybe we missed something," Sweetheart said.

The beam of light darted like a frightened bird around the room, briefly illuminating the glass case (just above eye level) with a fire extinguisher and the red notice EMERGENCY BOX 3456.

Still cradling Molly in his right arm, Sweetheart shifted

his body to study the case. "From here, it looks clean," he said finally. Sylvia realized he was weighing the possibilities of an IED booby trap versus the chance to get Molly vital medical assistance. "Do you see anything—wires, any sign of tampering?"

"Nothing."

Abruptly, Sweetheart raised one arm above his head. He smashed the glass with his fist, ripping the cover from the hinges. Then he lifted the receiver on the emergency phone.

Almost instantly, he whispered, "*Shit.*"

Sylvia saw it in his eyes—the fear. She made the connection—the box was wired—and she braced for explosive impact, crouching down.

Sweetheart sheltered Molly with his own body.

For thirty seconds nothing happened.

Then the explosion shook the earth like a quake, rattling the concrete vault. Shock wave after shock wave hit, rolling in on a molecular tide closing off one means of escape—the tunnel they had just left—and ripping a hole in the opposite wall. The final wave tore metal paneling from its hinges, propelling it into darkness—

And then the heavy overhead ladder crashed down on them like a falling sky.

CHAPTER FORTY-SEVEN

That night, as I wander downtown, past the Nickel, where fires rage in oil drums, past the sleeping streets of commerce, the ziggurat gleams like the Tower of

Babel and Broadway flows like a holy river toward the promised lands of San Gabriel, Rosemead, El Monte.

John Dantes

6:31 A.M. Just outside Dantes' basement cell, U.S. Marshal Fitz nodded to Officer Jones. Through the window, both men could see what appeared to be the prisoner stretched on the bed, his body almost hidden by a blanket.

"Let's go," Fitz snapped.

Jones glanced at his watch and frowned. "You're early."

"Security move," Fitz said gruffly, as Jones unlocked the door.

Marshal Fitz entered first, followed by Jones, who stepped reluctantly into the darkened cell.

"Put your hands where I can see them," Marshal Fitz ordered. "I need you to stand up—slowly—and move away from the bed."

Dantes' head emerged from under the blanket. "We're leaving now?" He sounded groggy and confused.

"Put your hands where I can see them," Marshal Fitz repeated. "Over your head, *now*."

Dantes stared down at the blanket. Then he looked back at the marshal. "I may need some help," he said softly.

Marshal Fitz took one step forward. That was enough. Dantes swung the section of pipe like a baseball bat, and it connected with the marshal's right arm with a sickening crack. A second blow landed on Fitz's temple, and he stumbled backward.

Dantes had already lunged off the bed, and he grabbed Jones, pulling him forward so his head thumped against the wall.

There wasn't time to do anything else.

The explosion ripped up the floor, blasting through

concrete, sending a spray of shrapnel 360 degrees around the cell; like some fuming satanic beast, it tore its way up from hell, clawing through earth, through metal, spewing refuse, devouring life with its toxic breath.

Bringing darkness.

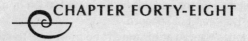

CHAPTER FORTY-EIGHT

I neither died, nor kept alive—consider
With your own wits what I, alike denuded
Of death and life, became as I heard my leader.

The Inferno of Dante, canto XXXIV; translated by Robert
Pinsky

6:34 A.M. Sylvia opened her eyes to discover darkness.

She struggled to orient herself. Had it been minutes since the explosion? She didn't know if she'd been unconscious. She felt dazed, stunned.

Dust clogged her throat and lungs. She was trapped. An unbearable weight was pressing down upon her body.

If she tried to move, pain shot through her muscles. She couldn't see Sweetheart and Molly. She was deaf to every sound except the rush of blood through her arteries.

Abruptly, the sky seemed to lift up, dirt and rubble rained down, and then she could breath again—and move. She gulped air; wiping grit from her eyes, opening them to see a gray ghost. He was inches from her, on bent knees, straining to lift half a ton of rusting metal.

Sweetheart, illuminated by a faint glow, covered with dust.

"Get going," he groaned, heaving the deadweight of the fallen ladder. Molly lay crumpled at his feet. "Find Purcell or Pete. They'll know how to get us out."

Sylvia scrambled for the opening they had used to enter the vault; but it was gone, covered by debris.

"The other way," Sweetheart whispered.

She turned slowly, searching for the only other possible exit. The flashlight on her hard hat still emitted a faint light. Her eyes found the outlines of an opening.

"You know where we are—I'll make sure we stay alive. Get help."

Sylvia scrambled through the gaping black hole.

6:41 A.M. Here in the earthen tunnel, hot dark air pressed in on her like the breath of some massive enveloping beast. The passage was large enough so that she could pick up speed, moving at a crouching jog. At first the tunnel ran straight, and she had visibility up to ten or fifteen feet. But soon it took on more of a slope, angling up, then down. She was beginning to hyperventilate, and her legs threatened to cramp from the strain of maintaining the stooping posture.

Water trickled onto concrete; she splashed through the fetid puddles. As she moved, the space narrowed and flared, again and again.

At one point in the tunnel, the earth was so damp, water drizzled like misting rain, soaking through her clothes, stinging her eyes. The smell of wet earth was pungent; sticks and roots scraped her skin. She protected her face with raised arms, not stopping, afraid to slow down, all the while trying to gain some sense of orientation.

She must have been between ten and twenty feet belowground. At most, she'd traveled a quarter mile since leaving the vault where Sweetheart and Molly were trapped. She had no way of knowing if she had moved west, east, north, or south.

The beam of her flashlight flickered.

This is a dead end. The tunnel will collapse.

The internal voice taunted.

I'm crawling into my own grave. I'll be buried alive.

Angrily, she fought off the dread, ignoring the threat of another explosion, moving forward until someone grabbed her shoulder.

She cried out, slapping away rough arms. Adrenaline flooded her system; it took seconds to comprehend that her attacker was a *thing*, not a person. She gripped the loose segment of vertical pipe, groaning in frustration and fear.

Dirt stung her eyes, and she wiped her sleeve roughly against her face. For the first time, she realized minuscule splinters had penetrated her body and tiny dots of blood freckled her skin. She steadied herself, taking a few deep, slow breaths.

Her flashlight flickered out.

She was alone in the dark—alone with the quickening rhythm of her own heart.

She wrapped her arms around herself, rocking like a lost child in need of comfort. There was no going back—no going forward.

This is what it's like to die, she thought.

She pictured Serena's face.

This is dying.

Then she thought of Sweetheart and Molly trapped in the ruined vault.

M and Dantes had enticed them into hell. She would fail to find help, and they would suffocate beneath the City of Angels.

She let out a single sound, and it echoed.

It echoed . . .

She felt around in the darkness, touching cold, clammy earth, rocks, sharp objects that cut into her palms. She shifted her body, scrambling 360 degrees until she caught it—

Light. A faint circular stream seeping up through the ground.

She began to inch forward.

She crawled until she reached a ledge—and a black hole. The air was cooler here. Her pupils had dilated to absorb even a hint of light. She found herself staring down a twelve- or fifteen-foot drop.

She could barely make out the live gleam of water, a brackish stream, and the double thread of tracks directly below. This must have been a railroad tunnel (now abandoned) that connected to Union Station.

She looked for a way to lower herself into the tunnel. Within reach, a tangle of exposed re-bar extended into space.

Inching herself out over the edge of the hole, she gripped ridged metal. She crawled another few feet until her torso was suspended in air. She was using her body as a counter-weight.

Her feet slipped free, pulling the rest of her down through the opening. She clung to the re-bar as she reached full extension, swinging in midair.

She moved her hands slowly along rusting metal. The muscles in her shoulders and arms burned. Halfway out, the re-bar began to bend, giving way in slow motion.

Don't let it snap, she prayed.

When she was only a few feet from the end of the bar, she lost her grip. Abruptly, she was falling.

She landed hard. The flashlight on her hat flickered to life.

She lay stunned. When she finally moved, she did it

slowly. She made it to her knees. After a few moments, she righted herself, gingerly standing to survey the surroundings.

Apparently, she was inside an old railroad service and storage area. The space was cavernous, and the walls had been shored with beams and lined with metal transport crates.

The tracks were centered like a seam. She began to follow them, searching for daylight, air, freedom.

Within minutes, she reached a dead end. Long ago the tunnel had collapsed, or it had been intentionally sealed off. She retraced her steps.

Only to discover another dead end.

Fear made her light-headed. She forced herself to concentrate.

At some point, this tunnel had connected to main tracks. No longer. Entry and exit had been walled off.

Sylvia circled, letting the thin thread of light illuminate crevices, curves. But she found no evidence of a passage, a door, an egress. She sat down abruptly, exhausted.

That's when she saw the word sprayed in red on the earthen wall. COCYTUS.

She recognized it. Cocytus was the name of a river in the ninth circle of hell. A river where damned souls stayed immersed, frozen to the neck.

There was an opening above M's graffiti. The mouth of a narrow crawlway, roughly three feet by three feet. She'd missed it before because it was well above eye level.

She guessed she was near the site of the old Spanish pueblo of Los Angeles. Perhaps the passage had been part of an aqueduct, or maybe a primitive pipeline left over from the oil boom in the twenties? If so, it might provide escape.

She tried to gauge the distance to the opening. It was

out of reach. She'd never make it without a boost.
rolled a metal drum slowly across the floor.

When it was finally in place, she had the leverage she
needed. She vaulted, pushing off with one foot, scrambling
with the other. She dove headfirst into the hole, using her
entire body to boost herself forward, gaining a few more
inches.

The flashlight died.

She lay still in darkness.

It was a kind of surrender. For a few minutes, the fear
evaporated. When she was ready, she moved. The passage
was just large enough to allow her to belly-crawl.

*To lose track of time. And space. To become completely dis-
oriented.*

She reached a section so narrow, she found herself
wedged in place. Her pulse—already fast—accelerated, and
her breathing became quick and shallow. She could only
wait out the worst: the dizziness, the nausea. She felt faint,
and then her body became weightless; all pain dissolved as
she called out . . .

Sound faded until there was only a ghostly, plaintive
wind that whispered back.

" . . . and demons from the deepest circle of hell would
journey up to earth to steal the souls of the dead . . . but
for earthly traitors these demons were not forced to wait
for death . . . they could steal the soul at the very moment
of betrayal . . . from which point, the soul would reside in
hell, but the body would remain on earth, inhabited by
the demon . . . they took your soul fifteen years ago, my
friend, my enemy . . ."

"Dr. Strange, welcome."

Blinding light exploded. Hot. White.

To reveal a metal-lined bunker, a type of Quonset hut.

Boxes, tanks, lumber, utility containers were stacked along the walls. The floor was dirt. The air smelled faintly of gas.

A figure came into focus. A man with short blond hair, a compact muscled body, striking features.

"You're just in time," he said, squatting down until he was at eye level. He gripped a small knife in one hand.

"I know who you are," Sylvia whispered, shifting her body gingerly so she could lean her weight against the wall. Her shoulders, her spine felt bruised and tender.

For the first time she noticed John Dantes, fifteen feet away, seated on a crate; his wrists were bound with duct tape, which was attached to a hook overhead.

"And you know John. It simplifies matters if you call me M." He smiled ruefully.

"When you've caught your breath," M began, "you might notice you are attached to an explosive device."

She looked down. Her left arm was taped to a large, rectangularly shaped bomb.

"No sudden moves," M said gently. "What with the explosives, and the tanks of acetylene. And I'd ignore any urge to smoke if I were you. Isn't that right, John?"

Dantes didn't respond.

Sylvia stared at him; there it was—the familiar sense that some unknown soul lived inside his skin. "Why are you doing this?"

M clapped his hands twice. "Excellent question. We were in the middle of something when you dropped by." He eyed her speculatively. "Actually, I thought by now you'd be dead, suffocated, along with Sweetheart and his precious niece." He shrugged.

"We don't have time for this." Dantes sounded bored.

M waved him away, saying, "I was reminding Dantes that the *Inferno* was a journey of self-discovery—a journey to God. Historical and eternal. You're a student of the human psyche—wouldn't you agree it's a journey to God?"

"On one level," Sylvia began slowly. Her voice was weak. "It's also a journey through the unconscious mind."

"Exactly." M smiled. "Compared to Dantes, I'm a simple man. After my hero killed my sister and destroyed my illusions and my innocence, I reinvented myself. I eliminated my parents. And I joined any revolution I could find. I interned with the IRA, with the PLO, with Qaddafi's and bin Laden's soldiers—until I was master of my trade. Only then could I take the name of Ben Black—"

"Get on with it," Dantes interrupted sharply.

"Dr. Strange," M said. "Dantes has elected you to be his Beatrice. My friend believes he's in love. I can see it in his eyes. That's the good news. The bad news is, he loved my sister, Laura, too. And look what happened to her; he let her blow sky high. Why? Because he is a *coward*." M paused, abruptly discomfited, as if his own words had penetrated his facade. "Why does a man become a fanatic, a revolutionary, Beatrice? Could it be to escape the truth—that he is a coward and a fraud? Could that be why?"

"It's possible," Sylvia whispered.

"And could a man become a zealot of the faith to escape another truth—that he will betray his closest friend, his cause, his kin?"

"It's called projection—reaction formation," Sylvia said deliberately.

"See, John, the doctor has a name for it." M turned, moving toward Dantes. "A demon stole your soul the day you let my sister die."

Dantes gazed up at him, eyes dull, face impassive. He shook his head. "Sorry to disappoint you, Simon. But I lost my soul long before I met you."

"You always have to have the last word," M said sharply, backing away. For an instant he resembled a peevish schoolboy; then his expression hardened. "We have two possible scenarios. The first belongs to the *demon*. You, Beatrice, remain with the bomb. Dantes and I leave. When the explosion occurs"—he glanced at his watch—"in three minutes, twenty-nine seconds, you're blown to shit and a series of secondary explosions at strategic locations are triggered." He shrugged. "Basically, Los Angeles is crippled—possibly beyond recovery."

M hadn't taken his eyes from Dantes, but now he checked his watch again. "Three minutes, four seconds. Almost time to skeedaddle, but there is a second scenario—and this one belongs to the *fallen hero*." He smiled. "It goes like this. I leave Dantes with you, Dr. Strange. He just has time to cut you free—in the process, he triggers a booby-trap, another switch on the bomb. Do you see that bright orange wire by your elbow? That's the one. LA is saved—the explosion is contained inside this bunker—and it's possible that Beatrice can escape—she has a good thirty seconds to make it out of here and up a ladder to the man-hole. But that's only if Dantes keeps his finger on the little button. When the time is up—*boom!* John Dantes sacrifices himself—he *dies* a hero."

M sighed. "Two minutes, thirteen seconds. Two minutes, ten seconds. Two minutes, seven seconds." He paused, studying his audience, apparently puzzled by their lack of enthusiasm.

Finally, he turned to Dantes for corroboration. "She dies, *yes?*"

Dantes nodded. *Yes.*

"Yes." M tipped his head toward Sylvia. "My fair Beatrice—where is your precious faith now? Don't deny it—you *believed* in John."

M was moving, strolling close to the tanks of acetylene that were lined along the far wall. Sylvia saw the labels, DANGER—PELIGROSO, inscribed on metal. She remembered Dantes' words: *acetylene . . . unstable at twenty-five pounds . . . just a little bit lighter than air . . .*

"Not that it matters," M was saying. "But Dantes would like to kill me and escape. Unfortunately for you, that would be too much like the past." He continued walking, covering space very slowly. When he was a few feet from Dantes, he bent forward quickly and sliced the small blade through the binding tape.

"'Which way shall I fly, infinite wrath and infinite despair? Which way I fly is hell; myself am hell,'" M whispered.

Now that Dantes' hands were free, he massaged his wrists and forearms. He made no move to stand.

"This will interest you Dr. Strange," M said, running his tongue across his lips. "Dantes believes his conversion disorder was all a sham. He conveniently forgets about UCLA—*that* was real. Although he tells himself he's confused things in his memory. But we know better, don't we?"

Dantes looked straight into Sylvia's eyes; there might have been the slightest tinge of regret in the gray-green pupils. "M's right. Bombing is a coward's crime," he said softly. "I lost my faith too long ago to be worthy of yours."

Sylvia stared at him, refusing to let him go, thoughts racing through her mind—Dantes' rigid ideals, his obsession with his mother and his parallel obsession with Los Angeles, his relationship with Simon Mole; a story complete with all the elements of love and revenge.

Except Sylvia still didn't know the story's ending—she couldn't quite believe Dantes would condemn himself to hell. She looked straight into his eyes; he met her gaze, and the energy was still there, still alive.

Sylvia shook her head. "You're not a coward, Dantes."

She saw Dantes react—M saw it, too, and at that same moment shifted, as if to break the connection between Sylvia and Dantes.

M's foot caught the edge of a metal canister; it rolled, raising a clatter. The noise, the movement, was enough to distract his focus.

Dantes lunged forward, and both men went down, cursing. They were on top of each other, hands at each other's throats.

M forced Dantes toward the wall, where acetylene cans tumbled to the floor.

Dantes reached out blindly, grasping a piece of metal pipe. He brought it down hard. There was a dull cracking noise, and M went limp. He lay on his back, eyes wide open in surprise.

"You . . . broke my back," he whispered. "That was never part of the plan."

But Dantes was already beside Sylvia. He ripped through tape with the sharp edge of pipe. Clasping the hot orange wire between his fingers, he whispered, "You knew I'd never let her down—not LA, not you."

"Dantes—"

He wrenched a wire back; there was a sharp clicking sound. "Now get the hell out of here."

She turned, stumbling, facing darkness.

"Go!" Dantes bellowed.

She ran down the tunnel stealing one quick look back. She caught a glimpse of Dantes as he hovered over the bomb.

Sylvia found the metal ladder, climbed—half heaved herself upward to hit solid metal. The cover gave—breaking open—and sunlight warmed her face.

Then she was out, slamming down the manhole cover,

diving across the hood of a parked car, hitting the ground hard.

When the bunker exploded, flames shot skyward through the manhole, the earth shivered, and a roar reverberated through the City of Angels like the echo of winds racing across the desert ruins of Babylon.

EPILOGUE

Seigen jikan ippai!
> Referee (Time's up!)

June 30—two months later . . . Neon bruised the street, pulsing red, blue, orange against slick asphalt. The night was quiet, sounds of traffic muffled by light rain, and the only other pedestrian was a slender woman in a black slicker poised gracefully beneath a white umbrella. Sylvia wiped mist from her eyes; when she looked up again, the woman had disappeared.

She glanced down to see Serena smile, eyes bright with excitement.

The club was located at the intersection of a bitumen trail, Chunking Alley, running west to east. Luke moved casually, in the lead, through a low, narrow doorway that Sylvia would have missed. Just below the sleeve of his T-shirt, and signaling the way, the tattooed flying fish hovered against pale flesh. Purcell and Pete (who was now a hero at county flood control) were meeting them later. Gretchen followed Sylvia and Serena through the doorway to ascend a long flight of stairs.

Sylvia was startled when they emerged onto a long balcony overlooking a small sports arena fifty feet below.

Luke whispered in Sylvia's ear, "It's called the *dohyo* . . . the ring."

Quiet and expectant, an audience of more than a hundred people waited, backed by rainbow-colored flags. "Those are *nobori* banners, Serena," Luke explained. "They list the names of the *rikishi* . . . the 'strong men' . . . those who compete."

Sylvia was looking around curiously. "Where's Sweetheart?" she asked, slightly puzzled and touching the empty seat to her left.

"He's here somewhere," Luke said vaguely. "There's going to be an overload of ritual . . . such as . . ." He proceeded to overwhelm Serena and Sylvia with vocabulary. He said, "This isn't *honbasho*—a major tournament. There are only six of those a year, all in Japan. This is *jungyo*—a ritual exhibition. Even these are extremely rare outside Japan. We're lucky to be here." He smiled. "It's great you two could fly out from New Mexico."

Gretchen touched Sylvia's leg and said, "The wrestlers join a *heya*, a stable, usually when they're just out of college. They work their way up through divisions . . . "

"Serena?" Sylvia said, smiling.

"I love this," Serena said.

Luke's voice asked, "When you going back to Santa Fe?"

"Tomorrow morning, early." Sylvia gave the map man a smile. "Unless we can convince Matt to fly out."

"We can," Serena said, quickly.

A murmur of excitement went through the crowd. Sylvia looked down to see several men enter the ring. The two wrestlers were wearing traditional sumo belts.

One looked familiar . . .

"It's very rare that non-Japanese ever become sumo," Luke said. "They're tossing salt, an offering for the gods. . . ." He looked up, over Sylvia's head, and smiled.

She turned, expecting to see the professor. It was Molly Redding who took the seat to her left. Sylvia reached out, clasping Molly's hand. Molly gently squeezed her fingers in return. She caught Sylvia's eye—*I'm okay*. She smiled at Serena and leaned down to give the child a quick hug.

A cry went up from the crowd. Sylvia, Molly, and the entire audience glued their eyes on the ring. The match had begun.

It was at the moment of first contact that Sylvia thought she recognized the smaller wrestler: something in the posture, the stature, the grace. Her eyes went wide, she turned toward Luke—but he kept his gaze straight ahead.

ABOUT THE AUTHOR

Sarah Lovett worked as a legal researcher for the New Mexico Office of the Attorney General and at the Penitentiary of New Mexico. A former resident of Los Angeles and a native Californian, she now lives in Santa Fe with her husband Michael and assorted dogs. Her Web site address is: *http://www.sarahlovett.com/*

SIMON & SCHUSTER
PROUDLY PRESENTS

DARK ALCHEMY

SARAH LOVETT

Available in hardcover March 2003
from Simon & Schuster

Turn the page for a preview of
Dark Alchemy. . . .

Prologue . . .

Doug Thomas fed the cat, walked the dog, and left for work in his two-year-old Subaru Outback. It was business as usual for the thirty-six-year-old molecular-toxicologist except for the headache. A doozy. Gene Krupa playing sticks on his gray matter.

Doug popped two extra-strength Tylenol and donned his sunglasses. Must be his sinuses acting up again; he'd been having trouble lately. His fingers had been tingling and now his field of vision was blurry around the edges. Bad headaches could do that. When his ex-wife called about the child support check, she always had the same three complaints: men, money, migraines.

Headache or no, Doug couldn't afford to stay home. No rest for the wicked, he thought to himself with a tight smile. Stay on schedule, business as usual, no break with routine. Nothing to tip them to the fact he'd pulled off another extracurricular assignment. Ten minutes work—only moderately risky—and this time he'd bought himself the chance to erase his debts once and for all.

Keep up appearances—that's all I have to do. Can't afford to miss a minute at the lab.

This was a crucial "window" for Project Mithradates. The "Mith Squad" had made a major breakthrough— "Building a better biotoxin," he whispered—they'd developed an entirely new manufacturing process (not to mention quantum improvements in the delivery system) using their quarry.

And a fascinating quarry it was—a relative (third cousin twice removed) of *Gymnodinium breve*, the dinoflagellate responsible for Red Tides, and *Pfiesteria pisicida*. Lethal little bastard. Still, you couldn't help but admire its chameleon nature: opportunistic, unpredictable, changeable.

Got to hand it to their project head, the Ice Queen—for all her bitchiness, she is truly amazing—come to think of it, not unlike their killer tox: opportunistic, unpredictable, lethal.

What was a headache compared to everything he'd been through over the past months, he wondered bitterly. He'd vowed he wouldn't let the petty personality differences affect his concentration. Territorial disputes were part of every research project, federal, state, private—just like they were part of every family. In a field as narrowly focused as his, fellow researchers interacted like some extended clan complete with feuds and alliances. He'd been down this road before. He told himself it would go no farther than disputes over territory; in the end it would all work out. The bastards were always on his case anyway—he'd yet to see eye-to-eye with his supervisors on any project.

But hell, a little bickering never killed anyone.

In fact, all in all, Dr. Doug Thomas was looking forward to his day. His thirty-five-minute commute—he lived in a sweet little river valley and the lab was on a mountaintop—allowed him to organize and prepare mentally for the work ahead.

He usually finished his PB&J sandwich before he reached the main highway, and he almost always swallowed the last of the Earl Grey tea in his thermos at the alpine tree-line where the view was awesome.

But this morning he'd forgotten to make his sandwich; the jar of Jif was sitting on the counter at home, as was the milk for his tea. And when Doug tried to open the thermos, his fingers felt stiff.

He spilled half of the contents into his lap; the other half tasted like bitter water, and it was *cold*, not hot. A sudden, fleeting bout of nausea hit—he managed to keep from vomiting—he did not remember that he'd been sick the night before.

In fact by the time he approached the main highway, Doug Thomas wasn't registering much of anything. He was functioning on auto-pilot. A faint internal voice warned him that he should take his foot off the gas pedal. The voice was meaningless because Doug could no longer respond to voluntary commands from his brain. He was traveling in a deep fog.

The thermos toppled, spilling the last of the tea onto his

thigh, but he didn't feel the liquid contact. Sunglasses couldn't ease the bright blinding light because it came from behind his eyes, an explosion of illumination. Fear came and went. Terror turned his skin cold—and then that emotion receded, too.

A weary sigh escaped his lips. A heavy calm slowed his body. He moved through molasses. His right foot grew heavy as it pressed down on the accelerator. The dark blue crosstrainer with the white laces seemed to belong to someone else.

As Doug Thomas drove his Subaru across four lanes of oncoming traffic on the highway, he did experience a moment of bewilderment: *You'd almost think I've been poisoned.*

The two-ton truck hit the Subaru broadside and Doug Thomas was killed almost instantly.

One . . .

    redrider: well done! bravo!
    alchemist: have we met?
    redrider: call me an admirer
    alchemist: ?
    redrider: I was impressed with the way you handled your
              associate
    alchemist: sorry?
    redrider: Dr. T—brilliantly done
    alchemist: don't know what you're talking about
    redrider: I'm still not sure how you managed the expo-
              sure
    —
    redrider: hello . . .
    —
    redrider: I know you're there
    —
    redrider: take all the time you need I'll be waiting

Two . . .

"One of the most problematic aspects of the case is the longitudinal factor; the deaths have occurred over a span of at least a decade," Edmond Sweetheart said. He was standing on the balcony of his room at the Eldorado Hotel. Behind him, the New Mexico sky was the color of raw turquoise and quartzite, metallic cirrus clouds highlighting a blue-green scrim.

"Why did it take so long to put it together?" Dr. Sylvia Strange had chosen to sit at one end of a cream-colored suede sofa in front of a polished burl table, the room's centerpiece. For the moment, she would keep her distance—from Sweetheart, from this new case. Her slender fingers slid over the black frame of the sunglasses that still shaded her eyes. Her shoulder-length hair was slightly damp from the shower she'd taken after a harder-than-usual workout at the gym. She studied the simple arrangement of flowers on the table: pale lavender orchids blooming from a slender vase the color of moss. Late afternoon sun highlighted the moist, fleshlike texture of the blossoms. The air was laced with a heavy, sweet scent. "Why didn't anybody link the deaths?"

"They were written off as unfortunate accidents." Sweetheart frowned. "Everyone missed the connection—the CID, FBI, Dutch investigators—until a young, biochemistry grad assistant was poisoned in London six months ago. Her name was Samantha Grayson. Her fiancé happened to be an analyst with M.I.6—the Brit's intelligence service responsible for foreign intelligence. He didn't buy the idea that his girlfriend had accidentally contaminated herself with high doses of an experimental neurotoxin. Samantha Grayson died a bad death, but her fiancé had some consolation—he zeroed in on a suspect."

"But M.I.6 chases spies, not serial poisoners." Sylvia stretched both arms along the crest of the couch, settling in. "And this is a criminal matter."

She was aware that Sweetheart was impatient. He reminded

her of a parent irritated with a sassing child. "So who gets to play Sherlock Holmes, the FBI?"

"As of the last week, the case belongs to the FBI, yes."

She nodded. Although the FBI handled most of its investigations on home turf, in complex international criminal cases the feds were often called upon to head up investigations, to integrate information from all involved local law enforcement agencies—and to ward off the inevitable territorial battles that could destroy any chance of justice and the successful apprehension and prosecution of the guilty party or parties.

"And the FBI is using you—?"

"To gather a profile on the suspect."

Sylvia shrugged. "Correct me if I'm wrong, but the last time I looked, you were a counterterrorist expert. Is there something you're leaving out of your narration?"

"There are unusual facets to this case."

"For instance."

"The suspect deals with particularly lethal neurotoxins classified as biological weapons. As far as we know, at this moment, there's no active terrorist agenda; nevertheless, more than one agency is seeking swift closure."

Sweetheart had his full weight pressed against the balcony's railing. The carved wood looked too delicate to support his 280 pounds. "The suspect is female, caucasian, forty-four, never-married, although she's had a series of lovers. She's American, a research toxicologist and molecular biochemist with an I.Q. that's off the charts."

"You've got my attention."

"She received her B.S. from Harvard, then went on to complete her graduate work at Berkeley, top of her class, then medical school, and a one-year fellowship at MIT—by then she was all of twenty-six. She rose swiftly in her career, she cut her teeth on the big shows—Rajneesh, Aum Shinrykyo, the Ventro extortion; she had access to the anthrax samples after nine-eleven— worked for all the big players, including Lawrence Livermore, the CDC, WHO, USAMRID, DOD. As a consultant she's worked in the private sector as well." Sweetheart knew the facts, reciting them succinctly, steadily, until he paused for emphasis. "Two, maybe three people in the world know as much about exotic neurotoxins and their antidotes as this woman. No one knows more."

Sylvia set her sunglasses on the table next the moss-colored vase. She rubbed the two tiny contact triangles that marked the bridge of her nose. "How many people has she killed? Who were they?"

"It appears the victims were colleagues, fellow researchers, grad assistants. How many? Three? Five? A half dozen?" Sweetheart shrugged. "The investigation has been a challenge; five days ago the target was put under surveillance; we both know it's a trick to gather forensic evidence in a serial case without tipping off the bad guy. Add to that the fact that she doesn't use mundane, easily detectable compounds like arsenic or cyanide. Bodies still need to be exhumed; after years, compounds degrade, pathologists come up with inconclusive data. Think Donald Harvey: he was convicted of 39 poisonings, *his* count was 86. We may never know how many people she's poisoned."

"Who is she?"

"Her name is Christine Palmer."

"Fielding Palmer's daughter?" Sylvia was visibly surprised.

Sweetheart nodded. "What do you know about her?"

"What everybody knows. There was a short profile in *Time* or *Newsweek* a year ago—tied to that outbreak of environmental fish toxin and the rumors it was some government plot to cover up research in biological weapons. The slant of the profile was 'daughter follows in famous father's footsteps'." Sylvia shifted position, settling deeper into the couch, crossing her ankles. She toyed restlessly with the diamond and ruby ring on the third finger of her left hand. "That can't have been easy. Fielding Palmer was amazing. Immunologist, biologist, pioneer AIDS researcher, writer."

"Did you read his book?"

Sylvia nodded. Fielding Palmer had died of brain cancer in the early 1990s, at the height of his fame and just after the publication of his classic, *A Life of Small Reflections*. The book was a series of essays exploring the ethical complexities, the moral dilemmas of scientific research at the close of the 20th century. He'd been a prescient writer, anticipating the ever deepening moral and ethical quicksand of a world that embraced the science of gene therapy, cloning, and the bio-engineering of new organisms.

Sylvia frowned. It jarred and disturbed—this idea that his only daughter might be a serial poisoner. The thought had an obscene quality.

She saw that Sweetheart had his eyes on her again—he was *reading* her, gleaning information like some biochemically-sensitive scanner. Well, let him wait; she signaled *time out* as she left the couch, heading for the dark oak cabinet that accommodated the room's mini-bar. She squatted down in front of the cabinet, rifling the refrigerator for a miniature of Stolichnaya and a can of tonic. From the selection of exorbitantly priced junk food she selected a bag of Cheetos.

"Join me?" she asked, as she poured vodka into a tumbler.

"Maybe later."

Sylvia swirled the liquid in the glass, and the tiny bubbles of tonic seemed to bounce off the oily vodka. She turned, holding the glass in front of her face, staring at Sweetheart, her left eye magnified through a watery lens. She said, "That's the beauty of poison—invisibility."

"Toxicology protocol is much more sophisticated than it used to be," Sweetheart said. "But there will always be undetectable poisons. Even water is toxic in the right dose. You have to know what you're looking for—there are new organisms, new compounds discovered all the time—you have to know what to culture, what to analyze, which screens to run."

When Sylvia was settled once more on the couch, she balanced her heels on the table, and she tore the snack bag open with her teeth. She ate a half dozen of the orange puffs before tossing the bag onto polished wood. "Okay." She held up her index finger: "Why you?" Her middle finger: "Why me?" Her ring finger complete with precious stones: "Why now?"

"The FBI has a problem—their strongest tool is a psychological profile because there are no eye-witnesses, no secret poison cache has been found in Palmer's basement—all the evidence is circumstantial. The purpose of the profile is two-fold: to track her patterns, her m.o., to look for a signature—and to prime investigators for the interrogation process. I'm their profiling consultant, I've got carte blanche."

"And you want me because—"

"Adam Riker."

The answer in a name.

Sylvia nodded, not surprised, but discomfited all the same. Months after the investigation, she still had nightmares about the Riker case. Adam Riker had been a nurse, a hospice specialist, who'd worked at nursing homes and V.A. hospitals in Texas, California, and, most recently, at an Indian hospital in New Mexico. He'd had another speciality in addition to nursing—serial murder. He'd poisoned at least thirty-five victims, ranging in age from an unborn child to a ninety-nine-year-old war veteran. And Sylvia had been part of the profiling team. In they end they'd brought him down—but not before more victims died.

"The Riker case is fresh in your mind," Sweetheart said, interrupting her thoughts. "You know better than I do that poisoners have their own special *tics*."

Sylvia didn't respond; she was looking straight at Sweetheart—not seeing his face, but the faces of Riker's victims, instead.

"You'll work with me on the psychological profile—that means some intensive travel, interviews, assessment of the data we've already got, and the retrieval of new data. It will be down and dirty, no time for anything *but* down and dirty. We'll stay in close touch with Quantico—running our data past their guys—and our local contacts will be the field agents on surveillance and their SAC. It's a short list—intentionally *short*—to avoid attracting attention. We'll have to give the investigators the tools they need for interrogation. We'll give them her stress points, her soft spots, her jugular. Once they have enough to bring her in, they're going to have to break Christine Palmer."

"A confession?"

"As I said, so far all the evidence is circumstantial."

"They'll need hard evidence."

"What they need is a homicide on U.S. soil."

"Are you certain she's your poisoner?"

He barely hesitated. "Yes."

"So Palmer had the expertise and the access, the method and the means. What about motive?" Sylvia thought Sweetheart's energy belonged to a caged cat—behind steel bars he was pacing a path in concrete.

He turned his head, avoiding her scrutiny, and said, "Before Samantha Grayson's death, she confided in her fiancé—the analyst; his name is Paul Lang. Samantha said she'd been spooked by Palmer. There was an incident where Palmer criticized Grayson's protocol—she flew into a rage and threatened Grayson. At the time Lang encouraged his girlfriend to go to someone with more authority to mediate the dispute. Grayson said nobody had more authority than Palmer."

"That's unpleasant, but it's not motive."

"After Samantha Grayson died, Lang started investigating on his own and found a string of incidents: abrupt arguments; paranoia, accusations of misconduct and negligence leveled by Palmer against her coworkers. He also found a disturbing number of 'untimely' deaths—accidental and 'natural'. Together, the incidents and the deaths began to carry weight."

"Were the accusations of negligence and misconduct groundless or did Palmer have a point?"

"Either way, a punishment of death is a bit harsh," Sweetheart said, his expression flat, his voice deadpan.

Sylvia took a drink of her vodka tonic. Ice beaded on the

glass, dripping onto her fingers and then onto deep mahogany wood. "In her line of work, psych screens are a given. Is she a full-blown psychopath? Is she paranoid? Schizotypal?"

"Her test scores fall within normal range."

"So she's smart enough to fake good."

"As far as the world's concerned, she's hyper-functional. She's *abnormal* only because she's brilliant, ambitious, highly moral, and charismatic."

"Since when do you care what the world believes? What's the real story?"

"The surveillance team has seen some eccentric behavior." Sweetheart crossed his arms over his broad chest. "And there have been fleeting rumors of a breakdown, time spent at private retreats—we'll have to look more closely at the rumors. It's our job to figure out why she kills, her pattern, her particular system of reference." He paused, his expression shrewd, opting then for understatement. "It's an interesting case."

Sylvia didn't speak immediately. In her glass, the last of the ice was melting in front of her eyes. *What's there, what's not there?* It took her a moment to focus on Sweetheart's face. She said, "Why do I have the feeling you've left something out?"

He didn't blink, didn't react. From a distance Sweetheart could almost pass for a tourist. *Almost.* He was dressed in slightly rumpled linen, his hands thrust deep in the pockets of gray slacks, his broad, muscled shoulders softened by the casual yellow shirt. But even in shadow his symmetrical features teased the viewer with alternating glimpses of European and Polynesian ancestry, the power of his body was undeniable, and the dark eyes gleamed with extraordinary intelligence.

The dead cases, the inactive files—there were no such things in Sweetheart's language. She'd heard whispers of his alliances with the CIA and M.I.6, as well as the FBI. (She didn't know how much was truth versus lie.) But his specialty could be summed up in the phrase, *The ones that got away.*

She stared at him. She didn't know exactly what drove him—hadn't figured it all out yet. But she would. She was filling in the pieces slowly. Constructing her own profile of the profiler. The ice clinked softly in her glass as she set it down.

The first fugitive she'd known about was Ben Black, a terrorist with ties to the IRA and Osama bin Laden. Sweetheart had pursued Black for years—he'd seen Black 'killed' more than once. In the end, Black had died in an explosion of his own design. And there were others on his 'most-wanted list.' A bomber responsible for a plane crash in British Columbia that claimed 221 lives. A sixties radical who had participated in a bank robbery that ended with three civilians dead, including a pregnant woman. (This one arrested a month ago, tracked down with the help of Sweetheart's profiling system, MOSAIK.)

And now, this—a serial poisoner . . .

Sweetheart shook his head, a gesture meant to dismiss her appraisal.

But Sylvia felt his hesitation. She considered the fact that he hadn't told her the whole truth; she didn't press him. She'd learned not to push Edmond Hommalia Sweetheart.

As partners she and Sweetheart made interesting chemistry. *He*—analytical, obsessed with empirical data, prone to intra-psychic denial. *She*—an equal mix of intellect and intuition, capable of faith under pressure.

Officially, Sweetheart was an expert in psycholinguistics, an anti-terrorism specialist, and the creator of a multi-tiered computer profiling system known as MOSAIK. In his spare time he practiced Sumo, collected rare timepieces, and consulted with federal and international agencies.

Officially, Sylvia was a forensic psychologist who had extensive experience with criminal and institutionalized populations; she was the author of several books, including one that had brought a popular readership. She had a mother in San Diego and a father who'd been missing for more than two decades. She had a highly perceptive eleven-year-old foster daughter named Serena, two dogs (a scrappy terrier with chronically "bad hair" and a three-legged Belgian Malinois who snored), and a lover named Matt England whom she adored and was about to marry and who shared her tendency to prefer an adrenalized life in the trenches over mundane, day-to-day problems. In her spare time she ran miles, played "Mom", and consulted with law enforcement agencies and private parties.

Placing the empty glass on the table, Sylvia stood and stretched her arms above her head. "You haven't asked about my life." She crossed the room to join him on the balcony. When she reached his side, she waved her ring finger in front of his nose. Light made the ruby shimmer. "You haven't said a word about my wedding."

"How was it?"

"Do you work hard to be this—*obtuse*—or does it just come naturally?"

"I want you on this case."

"Why?"

"Because you'll understand Palmer in a way I can't." He waited a beat, waited for the question she refused to ask, before he finished his answer. "Because you worked Riker."

Sylvia turned away from him, from unbidden memories and the vague daylight hangover of a nightmare, to stare out at the city—a shadowy, muted Santa Fe at sunset, purple and peach waves across a turquoise sea. Sounds drifted up from the streets: a car horn, laughter, radio songs. At that instant she felt poised between two worlds, between dark and light, between bad and good. "Hey, Sweetheart." Her voice was soft and flat. "What do you think of my city? How do you like this view?"

He shook his head, his gaze impolite in its intensity. His carotid artery was responding visibly to his heart. She felt as if she'd been penetrated and recognized.

"You want me on this case because of what I saw in Riker," she said. "It's what I saw in *me* that gives me nightmares. Riker made me touch a place within myself that knows no compassion, no mercy, no humanity." She turned away for a moment and her eyes were drawn toward the glass, but what she saw was her own reflection, her face distorted, a softening that read as compromise, a blurring of line. Her voice came out as a whisper. "That's a horrible realization when compassion is what keeps you safe and mercy is what separates you from the monsters. And you know that mercy and compassion must be the lifelines that offer the only glimmer of salvation—if not humanity, what's left? But all I touched was emptiness. A dark, cold place that made me too akin to the Rikers of this world. Do you understand why I can't keep going back?"

"I know you can't turn away." He reached toward her, she shook her head, and he said, "You're burned out from the Riker case, I understand that. You've lost your balance, but just for a moment—"

"It's more than that."

"I need you, Sylvia."

She heard the urgency in his voice and when she looked into his eyes she saw an almost desperate entreaty that left her shaken. She took a breath, trying to retreat, but feeling the internal pull. Strong. Sharp.

She sighed, abruptly exhausted—taking the first step in his direction. "What's the timeline on Palmer?"

He nodded. "Four months ago she joined a team of researchers who've been working on a highly sensitive contract for the DOD—potent marine toxins, which are being analyzed and manipulated in a way that's cutting edge," Sweetheart said. "There's no evidence to arrest, and she's too valuable to freeze off the project."

"I can spend the next few days reviewing the files. I'll let you know—"

"Not acceptable. I need you now."

"I can't do that." She pushed away from the rail—physically distancing herself once again, as if she were freeing herself from some invisible force-field. "Not until after the wedding."

"As of last Friday morning, we have a new victim. A molecular-toxicologist. Part of the original research team in England."

"What did she use?"

"We're not sure." He faltered. "A neurotoxin—"

Sylvia shook her head, and Sweetheart countered harshly: "You said it yourself, the beauty of poison is invisibility. The toxicology screens will take time. They're not looking for the standard compounds."

"What happened to him?"

"The victim drove his car at seventy miles per hour directly into the path of oncoming traffic. Yes, it might have been a vehicular malfunction, it might have been an accident, it might have been suicide. But I'll stake my career it was murder."

"Can't they temporarily shut down the project on some excuse?"

"They'd lose valuable research, and they'd tip her off." He shook his head. "She's under 24-hour surveillance. The feds need to catch her in the act. Or, they need a confession. That's where you and I come in. Sylvia, I'm asking you—give me five days—then go have your life."

"She's in England? What—London?"

Sweetheart shook her head. "Dr. Thomas died on U.S. soil—and his murderer's in your neighborhood. Why do you think I'm here? Dr. Palmer's heading up this project at LANL."

Visit the
Simon & Schuster Web site:
www.SimonSays.com

and sign up for our
mystery e-mail updates!

Keep up on the latest
new releases, author appearances,
news, chats, special offers, and more!
We'll deliver the information
right to your inbox — if it's new,
you'll know about it.

SIMON & SCHUSTER
A VIACOM COMPANY
www.SimonSays.com

POCKET BOOKS

SONNET
BOOKS